WOLF TOUCHED

THE FORBIDDEN MATE TRILOGY
BOOK 3

JEN L. GREY

Copyright © 2024 by Grey Valor Publishing, LLC

All rights reserved.

No part of this book may be reproduced in any form or by any electronic or mechanical means, including information storage and retrieval systems, without written permission from the author, except for the use of brief quotations in a book review.

CHAPTER ONE

My heart squeezed, and fear clawed inside my chest. I stood under the partially covered moon in the woods right outside the women's apartments at Evergreen Elite University. My wolf howled in my head as she inched forward, wanting to be released.

The question I'd asked Octavia, the blonde-haired woman standing before me, hung thickly between us.

A question so simple but one she struggled to answer.

Are you my biological mother?

Silence blanketed the air. We were only feet apart, but with emotions strangling me, the distance felt like miles.

My blood jolted, and I could easily read her emotions, with one being the most dominant.

Fear.

"It's complicated." She licked her lips, and her brown eyes widened as she took in the mountainous outskirts of Portland, Oregon, surrounding us. "And I don't have time to explain, not after the earthquake you caused. The nearby coven members will know where you are."

Baffe wrapped an arm around my waist, anchoring me

to him. Our fated-mate bond buzzed to life, reminding me that I wasn't alone. His ice-blue eyes narrowed, and his jaw was set.

I'd never be alone again. There was no question that Raffe would always be at my side.

"It's a yes or no answer, but this woman has a point," he sneered, his disgust swirling so heavy within him that I shivered. "We need to move."

Here was the thing. Her nonanswer confirmed that, even if she wasn't my mother, she knew who she was, and she had chosen to leave me alone in this world without any knowledge or guidance about my powers. Going along with someone else's poor decisions was as bad as making your own. I'd learned that the hard way while being bullied my entire life until I came to EEU and began to learn about myself.

I laughed humorlessly. "You know what? Forget I asked." I waved a hand, eager to get away from her. "The answer won't change the past." I'd wanted answers, but now that they were possibly here, I wasn't sure they mattered. I now had a pack, friends, and family.

Raffe tugged me behind him and stood between me and Octavia. With his six-and-a-half-foot frame, he easily blocked me, and his rage was so hot that it had to be palpable even to her. "I knew something wasn't right with *you*." His voice lowered so it sounded more animal than human. Dark fur that matched his hair sprouted along his arms, indicating that his shift was near. "This ends—"

"Wait," I interjected, placing my hand on his back. With my palm on his bare skin, our fated-mate connection buzzed harder. "She's not a witch." I still didn't understand what that meant. She barely had any power, but the faint traces within her felt exactly like mine.

What do you mean? Raffe's jaw popped. *You said something was wrong, and it was like you couldn't let go.*

"She's human, but my blood recognizes something inside her," I said out loud, hoping she would interject and clarify things for me. "It's like she's also arcane-born, though I can only feel a faint echo of power. She's a little more than human."

"My power was never activated, but I carry the genes." Octavia rubbed her hands together. "And I've never experienced anything like that before. For a moment, I swore my blood jarred."

I'm approaching, Lucy connected to us. *Don't attack me or anything.*

With all the chaos, I didn't blame her. Between Dave, Josie, Octavia, and King Jovian, I feared we were all about to lose our damn minds. There were too many active threats and strange occurrences going on at one time.

King Jovian had gotten Raffe and me to follow him into the woods for an unpleasant discussion. The last time I'd gone into the woods like that, a coven member had created a barrier to separate me from Raffe and the others, and three Eastern wolf shifters had attacked me. Raffe suspected his dad might be behind the attack.

I'll get Josie's clothes while you shift, I said to Lucy as I glanced at Josie. She was sweating even more, her bronze complexion pale from how much blood she'd allowed Dave to drink from her. Even her long, wavy dark hair seemed more limp. We needed to get her inside and fed and hydrated as soon as possible.

Surprisingly, Dave didn't appear worse off despite drinking wolf blood, which was supposed to be deadly to vampires.

I didn't hesitate, marching past Raffe and nearing Octavia, heading into the woods.

"Hey, where are you going?" Octavia asked, pivoting to block me.

My wolf inched forward and snarled, echoing through my head. "I'm getting my friend's clothes so we can take her someplace safe."

"You don't need to leave." She shook her head, the warmth in her eyes fading. "Someone could be out there, waiting to attack. You need to stay here with people who'll protect you."

Laughter bubbled from deep within my chest. "First off, you have no authority over what I do and don't do, and second, Josie has lost a lot of blood. We need to stabilize her."

Raffe's rage cooled into icy tendrils of concern. *Keith, keep an eye out for threats while we get ready to move Josie, and so Dave can recover enough to provide answers before he succumbs to his injuries. Lucy, shift and bring Josie her clothes. I can't risk Sky leaving my side.*

Keith's dark wolf darted off in the direction we'd come from.

I twisted toward Raffe, placing my hands on my waist. *What the hell? What was that?*

Raffe's olive complexion seemed a shade paler. *Look, I don't like her or trust her, but I agree that you shouldn't run off on your own, even to Lucy. It's best if we both stay with Adam. At least if she tries something and uses magic, we'll be together. Remember what has fucking happened every time we split up? And we both can't run to Lucy. It's better if we stay where we know nothing weird has been set up.*

He had a point, though I didn't like it. *Fine.*

Branches snapped, and Lucy's rose scent drifted in on the breeze.

She was here.

Thank God.

I feared that if we didn't move Josie soon, she might not make it out alive. I couldn't imagine her and Dave dying like this.

"You're pack-linking with them, aren't you?" Octavia gaped. "How is that possible? Unless you completed the bond, but even then ..."

My breath caught. "How do you know all of this?" I faced her again. "You might have dormant power similar to mine, but that doesn't explain how you know about supernaturals. I didn't, and I grew up with weird things happening around me all the time." It didn't seem fair, her being aware of all this when I hadn't been. How was it possible?

She crossed her arms and stared at the ground. "I was raised with knowledge about supernaturals. Though I don't interact with all species, I know about their existence, along with the heritage of my ancestors."

Her words were a punch to the gut. "That must have been nice." A sour taste filled my mouth. "I didn't have that luxury. Humans adopted me. The adoption was arranged while my birth parents were alive, so it wasn't like I was orphaned." I tried never to think about that part, but now I couldn't ignore it. "How many of our kind are out there?" I'd assumed I was alone, and I'd hoped that my parents had known they were under threat and gave me up for love, but I wasn't sure I believed that. What if they hadn't wanted me because I was odd?

"Not many." She mashed her lips. "But there are a few."

"Where?" I asked.

Lucy burst through the firs, cutting off the conversation. Her haunting gray eyes focused on Octavia for a second as she hurried past with Josie's clothes in hand. When her attention landed on Josie, the skin around her eyes tightened. "Shit! She looks awful."

That was putting it mildly.

She rushed to Josie, and I followed. Lucy worked on dressing Josie's top half while I worked on the bottom. As soon as Josie was covered, my wolf calmed. One less thing for her to worry about.

I straightened and noticed that Adam was gone and Raffe was looming over Octavia, not batting an eye. The way he had his hands clenched at his sides screamed that he was ready to attack her.

Did that woman hurt Dave? Lucy asked.

She said she didn't, but when we found them, she was hovering over him, and there was a dagger in his chest. The image popped into my brain again. *She's not a witch, and I don't believe she's spelled, so I'm inclined to believe her.*

That doesn't mean we can trust her, Raffe added, then filled Lucy in on everything.

When he finished, Adam joined us in human form. He was about four inches shorter than Raffe's six-and-a-half feet, and his loose, curly brown hair had a few twigs in it.

Now that he was here and Josie was dressed, we had to determine our next steps. *What's the plan?*

I don't fucking know. Raffe ran a hand down his face, his muscles tensing and on display due to his bare chest.

I tried not to let his muscles distract me, but my stomach fluttered.

I want her to come with us. I needed to make that point clear. *She knows about the arcane-born, and I have so many questions that maybe she can answer.*

Don't worry. She's not going anywhere. Raffe pursed his lips. *Let's take them to Adam and Keith's apartment. They can stay in the extra bedroom, and we can take turns watching them.*

You mean your room? Keith linked, adding to the conversation even though he wasn't here. *The one you've clearly forgotten about?*

Growling, Raffe snapped, *It hasn't been my room since Sky and I bonded, so make sure you get that shit straight.*

I swore Keith just liked getting a reaction out of people. *So, take Josie back to her place and Dave and Octavia to the men's dorm. How do we get Dave inside in this condition?*

Adam removed his shirt. *He can wear this. It'll cover most of the blood, and people might think he passed out. Luckily, a lot of students are drinking since tonight was a home game. Most will still be at the bonfire.*

The bonfire. I'd forgotten all about that. It was a campus-wide event held at night after home football games. I'd gone to one with Slade the night he'd pressured me to kiss him. It'd been awful and awkward, but it had helped Raffe and me get to *this* point.

You're right. That's our best bet, Raffe agreed and scowled at me before continuing, *You can stop staring at him now.*

I blinked, coming back to the present. I hadn't noticed that I'd zoned out while staring at Adam. He strolled past, and I couldn't help but notice that his body was leaner than Raffe's more muscular frame.

I arched a brow, refusing to feel guilty. *At least he wasn't completely naked,* I shot back.

Out of the corner of my eye, I saw Adam squatting by Dave. He ripped the vampire's shirt off and kept my shirt wadded in place. He slid the shirt over Dave's head.

The vampire's eyes cracked open, and he rasped, "Josie?" He lifted his head and locked on her still form beside him. "Is she all right?" His voice was hoarse, concern laced throughout.

None of us replied.

Dave opened his eyes wider, his head wobbling as he tried to look around. "Josie?"

"She's here. She let you drink too much from her," Adam answered, his voice growly. "We need to get her back to the apartment, which will go a lot quicker if you stay fucking calm."

Lucy bent down to lift Josie into a sitting position. Her bottom lip quivered. *Sky, she feels cold ... abnormally cold.*

We didn't have time to lose. My blood jolted as I hurried to Lucy. She needed help getting Josie back to the apartment. *We need to move,* I linked with everyone.

Just like Lucy had said, Josie's body was cold and clammy. Lucy and I worked together to lift her.

Is anything out of the ordinary? Raffe linked with all of us despite directing the question at Keith.

Looks normal here, he replied.

Head back. We need you close as we make our way to the apartments.

Adam tugged Dave to his feet and murmured, "It'd go a lot faster if you'd help me." But Dave's eyes were closed, his body limp again. He was out cold. Luckily, Adam was taller and stronger than the vampire, and he didn't seem to have issues helping Dave, especially since Raffe remained in front of Octavia, watching her every movement.

The sound of paws approaching indicated Keith had reached us.

"Let's go," I said. Josie was taller and heavier than me,

and I didn't want to drag this out longer than needed, especially if we could be attacked again.

"You should help them." Octavia waved a hand from Raffe toward Lucy and me. "They're struggling. I'll just head out and—"

"*You're* not going *anywhere*," Raffe gritted out and snagged her arm. "You're staying with us."

Octavia's nostrils flared, and she jerked back. "I'm human, and you're not my alpha or leader. You don't make those decisions for me. I'd hate to inform the other supernaturals that yet another wolf shifter has stepped out of line." The disgust in her voice was evident, reminding me of the secret society.

My stomach churned. Raffe was right that this could be a setup, but Dave was injured and needed help. That wasn't an act.

"Inform them, and I'll point out how you, a human, were holding a dagger lodged in a vampire's heart," Raffe snarled. "Your awareness of supernaturals changes your position here, especially your knowledge about arcane-born heritage. You don't have a fucking choice but to come with us, and then I'll decide your fate depending on your answers."

"Dru told me not to come here, and I didn't listen." Octavia sighed. "Don't do this. Don't force my hand and make us enemies."

Raffe chuckled darkly. "You act as if I don't already view you as a threat."

A low growl came from behind her as Keith returned. He hunkered down, ready to strike Octavia.

My blood jolted. We couldn't let her go, but I didn't want anything to happen to her. She might have answers.

"I'm sorry. I didn't want it to be like this." She glanced

at me, a deep frown on her face, then reached for something at her ankle and straightened, holding a small gun. She pointed it at Raffe's chest. "Let me go, and I won't harm any of you."

Fear choked me as my blood hummed. My wolf howled loudly and tried to inch forward, but I pushed against her, not wanting her to interfere with my blood.

Shifting would take too long.

Fur sprouted on Raffe's arms as his wolf fought for control. "And risk my mate's life? Not happening. I'd rather die and have Keith kill you than risk any more harm coming to her."

"Fine, we'll both die," she gritted out.

I yelled, "No!"

My vision darkened, and my power funneled through my feet and pushed into the ground. The earth began to quake right underneath her.

Her attention flicked to me, and her eyes widened, telling me everything I needed to know. She feared me as much as I did myself.

Keith lunged and bit the hand holding the gun. Octavia cried out. Keeping his teeth in her flesh, he jerked, and the gun dropped to the ground. Keith released her, blood coating his chest.

It wasn't enough. She'd tried to take my mate from me. She deserved a worse punishment.

"Skylar, let me take her," Lucy whispered in a shaky voice, taking the brunt of Josie's weight and freeing me as my power ravaged me.

Now, I could get closer. The ground shook harder beneath Octavia with my every step as my anger at her attempt to kill my mate took control.

The ground cracked underneath her feet, and Raffe

linked, *Babe, you need to calm down.* He pushed calmness toward me. *I don't want you to implode. I'm okay.*

He was right. If I used too much power, it could kill me, and she'd dropped her weapon. But my rage clung to me. My wolf was angry. Not only had she threatened Raffe but my pack as well.

Raffe took my hand. His touch ebbed my power back to a high fizz, and my head became clearer. The ground stopped shaking, and Octavia raised her uninjured left hand as she held her right one close to her chest.

"Skylar, I'm sorry. You need to calm down before anyone realizes you're out here." Her voice shook.

Now she was acting like she cared? "You tried to kill my mate. Why should I believe you?"

"You don't understand." Her eyes widened, and tears streamed down her cheeks. "I wouldn't have come here if I'd realized you completed the mate bond to the wolf prince. I thought you were in trouble. I came here to take you back with me, but he can always find you now, and I can't stay."

I laughed, though I could read she was speaking the truth. "Why come? It's not like you know me. You don't owe me anything."

"But ... I do." Her body quivered from shock, fear, and pain. "I'm the person who did this to you. There's a reason your power recognizes me. I can't abandon you *again*, knowing that my decision made you this vulnerable. I thought it would keep us safe, but I was so wrong, and I'm sorry. Either way, I *have* to go."

My heart panged as I sensed her true sorrow, but we couldn't let her leave.

I shook my head. "You're not going anywhere."

CHAPTER TWO

"Adam, take her to the extra room with Dave," Raffe commanded. "She'll stay there until we figure out what the hell to do with them."

"If you're forcing me to stay, I want to be with Di— Skylar." Octavia's shoulders slumped. "We need to talk *alone*. There are things I'm not comfortable with everyone hearing."

I arched a brow, feigning indifference. The nagging questions I'd had throughout my childhood appeared, but I pushed them away.

"No." Raffe's fingers dug into my side. "You don't get to make demands. You held a gun on me. You're lucky to be alive."

"Maybe, but I have answers that no *Book of Twilight* or history book contains," Octavia countered, lifting her chin high once again. "So ... if you're willing to take a little risk in exchange for the help I can give to your *mate*, let me go with her. But let me guess—that doesn't matter to you." Her irises turned damn near black. She tilted her head at me as if to send me a message.

I wasn't sure what she was getting at. Raffe was an amazing mate. *Let's bring her back to our apartment. We can get Slade or Hecate or someone to spell the perimeter so she can't leave.*

He cut his eyes at me and frowned. *I don't like this.*

Me neither. Before tonight, if anyone had asked me if I would love to meet someone like me, I would've said yes without a second thought. But I was with Raffe. I didn't trust Octavia, and the timing was suspicious. *If she doesn't follow through on her promise, we move her to the guys' apartment.*

"Fine, you can stay with us unless you don't follow through on your promise," Raffe said and turned to Keith. "Watch us until we're out of the woods. Once we're on campus, shift and join Adam at the apartment."

Octavia's mouth opened, but she didn't say anything. Keith shook out his fur, and spatters of Octavia's blood hit the forest floor. He linked, *Got it.*

With things settled, I hurried over to help Josie and our group. Raffe stayed close to Octavia, never taking his gaze off her.

I remembered how I'd felt the first time I saw him.

He was intense, sexy, and had a dangerous edge. Even then, he'd saved me multiple times, showing me there was more to him than his careless demeanor, and boy, had I been right. Once someone earned his trust and loyalty, he was the most amazing person anyone could know.

Do you think that's your mom? Lucy linked with me as we tried to walk in sync so we didn't jostle Josie too much. Her head bounced with each step we took, and there was no doubt that she and Dave would have sore necks when this was over and done.

I tried cradling Josie's head against my shoulder and

sighed. *I don't know, but it doesn't matter. At the end of the day, she left me to struggle on my own.* There was no telling how many arcane-born existed, even if their magic wasn't activated, and I wondered if they all lived near each other.

My eyes burned as the void inside my chest reemerged—the void I hadn't felt since Raffe and I had completed our bond, but clearly, the completed bond didn't take away my baggage.

Babe, what's wrong? Raffe asked, his concern causing his spot in my chest to tighten.

Even though it wasn't the best sensation, it reminded me that he was there and loved me unconditionally. *I'm just ready to get home and crawl into bed with you.* There was no lie there, and Raffe's body had a way of taking my mind off everything.

Same. He sighed loud enough that I could hear him. *This day feels like a fucking year. I woke up thinking it would be amazing, and it crashed from there.*

At least you guys won the game.

I'd rather lose every fucking game than have you feel like this. The warmth of his love cut through the cold.

Despite Josie's body getting heavier and my back aching, my cheeks lifted, proving that even in the worst situations, Raffe could make me smile.

Josie moaned and shivered. *Dave?*

Adam's carrying him, Lucy replied. *We're taking you both back to campus so you can rest.*

He's alive? Josie lifted her head, but her lids were heavy. *He's still here?*

I don't know how, but your blood helped him. I chose my words carefully, not wanting to give her false hope. *We need to get you both settled, and you need to eat and drink orange juice or something.* We needed to get sugar in her fast—before she crashed.

The trees thinned, and the apartment buildings came into view. As expected, no one was on the lawn. Now that darkness surrounded us, most everyone would be at the bonfire. In fact, I could smell the hint of smoke in the air.

We were bound to run into a few people because not everyone hung out there. *What are we going to do when someone sees us?*

Just pretend they're drunk. Keith laughed, and in animal form, it sounded like he was choking. *Everyone will believe that.*

As long as they don't see the blood on Dave's chest, Adam added.

With my focus on carrying Josie smoothly, I couldn't check.

I'm going to shift, Keith added, and he trotted off as we stepped out of the woods.

The end was in sight. Lucy and I kept a steady pace, heading toward the double-door entrance to the women's apartments.

Do you have it from here, Adam? Raffe asked. *Or do you need Lucy to help?*

I wasn't surprised that he didn't offer to go with Adam. Raffe wouldn't leave me alone with Octavia.

I'm fine, man. Go be with your girl and keep an eye on that woman. Something doesn't feel right. If I need anything, I'll let you know, but Keith shouldn't be far behind.

My arms began to scream, but I swallowed my complaint. Raffe wanted to watch Octavia. Not only that, but the thought of him carrying Josie didn't sit right with me. Damn the possessive wolf inside me.

When we reached the doors, Raffe nodded for Octavia

to go first. She scowled but didn't say anything as she obliged. Raffe then held the door open so Lucy, Josie, and I could get through.

Within a few minutes, the five of us were entering our hallway. A couple was making out a few doors down. We'd have to pass them to get into the apartment. And here I'd been hoping luck was on our side.

"Say one thing, and I swear, you'll wish you had shot me back there," Raffe whispered into Octavia's ear. "One wrong move and I won't hesitate to kill you."

Octavia scoffed, and she marched past Lucy and me toward the couple.

My stomach clenched.

Raffe followed close on her heels. She cleared her throat rather loudly.

The couple froze before jerking apart.

"What are you two doing out here?" Octavia placed her hands on her hips and tapped her foot, looking every inch like a mom. "This isn't the place for you two to be mauling each other. No one wants to see that, especially *me*."

The guy's jaw dropped, and Lucy and I used the opportunity to continue past the couple. Raffe remained beside Octavia, and Lucy and I got Josie into our apartment before the altercation ended.

I didn't know why Octavia had covered for us, but I was glad she had.

Leaving our front door open, we placed Josie on the couch. I heard a door down the outside hall shut and then a threatening growl. Raffe murmured, "Don't do anything stupid."

With my wolf ears, I could hear the exchange. If I'd still been human, it would've been a different story.

Lucy dropped onto the couch next to Josie, holding her

torso up, and I hurried into the kitchen to the refrigerator. Though we didn't have orange juice, I had a twenty-ounce Dr Pepper I hadn't opened yet.

Snatching it and a pack of peanut butter crackers off the four-seat table, I rushed back to Josie. Raffe and Octavia walked in as I handed the items off to Lucy, who worked on getting Josie conscious again.

I removed my phone from my back pocket. I had a missed text from Slade from two hours ago.

Slade: Hey, you coming to the bonfire? Hecate, Zella, and a few more coven members are here, wanting to hang out.

Such a simple question but one that held so much significance. The wolf shifters, coven members, and vampires didn't get along. Even though most species kept to themselves, the coven members and vampires were more likely to hang out together because both groups had a common enemy—wolf shifters. And I was caught between species. I was a wolf shifter, but before, I'd been accepted as part of the coven because my blood worked similarly to that of the witches.

I'd planned on asking Slade to help us, but if he learned about Octavia, he'd probably want to alter her mind. I couldn't risk it, but I still had to reply to him.

I sighed and typed a reply.

Me: Sorry, just now seeing this. I'm tied up.

My phone dinged within seconds.

Slade: Thank goddess you replied. I was worried. Okay, see you soon.

I put my phone back into my pocket and looked up to find Raffe scowling at me with his arms crossed. His unhappiness radiated so intensely that I didn't have to feel it in my chest to sense it.

"Let me guess... you texted Slade, and he's rushing here to help." Raffe grimaced.

Octavia lifted a brow and glanced between the two of us.

"Stop. You're my mate. He knows it. We're just friends." Even though Raffe was being silly, I couldn't blame him. Slade had tried to kiss me and had wanted to date me. "He never stood a chance even before that, and he helped me escape the underground bunker and trained me with my power. And no, I didn't ask him to come over, though I thought about it." I walked over to my mate and placed soothing hands on his chest.

Some of his tension eased as he wrapped his arms around me and pulled me to him. His chest rumbled with a growl. "Yet, if you did, he'd run here without a second thought. Anytime you ask, he's like a dog at your heels. Son of the supreme priestess or not, I'll kill him if I suspect he's up to something."

"Wait. You're close to a coven member?" Octavia tensed. "Why?"

"He helped me when no one else would. He saved my life." I hated how even the stranger didn't like the fact that I was close to supernaturals. "What did you expect? For me to remain alone and misunderstood all my life?"

She averted her gaze to the laminate wood-like flooring, avoiding mine.

Not wanting to analyze her reaction, I watched Josie sip the Dr Pepper. Her movements were still sluggish, and Lucy had to help her, but she was getting sugar and caffeine in her. That should help.

Octavia shook her head, her voice cracking. "We were so wrong to leave you."

My breath caught, and despite everything inside me screaming not to, I found myself looking at her. "What do you mean?" Though I already knew, I just needed to hear her say it.

"At that hospital"—she hung her head—"we gave you up, hoping if you were away from us, your power wouldn't grow. We wanted to keep you and your brother safe, but instead, I threw you into the arms of our enemies."

Knowing she was a relative was one thing, but hearing her confirm that not only was she my mother, but I had a *brother* ripped my heart in a way I'd never imagined possible. I wasn't sure what to lock on to, but Raffe didn't have the same problem.

"I will *never* be Skylar's enemy, but you ... that's a whole different story." Raffe released me and got in her face. "You left my *mate* alone, knowing her power was activated. What did you fucking think would happen?"

"In..." She licked her bottom lip. "I thought it was best ... for *all* of us. Her power would have put us on the radar and risked all of our lives."

She tried to make it sound like she'd wanted to help all of us, but that wasn't fair. She'd known my power was activated, and if she was aware of the history of arcane-born, then she also knew that Foster had imploded because of it. I murmured, "No, you thought it would be best for *you*. My power was already activated." I paused. "Do you know the hell I lived with growing up?" My voice was trembling. "Never fitting in, people calling me a *freak?* Do you know how many times people suggested I should kill myself, that the world would be a better place without me in it?"

White-hot anger rolled from Raffe into me as he linked, *You never told me that.*

It doesn't matter. It was my past ... my baggage. He couldn't do anything to change it. *Things changed when I got here ... well, after you stopped being an ass.* He had rejected me in front of everyone to get people not to hang around me.

Give me a list of those people. I'll kill each and every one. Guilt clung to him, and he stepped up beside me and took my hand. *And I'm sorry for acting like an idiot when you arrived.*

My chest expanded. I liked that he meant it. Still, I didn't want to live in the past anymore. I didn't want anyone to have that power over me, though I'd have to take things day by day.

"Listen, I messed up—I understand that—but we need to focus on the pressing matter. You can't trust the coven." Octavia lifted her hands. "You need to keep your distance from this warlock, especially if he's the priestess's son."

"It's too late for motherly advice." My breathing quickened, and the room spun. "So forgive me if I decide it's not worth taking. Slade has tried to help me control the power in my blood, and he discovered what I am. No one else gave me the time of day when I arrived. Only Slade."

Octavia flinched. "Of course he did. He could feel your magic as soon as you rolled onto campus. Supreme Priestess Olwyn knew exactly what you were when you arrived. I bet he didn't tell you that right away."

I hated that she knew that. What sort of contacts did she have? "Yes, but they did eventually inform me."

She leaned forward. "Did they tell you about the role you're predicted to play?"

"Role?" I asked.

She wrinkled her nose. "Of course they didn't. They dangle information in front of you whenever you stray to keep you close and make you trust them."

I froze. No. That couldn't be what Slade was doing. He'd gone to the library each night to search through the *Books of Twilight* for answers. He'd given me information as he'd found it.

"Sky—" Lucy's voice sounded strained.

Don't, I linked to her and Raffe. *Don't give her any reason to think she's right.*

But he did pull that card on you after he tried kissing you that night, Raffe interjected and clenched his hands at his sides. *And you didn't want to talk to him.*

I hated that he was right.

Someone pounded on the door. "Sky, let me in." It was Slade. "Someone said they saw you outside with Dave and a strange human lady."

Shit. He was here, and he already knew everything.

CHAPTER THREE

My ears rang from how hard my heart was pounding, and if Raffe hadn't been touching me, my blood would've been at hum level. Still, it was fizzing, on the brink of tipping over.

Of course a coven member saw us outside. We're lucky Slade's here and not Supreme Priestess Olwyn, though I bet she's coming. Raffe squeezed my hand comfortingly, feeling the turmoil inside me. *A coven is like a pack with how close they are, and Olwyn knows everything that happens pertaining to you.*

Another round of knocking was followed by Slade saying, "Sky? I'll call Mom so she can get the code from Lafayette if you don't open up."

He sounded concerned, easing some of the weight from my shoulders. He reminded me of the Slade I knew ... my friend. He'd saved me to his own detriment, and maybe he wouldn't inform his mom about Octavia if I asked him not to. I was letting Octavia's manipulation get to me.

Will someone get the door? Lucy linked. *I'm kinda busy here, and he already knows everything.*

I winced and glanced over as she held a cracker to Josie's mouth. Thankfully, Josie was conscious enough to take nibbles.

"Pretend we're not here," Octavia muttered, placing a finger to her lips. "He might think we left."

"Fine, I'm calling Lafayette. I know you're in there."

Shit. If a vampire came here, they would definitely want to erase Octavia's mind, and I wasn't sure that was possible. I also didn't want to chance her forgetting anything.

I released Raffe's hand and marched to the door.

A witch somewhere on this floor must have noticed us walk by. Raffe hit one hand on his other palm. *I swear, he's like the plague, always hanging around.* He then said out loud, "If you don't want him to know who you are, you'd better play along and act like you're not afraid."

He had a point.

I opened the door and found Slade standing there—alone. His spiky blond hair was ruffled, and his emerald eyes were glassy as if he'd been drinking.

"Skylar," he exhaled, his breath smelling of beer.

My stomach revolted at the foul scent, but I swallowed the acid down.

Slade pulled me to his chest and hugged me. "I'm so happy to see you."

His touch felt wrong. I leaned back to get away, but Slade held on tighter.

Rage blasted through Raffe and into me as he marched over, snarling, "Get your hands off my mate."

"Right. *He's* here." Slade loosened his grip with a frown. "I hoped Sasha was mistaken."

Sasha.

I'd never met her.

That must be why I hadn't recognized the witch when we headed in.

I took several steps back as Raffe came to my side. His nostrils flared as he glared at Slade and fisted his hands.

Given this already tumultuous situation, I looped my arm through Raffe's. With Slade and Octavia watching, I didn't want to try to unclench his hands. As soon as our bodies touched, some of his tension ebbed, but barely.

"You know better than to touch someone's mate." Raffe's face twisted in fury.

Slade rolled his eyes. "Sky and I are friends. Friends hug from time to time."

Even though Slade was my friend, he liked to piss off Raffe when he could.

I blew out a breath. "I've never been a big hugger, especially now that I'm mated with Raffe." I had to draw boundaries, and Raffe's feelings were more important than anyone else's. Besides, my skin crawled whenever another man touched me.

"Whatever." Slade scoffed and glanced over my shoulder. His back straightened. "What the hell happened here? And where's Dave?" He'd noticed Josie. He shut the door behind him and walked farther into the room. Then his attention landed on Octavia.

She stood in front of the television across from Lucy and Josie with her arms crossed. She'd schooled her expression into one of indifference, but the corners of her mouth were tipped downward. I could only hope Slade didn't notice that.

"Did you all get attacked?" Slade's brows furrowed. "And who is this?"

"A visitor who helped us find Dave." I didn't want to say she was supernatural, but I also didn't want to willingly admit she was human. Coven members didn't have the sense of smell that wolf shifters did, so he might not notice if he kept his distance. "And Josie lost a lot of blood." I told him about Dave.

Slade rubbed his forehead. "Shit. This is a huge mess." He arched a brow. "Dave's alive? After all this?"

If that didn't prove he cared about us, I didn't know what could. He and Dave were friends. Guilt churned in my stomach over doubting him again. I couldn't let Octavia influence me.

"He's fine." Raffe shook his head. "I don't fucking understand it. He should be dead from drinking wolf blood. I don't know what made Josie do it."

Swallowing a small bite of cracker, Josie cleared her throat. "I ... I don't know. I had the overwhelming urge to save him, and it wasn't like we had options." Her words slurred as if she'd been drinking, but she was speaking in full sentences. Between getting her some calories and her shifter healing, she was improving, but fatigue had hit her hard. She needed rest just as much as calories.

"That is odd. I'm sure Mom will want to visit him and figure out what's going on." Slade rubbed a hand over his chin. "I've seen vampires die from drinking wolf's blood. Is he here or back in his room?"

"That jackass is the one who drugged Sky so those crazies could capture her." Raffe's hands clenched tighter until his knuckles blanched. "We're keeping a close eye on him, and I don't want him anywhere close to her. I don't care if he fucking dies as long as he lives long enough to tell us everything he knows about that secret society."

"He's a student, so he's Mom's responsibility. She'll want to check on him." Slade removed his cell phone from his back pocket.

Raffe snarled, "She may be on the board, but *we* found him. Therefore, he's under wolf shifter watch and protection."

The two guys glared at each other, and when Slade swiped his phone to show he was going to text her, Raffe coiled, ready to snatch it away.

I'd hoped that one day we could all get along, but clearly, that wasn't today. "Slade, I get that she'll want to check on him." I held on to Raffe's arm tighter, trying to squeeze sense into him. Being all alpha-y and throwing his weight around would only get Priestess Olwyn over here tonight. Selfishly, I was exhausted and didn't want to deal with any more drama. I needed to come to terms with Octavia and get some sleep. It'd been a long-ass day. "But he's unconscious and needs to rest. She won't get anything out of him until he wakes. Believe me, if we could, we'd all be over there with him."

Slade lowered his hand, my reasoning hitting the mark, unlike Raffe's. He pursed his lips. "He's that bad off?"

I nodded and glanced at Josie, whose eyes were closed. Good. I didn't want her to hear what I was about to say. Whatever connection those two had, she'd been willing to risk death to save him. "Honestly, even after her feeding him, I'd be surprised if he survived."

"What the hell is wrong with this university?" Lucy placed her head in her hands. "Ever since the school year began, there's been one attack, chaos, or kidnapping after the next. If I hadn't attended school here last year, I'd be certain this place was cursed."

Cursed was another word people threw around to describe me, but not as often as *freak* and *weirdo*.

"Fine." Slade placed his phone back into his pocket. "I'll call her later and get her to put it off until in the morning. I assume he's at Raffe's apartment since the wolf shifters are monitoring him."

"Not my place anymore," Raffe interjected, placing an arm around my waist. "We're mated. I stay here now."

Maybe I shouldn't have appreciated the possessiveness, but dammit if my heart didn't flutter. My wolf wanted to trot in pride, knowing our man wanted everyone to know we belonged to each other.

Slade frowned. "This is the women's apartments. The rules state—"

"We have a completed mate bond," Raffe cut in. "That's more than equivalent to marriage, and her roommate is my cousin. I'm not going anywhere, and if Lafayette tries to make it where we can't stay together, Sky and I will move off campus."

"Both of you, stop it." I'd forgotten how they acted when we were all together. I placed my hands on my hips. "We have problems, and I'm sick and tired of you two having a pissing match every time we need to work together." Sometimes, I wondered if Slade was meant to be a wolf shifter with how much posturing these two did around each other. "Raffe is my mate—you need to accept that." I pointed at Slade.

From the corner of my eye, Raffe beamed.

But I wasn't finished.

I turned to Raffe, our chests touching. "And Slade is my friend, so it'll be easier if you two could pretend to get along."

That'll be the day, Lucy linked to me. *They've always been hostile toward each other, but it's been over the top since you came along.*

Something else my presence had impacted. Everywhere I went, something bad followed. Those weren't good things to bring, especially for a future vet, and only validated what King Jovian thought as well.

"Fine." Slade sighed and waved a hand. "I'm just trying to come to terms with you two being together."

"Get there faster," Raffe spat.

Raffe, I linked, wanting him to defuse the situation. *Aren't you a political science major? Shouldn't you be skilled at working across species and with negotiations?*

Not when the person has the hots for my mate. Raffe's body vibrated with anger. *Imagine if a girl came sniffing after me all the time. You wouldn't be all logical.*

Uh, did you forget about you and Josie? I shot back. *Yeah, you might have been pretending, but you guys were excellent at it. And your dad would be way more accepting of her than me.*

Point made, I turned back to the matter at hand. I needed to be careful and not give away too much about Octavia. "Slade, I'm not trying to be rude here, but we're all tired."

"Yeah, okay." Slade bit his bottom lip and glanced at Octavia. "Who are you, anyway?"

Octavia's eyes widened slightly.

Great, no wonder she was freaking out about him. She couldn't think quickly on her feet, and I doubted she wanted me to use her full name.

I came up with a nickname for her because *Mom* wouldn't cut it. "Her name is Vi, and she came to visit. You know, today was a big football game for the school, and there are a ton of people here who aren't normally on campus."

"She's part of our extended family," Raffe added, and my stomach clenched.

I understood what he'd done—because he and I were

mated and she was my biological mother he hadn't lied, yet he'd made it sound like she was a wolf shifter.

"Great. More royal shifters on campus." Slade rolled his eyes.

He needed to go, and quickly. I forced a yawn to illustrate that I was tired. "Is there anything else you need? It's been a long day."

Slade tapped a foot like he was delaying. "But I'm calling Mom first thing in the morning."

Whatever it took to get him out the door. We would fight the next battle in the morning.

"Call me if you need anything," Slade said, patting my arm and then heading out the door.

As soon as it shut, a weight pressed even heavier on my shoulders.

The four of us stood in silence as Raffe, Lucy, and I listened to Slade's footsteps grow fainter.

Octavia frowned. "What's the plan?"

"You sleep in Lucy's room, and we'll tie you to the headboard so you can't escape or harm us." Raffe's eyes glowed, and when he didn't connect with me, I realized he had to be talking to Adam and Keith. "Lucy, are you okay sleeping on the other couch?"

"That's fine. I want to be close to Josie anyway." Lucy stretched. "There's only a small window in the room, so she can't get out."

"There won't be any chance after I tie her up." Raffe kissed the top of my forehead and linked, *Why don't you take a shower and get ready for bed?*

A shower sounded fantastic.

I glanced at Octavia, whose shoulders slumped. She knew she couldn't get out of this.

I won't be far behind. Promise. Raffe's concern engulfed me, and I felt the magnitude of his love all over again.

Needing a moment to myself, I went into our room and grabbed some clothes before taking a quick shower to wash off the blood, grit, and dirt.

When I came out dressed in my favorite lilac pajamas, Raffe breezed past me into the bathroom. I glanced inside Lucy's room to find my cat, amusingly known as Cat-Keith, standing on the end table, staring at Octavia, who lay on her side with her hands tied to the headboard. Raffe had left enough slack for her to be comfortable.

Octavia's attention flicked to me, but I pushed away and went into my room. I needed the comfort of my own bed.

As I lay on my lilac comforter, listening to Raffe showering, I stared at the butterfly chandelier I'd made at home before coming here. It dangled from the light fixture, the darker purples at the top fading to lilac at the bottom.

I tried to push all thoughts from my mind, including the way my parents and King Jovian had reacted to Raffe and me being together. Both sets of parents disliked it, though mine thought our relationship was too intense, not understanding the supernatural, while King Jovian wanted Raffe to mate with the Atlanta alpha's daughter to fix the divide among their people. Instead, his son was mated to me, a human turned wolf shifter, which should've been impossible. I believed King Jovian feared me and what I was.

Our time together had been one disaster after another, culminating in the appearance of my birth mother, who'd abandoned me. How had my life changed so much in two months? Even though I wouldn't trade Raffe, Lucy, and the others for the world, I wouldn't complain if life got a whole lot easier.

The water turned off, and within minutes, Raffe joined

me in my room. His dark hair was damp, and he wore black sweatpants, remaining shirtless.

He slid into bed with me and pulled me into his arms.

I sighed. After today, I was so damn tired.

Are you okay? He cupped my face, watching me as I answered.

No, but I will be. I kissed his lips, needing to feel him all over me. *With you here by my side and pleasuring my body.*

He groaned, responding to my kiss, but when my hand went to his waistband, he caught my wrist. His tongue swept into my mouth before he pulled back and rasped, "You don't know how badly I want to do that, but I can't lose focus." He tapped an ear. *I need to listen in case Octavia tries something, and I'm pretty sure she will. Your safety and getting you some answers are more important tonight. That, and holding you.*

I wanted to pout, but I forced my bottom lip to stay firmly in place. He was right. With Octavia here and Josie recovering, we needed to listen for any signs of trouble. I forced a smile, knowing he was saying no *for me*. Everything he'd done had been to protect me, even when he'd rejected me in front of the school. Though he'd been in the wrong, he'd thought he was doing the right thing.

He held me against his chest, my head resting right over his heart. The comforting and steady beat of his heart soothed me while the buzz of our connection sprang to life and his musky sandalwood-and-amber scent wrapped around me. He trailed his fingertips along my arm and pressed his chin to the top of my head.

My chest expanded until it ached. I felt so special and loved. No one had ever made me feel this way before him, and I had no doubt he would always protect me, even at the cost of himself.

I felt the same way about him, and before I realized it, I fell into a blissful, peaceful sleep.

Raffe and Sky, Adam linked, stirring me from my rest.

My eyes cracked open, and for a moment, I couldn't remember where I was. It sounded as if Adam was standing right over us.

Raffe tensed. I realized I was turned away from him and he was spooning me from behind. The way my body thrummed from his warmth had me not wanting to move an inch. This was what waking up with him would be like every day for the rest of my life, and I *loved* it.

What? Raffe asked as he pulled me closer.

It's Dave, Adam said hurriedly. *Get here fast.*

CHAPTER FOUR

Despite the warmth from Raffe's body, my blood turned cool and jolted, and my wolf stirred. My breath caught. *Is he dead?* As much as I wished I was concerned because he was a person, it wasn't only that. He had answers that could get us closer to whoever had made him act for the Veiled Circle, the secret society that had kidnapped me.

He's not dead, but he's in a panic, demanding to talk to you, Adam replied.

Raffe's arms tightened, and his wariness swirled between us as he linked, *Then she's not fucking coming. He doesn't get to make demands.*

I turned to him, lifting a brow. Not wanting Adam to overhear, I spoke out loud. "You actually think I'm not going?" There was no way in hell I was letting him exclude me. "I was the one he drugged, and I want to hear his explanation."

He opened his mouth, but I wasn't done. "And I'm *not asking* for permission. You're my mate, not my boss. Be careful what your next words are."

Raffe? Adam asked. *Are you on your way?*

A chuckle vibrated through the pack link, and Keith interjected, *I bet Skylar is scolding him right now and informing his sorry ass that she will, in fact, be coming. Raffe's preoccupied and not in the way he likes when it comes to her.*

My face burned, and I was thankful none of them could see my reaction. I wasn't ashamed of enjoying sex with Raffe, but there was something mortifying about getting called out on it.

Raffe scowled. *Shut the fuck up. You're making her uncomfortable.*

As much as I understand where you're coming from, Skylar should come. He's refusing to talk to anyone but her. Adam sounded resigned. *He said it's something we should all know, and if Supreme Priestess Olwyn gets here before he can explain himself to Skylar, he'll never be able to.*

My heart dropped into my stomach. I didn't like the sound of that. "Raffe."

"Yeah, okay. I won't argue with you." Raffe jumped out of bed. "Let's get over there."

I wasn't sure whether to be relieved or frustrated about what had made him change his mind. I'd save further argument for another time when he got all protective and growly.

I snagged my darker-purple jacket and slid it on as we hurried out of my room. Putting on the jacket was quicker than fully dressing in a bra and a new shirt.

Lucy, get up, Raffe linked as we hurried into the living room. *I need you to keep an eye on Octavia while we're gone.*

She blinked and sat up on the couch directly across from us, where she had a view of the hallway. *What time is it?*

Six, Raffe answered as he reached the door and opened it. *Dave is awake and wants to talk to us before Supreme Priestess Olwyn gets there. Whatever it is must be important if he wants to discuss it at this hour when he knows how much I despise him.*

I stayed on his heels, knowing Lucy would pull through for us. She always did.

Or gloat. Lucy sighed. *And yeah, I'll get up and see if I can get Josie to eat and drink a little more.*

That wasn't a bad idea. *Let me know if you need anything or if Octavia does anything suspicious.*

I will. I don't want to be the only one handling any of that.

That was fair. I wouldn't want to be either.

Raffe took my hand, still inching in the lead because of his longer legs. Damn sexy, tall man who towered over me. Despite all that, he didn't drag me like I knew he could.

Soon, we were exiting through the front double doors, racing toward the men's apartment building. That was when it struck me. I'd never been to Raffe's place. That couldn't be normal ... surely.

The cold, dark October morning air blanketed me. The faint drizzle had returned. The normal weather conditions comforted me. At least I could rely on one thing, even if it was the shitty weather.

The men's building looked identical to the women's, right down to the paint. We hurried inside and took the elevator to the sixth floor. Their building had one more floor than the women's.

The hallway also looked identical, but there were two fewer apartments on either side of the hallway. That made sense, given that the guys had three people in each apartment instead of two.

Why do they have more students per place than the women do? I linked as he turned right and raced down the hallway.

Floors one through five are just like yours. The football team is assigned to this floor, and they wanted to put more of us in a space together for camaraderie or some shit like that.

I didn't need to see his face to know he was rolling his eyes; I could feel his slight annoyance in my chest.

Their apartment was the last one on the right, and before he could type in the code, the door opened, revealing Keith. His hair was messy for him, and he was rubbing his temples like he had a headache. *He won't shut up. He keeps talking about Skylar and freaking out. He's petrified of something, but he won't tell us what.*

"I only hope she understands," Dave said loudly. "And Raffe gives me a chance to explain before he kills me. After everything they've done, I'd rather he do it than *them*, anyway."

"Man, they're here. Okay." Adam sounded tired. "You'll get to tell her. Give her a minute."

The only thing different about this apartment was that there was a room to the right behind their couches since their layout was the opposite of ours. I didn't know why I'd expected their space to be different, especially since the buildings appeared to have been built at the same time.

Voices were coming from the room on the right, so we shot past Keith and through the living room. Inside the bedroom, Raffe's scent was mixed with copper and a faintly sweet smell.

Adam towered over Dave in the queen-size bed. The vampire had an evergreen comforter over his body, which shook with cold, nerves or a combination of the two.

I took in a picture of Raffe's motorcycle stuck into the

mirror of his dresser. I wasn't surprised to count ten trophies on top of the dresser, but I blinked when I noticed one was of a guy holding a bowling ball. *What the hell?*

Before I could ask, Dave's hazel eyes focused on me, some of the golden flecks showing now, further proof he was healing.

The betrayal by this guy, whom I'd thought of as a friend, hit me. My blood fizzed, and a lump formed in my throat.

He tried to sit up but groaned and fell back. "Sky." His voice cracked. "I'm so damn sorry. But you're already smelling more alluring now."

The fizz allowed me to read his remorse and sincerity. That was the only benefit of my emotions stirring my blood, but if I didn't calm my blood, he could lose control and try to attack me again.

"Don't fucking *look* at her," Raffe growled, edging in front of me. His protectiveness and concern made my heart race faster.

Babe, he feels bad, and he wants to explain what happened. I pushed calm toward Raffe, but his back tensed more. I wanted to touch him and calm him down, but I also wanted my blood to remain at a fizz so I could read Dave's emotions. *Give him a chance.*

Asking me not to protect you is like asking me not to breathe. I need to do both to survive.

Butterflies took flight in my stomach. Even though I knew how much I meant to him, hearing him admit it so openly made me swoony. *Let him give you a reason to get that way in this meeting before you do. Otherwise, be nice.*

He glanced over his shoulder at me and pouted.

Stepping next to Raffe, I cleared my throat to get Dave

to focus on me. "Raffe just needed to make sure you understand that if you try something against me, he'll hurt you."

"I'm aware." Dave shivered and flinched from what had to be the pain from his chest wound.

"What's so urgent?" I wanted to get straight to the point because I didn't want to be here when Supreme Priestess Olwyn arrived.

He nodded and swallowed. "First, I need to explain why I did what I did."

"I'd love to hear this explanation as well," Raffe rasped, making sure Dave didn't forget he was there. Not that he could anyway.

Dave licked his lips. "I did something that would make the wolf shifters want me dead." He stopped, his hands clenching at his sides.

I tried to be patient, but if he didn't continue, I might scream.

"I ... I lost control and drank from someone." He cut his eyes at the wall between Adam and me. "Another supernatural."

Adam scratched the back of his neck. "Drinking from another vampire isn't forbidden. Most mated couples do that from time to time."

"It wasn't another vampire." He blinked and cracked his neck. "It was a wolf shifter."

I shook my head. "I thought wolf shifter blood was toxic to vampires, and now you're telling me you drank from *two* wolves and survived?"

"It wasn't two wolves." He stared at the smooth white ceiling. "It was the same wolf shifter both times. Josie."

"*Josie?*" Keith stormed into the room and stopped between Adam and me. "No way. Not possible. She'd have told us."

"She didn't because she let me do it, and then she freaked out." Dave placed a hand over his mouth. "I realized if you all found out what she let me do and that I lost control, we'd both be punished, so I asked Slade for help."

I tensed. "When was this?" Even as I asked, I suspected it had something to do with Dave drugging me so that the Veiled Circle could kidnap me.

"At the beginning of the school year. He and Supreme Priestess Olwyn showed up along with Lafayette." He sighed.

Every time I heard Lafayette's name, it took me back to the night he tried to make me forget about the vampire attack, which had revealed that the stronger the power coursing through my blood was, the more appealing I smelled to vampires, causing them to lose their rational mind and become desperate to drink from me. Lafayette was the vampire people called to handle such things, and I wondered if that was part of his job description as the head of housing here at the university. He was responsible for keeping supernaturals and humans separated, which would involve altering human memories when needed.

"Why?" Adam's brows pinched together. "Lafayette can't do anything with a supernatural's memory. And why wouldn't Josic tell us?"

An unreadable feeling passed from Raffe to me.

"Lafayette came because they thought I drank from a human, but when Slade and Olwyn realized it was a wolf shifter, they went to the—" He cut himself off.

I suspected I knew where this was heading. "They know about the *Books of Twilight* and the hidden library. But the coven isn't aware that Raffe knows."

Dave's jaw dropped. "Oh."

"Wait." Keith lifted a hand. "You're telling me the books

that were supposed to be destroyed centuries ago are in a fucking hidden library somewhere, and we haven't done a damn thing about it?"

My head spun. I hadn't thought about how Adam and Keith would react to that news, but I didn't want Dave to hold back information.

Raffe growled. "I didn't tell anyone because Slade was using the books to find answers about Sky's heritage and how her power works. I didn't want the books destroyed until Skylar learned everything we could to help her control her magic so she didn't fucking implode. I also wanted to protect you all from my dad's wrath." He lifted his chin, staring at his friends.

"I asked him not to." I wouldn't let Raffe take the blame for all that. "So if you're going to be upset with anyone, it should be me. I'm his mate, and I asked him to keep that a secret." What I said wasn't technically a lie. I'd been his fated mate even before we completed our bond, but I tried to imply that I'd asked him after the bond completion, giving my claim more power.

"As much as I hate to interrupt to tell on myself some more, this needs to come out. Supreme Priestess Olwyn won't hesitate to come here and finish me."

My head jerked back. "Finish you?"

"That's what I'm trying to tell you." Dave moaned as he sat upright, his face flushing. When he got situated, he exhaled noisily. "Slade and Olwyn found a memory-wiping spell in one of the books, and Slade waited for Josie to return from a run in the woods after our connect—er, my need to feed from her snapped. They were able to erase her memory and ease whatever might have happened when I fed from her."

I swallowed. He'd almost said *connection*. Were they

fated mates? "What does any of this have to do with you drugging me?" Slade was friends with Dave, and when he learned Dave was here, he'd cared enough to ask about him.

"Supreme Priestess Olwyn told me I had to drug you." He winced. "And Slade came to get you after I told them you were unconscious. It was the only way they wouldn't rat me out to the wolf shifters."

I shook my head. This *couldn't* be true ... but my blood was at a steady fizz, and I could read it was all truth.

"Are you saying Supreme Priestess Olwyn and Slade handed her over to the secret society?" Raffe whispered scarily.

"No." He steepled his hands. "I'm telling you, they're part of the secret society and planned it all, including knocking me out when they came to get Skylar."

My blood neared a hum, and I touched Raffe to ground myself. "But Slade was *kidnapped*." My voice rose so high it was almost inaudible. "He *saved* me."

"I don't know anything about that. I was locked up. But I know for a fact that Slade has been testing you the entire time you've been here." Dave held out his hands, palms up. "He told me he found you the first night you were here and watched you in the woods. He saw a deer walk right up to you."

Acid churned in my stomach and inched up my throat. Dave hadn't known about that.

"Fuck, man." Keith fisted both hands. "I smelled him in the woods that night, but I thought he was out there practicing magic."

"That's not all." Dave sighed. "That day at the bookstore when the books fell, when I returned to the stand, I glimpsed Slade outside, watching you."

My eyes burned, and my heart felt like it was being

stabbed repeatedly. "By making the books fall like that when my blood wasn't humming, he had me thinking I was going crazy." Between that and feeling like someone was stalking me, I'd been anxiety-ridden, making my emotions more volatile. Worse, my blood was still fizzing, and I knew Dave wasn't lying.

Boy, how I wished he was.

Slade had pretended to be my friend while manipulating me the entire time, even pretending to be kidnapped to make me think he'd saved me.

To get me to trust him again.

I placed a hand on my chest and pressed. The pain was so intense that I wouldn't be surprised if my heart ripped right out of it. The first person I'd trusted here, the one who'd made me feel as if I'd finally found a friend, had been behind my captivity.

My blood hummed, and I stepped into Raffe.

Dave rasped, "I was supposed to die in the woods. I should have. Lafayette was upset because he was the one who carried me to the spot. Skylar, you need to leave. This university isn't safe for you. It never was."

Raffe's protective instincts flared, and he looked at me, his eyes glowing. "*We've* got to go."

"If we disappear, they'll know, and our friends will be at risk." There was only one clear answer—we *all* had to leave. Everyone who was tied to us, including two people Raffe would object to.

"Fuck, she's right, man. We gotta figure this out." Adam sighed, glanced out the window across from him ... and froze. "And we don't have long."

CHAPTER FIVE

I dropped my hand and Raffe and I glanced out the window, which faced campus. Even though I didn't have the same view as Adam, I had no doubt what he saw—Priestess Olwyn heading toward the apartments.

"We've got to get out of here." I breathed through my teeth, rushing toward Dave.

Keith grabbed me around the waist and tossed me into Raffe. He linked, *You're going the wrong way.*

My back hit Raffe's elbow, and a sharp pain shot through my shoulder blade.

Raffe snarled as he placed his arm around me and tugged me behind him. His rage slammed into me, squeezing my already battered heart like a vise. The only time I'd ever come close to feeling this intensity was a couple of weeks after Raffe and I had broken up.

Touch her again, and I'll kill you, Raffe commanded through the bond.

Raising both hands, Keith widened his eyes. *Man, I was trying to move her out the door, especially since we now know who Supreme Priestess Olwyn is.*

We didn't have time for grandstanding. "We need to get Dave the hell out of here."

"Dave?" Raffe spun around, his face tight. "No fucking way."

"I'm not asking." Even though I loved this man with my entire heart and soul, he wasn't my boss. I couldn't be in a relationship with someone who tried to control my every move, and the only reason I wasn't angry with him was because he was protecting me out of love. "I'm not leaving without him."

"Listen, I appreciate what you're trying to do." Dave sighed and winced. "But I'm injured and will only slow you down. You should all go now while you still can."

This was further proof that Dave was a good guy. There was no way I was leaving someone behind who'd been threatened, and he hadn't known what they were going to do with me. He'd been put in an awful spot, one he regretted. "Then you better get moving."

Skylar, you can't be serious. This guy drugged you and wanted to drain you that day you were heading back to the apartments by yourself. Raffe stepped in front of me, blocking my way. *He got blood-crazed and drank from Josie. He should die before he loses control again.*

I placed my hands on my hips. *Have you ever made a mistake? Say, like, treating a girl like shit and adding to her losing control of her magic? You weren't nice to me. What would you have done if I'd decided you could never change and treat me differently? And don't forget, yes, he wanted to drink blood from me that night, but he controlled himself and told me I needed to walk away, not run. If he'd lost control, he would've jumped me. He's the only vampire to hold back once my blood had been activated.* I rocked back on my feet. *And how would Josie feel if you left him to die or be tortured after she risked her life to save him? I suspect she wouldn't be happy.*

"Fuck. Fuck. Fuck!" Raffe ran his fingers through his hair and pulled.

Guys, she's almost at the door. We need to go. Adam tapped his wrist. *We'll run out of time if you two keep standing here and arguing.*

Yeah, man. Just alpha-will her, and let's get the fuck out of here. Keith motioned to the door.

My stomach hardened, and I gritted my teeth. *I'm not leaving, and if you do something like that to me, our relationship will never be the same. Fated mates or not.*

He sighed, and the pressure on my chest released. He linked, *You better realize how damn much I love you.* He stalked past Adam and lifted Dave up like a princess.

Dave whimpered and his face twisted in agony.

"What the hell?" Keith gasped. "Are we seriously taking him? He'll slow us down."

"So will arguing about it." Raffe shoved past them toward the door. "This is important to Skylar. Let's fucking go." *And grab the keys to all our vehicles and the bike.*

The warmth of my love for Raffe rushed through me. Even when he didn't agree with me, he put my needs before his own.

Stay behind me, he linked as we hurried out the door. He added Lucy, Josie, Keith, and Adam to our connection. *Get your asses to the cars. We've got to get the hell out of here.*

What? Lucy replied. *What's going on?*

No time to explain, but bring Octavia and Josie, and hurry, Raffe replied.

But—

I understood that Raffe expected to bark a command

and be followed, but sometimes, taking an extra five seconds to explain things made people move faster. We hurried into the hallway with Keith and Adam a few steps behind me. Raffe opened the door to the stairwell as I explained, *Slade and Supreme Priestess Olwyn are part of the secret society that's trying to kill Dave and potentially me. We're all at risk, so we need to leave.*

I appreciated so much that their room was positioned right next to the stairwell, but as Raffe took the stairs, Dave grunted and groaned loudly.

"Man, be quiet," Keith muttered under his breath as they caught up. "You're going to lead her to us."

"I can't help it," Dave gritted back.

Raffe reached the first landing, and Dave clenched his eyes shut. His hand clutched the stab wound in his chest, and his face paled even more.

Try to take the stairs easier. I despised saying it because this was one of the two main reasons Raffe didn't want to bring Dave, but I had to stand by my decision and deal with the consequences. *Which means slow down. Otherwise, he will get louder.*

This is why Raffe should've alpha-willed her ass to leave him, Keith interjected.

My blood rose to a near hum, and my wolf edged forward. If we hadn't been running for our lives, I would've spun around and put him in his place, but I'd kept my wits about me for twenty-two years. I'd hold my temper, even though it was more difficult with my wolf's influence.

Drop it, Adam said before my mouth got the best of me. *What's done is done. Bitching about it won't change matters.*

Keith, do I need to remind you what I said about how you treat my mate? You're one claw's width away from crossing a line you'll never come back from. Raffe's jaw twitched as he took the next set of stairs slower.

Dave stopped making such loud noises and breathed through his teeth.

We were still moving quickly, but not fast enough with Supreme Priestess Olwyn on our tail. As each platform transitioned to another set of stairs, my heart rate picked up. I kept waiting to hear the door open and the priestess proclaiming she'd found us while spelling us. I'd never considered myself a dramatic person ... until *now*.

Babe, I won't let anything happen to you. I swear. Raffe moved easily as if he wasn't carrying a grown-ass man.

Here I was, out of breath from anxiety. He and I were definitely not the same type of person. *I'm not worried about me. I'm concerned about all of you getting caught in the fallout of whatever they want to kill or recruit me for.* What Warin had said to me in the bunker rang in my head: if I didn't join them, they would end me. I was either their weapon or a threat—there was no in-between.

You're my main concern. So, as long as we get you out of here, I'll consider it a win. Raffe picked up his pace, and Dave groaned.

The sound was loud and echoed down the hallway.

Shit.

We had one set of stairs left to go, but then my worst fear happened.

A door above us opened.

My heart hammered in my ears, distorting sounds.

"What in the goddess—" Supreme Priestess Olwyn's voice cut off. She must have looked over the rail as we reached the door that led outside.

"You're going to have to deal with the pain," Raffe

rasped as he opened the door. "You deserve to feel it anyway after all the shit you pulled."

As I ran out the door and the drizzle hit me in the face, I heard Supreme Priestess Olwyn say, "They've taken Dave and are running. Get the word out and stop them. I told you I should have—" The door to the apartments slammed shut, cutting off her last words as the four of us ran toward the vehicles.

It was past six thirty, and some students were out and about. A guy jogging on the road that circled the campus paused to watch us. I could only imagine how we looked to observers with Raffe carrying a man like a baby.

As we reached the edge of the women's apartments, the double doors of the men's apartments opened. Slade yelled, "Sky! What's going on?"

My heart ached, and I couldn't swallow around the lump lodged in my throat. Hearing his voice right after learning what he'd done to me made my mouth taste salty and bile churn in my stomach. I wasn't sure what to say. It was clear what we were doing. But maybe that was the point—for him to see what we'd learned.

Where are you guys? I linked with Lucy and Josie. I didn't see them, which meant they were likely still inside. Raffe had tied Octavia extremely well to the bed, so it wouldn't be easy to free her.

We're leaving the apartment. We'll be down in a few minutes, Lucy replied.

Shit. We had to buy them time.

Forcing my legs to slow, I rolled my shoulders and pushed the hair out of my face. The rain was coming down harder, making it more difficult to see. I was about to tell a big ol' fat lie, so I hoped like hell the coven members couldn't smell it. The rain should keep the smell from reaching too far. "Hey, sorry. We're in a hurry."

"I can see that." Slade chuckled, jogging toward me.

Two male coven members I'd never seen before were with him.

What the fuck are you doing? Raffe linked, his fear like a choke hold.

Keep going. Lucy and Josie aren't here yet. I have to buy us time. I knew it wouldn't go over well, but I was already stalling.

Slade stopped a few feet from me, his blond hair more of a medium brown in the precipitation. He shook his head, reminding me of a dog, and asked, "What's going on?"

"Dave ... he's not doing well." I chose my words carefully.

The nape of my neck tingled, which always happened when Raffe watched me from afar. I knew he was passing Dave off to one of the others and circling back to me. He wouldn't leave me alone with a threat.

But that was the thing. The Veiled Circle *needed* me, so they wanted to play nice in the hope I'd turn against my mate.

"He's still alive?" Slade's eyes flicked to the retreating figures behind me. He pursed his lips. I used to think his reaction was over Dave's well-being, but now I was certain it was consternation because the vampire was still breathing. How sad was that? What sort of people thought they should be in control when they didn't value the lives of others? At least the wolf shifters weren't killing other supernaturals just because someone had dirt on them.

"Yeah, he's hanging on." Raffe's deep voice came from a few feet behind me. He took my hand and stood stiffly at my side.

A shiver from how raspy and low his voice was shot down my spine. "Is there something you need? We're trying to get him help."

"Help? He's a supernatural. He can't go anywhere." Slade laughed forcefully. "Just take him back to his apartment. Mom wants to check on him. If anyone can help, it's her."

Shit. I hadn't thought this through, but we couldn't abandon Lucy and Josie. The Circle would use them as leverage over us, and I couldn't live with myself if something happened to those two ... and even Octavia. She might have been a shit biological mother, but that didn't mean she deserved to die, especially not if I had a brother. I didn't know anything about him, but no one deserved to lose their mom.

"He needs blood." Raffe lifted his chin. "Lots of it. The best thing we can do is take him somewhere isolated and steal some bags. If he drinks from a human, he'll kill them."

Slade scowled. "He's a vampire and none of your concern. He's an EEU student, and Mom should be taking point on this. I don't understand why you two are fighting against it. I honored your request to wait until this morning for Mom to come, and now you need to bring him back inside."

This stall tactic wasn't working. Josie and Lucy needed to come out *now*. We'd done everything we could to give them time.

Time we'd officially run out of.

Thankfully, they and Octavia rushed from the women's apartment building, but unfortunately, their timing was almost simultaneous with Supreme Priestess Olwyn stepping out of the men's apartments. The high priestess's emerald eyes locked on me.

We've got Dave in the car. You need to get away from them, Adam linked.

Just go. Sky and I will take the bike, Raffe linked back. *Take your cars if that's what you want and leave.*

The three women rushed toward the parking lot, and Slade's eyebrows rose. "What the hell is going on?"

Josie was stumbling, but she was holding her own. I hoped that meant something. "Josie isn't feeling the best either. We thought it'd—"

"Everyone needs to go back to their rooms," Supreme Priestess Olwyn huffed. Her long, light-blonde hair became wet, and her black dress suit clung to her figure. Her lips were crimson, a color that struck me as bloodstained now that I knew what she was. She puffed out her cheeks, making her cheekbones appear less sharp. "What in the goddess are you all thinking, running around in the rain like this, especially with two unwell students?"

Hatred flared inside me, more than what I felt toward Slade. He'd betrayed me, but Supreme Priestess Olwyn had done worse. She'd claimed me as one of her own coven members. *Let my hand go,* I linked.

Immediately, I felt the hurt roll off Raffe.

I need my blood to activate; otherwise, I don't think we'll get out of here. I could never rely on my blood to do what I wanted, but I knew one thing. It helped me survive, or at least tried to.

Raffe's emotions steadied, and I released his hand. It wasn't hard for my blood to hit the hum, and my wolf inched forward, but I couldn't risk shifting out here.

"No." I shook my head. "We aren't bringing them back." There was no point in keeping up pretenses. They already suspected that we knew; we'd just played the game a while longer.

I heard the car doors shut, telling me that everyone was settled.

"What happened?" Slade spoke slowly, controlling his voice. "Why are you fighting us?"

I tilted my head, tired of playing games. "Why would you ask? Are you worried about something?"

He laughed. "No. Of course—"

The smell of sulfur hit me, along with his fear and tension.

"Shut up," Supreme Priestess Olwyn snarled. "She's a wolf shifter."

My heart pounded, the power funneling into my hands and not my feet. I wasn't sure what would happen.

"They know." The supreme priestess lifted her hands.

Then something shattered.

CHAPTER SIX

Before I could turn toward the apartments, shards of glass pummeled Slade, Supreme Priestess Olwyn, and the two other students standing behind them.

I looked around. The glass was coming from the women's and men's dorm windows and was circling Raffe and me, leaving us untouched.

"Holy shit! Something exploded!" someone shouted from midcampus, near the cafeteria.

Then I noticed the shards were in tune with my pulse.

My breath caught. *I'd done this.*

The coven members crouched, hands over their heads, blood trickling from where the glass had hit them.

I spun and linked, *Run!*

Raffe didn't question me, and we took off toward the parking lot.

"They're getting away!" Slade exclaimed, but I could still hear the glass attacking them.

Get on the motorcycle, Raffe ordered me, holding the keys in his hand. *We'll get off campus and put our helmets on then. We don't have time for safety.*

We ran to his black bike and slid on, and he started the engine. I wasn't thrilled with riding the bike in the rain, but we had to get out of here. My blood still hummed, my heart racing in sync as I glanced back at the coven members, who were getting back on their feet.

The glass assault was over.

Raffe started the bike and backed up enough to shift into drive, then gunned it and wove around the cars to the exit, away from the apartments.

"Stop them!" Supreme Priestess Olwyn yelled.

I glanced back and cringed. All the windows I could see on both buildings had shattered, giving the place a dystopian look.

Yet another attribute I could add to my ever-increasing list of skills I couldn't control.

Hurry. Slade and the supreme priestess can control water. I wasn't sure whether Raffe knew that, but with how hard it was raining, I hated to think what they could do.

Two women appeared between the buildings; their wide eyes took in the sight. I hoped they were human, though I doubted that mattered. Supreme Priestess Olwyn would get Lafayette or another vampire to erase their memories.

Raffe pulled onto the road, and suddenly, we were hydroplaning. The bike tilted to the left, and a scream lodged in my throat. We were going to fall, and it would hurt like hell.

Hold on tight to me. Raffe growled as he kicked out his leg and pushed off the road to keep the bike upright.

I tightened my thighs against his body, but for once, his touch didn't comfort me. I grew dizzy, and my blood increased in strength. Then I noticed something strange. All this time, what I'd assumed was my blood began thrumming faster than my actual heart rate. It swirled around me like my blood but was somehow separate. What the hell? It felt like my wolf magic but stronger and more in sync with *me*. Was that my actual power?

Not wanting to cause more balancing issues, I buried my head against the center of Raffe's muscular back and wrapped my arms around his waist ... as much as I could. Even though he played quarterback, he was way more built than he appeared because of his height.

The tires skidded again as we hydroplaned to the other side. This was definitely Olwyn's and Slade's doing because it hadn't rained enough for the roads to be this treacherous.

"Fuck," Raffe snarled as he shifted his weight to compensate. Had we been human, we would have crashed, but Raffe held his own. Pain radiated from within him.

The sensation I'd always thought was my blood increased to a new level. The best way to describe it was singing. The humming was louder and stronger than ever, pulling closer to my skin and causing it to buzz, similar to my fated-mate bond with Raffe. The power merged with my connection to Raffe and my wolf.

This time, when Raffe righted the motorcycle, the wheels remained level. Every few seconds, I felt something push against me, hurting my insides.

More jolts came as if someone were kicking my chest and intestines from within. I'd never experienced pain like this, and I swallowed to keep in my agony.

Why are you hurting? Raffe asked.

I ... I don't know. My power hadn't felt like this before. Maybe this was what imploding felt like? *My power has gone crazy. Every few seconds, it's like it's fighting me.*

I lifted my head to determine what might be causing my internal attack and saw that we were driving past the brick administration building and the soccer fields. The iron gates to the campus loomed in front of us, and the rain eased back to a drizzle. I glanced back and couldn't see the coven members. The attack within me eased.

I'm hurrying, but I can't be reckless, not with you on the bike with me. He tensed more, and his worry added an extra edge to my hysteria, making me dizzy again.

I leaned my head against his back, not burying my face in it like before. With his body coiled so tightly, I felt like I was hugging a brick wall but one that smelled nice and was warm.

As soon as we breezed through the gate and were off campus, my lungs filled more easily. I focused on my breathing and the way my body tingled where it was pressed against Raffe.

Needing to feel his skin, I slid my hands underneath his shirt, and the strong buzz of our connection sprang to life.

He fidgeted. *You're going to make this hard on me.*

I snickered, my blood calming to a hum. I'd never imagined a day when I would consider a hum calm. *I'm not opposed to making you hard.*

His chest shook, his shoulders relaxing marginally. *Nor am I, but not when we're on two wheels speeding without helmets, and I'm carrying precious cargo. Besides, would you want me to wreck? My pretty face could get scarred.*

My blood eased to a fizz, settling quickly with our banter. Oh, how I missed feeling carefree. It felt like it had been ages. *It might make you look more rugged.*

Hey now. He snorted. *I'm already tall, dark, and mysterious. Why mess up what's working for me?*

I rolled my eyes, though he couldn't see it, and Lucy linked with all of us, *Please tell me you got away. I'm about to turn around.*

The easy moment between us vanished, and Raffe replied, *We did.*

Thank fucks, Adam interjected. *We were worried but didn't want to link in case you were under attack and needed to focus.*

When someone says thank fucks, is that singular or possessive? Keith asked, posing what he must have felt was a significant question. *'Cause I'm sorta torn. I could see it either way, so I guess it depends on how many fucks the person speaking has left.*

Raffe growled. *I have one fuck that I'm about to take care of if he doesn't stop interrupting with stupid shit.*

Possessive it is, Keith amended and went quiet.

"Sometimes, I wonder why I'm friends with him," Raffe grumbled to himself and shook his head.

As entertaining as this is, where are we going? Do I have time for a nap? Josie linked. *I'm exhausted and wound up riding with Lucy in Raffe's car so I can keep an eye on Octavia and deal with the demon cat.*

My body sagged against Raffe's. I'd been so focused on making sure we didn't leave Dave that I hadn't even thought about Cat-Keith. If that wasn't proof that Lucy was now his official owner, I wasn't sure what was. *Thank goodness you got her.*

Wouldn't have been upset if the mangy beast got left behind, Keith added. *I'd rather that if you guys refuse to change her name.*

And that right there is why it's never changing, Lucy said. *We know how much it infuriates you.*

Raffe glanced in the rearview mirror. *Head back to the pack. They won't risk coming there to attack right away. We need to inform Dad and his advisors of what's going on, but I don't want to tell him before we get there, not after how our last meeting went. I need him to see us and smell we aren't lying.*

A shiver racked me. Though my body temperature was naturally warmer now, between the rain and having caused the chasm between Raffe and his father, I was an emotional mess. I wasn't cold; it was all stress.

Raffe growled. *We're stopping soon to get jackets and helmets. I just want to put some distance between us and campus and make sure no one's following us.*

I hadn't considered the possibility that they'd get into their cars and chase us, not with the injuries they'd sustained and the glass shards lodged in their skin from the exploding windows. With the shattering windows and the scared students who had to be racing from the building, not understanding what was going on, the coven members would be forced to handle chaos. But we had no clue how many members the Veiled Circle had. They might have the resources to send someone after us.

A Chevron appeared on the left, a little more run-down than the gas stations in the city. Raffe slowed and coasted onto the gravel road and parked at one of the pumps out of the drizzle.

He went to the back, opened the storage container, then removed two full-face helmets and two leather jackets, one of which seemed to be my size.

Should I be jealous about the second jacket? I didn't like the icky sensation that crawled over my skin and the way my wolf edged forward, wanting to hurt whoever he might have bought it for. I wondered if it was Josie. She had pretended to be his girlfriend for *years*.

Raffe mashed his lips together. A raindrop fell from his dark hair and rolled down one cheek. "I ordered it when we were secretly dating." He winced as the tightness of his shame flowed between us. "It got here while we were broken up, and I didn't have a chance to think about giving it to you until now." Then the corners of his lips tipped up, and a smile broke through. "I told you no one has ever ridden with me before, and the only other person who's driven my bike is Keith. That was only because you were frozen and needed to get warm."

Warmth swarmed my chest, and I stepped closer to him. I stood on my tiptoes and kissed him, linking, *Right answer.*

I'm glad I didn't disappoint you. He leaned back and booped my nose. He then placed the larger jacket and the two helmets on our seats and held my jacket up for me. *I hate to cut this moment short, but we need to get going.* He frowned and said out loud, "We probably should've taken the car, but the bike is faster in case they followed us."

He had a point, and honestly, I didn't mind the bike, though I wished we were riding it for pleasure rather than fleeing for our lives. At least I could snuggle into my mate and feel him between my legs for the entire ride to Seattle. Best of all, I didn't have to share him with anyone. Now look who was being possessive, but I didn't feel a bit of shame for it.

As I slid into the jacket, he asked, *Do you want to see if we can meet up with Lucy and you can ride with them?*

I shook my head so hard that my neck popped, and I wondered if I'd given myself whiplash. Being parted from him was the worst thing I could do. *That never turns out well for either of us.*

He exhaled. *You're right. But I still—*

Stop. I placed one hand on his chest and, with my free hand, snagged the helmet. *There's no getting rid of me.*

Now, let's go to Seattle and talk to your dad—and maybe finally relax for a moment.

He glanced over his shoulder and tensed. *Yeah, you're right.* He quickly put on the jacket and his helmet, and we climbed on and took off, barreling out of the parking lot.

I glanced over my shoulder and saw a car getting smaller as he pushed the bike faster. *Is that someone from EEU?*

I'm not taking any chances.

With that, I leaned against the backrest, not wanting to crowd him while he drove, and settled in for the long ride.

THREE HOURS LATER, we were swerving up the twisty roads of Cougar Mountain, and my ass was sore—a little fact I hadn't expected. All I was doing was sitting on the back of a comfortable bike made for long rides, but my butt was numb and aching.

I'd expected to dread pulling into the long driveway that led to Raffe's pack home, but I was practically panting. I was ready to get off this bike, even if that meant King Jovian glaring at me.

I shifted and groaned. *I thought you said this was a cruiser bike.*

You hurting? Raffe turned the bike onto the road.

Let's just say there's no way we're having sex like I'd hoped. I dreaded getting off the bike.

Raffe wiggled. *You should've told me. I felt your discomfort, but I thought it was from coming here. It increased the closer we got.*

I've only felt like this one other time when I went horseback riding, and it wasn't even half this bad. I'd been sore for days, and I didn't want to think about how long it would take to recover from this.

I'll rub you down when we get to our room.

I guess that will do. Desire knotted in my stomach, making me reconsider my stance on sex.

The huge mansion towered ahead, thick woods of maple, cedar, and hemlock behind it. Stones framed each window with tan siding everywhere else.

Octavia, Keith, Josie, Lucy, Dave, and Adam stood on the stone path in front of the six stairs leading up to the gigantic wooden front door.

Aldric stood across from his daughter, looking every inch Marcel Gerard from *The Originals*. I still couldn't get over how uncanny his resemblance was to the vampire on that show. He stood in front of five other men, all giving off strong alpha vibes. But one key person was missing

King Jovian.

Instead of slowing down, Raffe sped up and parked the bike between his black BMW and a white Porsche. Tension radiated from him, and the spot in my chest where we were connected shrank, giving off dread.

What's wrong? I linked, removing my helmet. As soon as I did, I regretted it, feeling how my wet hair had dried underneath it. I must look like a train wreck.

Lovely.

Raffe replied, bringing Lucy, Josie, Keith, and Adam into the connection, *I'm not sure, but I'd like to know what's going on as well.*

The king isn't here, and Dad and the advisors want to talk to Raffe. Josie glanced at us, biting her bottom lip.

I noticed how close she and Dave were standing, their arms just brushing. Clearly, Aldric had noticed the same thing because his scowl flicked between them and us.

And you guys didn't think to inform me before we got here? Raffe replied, his jaw clenching. He took my hand and led me toward them, making it clear we were together.

Somehow, that made me fall more in love with him.

My ass ached with every step, but I stood tall, keeping my strides confident, even if I looked straight out of a horror flick.

Raffe stood tall and radiated alpha wolf power, which was stronger than any of theirs. He seemed more powerful than before, but maybe that was because I was a wolf shifter and could finally notice it.

"What's going on here?" Raffe asked, his voice deep and commanding. "Where's Dad?"

Puffing out his chest, Aldric sneered. "Why are you here?" He acted as if Raffe hadn't asked a question.

I swallowed. Something was off.

"Why am I here at my *home?*" he rasped.

"It's not your home anymore." Aldric pointed at Raffe. "You need to leave."

CHAPTER SEVEN

My mate released a ruthless snarl I'd never heard before, and I feared what it meant.

"What do you mean it's not my home anymore?" Raffe's nostrils flared, his mouth set in a firm line.

Every inch of me wanted to step closer to him, but I kept my feet firmly planted. Standing beside him would make it all worse. They needed to see *him*, their future leader and alpha, not me.

Aldric flicked his attention to me then back at Raffe. "Son, you chose a human—"

My patience snapped, and I stepped up beside Raffe anyway, allowing my wolf to surge forward. I rasped, "I'm not human anymore, so that's not a valid complaint."

Pride surged through our connection, catching me off guard. I'd thought Raffe would be annoyed with me for speaking up since he was the alpha heir, but the opposite was true.

"That's impossible." Aldric's forehead creased, and he leaned toward me and took a huge sniff. "That ... that has to be from the partial mate bond."

"It's completed now because she's a wolf," Raffe said and moved so Aldric could get a strong whiff of him as well. "Our scents are combined in *both* of us."

"What is this sorcery?" The older man's eyes bulged. "She must be a witch. Someone we can't trust. This goes against nature."

Raffe's jaw clenched.

Despite holding my tongue my entire life, I couldn't anymore. I was tired of people disregarding me and pushing me aside. "Even if that were the case, I was still *human* first. Either way, I'm supernatural now, whether you like it or not."

"Wolf shifters can't be turned." A man with ash-blond hair crossed his arms. He appeared to be in his fifties, slightly older than the king and Aldric. "Because inevitably, some weak *fool*"— he paused, glaring at Raffe—"falls in love with a human and hopes he can change her so they can be accepted by the pack. But that's not how it works."

"Yet, she's proof that it did." Raffe gestured at Aldric. "You met her before the bond was complete, and you could tell she was human."

"The rest of us can vouch for it as well." Adam moved forward, flanking my left side. "And she's not a witch. She's never smelled like one."

"Son, be quiet." A man with light-brown skin and curly dark hair broke in front. "You don't need to remain loyal to someone unfit to lead, especially when the king has ordered that his son may not return here. Even the king has turned his back on Prince Raffe."

The sharp slice of pain that came from Raffe stole my breath. Even though Raffe had said that if being cast out was what it took for us to be together, so be it, hearing that his dad had actually come to that decision hit hard, especially when the news had come from someone else. His dad should have informed Raffe himself.

"Not only has he decided to mate with *her*, but he had you bring a human and a vampire to our pack home." Adam's dad's expression twisted in disgust. "Someone so reckless can't take over the alpha position and lead us."

Between his words and Raffe's pain, I couldn't take any more. "You mean someone who isn't bigoted and who can see things beyond the wolf shifters' point of view? Because, let me tell you, narrow-minded people actually hinder progress and alienate anyone different from themselves. True strength and courage are in seeing the world from other perspectives because not all things are right or wrong. There's a shit ton of in-between."

"This is exactly what they're referring to." A man with bronze skin scoffed. "You have no respect for tradition and supernatural law. I'm just glad my son, Adam, Josie, and Lucy can now be free of Raffe's recklessness."

A lump formed in my throat. I hadn't considered it could be just Raffe and me when this was all done. My heart ached at the thought of not having Adam, Keith, Josie, and Lucy around. And lumping Keith in with the rest of them made me question my sanity. But Raffe and I could get through anything, even as a pack of two, as long as we were together.

I couldn't gloss over what Keith's dad had accused me of. "I do respect tradition and laws, as long as they make sense. There's value in all of that, and even in past mistakes. But standing between fated mates ... there's no justification in the world for that."

"I agree." Keith stepped forward, dragging Octavia along slightly behind him. "Dad, they love each other. Believe me, I was against it before, but if you just—"

"*No!* Stop right there." Keith's dad's eyes darkened to onyx. "You will not get more involved in this mess than you already are. This ends *now*."

"That's something I can agree with." Raffe arched a brow, and his gaze settled on Aldric. "Should I link with my father, or do you want to inform him that I'm here to speak with him?"

"Your father isn't here. He's in Atlanta delivering this unfortunate news." Aldric clasped his hands together. "That's why I'm here, delivering *this* news since your mother went with him. He doesn't want to be interrupted unless it's a life-or-death emergency, which this isn't."

I snorted. A person *could* call it life or death. "What do you consider a situation where we show up with a human, a very injured vampire, and Josie at half strength?"

"An unfortunate inconvenience." Aldric's expression softened as he glanced at his daughter. "One I'm looking forward to hearing explained."

I had no doubt he *didn't* want to hear it, but I wouldn't contradict him.

As if reading my mind, Josie and Dave flinched, and Josie leaned away from Dave, biting her bottom lip.

You've got nothing to be ashamed of, I linked with her, wanting her to know she had my support. *Other than the almost-dying part.*

The corners of her mouth tilted upward, and Aldric's concern faded into a scowl.

"What's so funny?" he asked.

"So damn much," Raffe interjected and took my hand. "This whole situation is appalling because I did *nothing* wrong. If Dad wants me gone, so be it." His eyes glowed, and he lifted his head high. "He's not my alpha anymore. I can't be part of a pack that doesn't support the woman I love."

A short man in the back who hadn't spoken gasped, and the other four men grimaced. Aldric's nose wrinkled.

What's going on? Whatever he was doing must be huge.

I've left Dad's pack. Raffe winced as if in agony. *I'm technically a rogue and can't link with anyone here anymore.*

Rogue. That wasn't good. Even in nature, wolves preferred to stay in packs. *Wait, but we're still communicating like this.*

He squeezed my hand and answered, *We're fated mates.*

Well, there was no way in hell I'd abandon him. "That goes for me too. I don't see King Jovian as my alpha, though in fairness"—I pursed my lips—"I never did."

"Who would've thought you'd grow on me?" Keith snorted. "And if you're trying to join Raffe's pack, this is how you do it." He handed Octavia off to Adam and strolled over to stand in front of Raffe.

"Keith, what are you doing?" his dad growled and clutched his arm.

Keith jerked his arm away while his eyes met Raffe's. He then averted them to the ground. Just like that, I felt a warm link I was familiar with vanish. It was so strange, and I missed the connection.

"What did you do?" His dad's voice shook with rage.

"So, I just look at him and then look down?" There had to be more to it.

You have to challenge me, then avert your eyes and submit.

Submit.

I didn't like the sound of that, but if that was what it took to have Raffe lead our little rogue pack, I'd do it.

I released his hands and shook out my own, preparing to

look away. Not that it would be that hard. Raffe was strong, more so than me. I just wasn't sure what to expect.

You're just locking eyes with me, not preparing for a fight. Raffe mashed his lips together, a bit of lightness emanating from him.

The slight reprieve from the hurt was much needed.

Fine. I rubbed my hands, wanting everyone to see that I supported Raffe just as much as he supported me. Then I met his gaze.

My wolf inched forward, embracing the alpha challenge. Raffe's crystal-blue eyes lit up like the summer sky, gorgeous and pure, exactly like his soul. I told my eyes to look downward, but they didn't listen. Instead, they remained in place, engaged in the battle.

Shit.

"You need to look down," Keith spoke slowly, like I hadn't understood him the first time. He stomped his foot on the concrete, emphasizing his point. "Right here, where your feet touch."

Adam sighed. "Man, I think she knows what you meant by down."

Something's wrong, I linked, not wanting anyone to hear me say it. *I can't. My wolf is refusing to listen to me.*

Raffe's irises brightened. *It's your wolf. Damn, she's strong. If you don't want to chance being the alpha, you'll have to rein her in and force her to listen to you. Her animalistic side is showing.*

Great.

Yet again, I had to control something I didn't understand at all.

"That's what he gets for splitting off." The smaller man in the back laughed. "He's going to have to follow a woman. I knew he wasn't king material."

When we're done here, I'm kicking his ass first. My power jolted in tune with the beating of my heart. The power coursed through me the same way blood filled my veins.

Even with me threatening his dominance, Raffe smirked and replied, *I'm fine with that. And if you want or need to lead, I'm okay with that as well.*

Even though my wolf wanted to *win*, there was no way I could do that to him, especially in front of these sexist men. His reputation would be ruined.

I took a deep breath, concentrating on the magic swirling in my chest. I visualized a lilac thread surrounding it—something I'd never noticed before or couldn't concentrate on. Imagining my favorite color comforted me ... made my wolf feel less foreign. I yanked on the thread to force her to retreat.

A drop of sweat dripped down my forehead, and perspiration beaded on Raffe's upper lip.

This was going on too long.

Desperate, I jerked harder on the thread, trying like hell to shock my wolf. I felt her retreat, and before she could surge forward again, I broke eye contact with him.

The thousands of warm spots in my chest vanished, and the spot that had been Keith's popped back up inside my chest.

It's about damn time. Keith tapped his foot exactly where I'd wound up staring.

I cut my eyes at him and retook my spot at Raffe's side.

For a minute, I thought you might win. Raffe took my hand, raised it, and kissed the back.

Maybe I would have. I'd never know. Which I would forever be good with because being arcane-born was challenging enough. I didn't want to be a pack leader, especially of people who understood this world and what being a wolf shifter was about far better than I ever would. *Better you than me. You're an amazing leader.*

"Okay, you've made your point." Aldric flicked his wrist, his face flushed. "Now leave and take your human and vampire with you."

Raffe's neck corded, and I could feel his anger take hold.

"That's more than fine with me," Adam muttered and dragged Octavia behind him toward Raffe.

His dad lifted his chin. "Yes, give that woman to him, and let's go home."

Unlike Keith, Adam didn't make a production out of it. Instead of proclaiming his intention, he met Raffe's stare. Their wolves emerged, but like Keith, he submitted to Raffe seamlessly, and his warm spot returned inside my chest.

Adam's dad stumbled back as he paled.

Lucy followed suit, leaving Josie standing alone next to Dave a few feet away. As each of them transitioned to Raffe's pack, they moved next to him or behind him, effectively drawing a line in the sand.

Adam's and Keith's dad's nose wrinkled, and Aldric grabbed Josie's arm.

"Come on, Josie," he said loudly. "At least you haven't lost your mind, other than standing so close to a bloodsucker."

When she didn't move, Aldric tugged on her again, but she glanced at Dave and then at us.

"I'm sorry," she muttered.

I forced a smile, wanting her to know I didn't blame her. She had a dad who wanted her in his life—something Raffe no longer had.

"You don't owe them an apology for *anything*." With his

free hand, Aldric rubbed his forehead. "Their recklessness will end up killing them."

Dave turned to us and swayed. He still wasn't doing well.

"I'm not apologizing to them." Josie leaned back and frowned. "I'm apologizing to you. Even though I know you love me and want to protect me, I believe Skylar and Raffe should be together, and I can't remain with a pack that's biased."

My breath caught. Once again, Josie had surprised me. Her character was rather meek and mild, but she had a backbone I hadn't seen before.

"Stop this." Aldric scoffed. "Right now. You don't know what you're going up against."

"Neither do you, Dad." Unlike the others, Josie remained in her spot, but she completed the stare-off and, seconds later, joined us.

"No." Aldric dropped his hand like he'd been touching something hot. "Josie—"

Raffe wrapped an arm around my waist and straightened. "I think it's time to head out." He spoke loudly with command, sounding every bit like a leader.

Warmth spread through me. He might be the leader, but I'd be in control in bed. But damn if I didn't find his sense of command sexy.

Josie kissed her dad's cheek, then looped her arm through Dave's and headed back to the vehicles.

We all turned that way, and Octavia's brows furrowed as if she were trying to figure out the most confusing puzzle in the world.

I nodded toward the cars, and she sighed before following Adam and Keith.

"Wait!" Aldric called out. "Maybe we can work this out."

Raffe paused, and I stilled beside him.

"It's too late for that. You all made your intentions and how you feel about my mate clear."

We continued, and when we reached the vehicles, Raffe tossed the motorcycle keys to Keith. "Lucy, Josie, and Dave can take your car with the cat. Sky can't handle riding on that again. Octavia can stay with us."

Raffe got the BMW keys, and soon, I was sliding into the orange leather passenger seat. My ass ached when I sat, but the seat was so much more comfortable than the bike.

With everyone in the vehicles, Raffe turned on the child lock so Octavia couldn't get out. He backed out first and sped a little too eagerly toward the road.

I couldn't blame him. I wanted to get far away too.

As soon as we'd all pulled out, Raffe turned in the direction away from Seattle.

So, I hate to be like this, but where are we going? Keith linked, asking the question no one wanted to address.

We couldn't go back to campus, nor could we stay in their childhood homes.

Despite my reluctance, I suggested, "We could go to my parents' house."

Raffe's hands tightened on the steering wheel. "That's the first place the coven will look. But they shouldn't bother your parents if you aren't there. We'll have to rent a cabin or something."

"Actually, I have a suggestion." Octavia cleared her throat. "But you won't like it."

CHAPTER EIGHT

"If you're going to suggest we let you go, it's not happening." Raffe glanced at her in the rearview mirror. "You're stuck with us. I won't let you run back and report to the society or whatever group you belong to."

I didn't trust her either. This woman had abandoned me because of who I'd become. What sort of parent did that?

She leaned forward and sighed. "What I saw back there made me realize this group is different, and I'm offering to take you all to my home."

I turned to her to see her reaction. I hated that my blood ... power ... or whatever gave me my abilities was calm, so I couldn't read her intent. Learning to access those abilities on my own would be *amazing*.

Her expression was smooth, and her heartbeat was faster than normal, but that could be from being our prisoner.

Raffe chuckled grimly. "You think we're desperate enough to trust you? No fucking way."

"Where else are you going to go? You don't have many options." She leaned back and crossed her arms. "Believe me when I say that this offer is a big deal. Dru will be pissed as soon as he sees that I've brought wolf shifters and a vampire to our home."

My ears perked up. "Dru?" I asked, then wanted to clamp my hands over my mouth. I despised that the name caused so many questions to spin around in my head. I hadn't meant to sound interested because I wasn't. I mean, how could I be? They'd tossed me out like garbage.

She grimaced. "Your fath—" But she cut herself off.

My lungs seized, and my heart ached. There was no doubt what she'd been about to say.

Raffe reached over the center console and squeezed my hand. The comforting buzz of our connection sprang to life, but the pain didn't ease much.

Granted, being strange, not fitting in, and feeling like my birth parents hadn't wanted me were three things I'd battled my entire life. Facing my birth mother now meant staring down one of my biggest demons; she had admitted those reasons were, in fact, why they'd given me up.

After a long moment, she ran her hands down her jeans and finished, "I mean, my husband."

The two people who were supposed to have been my protectors as a child now had names, and I knew the face of one better than I wanted to admit. You'd think, at twenty-two, I'd be past all the betrayal and anger, but I felt like a child again, wanting to know why I wasn't worthy of their love.

"If *Dru* would be pissed, why are you even offering?" Raffe focused on the road, taking a sharp turn as we headed east from Seattle.

"Skylar needs my help and a safe place to stay." Octavia closed her eyes a beat longer than seemed normal. "No one knows where we live. We stay away from most every supernatural."

Did she not think we'd pick up on "*most* every"? I rolled my eyes. "So some supernaturals are there. We can't risk anyone discovering our presence, and that's if we even agree to trust you. It sounds like a horrible idea." I pushed aside my desire to agree so I could meet the brother I'd never known I had. He was the only one who was truly innocent. I assumed he had to be older, but she hadn't mentioned him.

My heart stopped. What if something had happened to him?

"The supernaturals around us stay out of all that drama. They keep to themselves, much like we do."

Babe, I know you want answers, but she could be walking us into a trap. If Slade was pretend-kidnapped to make it look like he saved you, this could be another act. She's potentially not even your mother. The coven could be trying to manipulate us again.

I faced forward, staring out my window at the trees blurring by. The sun peeked from behind a gray cloud, but that didn't stop the drizzle. My body went numb as I processed what he'd said, but he was right. There was no proof that this woman was my mother. The information she'd shared she could've gotten from the Veiled Circle.

The problem was I didn't like thinking that way. When I checked her for magic earlier, she hadn't had any, but that didn't mean she wasn't choosing her words carefully. It had been a highly volatile moment. I could ask her again, but I wasn't upset enough to sense the truth of the answer.

My emotions were a hot mess. I both wished she hadn't come but also wanted to know more. I wasn't sure I could handle finding out she was pretending.

"Thanks for the offer, but we'll pass." Raffe leaned

forward and turned on the Rolling Stones, indicating that all conversations were over.

And I loved him for that.

SIX HOURS LATER, we pulled up to a rental house Josie had found online. We were outside of Spokane, Washington, close to Riverside State Park. We'd stopped at Walmart on our way in to grab clothes, food, and other essentials, so we had a ton of things to carry in.

Sky, Josie, and Lucy should go in with Dave and Octavia while the three of us unload the vehicles, Raffe linked with everyone he could and opened his door.

Even though I wanted to help, I didn't have it in me to argue. The entire ride here, I'd struggled with everything we'd lost because of me. If I hadn't come into the picture, Raffe would still be making his dad proud, and they'd all be at school, completing their education.

I took in the gray brick house and headed up the slanted porch to the front door, then punched in the code.

By the time the door opened, Octavia and Dave were behind me, with Josie and Lucy, Cat-Keith clinging to her neck, taking up the rear.

We stepped right into the living room, my dark-purple sneakers squeaking on the maple floor. Right across from me, a large window overlooked the side of the yard where a basketball court connected to the woods that led to a park.

Lucy said, "Why don't you four sit while I put things away in the kitchen?"

The house had an open floor plan, and I could see the dining room and the kitchen from here.

I can help, I linked with her, wanting to pull my own

weight.

One of us needs to stay with Octavia and Dave. Josie's still a little out of it, so if they try something, she might not be able to handle them, and honestly, I need to be busy.

Okay. That was different. *Let me put Keith somewhere so she doesn't get in the way.*

"Come on." I took the cat, waved for them to follow me, and headed to the L-shaped, dark-brown pleather couch. I hurried and put Keith inside the first door to the left, which was a bathroom. I cracked open the window, letting in cool air. Keith jumped off me and hurried to the window, lay down on the wide sill, and started licking her paws. I plugged the sink and filled it partway with water for her.

With Cat-Keith settled, I went back to the others and sat on the end of the couch closest to the door and kitchen so I'd have more time to react if Octavia tried something.

From the way Dave continued to grimace as Josie helped him into the room, I had no doubt he wasn't fully recovered.

Raffe, Keith, and Adam brought in the food first and then other items. Each time my mate walked by, my eyes locked onto his ass and the way it moved with each step.

He was so damn sexy and, even better, the most caring person I'd ever known.

I eventually snatched the remote from the light-gray coffee table and turned on the television, needing something to do other than watch people work while the rest of us sat in awkward silence. I flipped channels, wishing like hell this place had a smart TV for Netflix.

Then Josie cooed, "Let's watch that!"

My lips tipped up. The movie was *How to Lose a Guy in 10 Days*, and for some reason, her liking it made things feel more normal. Though I had no interest in the movie, I tossed the remote on the table as the guys came in with the last load.

As soon as the door shut, Raffe came over and pulled me to my feet while holding the bag with our things. He asked, "Which one is our room?"

Josie pointed to the stairs on the other side of the living room. It was a split foyer with one set going up and the other side down. "Upstairs. The other three rooms are downstairs."

"Sounds good to me." He tugged on my hand.

I glanced at Lucy, who was still putting things away. "I should—" I started.

Fuck no. I need—he replied, tugging me to his chest and forcing me to stare into his eyes. *You.*

My body warmed.

"Man." Keith set his bag on the floor and waved a hand in front of his nose. "Can you two not make it obvious why you're leaving? We knew when he asked where the bedroom was, so you don't have to go and make it smell like a Bath and Body Works shop in here. Those damn places give me headaches 'cause the scents are so strong."

I snorted so loud that my throat burned. "You frequent Bath and Body Works that often? What scent's your favorite?"

Lucy stood from behind the white island in the center of the kitchen. "Oh, I bet it's Japanese Cherry Blossom."

"Nah." Josie beamed. "He seems like a Perfect Peony sort of guy."

"Ha ha." Keith's cheeks flushed, but he stood tall. "If you must know, it's Warm Vanilla Sugar, so beware. If I smell it on any of you three, I'll know you're trying to get my attention."

Raffe snarled, his nostrils flaring while Dave hissed

lowly.

"Keith," Adam sighed. "You're a dumbass."

Raffe marched toward Mr. Fragrance, dropping the bag, and rasped, "If you ever lump my mate in with other women like that again, I'll teach you a fucking lesson."

Keith lifted his hands in surrender. "I was kidding. *Gods!*"

"You don't joke about someone's mate like that." Dave's nose wrinkled. "You should know better."

To defuse the situation, I took Raffe's hand and tugged him to the stairs. *Let's get settled.* Even if we didn't have sex, he needed a break from everyone else. We'd been stressed for over twenty-four hours, and we'd lost so much, including a roof over our heads.

He followed me, though he kept glaring at Keith.

You guys relax. I'm going to marinate some steaks, wash our clothes, then cook some dinner. Go ... rest for a couple of hours, Lucy linked.

At the top of the stairs, a door opened to a large room. The wooden floor was more of a gray, and a king-size bed sat against the wall with four spotlights above it. Right across from the doorway was a full bathroom with a barn door. The door didn't seem to lock, so I was thankful it was in our room.

Raffe shut the outer door and pulled me into his arms. He cupped my cheek and pressed his lips together. *What's wrong? I've been sensing your emotions the whole ride here.*

I lifted a brow. *Really? What's wrong? You have to ask?*

He huffed. *Okay, fair, but it feels like guilt's mixed in.*

Damn fated-mate bond and his ability to sense my feelings. I hadn't meant to be so obvious, but he knew me better than anyone. I turned my head, not wanting to answer that, and a lump formed in my throat.

Hey. He pivoted, remaining in front of me, and placed a finger under my chin to lift my face so our eyes met. *Don't hesitate to meet my gaze now. You've already submitted.* He winked, but the joke fell flat.

He frowned and stiffened. "Sky, what's going on? Tell me."

I closed my eyes, not wanting to see his reaction. *If I hadn't come to EEU, none of this would've happened. Maybe it would've been better if I hadn't accepted the scholarship.*

Hurt pierced his spot in my chest, forcing me to open my eyes. Immediately, I wished I hadn't.

He took a step back and dropped his hands to his sides. *Is that how you really feel? Because I'm fucking glad you did. Yeah, life got a whole lot more chaotic, and I was a jackass until I figured my shit out, but finding you and completing our fated-mate bond is the best thing to ever happen to me. No matter the cost. It sucks that you don't feel the same way.*

The breath whooshed out of me like I'd been kicked in the gut. *Of course finding you has made me happier than anything. I wouldn't give you up for the world, not now or ever. You bring me more joy than I ever thought possible.*

Then why did you say you'd be better off if you hadn't come? He raised his hands, threading them through his hair.

Not me. I placed my hands on my chest, feeling as if I were underwater. *All of you ... but especially you. You can't go home anymore because of me.*

If this hadn't happened, I never would've found out what a selfish asshole my father is and would still be blindly following him. He placed his hands on my shoulders. *You make me a better man and make me see things in a different way, even when I don't want to. Every sacrifice is worth it as long as you're next to me, loving me.*

My chest expanded, feeling so warm. *That's exactly*

where I want to be too, but dammit, all I do is cause you problems. Hell, I struggled to submit to you when no one else did, and that made things worse for you with your dad's followers.

Babe, those four wolves downstairs grew up with me. We had stare-offs all the fucking time, so their wolves already saw me as dominant. He placed his forehead against mine. *That was the first time for you, and damn, your wolf is strong. I don't know what you did, but I was beginning to think you'd win. And you know what? If you had, nothing would've changed between us. I love you and don't give a damn if you're stronger or weaker.*

I chuckled. *What about equal? I like the sound of that a whole lot better.*

We're definitely equal. He grinned. *You putting Aldric and the others in their place had me so hot for you, and I'm hoping that maybe, just maybe, you can help me out with that.*

I smiled so large my cheeks ached. *I might do you a solid.*

Oh no. I'll be the one who's solid. He winked, sliding his hands up the side of my shirt.

I leaned back and arched a brow. *Really? That was a horrible innuendo.*

All my brainpower has gone to my dick, he replied, tugging me against him so I could feel his hardness against my stomach.

Just like that, my body heated, and he kissed me.

Eager to taste him, I brushed my tongue over his lips. He opened, allowing me entrance. He matched every stroke of my tongue, and his fingers dug into my waist as he deepened our kiss.

I slipped my hand under his shirt and traced the curves

of his muscles. With each brush of my fingers, the buzz of our connection increased, and his abs contracted, driving me wild. The rest of the world disappeared until all I sensed were the two of us.

He tore his mouth from mine and kissed down my jawline and neck. My head spun as I leaned my head back, giving him better access. When he reached the juncture of my throat and collarbone, right where my pulse pounded against my neck, he grazed his teeth along the spot.

My wolf howled and my stomach tightened. Though our bond was cemented, there was something so possessive in the action that I melted into his arms. Mind hazy, I lowered my hands, fumbling to unfasten his jeans, *desperate* to touch him.

He chuckled throatily, feeling my need for him. He grabbed my ass and lifted me, and I wrapped my legs around his waist, rocking against him. He groaned as he carried me to the bed and laid me down.

Sitting up, I unbuttoned his pants and pushed them and his boxers down. He sprang free, and I wrapped my hand around him. I'd never tire of seeing him like this.

Here I thought I was the only desperate one. He moaned as he removed my shirt.

His hand slipped around my back and unfastened my bra. Then he tossed it to the floor. His striking blue eyes darkened as he scanned me, and I moved my hand, stroking him.

He growled, his body shivering, making me feel powerful.

What were you saying? I teased as I slowed my pace to drive him wild.

He leaned down, his mouth capturing a nipple as he easily removed my jeans and pushed them and my panties off. His tongue rolled across my nipple, and my back arched just as his fingers slipped between my legs and circled.

The sizzle of our connection and the way he worked my body had pleasure knotting deep inside me. I quickened the pace of my hand on him, wanting to work him into the same frenzy.

Fuck, Sky. He groaned, tugging on our connection. It opened, and I felt his emotions and sensations almost as if they were my own.

Wanting to reciprocate, I tugged on the lilac strand, and our emotions and sensations merged—something I hadn't realized was possible. I reveled in how erotic it felt.

Friction built in me, sending me over the edge. His fingers quickened, and my ecstasy slammed through our bond. My body shook, but even then, he didn't slow. I tried to move to get some relief, but his free hand reached out and held me in place. I was at the mercy of his torture, and I both loved it and felt overwhelmed by it.

When my mind cleared, a more desperate hunger took its place. That hadn't satiated me at all. I had to have him.

Clutching his shirt, I shoved him onto the bed and yanked the garment from his body. As his muscular body and wolf tattoo were revealed, I straddled him and sank down onto him.

I am so damn glad you came to EEU, Raffe linked, his hands gripping my hips as I rode him. *Don't ever think I'd want it any other way. I was miserable without you, and I'd rather die than lose you. We're stronger and better together. I fucking love you.*

Rocking against him, I pressed my hands into his chest. *I love you too, and I will* never *let you go.*

He lifted his hips and rolled against me, and we watched each other as we made love.

We moved in sync, sensation building in us. I moved my hips faster, and he cupped my breasts as we reached the edge. When he gently ran his fingers over my nipples, an orgasm rocked through me. My body shook with the ecstasy that flooded between us, and his body tightened. His mouth opened as his release joined mine.

Our breaths mingled and we watched each other come undone. The pleasure seemed never-ending. When my head cleared, I flopped onto the bed beside him.

This was the moment we'd needed. A moment to connect.

I cuddled into his side and let my heavy eyelids close.

LATER, I went out onto the covered back porch and sat at the wooden bar. We'd put on new clothes and had dinner, and I'd come out here to get some fresh, cool night air.

Raffe was cleaning up the kitchen while the others got ready for bed, and I wanted a moment to myself. There was no telling when I'd last had one.

A few owls hooted, and a pair of red foxes appeared at the edge of the woods, staring at me. Just as I was about to get up and head toward them, the sliding glass door opened, and Octavia's strawberry scent hit my nose.

"Mind if I join you?" she asked.

I wanted to say no, but the more she talked, the more she might slip up and say something she didn't mean to.

Do you need me? Raffe linked.

I could hear him running water in the sink, and I looked over my shoulder at him through the window. *I'll let you know if I do. Right now, it's fine.*

Octavia sat on the open barstool beside me and pursed her lips.

Silence hung between us, but I kept my mouth shut. She'd sought me out, not the other way around.

After several minutes, she exhaled loudly. "I assume you've heard the history of our kind."

I nodded, keeping my gaze on the trees as the cold October breeze rustled the needles.

"And what did they tell you?" she asked.

I wondered if this was a test, but it didn't matter. Whether she was who she said she was or part of the Veiled Circle, she already knew. By telling her the history, I wasn't revealing knowledge she didn't already have. So I told her about the first documented arcane-born, Foster, and how he'd caused an earthquake and almost imploded. That a coven had found him and taken him in and he'd had a connection with the local wolf pack alpha's daughter. That the wolves had attacked and Foster *had* imploded, allowing the wolf shifters to take over and rule.

She didn't respond, and when I turned my head toward her, I found her deathly pale.

Her brows furrowed, and she smacked her mouth as if she'd tasted something foul. "That's what they told you?"

My back straightened, and power jolted. "Yes. Why are you acting like that?"

"Because they left out a *lot* of information. Information you should know. No wonder you trusted the coven." She twisted in the chair to face me. "They made it sound like they only wanted to help the arcane-born."

Wait. I hadn't expected that.

"Don't worry." She touched my arm and smiled. "I'll tell you *everything*."

CHAPTER NINE

Her ominous tone had my back stiffening as my power jolted in tandem with my heart. Worse, I hated how her hand on my arm comforted me.

Tears burned my eyes as I fought back the surge of flaming anger that came with that realization. She hadn't been a mother to me, so she shouldn't draw any reaction from me except for distrust and disgust.

I blinked, holding back the liquid forming in my eyes, but didn't budge my arm. I didn't want to do something rash. If she thought I wasn't buying her act, she might not share the information with me.

After all, that was how Slade had played me.

"Sorry." She dropped her hands, her gaze heavy on my face. "I didn't mean to make you uncomfortable."

If only discomfort had been the sensation she'd shot through me. I faced forward, noticing a few raccoons had joined the foxes at the edge. All of the animals watched me. "It's fine." I was certain that whatever moment she'd wanted to share was over.

She cleared her throat. "An arcane-born was the first

bearer of magic. No one really knows why or how, but the one thing we have gathered is that when she died at age twenty-one, the other supernatural species were created. It was as if her power was unleashed and changed her children—aside from one—upon her death. Her eldest son fathered the first wolf shifter, her eldest daughter bore a witch, her youngest son fathered a male vampire, and the baby of the family seemed to have human children. That was how the different supernatural species were created over two thousand years ago."

A weight sank in my stomach, and I blew out a breath. I'd never imagined it all beginning like that. An arcane-born had created all the supernatural species—that meant every species started from the same family and was a grandchild of the original magic bearer. "Uh ... why wasn't I told this before?"

"Because the species became divided, and common interests and shared heritage go out the window when that happens." She stared up at the cloudy sky. "When you want to separate, you focus on what divides you, not what you have in common."

Being labeled a freak and teased my whole life had taught me that hard lesson. "What happened?"

"At first, they were raised as a family, the way supernaturals were always supposed to be. But a few generations later, egos got the best of everyone. The wolves thought they were the strongest, the witches believed they were the most powerful—and at the time, they were—and the vampires prided themselves on being the most cunning."

That sounded right, but each species also had its shortcomings. The wolf shifters weren't as strong magically as the coven members and couldn't move as fast as vampires, but the witches tired out quicker, and the vampires died if they were clawed by a wolf or drank their blood. Each one had weaknesses, just as they had advantages.

"The coven members were the fastest to populate because the women were fertile, and a full-blooded witch could be born even if the other parent was human. Not only that, but most women birthed more girls than boys because, in that species, typically, women are the strongest. That's how the witches became the first real leaders of the supernatural world, pushing their will and way upon the shifters and vampires."

My stomach roiled. "What about the vampires and shifters?"

"They struggled, and several times, they almost died out. You see, when the wolf shifters and vampires obeyed and allowed their blood to be used in the witch's spells and sacrifices, the covens would bless whatever human woman a supernatural mated with to make them strong enough to bear supernatural children. Each pregnancy required an exchange of magic between a coven member and the woman, usually in the form of a charm they had to wear the entire time. If someone upset the coven, they wouldn't offer the woman this blessing, and usually, the woman and the child died during the pregnancy because a human body isn't strong enough to carry a supernatural to term. The women of those species could marry human men and reproduce, but their children were only halflings, which caused more problems. If they were given a charm to wear, their child would genetically be fully that species."

A shiver ran down my spine. The witches were upset about the shifters trying to take away access to the *Books of Twilight*, and I completely understood that, but their history of leadership was darker than anything wolf shifters had done. By choosing not to help the wolves and vampires, they'd doomed human women to their deaths and the children born to be neither human nor supernatural. And boy, that was one struggle I understood—having one foot in both worlds but not fitting into either. I shuddered, considering the challenges a part wolf or part vampire would have. Could they shift or drink blood?

"The coven members used their magic to control the other supernaturals, but over the centuries, the populations of vampires and wolf shifters grew large enough that they could marry within their own species without any problems, and that's when things changed in the supernatural world. The witches began to lose their control over the other species, and their magic weakened because they also didn't mate with other species."

This painted witches and the covens in a different light. The supreme priestess had raised red flags with her lack of concern for Slade at times—she'd seemed almost nonmaternal—but when she'd taken me in as one of her members, I'd begun to trust her more. After all, the wolf shifters hadn't wanted to associate with me, and the vampires wanted to drink my blood when my power went out of control. At least the witches had tried to help me.

Now I understood their motivation.

It had all been about control.

Acid burned my throat as I thought about how Slade had controlled me by withholding information. I'd believed that he'd discovered new information, but after what I'd learned from Dave, I realized Slade had known everything *all* along. I'd been so desperate for a friend and answers that I'd believed him.

"So what happened?" There had to be more to the story because the shifters were in control.

"Foster." She ran her hand along the bar table. "He was born many centuries later."

"Was he a descendent of the youngest of the original arcane-born?" I wasn't sure how all this worked—for all I knew, a random arcane could be born another way.

She nodded. "He was—from the line the witches, shifters, and vampires cast out because they deemed their youngest sibling unworthy. Their mother seemed to not have passed on a piece of magic. Little did they realize that the youngest sibling had received the original magic—the strongest of all—but it was inactive. Now, the coven was correct about what activates the dormant power, so they didn't alter all the information, but they didn't learn that until Foster was born. The coven felt his power activate, and the earthquake had that same power signature."

The world tilted, and my power increased to a fizz. "Wait, I'm only the *third* active one of our kind?" I understood that the rare galaxy event happened infrequently, but I was a little perturbed that the number of my kind who'd had to handle their magic could be counted on one hand.

"That's why a lot of supernaturals don't know about us and why the knowledge of how your power works is very limited." She frowned and stilled her hand. "And why I freaked out when I felt your power activate. That was the horrible part of all this—knowing the history and the challenges you'd face. I ... I didn't want you to be targeted or for the supernaturals to discover who we were. Fear makes you do some truly stupid things ... things that your father and I have regretted every day since."

I blinked quickly to clear my blurry vision. "We're getting off track." My voice wasn't as clear as I hoped it'd be, and I wasn't ready for this conversation. With my power jolting, I could feel her emotions, and she was telling the truth.

"I know, but I need you to understand something." She inhaled deeply and met my stare. "I understand why you're keeping your distance. We abandoned you, and then I randomly showed up in your life and tried to leave again when everything came out. But your father and I think about you every day. Every holiday, and your birthday, the memory of you and of what we did haunts us. I'm sorry, and if I could go back in time—"

A traitorous tear trickled down my cheek, and I quickly wiped it away, hoping like hell she hadn't noticed. "Yeah, you did try to leave, so it's hard to believe you regret anything."

"Wolf shifters, vampires, and coven members haven't been good to our kind. The last time someone with our active power was born, each side tried to manipulate or abuse him. When I learned you were not only mated to a wolf but had completed the bond with him—the *prince* of wolf shifters—I feared that was how they'd gotten you on their side. My perception changed when I saw how everyone in that house protected you and after the prince gave up his crown to remain at your side. No arcane-born has ever had that."

I wanted to judge her and tell her how narrow-minded she was, but she'd been right about Slade and his mother. Her bias hadn't served her completely wrong. "I'm assuming the coven betrayed Foster?" I needed to get back on topic. My emotions were all over the place with tears threatening to slide down my face. Part of me wanted to forgive her, but another part was angry at myself for even considering it. I had to sort through my emotions before I attempted to determine how I felt about any of this.

Exhaling, Octavia rolled her shoulders and stared straight ahead again. "The coven and the wolf shifters. Both hurt him, resulting in his death."

I arched a brow, just as Raffe linked, *I've been trying to leave you alone, but I keep feeling your emotions. Do you need me out there?*

The truth was I did, but I suspected Octavia would not be as forthcoming if he joined us. *Give us a few more minutes. I don't want her to clam up, and she's sharing a lot with me.*

You do what you need to do. I'm not going anywhere.

My heart warmed, some of the pain ebbing. Raffe was one of the few people I believed when he said that. *I love you.*

Love you too.

I didn't end our connection, wanting to keep it open a little longer. It wasn't as nice as having him with me, but he was more accessible. "Can you be more specific?"

"Similar to what the coven did to you by trying to make you one of their members. They felt Foster's power and found him on the brink of death. A woman was leaning over him, touching his face. When she sensed the witches, she ran off."

I hadn't heard that part. "A woman? Was she human?"

"She was the alpha wolf shifter's daughter. She'd been coming back from the village and found him." Octavia steepled her fingers. "She was his fated mate, and her touch calmed the power inside him, which was the only reason he didn't die then. But he was bad off, so the coven took him back with them. He was out for days after causing a minor earthquake."

Everything but the woman leaning over him matched what Slade had told me. "Are you sure the wolf shifter was his fated mate?" That story sounded way too similar to mine.

"Unfortunately, I am. Foster kept a journal where all of this was documented ... until he imploded. His parents stayed with him and kept his things when the coven ran off. They filled in the pieces."

The wind picked up, and I wrapped my arms around myself. At least, I assumed the cold was from the wind, but it could have come from within me. "What is his version of what happened?"

She sneered. "Similar to yours. The coven tried to help him, but they didn't know how he could grasp his power. And each night, he snuck out to meet the alpha's daughter. Her presence was the only thing stabilizing him."

That I understood. Raffe eased my emotions when they were volatile, and if he hadn't come to me that one night, I would have imploded, just like Foster. The power had ravaged me and drained my strength, taking on a life of its own. My skin prickled at the memory.

"One night, the supreme priestess of the coven followed him. She'd become suspicious of him. She told the alpha what his daughter was doing. Let's just say the revelation didn't go over well. In the alpha's eyes, his daughter was spending time with a warlock ... a coven member. After spending centuries under the coven's control, the shifters and vampires despised the witches and anything that resembled coven power. He alpha-willed his daughter to never see Foster again."

I thought of King Jovian trying to alpha-will Raffe to marry the Atlanta alpha's daughter, and my heart ached. The only difference was that Raffe and I had partially completed our mate bond.

"Foster couldn't stay away, and his power became more

volatile on days he didn't see her. Eventually, the shifters had enough and attacked the coven to eliminate the threat. Foster tried to protect everyone, both shifters and coven members. In the end, he caused his own death, and the wolf shifters took over after that."

That was a horrible way to die, and knowing how he'd felt from my own beginning with Raffe ... no one deserved to end like that. "That's horrible." My chest throbbed, and I rubbed the spot to appease the ache.

"It is, and that's why we need to be careful. You're twenty-two, the same age as Foster when he imploded." Octavia placed a hand on the back of her neck. "We can't let that happen to you. We need to figure out how you control your power."

The sliding glass door opened again, but the tingles on my neck told me who it was—Raffe.

"It's late. We should all get some sleep," he rasped, his concern flowing into me.

I stood without a second thought. Though Octavia had shared a lot of information, I needed space. "He's right. It's been a long day." And we had to determine our next plan. We didn't have a large pack, we had no incoming money, and a secret society was on our trail. Not only that, but Octavia had told me that no activated arcane-born had lived past my current age. This was messy.

Octavia didn't say a word, and the three of us headed back inside. Lucy and Adam were standing in the living room, the television off. It was close to ten, and we were all tired, especially Josie and Dave.

Lucy arched a brow, taking in my appearance. *You need to talk?* she linked.

I smirked. She was becoming more like a sister than a friend. *I don't have the energy to tell everyone individually.*

I'll tell you everything in the morning after we get some sleep.

If you change your mind, I'm always here, she replied and hugged me. *And when things settle, we gotta get back on our* Criminal Minds *kick. I'll check on our favorite little monster before heading to bed, so don't worry about anything.*

Lucy nodded toward Octavia then the stairs that led below. "You're rooming with me. Let's get going."

Octavia didn't hesitate, and the two of them headed down.

Adam remained, his face tense. *Something weird is going on between Josie and Dave. I think his feeding from her created some sort of connection. We need to watch them carefully. I'm afraid she's in over her head.*

When she and Raffe had been pretending to be a couple, she'd tried to hide Raffe's jersey around Dave. And Dave had always asked about her. I was certain their connection went beyond him drinking her blood. But I doubted now was the time to mention it.

Raffe tilted his head back. *Noted. I'll keep a close eye on them tomorrow. In the meantime, you're sleeping in there with her, right?*

Yeah, I'll watch out for her. He patted his chest. *Speaking of which, she just told me she's done changing, so I'm going down there.*

We split off, and soon, Raffe was spooning me, his face nuzzled in my neck. Our connection buzzed, offering me solace as I told him everything Octavia had said.

As the story progressed, he held me tighter. Not that I was complaining.

When it was over, he sighed. Guilt blanketed him. *Babe, I'm so sorry.*

Not your fault. I pushed my love and warmth toward him. *You aren't responsible for a past you had nothing to do with.*

He kissed my neck, and I shivered. I wasn't alone anymore.

I'll always be by your side. I love you, he vowed, his breath warming my neck.

I turned around and stared into his crystal-blue eyes. *I love you too, and as long as we're together, I'll be okay.*

He pulled me to his chest, and we fell asleep in each other's arms.

The sound of a vehicle outside woke me. My eyes cracked open, and I glanced at the time.

Three in the morning.

That was odd.

Multiple car doors opened and shut, and my blood turned cold.

"They're here," a man whispered. "I'm glad she gave us the right address."

CHAPTER TEN

My pulse quickened, and my ears roared. The voice sounded familiar, but I couldn't place it. I tore myself away from Raffe, my head spinning and my power buzzing.

He groaned and reached for me, but I swatted his hand away.

People are outside, I linked to everyone. If I could hear the intruders outside, they might be able to hear us inside, depending on their species.

Raffe's eyes popped open, and he jumped out of bed. At least, this time, the unexpected visitors hadn't caught us naked.

Who is it? Keith's words were slurred, like he was still half-asleep.

If I knew, I would've led with that. I rolled my eyes, not feeling bad for calling his ass out. He would've done the same.

Raffe moved to the window on his side, about two feet past the end of our bed. He stood in the corner, barely moving a blind, and his body tensed. He released the blind, not even trying to be quiet, and snarled, "You've got to be kidding me." He rolled his shoulders back and marched past me toward the stairs. *It's Aldric, Valor, and Finley.*

I blinked, thinking I'd misunderstood. *Aldric?* Out of everyone, I hadn't expected it to be him. Granted, he was probably here to take Josie back with him. He hadn't been thrilled when his daughter left with us. *And who are Valor and Finley?*

Keith's dad is Valor and Adam's is Finley, he answered, practically jumping down the stairs.

My stomach clenched. If they were here to force their children to come home, that might be more problematic than if an enemy had come to attack us. I hoped that meant none of them were here to kill us.

I reached the bottom of the stairs as Raffe opened the door, not waiting for them to knock.

All three men were standing there, waiting.

Footsteps scurried downstairs as Adam and Keith rushed to back up Raffe.

"What are you three doing here?" Raffe gritted out, blocking the doorway so the three of them couldn't enter.

Aldric, from his spot in the middle, looked over Raffe's shoulder and straight at me.

A chill ran down my spine.

"Not going to invite us in?" Aldric arched a brow, yanking his attention back to my mate. "That's rude, don't you think?"

I moved next to Raffe, showing that I wouldn't hide, just as Adam and Keith strolled into the room behind us.

"We're just returning the favor." I smiled sweetly, looking as innocent as possible while making my point.

"She's right." Raffe placed an arm around my waist. "At least we aren't kicking you out of our pack and home."

Aldric winced. "That's fair, and that's why we're here."

"You need to come home." Valor stood in front of me, but his attention was behind me, on his son. "It should not have come to this."

"Yet it did," Keith deadpanned, emanating the resentment and malice he used to reserve for me. "And not by our own doing."

Scoffing, Valor shook his head. "You left the pack. I didn't make you do that."

"By not accepting Skylar and Raffe, you drove a wedge between us," Keith said, taking the other spot beside me. "I pledged my allegiance to Raffe years ago, and I will stand by my friend and *alpha*."

A lump formed in my throat, and my eyes burned. I never would've imagined Keith standing up for me, presenting a united front.

"Son, you and I can be the voice of reason." Finley sidestepped to see Adam. "Raffe's relationship with this girl isn't ideal. You must see that."

"All I see is a woman who grounds Raffe and makes him stronger," Adam replied stiffly. "I still love you, Dad. But my decision stands. Raffe is my alpha, and Skylar is my alpha's mate. I stand behind *both* of them the way you always taught me."

"Not when he takes a human as a mate. That was bad enough, but now she's somehow changed and has magic." Finley dragged his hands through his hair.

Raffe growled. "We had this conversation, and we left. Why come here in the middle of the night to rehash it?"

He had a point. I stood taller despite being several inches shorter than every man here. "A phone call would've been easier. And how the hell did you find us?" The latter question had my stomach clenching.

If these men had found us that easily, who else could?

"You don't think we've been trying to call?" Aldric scowled. "All your phones are turned off. Luckily, Josie used her credit card to pay for this place. I made a few calls since it's technically under my name and got the renter to provide the address."

Raffe's frustration put pressure in my chest.

None of us had considered that. Our funds were limited, and now we wouldn't have any unless we wanted to risk more of *this* happening.

"Well, you wasted your time." Raffe shut the door.

Before it could close, Aldric caught it with his hand. His jaw clenched, and he strained against Raffe's strength.

"Don't think I won't shut it," Raffe growled. "This is your one chance to move your hand before it gets slammed in the damn door."

Aldric sighed. "Your father linked with me, and he told me to come here and ask you and the others to come home."

"Did he now?" Raffe snorted bitterly. "The answer is the same. Skylar is my fated mate, and I won't marry anyone else. She is *it* for me, and she's a shifter, so her being human is irrelevant. You can tell Dad where to shove it."

"If it's not clear where he's referencing, he means good ol' Jovian can shove it up his—" Keith started.

"Keith Barren, you'd better not finish that sentence." Valor glared and puffed out his chest. "King Jovian was your alpha your entire life until not even twenty-four hours ago. You will show him respect."

My power jolted, matching the way my blood pulsed through my body. I hated when people used age and experience as a reason to show someone respect. Respect had to be earned and not given just because of some set requirements. "Tell me why King Jovian still deserves respect from his son and my pack members. He didn't listen to his son, he dishonored the sacred bond Raffe shares with me, and then he attempted to alpha-will his son into marrying someone else. He also tried to have me killed, *then* tried to bully this entire pack by not allowing them to enter their own home if I was part of the deal. What sort of leader does that to his pack members, let alone his only son?"

Can I say I like her logic now that we're on the same team? Keith linked, and out of the corner of my eye, I noticed the corners of his mouth tipped upward.

"The king has sacrificed so much for his people and is doing what's best for everyone, not a select few." Aldric lifted his chin, but some of the light in his irises dimmed. "And not all of those decisions came directly from the king. That's why we're here."

Raffe tilted his head. "And which ones were those?"

"Not allowing you inside the mansion and casting you out." Aldric fisted his hands. "King Jovian was concerned when your pack link vanished, and he commanded me to bring you home. That's why we're here."

There had to be a catch.

"We've already had this conversation." Raffe kissed my cheek and tugged me tighter to his side. "I'm not going anywhere without Skylar, and I won't be part of a pack that disrespects my mate."

Shaking his head, Valor leaned against the doorframe. "Oh, he's aware. Unfortunately, he's willing to take your *mate*. You all just need to rejoin the pack."

"So everyone can disrespect her?" Raffe's jaw clenched. "I'll pass. It's not just about the pack tolerating Skylar—they must treat her like a fucking equal, and it's clear none of you standing here will do that."

Babe, I'm used to being an outcast. This way, Raffe and

the others could have their family and pack back. Besides, everyone staying in this house already treated me as an equal, so I'd have that. *If we don't go back, we won't have access to any money.*

We're wolves. We can live in the woods. Our wolf form is made for that.

"We can't turn our backs on a sacred law. Humans are forbidden. There isn't a caveat about what to do if one could be turned." Finley dropped his hands to his sides. "Adam will at least understand that."

"She's never been a regular *human*." Adam crossed his arms. "Her turning proves that. You're being narrow-minded—the same thing you all accuse the Eastern packs of being."

"Raffe, your father never wanted me to turn you away." Aldric lifted his hands, his expression strained. "I did that without his support. Your issue is with me, not him."

Good ol' Jovian must have ripped Aldric a new butthole, Keith linked. *He's pretty much groveling, which tells you how pissed your dad is.*

We're not going back, are we? Josie asked, her words muted even via the link. *They won't let Dave come, and definitely not Octavia.*

Fair point. There was more at risk than me being the black sheep of the pack. "You do realize if we came back, we would bring Dave and Octavia with us?" I asked.

Valor sneered. "Absolutely not. They aren't pack."

"And neither are we!" Raffe bellowed, his deep voice raspy as his rage flamed into my chest. "That's why you're here. Remember?"

"We have to draw a line somewhere." Aldric karate-chopped the air. "Let them free or kill them. I don't care."

"It's time for you to go." Raffe gestured for them to move away from the door.

Moving so he was partially blocking the door, Aldric lifted a hand. "Don't be foolish. You have no money, and you can't live outside in the cold and rain with a human. You'll have to deal with her anyway, so you might as well be comfortable at home. We want our kids back. The way it should be."

"Not like this." Keith motioned between us and them. "Nothing is resolved, which means nothing has changed. The king doesn't want the Eastern wolves to know that not only did he lose control of his son but also the children of the men he trusts most. Our coming back won't resolve anything."

"And I don't trust that you won't try to kill my mate again." Raffe lifted a brow. "Can all three of you promise that you will ensure my mate remains safe, no matter the cost?"

Aldric flinched while Finley and Valor glanced at each other, their noses wrinkled in disgust.

"That's what I thought. You need to leave." Raffe edged in front of me and added, "Now."

"Not without my daughter." Aldric stood tall. "She doesn't need to be part of this mess. The same goes for Lucy, Keith, and Adam. Release them."

My power rose close to a hum. Did he think we were holding them hostage? Raffe hadn't made them leave their pack. They'd left of their own free will.

Keith crossed his arms. "We're not going anywhere."

"And neither am I, Daddy." Josie stepped up the stairs. "If you don't accept Skylar, you won't accept my fated mate either."

Raffe, Adam, and Keith tensed, and I couldn't swallow. No. She couldn't be doing this now.

"Fated mates are rare." Aldric exhaled. "There hasn't been a fated pair in decades. And if you do have one, I'm sure it's a strong, strapping wolf."

"He's not." Josie bit her bottom lip, and then she jutted her chin. "It's Dave."

Suspecting it and hearing it were two different things. Her words had me taking a step back.

"The *vampire?*" Aldric choked. "There's no way."

The story of how the supernaturals were created flashed through my mind. We all stemmed from the same ancestor. If I could become a wolf shifter, then it was possible that her blood wouldn't be deadly to her mate. They'd need to claim each other to complete the bond.

Uh ... why does it not smell like eggs in here? Keith linked. *Because Josie just told one big ol' whopper.*

She's not lying, I linked.

"It is, whether you want to believe me or not." Josie lifted her hands. "Like Raffe, I refuse to not be with him."

"None of you know what you're up against." Aldric rubbed his temples. "When your senses have returned to you, you know the way home. I just hope it's before any of you do anything more foolish. Your money is cut off, but we will leave your cell phones on so you can contact us."

"But—" Finley started, but Aldric's eyes closed, cutting the man off.

The three of them spun around, though Valor frowned as he stole one last glance at his son. The four of us remained by the door, watching them get into their car and drive away.

Shit. We were screwed, but at least we had the house for the next few days. We'd already paid for it.

When Raffe shut the door and the immediate threat was gone, my limbs grew watery.

"You were kidding, right?" Keith looked at Josie and pointed toward the stairs. "I'm not sure if you get that he's a whole different species."

Josie leaned her head back. "So is Sky."

"Wait." Keith turned to me. "Will Dave turn into a wolf too? Sky did, and she still has her weird magic. Will he be some sort of vampire wolf?"

"Man, I think exhaustion is getting the best of you. There's no way that combination can exist." Adam pursed his lips. "Wolf blood is deadly to vampires."

"I hate to say this, but I see his point." Raffe rubbed the back of his neck, but his emotions were leveling out. "Her blood isn't deadly to him."

This situation could drive anyone insane. I yawned, desperate to crawl back into bed and start fresh in the morning. "Can we leave this discussion for when it's not the middle of the night? I want sleep."

Raffe took my hand. "I agree. This isn't something we can solve in a few minutes. Let's get some rest. We'll need to figure out what the hell to do once the week is over and we have to go somewhere else."

Ever since I'd walked into their lives, I'd been a burden. Even though Raffe had made it clear he didn't care as long as we were together, I still hated that I was causing them trouble.

Josie wrapped her arms around her waist. "That's it? No one is going to say anything else tonight or threaten to throw Dave out?" Her skin blanched like she was waiting for us to react the way their dads had.

"I think the blood exchange you did with Dave has you

feeling like that." Raffe shrugged. "I don't think it's more than that."

She scowled.

"Even if that's not the case"—I cut my eyes at Raffe, giving him a warning look—"we'll support you and your happiness."

We will? Raffe's eyebrows rose. *He's a fucking vampire who drugged you.*

He was scared for his life and has been trying to make it up to us ever since. Dave seemed genuinely sorry. People had the right to make mistakes, and he hadn't known what they were going to do with me. *How can we not support her and Dave after everything she's done for me?*

He didn't respond, but I could feel his mixed emotions.

"Really?" There was so much hope in Josie's voice.

I watched Raffe fold under our pressure. He sighed. "Yeah."

Keith pressed his lips into a line. *"Really?"* His voice was a note higher than Josie's.

The air pulsed around me, feeling like sandpaper rubbing against my skin.

My heart stopped.

Coven magic.

I spun around and stared out the house's wide windows just as flames shot from multiple spots at the edge of the woods, where the raccoons and the foxes had been, and engulfed the side of the house.

CHAPTER ELEVEN

Flames ignited, and tendrils licked the doorframe while the floor underneath our feet quaked.

"It's the coven! We've gotta get out of here!" I yelled, needing Octavia and Dave—and not just the shifters—to hear my message. We had to get our asses out of here fast. We had no clue what we were up against.

My power hummed within my blood, and my wolf stirred restlessly.

The coven members who could harness the elements were the strongest of their species. The longer we stayed here, the more screwed we were, but I didn't want to freak out Octavia and Dave more than they probably were.

As the house's vibrations increased, the couch banged against the wall. It felt like an earthquake, but I guessed it wouldn't be over in seconds. I'd seen Slade and his friends use elemental magic before, and they could channel it for several minutes. I wasn't sure if I'd ever seen any of them tire out since Slade had betrayed me, so I wasn't sure how long they could last.

People scattered down the stairs, and I knew the coven

members wouldn't wait around to see what happened. They'd be surrounding the house.

The power wanted to leave my body, which meant I needed to go outside and direct it toward the threat. Otherwise, I'd assist them in ripping this house apart.

I was hurrying toward the door, ready to face them, when a large, rough hand grabbed my arm. The buzz immediately told me who it was, and my power calmed to a high fizz.

Where the fuck do you think you're going? Raffe growled. *We need to get out of here, not run toward danger.*

I lifted my chin. *You don't think they're waiting for us out there?*

He frowned. *Maybe, but we need to check before knowingly running into danger.*

The walls cracked, and I feared the structure might collapse and trap everyone inside. I had to do something to keep the house together, but I had no clue what or how. Damn lack of training. There *had* to be a way to control this power.

We need help! Josie linked. *Dave can't get up, and his room is filled with smoke.*

This kept getting better. I took off for the stairs, and Raffe cursed.

Keith and Adam, check outside. If you don't sense anyone, let us know, and we'll get the hell out of here, Raffe commanded as he followed on my heels.

The floor was shaking so hard that my teeth clacked together, and each step was unsteady. When I reached the first step, I jumped and landed on the bottom floor.

The reason the house was so unstable became clear. Earth, rock, and trees had cracked through the foundation and floor and kept growing.

My lungs seized. Our time was running out.

Octavia and Lucy were in the hallway, moving slowly. Cat-Keith clung to Lucy like she was her lifeline. Something new broke through the foundation every second, making progress difficult.

Which room is Dave in? Raffe asked, scanning the four doors in front of us. Of course, Lucy pointed to the one to the right, farthest from the stairs.

Raffe took off just as a tree jutted from the floor, knocking him back.

I had to do *something* so the coven couldn't focus all their magic on the house. But what?

We can't reach the vehicles, Keith linked, his panic surging through the pack link. *We're blocked from getting off the front porch. We're heading back to you.*

Not surprising. The witches were an all-or-nothing sort of species. We either faced them or died hiding. *Get Dave and Josie ready—I'll handle this.*

Not alone, you won't, Raffe linked as he stumbled down the hallway. *Stay right there. I need to get Dave and Josie out of here.*

As he continued, I pivoted and raced up the stairs with Octavia and Lucy behind me. Something shattered, and my heart leaped into my throat. We had to get out of this house.

In the living room, smoke hung thickly, and Keith and Adam had shifted into their animal forms. Lucy darted toward Cat-Keith, who blurred past me and out the door, which was missing its glass. I nearly sobbed, and I hoped she found safety. Flames now covered that side of the wall.

That must have been the noise.

"You need to use your power," Octavia shouted and grabbed my hand. Even with supernatural hearing, I could barely make out her words.

She was right. I needed to fight the witches; otherwise, Raffe, Dave, and Josie might die. "Let me see what I can do. Lucy, stay here with Octavia and get her out of the house as soon as you can."

"Focus on what you want to happen. Your power works through vibrations, so push it outward or at one person. Imagine it in your head—that's what the original arcane-born figured out. She closed her eyes and pictured her target." Octavia's eyes watered, and she hacked.

"Got it." I nodded and took off after Keith and Adam. Before I could take a few steps, my wolf surged forward.

Part of me wanted to fight her, but having her speed and agility might give me an edge against these well-trained coven members. I allowed her to begin the shift.

My skin tingled, and my bones broke. Soon, I stood on all fours. The shift was uncomfortable but not painful like the first time. I hurried to the back door.

That's not waiting for me! Raffe linked as white-hot rage filled the center of my chest. *What the hell?*

Never said I would, I replied. That was the one nice thing about Raffe—when he got all alpha-y, he commanded but never stuck around to make sure I agreed. Unfortunately for him, I had my own mind. *And if I stayed down there, we'd probably all die.*

I ran through the back doorway, glass crunching under my paws. The heat of the flames hit my side, and the smoke clouded my vision, but I didn't pause.

In the yard, the ground wasn't marred, reinforcing that the coven members' focus was on driving us out of the house.

My power hummed, nearing that new sensation of singing that I'd felt while on the back of Raffe's bike. Flames shot from the woods and hurtled toward the three of us.

Streaks of flame streaked toward Keith.

Watch— I started, but the fire hit Keith.

His body jerked to the side, and he yelped as he crashed to the ground. His fur was singed, and the awful scent filled my nose.

No! We couldn't lose anyone else.

Power pulsed from my paws, and I froze. If controlling my power required my full concentration, so be it. I'd rather die than save my own ass when one of my pack members lay helpless before me.

Flames from different directions sailed toward Adam and burned him on both sides.

What the hell was wrong with these witches?

The house behind me made an awful groaning sound like it was going to collapse, and I forced my eyes shut and concentrated.

Octavia better be fucking right, or I'd kill her.

Power seeped from my paws into the ground, and I imagined the tree line. I wasn't sure what I wanted to do, but I knew our attackers were out there. I pushed my power toward them to eliminate the threat. I didn't care what it did as long as the coven members stopped their attack.

Even as I channeled my power into the ground, the house creaked.

You need to get out of the house, I linked, the sharp claws of panic sinking into my chest. I shouldn't have left Raffe; I'd been foolish to think I could do this by myself.

We're up the stairs and rushing that way, Raffe linked, his frustration nearly boiling over.

I opened my eyes to find Keith and Adam trying to get up. No flames darted toward us.

"This will end if you come with us," a way-too-familiar voice called from the trees.

Cade.

Someone I'd thought was a friend. Yet, here I was, proven wrong again. Were *any* coven members my friends? The possibility of Hecate and Zelle being part of the Veiled Circle hurt almost as bad as Slade. But they were friends, so to be safe, I'd assume the girls were with them as well.

I hadn't had friends beyond Lucy, after all, and that thought burned worse than the smoke in my lungs.

I'd been so stupid and foolish while Raffe had tried to warn me all along.

We're out, Raffe linked, and his rage turned into something sharp and heavy.

Hate.

Of course that asshole would be part of Slade's circle.

I glanced over my shoulder. Raffe jogged to my side with Lucy, Josie, Octavia, and Dave behind him. Dave appeared ghostly pale again, and Octavia leaned over, hacking. Dirt smudged their faces, evidence that the smoke had gotten worse in the short time I'd been out here.

As soon as Dave got within a few feet of me, he inhaled, and his gaze landed on me. His face twisted in agony, and he gripped the sides of his head.

My blood was affecting him. Dammit, I'd forgotten about that problem. I linked only to Josie, not wanting to distract Raffe, *Keep a handle on Dave. He's compelled to drink my blood.*

Josie's head snapped toward him, and she frowned.

"You really expect me to let my mate hand herself over to you after you kidnapped, drugged, and contained her in a room, then tried messing with her mind?" Raffe pressed into my side. "There's no way in hell I'd let her walk over to you."

Cade pointed to the house behind us. "It's simple. If she

wants you all to live, she'll turn herself over to us. If she doesn't, you'll all die. We have you trapped, and what we did to the house, we can easily do to you." His brown eyes were near the shade of onyx. I couldn't believe I'd once thought they were warm and kind.

"You're threatening to kill *me?*" Raffe laughed bitterly, the cockiness sliding back into place like the first time I met him. "The *prince* of wolves and his *mate?*"

"You left your father's pack." Cade smirked, his light-brown skin crinkling around his eyes from his heartless smile. "If anything, he might thank us for getting rid of his heir problem."

My back tensed. *I didn't expect that news to be public knowledge.*

How the hell do they know that? Lucy chimed in.

"Aw. I'm tempted to pull out my phone and snap a picture of the expressions on your faces." Cade tilted his head back, laughing. "We have people inside your father's pack. People who are loyal to us. We know everything."

A chill ran down my spine, and my power began to sing despite Raffe's touch. We were so far over our heads that I didn't know what to do.

"How do you think we knew where to find you?" He winked.

"Dave, no!" Josie yelled, and I spun around to find Dave blurring toward me.

Shit. How did I protect myself without killing him?

Raffe spun and punched Dave in the head. The vampire hit the ground hard and stayed down.

Cade laughed. "They expect to win when they're turning against each other."

They'd caused the situation, and they were laughing at us?

My power swirled and met something, then merged with it. The responding magic pulsed in tandem. I didn't know what it was, but I tugged at it. Whatever was answering, I needed it to come to my aid and fast.

A loud rumble sounded from behind us, and our group turned just as the house fell in on itself. The noise was deafening, and particles flew everywhere. Pieces of the roof fell off, one hitting Dave in the back of the head, and a thick piece of wood ricocheted off the top of the porch into Lucy's back, knocking her over.

The houses on either side of ours had no lights on and stayed quiet. The coven must have cast a cloaking spell over the affected area.

We had a human, an unconscious and injured vampire, and six wolf shifters against coven members who hadn't even struggled to take down a house. I could only hope that they'd used a lot of their magic, but as I pivoted, my heart sank further. Cade wore a cocky grin.

"This is your last chance. Hand over Skylar, or everyone dies. We'll even take her in her *mutt* form." Cade shrugged. "Doesn't matter either way because, for the first time in centuries, the witches will win." He glanced at me. "If you fight us, we'll make sure you watch every single one of them die before we take our time breaking you."

If I'd believed that turning myself over to the coven would save any of our lives, I'd have considered it, but Supreme Priestess Olwyn, Slade, and now Cade had taught me something I would never forget.

Never trust a witch, especially those tied to the Veiled Circle.

I refused to stand here and accept death. I would fight until my last breath, especially if I could get Raffe out of this alive. I'd implode if that was what it took to save these people who were becoming my chosen family.

"She's not going *anywhere* with you," Octavia spat like she had a horrible taste in her mouth. "You'll kill her anyway because she won't do what you want her to."

I tensed.

"No, they won't," Raffe snarled. "Because I'm going to kill them *all*." *Attack hard and fast and take out as many as you can. Skylar, stay back.*

If we hadn't been about to die, I'd have laughed that he'd wasted energy saying that.

All of us took off, the power in my body overtaking my wolf.

Josie, Lucy, and Raffe charged in human form while Keith and Adam limped toward the tree line.

Octavia ran back toward the house.

What was she doing? But I didn't have time to focus on her. I had to move forward.

I stumbled, my wolf and power out of sync with each other.

Owls hooted in the woods, wings flapping, and animals scurried through the trees. The loud, chaotic noises added to the adrenaline pumping through me.

A woman with fair skin darted from the woods. Between the caramel-blonde hair pulled into a bun and the bright cobalt eyes, I immediately recognized her.

Priestess Sabrina, one of the coven members I'd met in the hidden library on campus when Slade had taken me there to learn about my heritage.

I could feel maliciousness emanating from her despite her innocent features.

A snarl pulled my attention from her to my mate, who was fighting Cade.

Cade raised the ground underneath Raffe's feet, but my mate leaped off each obstacle and kept racing toward him.

Priestess Sabrina grinned, cold and calculating. She lifted her hands toward Raffe, nasty, vengeful desire rolling off her.

She was going to hurt him, and she was going to like it.

I pushed myself like never before to reach her. The ground shook underneath me, but I closed my eyes and directed the sensation at her.

The bitch had to *die*.

A screech pierced my ears, and I opened my eyes to find Priestess Sabrina barely holding on to the edge of a hole I must have created.

How the hell had I done that?

I reached the edge and looked down.

Her bottom lip quivered, and her fingers scrabbled, quickly losing their grip. "Please, help me." Fear poured off her, but her nasty hunger to hurt still held on.

There was no way I would help her. She'd turn on my mate as soon as she hurt me.

Pain soared through my connection with Raffe, and I tore my gaze away to see that Cade had stabbed Raffe in the shoulder.

My mate gritted his teeth, blood pouring from his shoulder. He punched with his left hand, but Cade dodged and ripped the knife from his body.

CHAPTER TWELVE

Raffe groaned, and his agony churned in my chest. Nausea roiled inside me, and Raffe dropped to his knees. He grasped his shoulder wound, pressing over the bleeding.

No! I shouted to myself. *Raffe can't die. Something has to save him.*

My wolf took control. I threw my head back and howled, then took off toward him. The sound was so loud and strong that it echoed all around, even over the sound of the burning house behind us.

I kept my eyes on Cade, using hatred to push me forward as my power sang and radiated from my body.

In that moment, there was only one thing I knew for certain.

Cade was going to die.

Stay back, Raffe linked, his icy fear contrasting with my blazing anger. *You need to get out of here. Take the car and run. Their perimeter won't stop you if you can figure out how to get through it like you did the last one.*

His love and concern spurred me faster.

Cade paused, enjoying the moment. "Not so strong and princely now, are you?" He chuckled then winked at me cruelly. "Hope you got to say goodbye."

Dammit, I was still twenty feet from him. I wouldn't make it.

He swung, but Raffe rolled out of his way. The agony of his injured shoulder hitting the ground sheared through me. Cade must not have thought that Raffe would move to his injured side because Raffe was still breathing.

Rolling onto his back, Raffe kicked Cade in the stomach, and the warlock stumbled back into the woods.

As I reached my mate's side, a hiss came from the woods. I snarled, ready to protect my mate, but a bobcat leaped from the darkness and landed on Cade's back. It wrapped its front paws around his neck and jerked him backward. Cade stumbled and dropped his knife as his hands grasped the bobcat's paws.

Realization of what my magic had been calling slammed through me.

Animals.

The very ones who lived in the woods here.

That must be why the raccoons and foxes had been out here earlier. They'd been drawn to me and my power, and now nature was responding to my call for help.

My vision turned red as I locked on Cade. I would make the lily ass pay for everything he'd done to my mate and then some.

Move back, I commanded, hoping like hell the bobcat would understand.

The bobcat indeed dropped away, and my teeth sank into Cade's flesh. Blood poured into my mouth and down my snout as I clenched my jaw, making sure I killed this asshole. No one hurt my mate and got to walk away to tell the story.

He gurgled, and I jerked my head, ripping out his throat. Cade clasped his hands around his neck as if that would help. Then he dropped to the ground, and his eyes went glassy.

I spun around, ready to attack the next person who tried to hurt my mate, but what I found stopped me in my tracks.

Animals were everywhere.

Bobcats, coyotes, raccoons, foxes, and skunks were taking on the witches in the yard, and I could hear snarls and cries in the woods, where I assumed more animals were attacking the witches who'd been hiding.

Supreme Priestess Olwyn had sent at least fifty coven members here to fight us. I swallowed. None of us had been meant to survive. She'd wanted to make sure of that.

Raffe growled from beside me. He clenched his jaw, taking in the sight. Beads of sweat dripped down his face, streaking the soot. I wanted to cry, but we weren't free yet.

Even with the animals' help, Keith and Adam were still engaged in battle. Josie and Octavia had flanked Dave. Octavia held a long piece of wood from the fence in her hands, ready to use it as a weapon. That must be why she'd run toward the house earlier—to get something for protection.

This fight had to end before nearby humans realized what was happening. It would be hard enough to explain without the cops showing up.

My attention turned to three skunks fighting a warlock ten feet away. The skunks had their tails lifted, circling the warlock, hitting him all around. The warlock held out his palms, and fire blazed from them. The skunk spray lit up, and the fire rushed to the skunks' back sides. The three creatures screamed and took off running to the woods, away from the source of pain.

Chest constricting, I dug my paws into the ground and ran toward the warlock.

Sky, wait! Raffe called. *Let me come with you.*

I swallowed my laugh, not wanting to hurt his feelings. His injury was deep, and the last thing he needed to do was protect me. *I'll be fine.*

The warlock rubbed his eyes, the spray still affecting him.

I smirked inside. Water would've been a better power to have against skunks.

The smell grew worse the closer I got. When I reached him, I held my breath. Even my wolf didn't want to put my mouth on him. As I readied to knock him out, a woman shouted, "Leath, in front of you!"

I crouched, and he aimed his hand at my chest. Fire erupted from his palms.

Shit.

"Skylar!" Raffe shouted, his terror adding to mine.

Flames reached me, and I tried to stumble out of the way before I got too burned. Then I realized all I felt was the tingle of magic. I froze, my breath catching, and watched the flames dance around me without burning my skin.

What the hell…?

Octavia appeared behind the warlock, shouting, "No one hurts my daughter!" She nailed him over the head with the wooden panel. A sickening *thwack* followed, and the warlock crumpled with the wood stuck to his head.

Acid burned my throat. For it to stick like that, there had to be a nail involved.

Then, aside from the crackle of the burning house, there was silence.

I looked around. Thirty bodies littered the ground, as well as twelve animals—mainly skunks, with a few raccoons and a bobcat. Hurried footsteps sounded in the distance.

The witches were retreating.

Good.

Let them go back to Olwyn and tell her they'd failed.

Raffe dropped to his knees and pulled me into his arms. His agony intensified, but he didn't loosen his hold as relief and anger fought for dominance. He linked, *Are you trying to give me a heart attack? I thought you were going to die. Why do you keep running into danger?*

I stepped out of his grip, trying not to miss the buzz of our connection, and shook my fur. *I don't run into danger. It finds me. What am I supposed to do? Hide? Those animals came here to protect us, and anyone willing to do that deserves to have the favor returned.* Those skunks hadn't stood a chance against the warlock's fire magic. *And who's the one hurt?* I pointed my snout at his right injured shoulder. *Not me.*

By a fucking miracle. Raffe growled, his eyes glowing. *They were going to kill us all, including you. That's not an option.*

But you dying is? I understood he loved me and wanted to protect me, but that went both ways. *I don't want to live without you either, but I'm not telling you not to do what you think is right.*

"Why are they staring at each other like that?" Octavia huffed. "We need to get going. The neighbors are turning on their lights, and the animals are a problem."

I snapped back to reality. This argument could come

later. Raffe required medical attention, and the animals needed to disperse.

They all stood a few feet away, staring at me. Keith, Adam, and Lucy made their way back to Josie and Dave, their eyes wide as they took in the bobcats, coyotes, skunks, raccoons, and foxes.

I wasn't sure what to do, but there was one thing I wanted to say. *Thank you. I'm sorry for the lives that were lost and anyone who got injured, but I appreciate your help. Because of you, we survived, and I'm not sure how to repay you.*

The coyote and bobcat lowered their heads, making me feel nervous. But they felt my power, and I understood their intention—they were happy to help me the same way I would them.

I swallowed, my power swirling in a different way. Even though I wanted them to stay, they all needed to go back into the woods. The barrier would come down any second if it hadn't already. *Thank you again. Good night.*

They all melted into the woods, and their magic stopped responding to my power. My blood and power ebbed. My eyes were heavier than normal, sleep wanting to descend, but it was nothing like it had been before Raffe and I completed our bond and I'd become a wolf.

That wasn't fucking weird at all, Keith deadpanned. *Hell, maybe we should have stuck to calling her Bambi, though Cinderella or Aurora may be more fitting.*

Laughter bubbled in my stomach, and I remembered the first time I met the three of them. Keith had made fun of me because I'd mentioned seeing a deer in the woods.

The front door of the house to our left opened. Fortunately, there was a gate still up, so they couldn't see me in wolf form, but there was no hiding what had happened to the house.

"Barbara! Call 9-1-1!" a man yelled. "I'm going to make sure no one's hurt or stuck in there."

Of all the times to find a Good Samaritan, it'd be now.

We all froze then burst into action. Josie bent down and smacked Dave in the face. His eyes fluttered open. She muttered, "We've got to go." She and Octavia helped the vampire to his feet.

Raffe stood and held his shoulder. *We've gotta get out of here before they see you three in wolf form.*

I hadn't even thought about that. We needed to shift, but our clothes had been destroyed.

Raffe jogged across the yard to open the gate at the side of the house.

Keith, Adam, and I kept up with him, but I worried it wasn't just because we were in wolf form. Raffe kept stumbling, and his face blanched even more. Blood had soaked through his shirt, and the top of his sweats was crimson. We needed to dress his wound and quickly.

As we ran out of the backyard, the older man was at the halfway point between his house and this one. He froze, taking in Raffe's horrible condition. Then his gaze flicked down to the three wolves. The man clutched his chest, spun around, and raced back to his front door.

I rolled my eyes. He should've been thankful we weren't vampires because there was no doubt I'd be chasing his ass down with the fear in his eyes.

Raffe unlocked the BMW and waved for me to get in the back seat. I did, trying not to claw up the leather, as Keith and Adam raced to the other vehicles. I huffed when Cat-Keith hissed and pushed by me then jumped into the front passenger seat. The saying about nine lives must be true, and I was grateful.

Josie and Lucy are driving as well, Raffe linked, starting his car.

You're hurt, I linked to him. *You shouldn't be driving.*

We need to leave and get you all some clothes. Then you can drive.

What about your bike? With Adam, Keith, and me in animal form, no one could drive Raffe's favorite vehicle.

Fuck it. We'll get a new one when shit settles down. He waved a hand.

I swallowed. *We have no money.*

Babe, it's fine. As long as I have you, a bike is just a thing. He tried to turn around and groaned.

Sirens sounded in the distance, but thankfully, Lucy, Josie, Octavia, and Dave made it through the gate.

My heartbeat quickened, and my power fizzed. I feared we wouldn't get away in time.

As they helped Dave into the vehicle behind us, the entire situation came crashing down over me.

My mate was badly injured, and the place we'd rented for a week was gone, along with the food in it. We had no clothes, no money, no fucking place to go, and a ton of enemies. What the hell were we going to do?

I lay on the floorboard, not wanting to chance humans seeing me again, and the world spun. I'd thought I understood what being the underdog was like, but I'd had no clue.

Octavia pushed Cat-Keith to the floor and climbed into the front passenger seat, and then all three vehicles took off.

The sirens grew louder, the sound making my head pound as we sped away.

Lights flashed, and we passed three police cars. They

were heading toward the house. My stomach churned. I couldn't believe the shit we'd gotten ourselves into.

"Raffe," Octavia said. "You need to pull over."

"I'm fine," Raffe slurred.

Shit. My stomach wasn't upset due to the police cars and where they were heading. Raffe wasn't feeling well.

He was losing too much blood.

"Let me drive," Octavia pushed. "You need to rest."

"Like hell you will," he snapped.

His nausea and pain increased, making me feel ill.

There was only one way to handle this. I linked to everyone but Raffe, *Josie and Lucy, head to the Walmart down the street and grab Keith, Adam, and me the cheapest clothes you can find. Park far enough away that no one can see Adam and Keith, then come back this way, and I'll tell you where we are.*

It was either early in the morning or super late at night, depending on perspective. Either way, the local twenty-four-hour Walmart wouldn't be busy. At least, we had that going for us. *Raffe, turn off as soon as you can.*

No, I'll be fi—

If you don't, you're going to wreck. He had to realize how bad off he was. *And if you wreck, that means I get hurt too.*

His resistance melted, and my chest tightened with his newfound concern.

Good. I'd thought that would get him to hear me. You've lost too much blood, and I refuse to sit back here and hide while you bleed out. Pull the fuck over so I can shift back into human form and help you.

The car swerved, and then there was a slap.

"Pull over before you pass out," Octavia said with so

much authority some might have thought she was a wolf. "There's a turnoff right there!"

The car slowed, and I felt it turn. I lifted my head to see where we were.

There was a small parking lot off the road for a campground. Luckily, it was winter and closed, so the place was empty. Gravel crunched under the tires, and when the car stopped, Octavia got out.

I snarled while Raffe said, "Get your ass back in here." Or that's what I thought he said because he was slurring his words horribly.

The back car door opened, surprising me, and Octavia waved a hand. "Hurry, I need your help. I'm not sure what to do, so let's figure it out together."

That was more than okay with me.

I jumped out of the back seat and stood by the car. I didn't even have to ask my wolf to recede. She was already leaving my mind and heading back into the center of my chest.

My bones snapped, and my fur vanished, and within seconds, I was in human form, albeit naked. But the cold chill that brushed my skin didn't matter.

I had to help Raffe.

I spun to find Octavia's eyes wide. She must have watched me shift. The way she was staring at me while I was *naked* made me super uncomfortable.

Then I heard a *thump* from inside the car, and Raffe's connection went colder.

My pulse pounded in my ears. He'd passed out. If I didn't stop the bleeding, he'd die.

CHAPTER THIRTEEN

All modesty vanished as I shoved past Octavia and jumped into the front passenger seat to tend to Raffe's wounds.

Raffe was slumped against his door, head against the window. He was already significantly paler than he'd been just a few minutes ago. We had to stop the bleeding, and my blood turned to ice.

What if Cade had nicked an artery? Even though I'd taken a shit ton of science classes, I hadn't advanced to vet school or done any work on humans.

For the first time in my life, I prayed to Fate, the goddess —to *anything* that might have divine power—to save my fated mate.

I shook my head to clear it. I couldn't panic, or he would definitely bleed out. I needed to slow the blood flow enough for his shifter healing to kick in.

"Lean his seat back so he's lying down more, but don't lay him flat. Keep him slightly elevated," I barked loudly, not bothering to turn around and see if Octavia was listening.

Blood coated Raffe's pants, and I wanted to scream. Instead, I had to channel that exertion elsewhere, so I linked with Lucy and Josie, *Raffe needs new clothes too, and I need you to get some alcohol and tons of bandages.*

On it, Lucy replied. *Let us know if you need anything else.*

Pain medicine. Raffe would be hurting, even with his rapid healing, and I wanted something to take the edge off. *Advil—the biggest bottle you can find.* That was the best we could do under the circumstances, unfortunately.

Octavia hurried around the vehicle, and I ripped Raffe's shirt from his body as she opened his door. She pressed the lever and leaned him back, and I continued to shred the material so I didn't have to jostle him more. He needed to lie as still as possible to prevent further damage.

Any other time, I'd have taken a moment to admire his muscles and how cut he was, but not this time, with his life on the line.

I wadded up his shirt and pressed it against his wound. He grunted and flinched, but I kept the pressure on.

Dammit, that fucking hurts, he groaned, despite his eyes remaining closed.

I've got to stop the bleeding, so deal with it. I'd rather you whine than die, I shot back, increasing the pressure. *You need to stay awake.*

Can't … sle— His head turned to the side and hung limply.

When he was nearly flat, Octavia stopped pressing the button and straightened. "What do I do now?"

I wished there was something else, but this was all we had. I had to believe it was enough. "Hope this is enough for him to heal." My voice cracked on the last word. "I need him back to his normal health *now*." My vision blurred, and before I could stop them, tears trailed down my face. We'd finally gotten *our* shit together, and now we kept facing threat after threat. Something had to give because I needed way more time with him.

"He'll be okay," Octavia murmured and reached over, placing a hand on my bare shoulder.

It would have been odd and uncomfortable under any other circumstances, but right now, I needed comfort, even if it was from her. I needed someone to promise me that he'd be all right and I wouldn't lose him. "You can't know that."

"You're too strong to let him. Push your power into him, and see if that helps."

Wait. *Can I do that?* I wasn't sure if it was possible, but it wouldn't hurt to try. If sending Raffe some of my strength would help him, I'd give it freely. "Okay." I sniffed.

Closing my eyes, I tugged on my wolf. My arcane-born power was pure chaos, but maybe my wolf-shifter magic would know what to do. My wolf naturally wanted to protect my mate.

She uncoiled inside me, springing into action. I opened the bond between Raffe and me wider, allowing my magic to flow into him. In his slumber, he didn't reciprocate, but my wolfy magic surged through the bond.

As the bond warmed, I allowed my wolf to funnel whatever she wanted over to him. Even if I wound up passing out, as long as Raffe survived, that was all that mattered. If saving him meant that Octavia got away, so be it. It'd be one less mouth to feed.

I laid my head on the side of Raffe's seat, enjoying his amber scent as my eyes grew heavy. Still, I continued to place pressure on the wound, making sure I kept him from bleeding out as Cat-Keith curled into my lap.

I wasn't sure how long I stayed like that, but a hand

touched my shoulder, and Octavia said, "Your friends are here."

I blinked, trying to remember where I was. Memories crashed back over me. My arms ached, and I sighed with relief when I saw that I'd continued to place pressure on Raffe's wound despite falling asleep.

Our connection was still open, but my wolf was tired and back in her place in my chest. We'd given him as much of our magic as possible.

Josie and Lucy pulled up behind us, and Lucy got out with two bags and darted toward me. She jumped into the back seat.

When she reached Raffe's side, she frowned. "How's he doing?"

His color seemed slightly better. "I don't know. I've been putting as much pressure on the wound as I can."

"Here." Octavia held out her hands. "Let me do it so you can get dressed."

Even though she hadn't tried to escape, that didn't mean I trusted her. "No thanks." She'd abandoned me, and then she'd shown up at the university with suspicious timing. She hadn't proven we could trust her.

"Let me." Lucy tossed both bags at my feet. "You can trust me. Besides, if Raffe finds out that Keith and Adam saw you naked, neither of them will live once he gets better."

Snorting, I nodded. I'd needed that laugh. "Fine. But keep pressure on it."

Carefully, I pushed the cat from my lap, and Lucy took over. I grabbed the underwear, bra, jeans, and lavender shirt she'd gotten me. Realizing that Lucy had taken the time to get a shirt close to my favorite color—lilac—I smiled and felt my heart slow to a more normal beat.

I quickly dressed inside the vehicle, thankful she'd bought me underwear packaged in a box. Once I had clothes on, I felt better, though I wished Raffe would wake up. He was still out cold.

Snagging the gauze, I took a deep breath, ignoring the coppery scent of Raffe's blood. "Remove his shirt. Let's see what the wound looks like." I yawned; my eyelids were still heavy with sleep.

When she removed his shirt, my body sagged. His bleeding had slowed, and his breathing and heart were steady despite him being unconscious. At least those were good signs.

I packed his wound as tightly as possible then rolled the gauze around his shoulder several times, making it as snug as I could. I straightened, wondering like hell what to do next. One thing was certain—Raffe needed to be moved because he wouldn't be driving.

Keith and Adam, can you help me move Raffe to the passenger seat? He needed to stay slightly elevated.

By the time I got out of the SUV and walked around the hood, Keith and Adam were there. Adam stood closest to the door, his face lined with worry.

"The bleeding slowed, so that's something." I forced a smile, trying to reassure him and myself. "He just needs rest."

"We all do." Keith hung his head. "This is all bullshit. We left to hide and stay off the grid, and both our dads and the coven found us. At this rate, we might as well go back to campus. At least our place there is paid for. We just spent almost all the money we had."

I didn't ask how much money we had left. It had to be hundreds, if that.

"Going back to campus would be handing Skylar over

to Supreme Priestess Olwyn." Adam pinched the bridge of his nose. "And we all know Raffe wouldn't want that."

"So what do we do?" Lucy leaned against the back driver's side door. "Go home to our parents' pack?"

Adam wrung his hands. "Raffe will kick our asses if we do that, especially after forming our new pack. And for all we know, our dads brought the coven members to us."

I hated that he was right. If taking Raffe back to his dad would keep him safe, I'd do it in a heartbeat, but Raffe could find me now that our fated-mate bond was complete, and I had no doubt he would track my ass down if I tried to be noble and leave him. He was determined like that.

Even though I didn't want to know, the question had to be asked. "How much money do we have left?"

"Josie said about two hundred." Lucy bit her bottom lip.

Less than that, Josie linked. *More like a hundred and seventy-five, and guys, we have another problem. Dave needs more blood. He's hungry and can't heal without it.*

That must be why he'd been struggling back at the house and why he'd tried to attack me when my power sang.

Octavia huffed. "I already said we should go to my house. No one from the pack or coven knows where I live."

"Sounds great, except we don't trust you." Keith arched a brow. "So there's *that*."

Even though he was right, I didn't know what better option we had. We had hardly any money. Coven members and wolf shifters lived throughout the United States, and this group had such prominence that most supernaturals would recognize them. I didn't know where we could go or hide other than her place.

I gritted my teeth, hating the situation we were in and that Raffe had gotten significantly injured because of *me*. Dave wasn't far behind him unless we found him some blood. Guilt and regret made it hard to breathe. My power went to a fizz, and I wanted to scream and pull my hair out.

I was sick and tired of this. For once, couldn't things be easy for us? "Why should we trust you?" I pivoted to Octavia, needing to watch every expression and read her emotions.

She stood tall, meeting my gaze head-on. "I came to the university, despite all the risks, because I heard you were in danger. I understand how it looked when you found me, but Skylar, even though we gave you up, we never stopped loving you. You can trust me. I won't betray you."

I snorted, bitterness rising, but now wasn't the time to address my abandonment issues. We were in the parking lot of a closed campground. We had to move, and driving around aimlessly would waste what little cash we had left. We had to be strategic. "How do you know we'll be safe there?"

Skylar, Adam linked. *You can't be serious. Raffe wouldn't like this.*

My head snapped toward him, my wolf stirring enough to rise. *Well, he's not awake and healthy enough to offer suggestions, is he?*

Keith's head tilted backward, and he smirked. "It's a good thing that Raffe isn't awake right now, or he'd kick my ass because that right there was very se—"

"Don't"—Lucy smacked him in the back of the head —"finish that comment. Think it to yourself, but never say anything like that out loud or in the pack link. We're going to pretend you aren't that stupid. Just in case, I'll remind you that he wouldn't get mad at only you for saying something like that but at all of us for not telling him. But since you aren't correcting me, we all know you weren't about to say what it sounded like you were going to say." She glared at him, daring him to counter her.

I shivered, my wolf snarling in my head. No one was allowed to look at me in any way but platonically except for Raffe. Before Keith said something else that might provoke my mate, I asked, "How far away do you live?"

"About fourteen hours." Octavia rubbed her hands together. "If we get moving, we can be there by this evening."

"We need blood for Dave." Yet another problem I didn't have a solution for. "Can you help us with that?"

She nodded. "Both Dru and your brother are human. I can get them to donate some of their blood. Dru is a doctor—he has the supplies to draw blood and access to a blood bank. We should be able to take care of him."

Doctor.

My heart leaped into my throat. "And you swear no one will tell anyone about us?"

"I promise." Octavia placed a hand over her heart. "If I wanted to escape or hurt you, I could've done it."

She was right. When I'd passed out helping Raffe, she could have killed him. Instead, she'd kept watch by the door.

I felt myself soften. A place to stay where no one could locate us and with a doctor, and we wouldn't have to worry about money. *This is our best option. What do you all think?*

Raffe might need a doctor, and they can get Dave blood. Lucy leaned back on her heels. *I think we do it.*

Adam and Keith glanced at each other then nodded.

That was it. We had a majority, and Josie would be in if it meant helping Dave.

Still, that didn't mean I liked it.

I lifted my chin, letting my wolf inch forward. I needed

Octavia to see how serious I was with my next words. I growled, "Fine. We'll go. But if one wrong move is even hinted at by you or your *family*"—I couldn't help but spit that word—"and I will unleash my power. Got it?"

Octavia nodded. "I understand. Now, let's go before someone else finds us."

The four of us nodded at each other, and then Adam and Keith moved. Together, they gently lifted Raffe and carried him around to the passenger seat. I watched as blood soaked through the clean gauze.

My stomach sank. He wasn't healing as quickly as I'd hoped. We needed to get him somewhere to rest. That sealed the deal, and I was eager to go. He might not last the fourteen hours it would take to get to Octavia's home.

I gave Octavia my phone, and with my supernatural hearing, I listened as she pressed the buttons. After one ring, an older man answered, "Hello?"

"Dru, hey, it's me."

"Oh, thank gods." The man sighed. "Are you okay? We've been worried sick."

"Yes, sorry. There was a complication, but I'm fine." Octavia cleared her throat.

My mouth went dry as I heard the voice of my biological father. A sharp pain I hadn't expected pierced my heart.

"Is Divinity all right?" he asked with concern.

I tensed.

"She's fine. She's actually here with me. I'm bringing her and some of her ... uh ... *friends* home."

"Friends?" he parroted. "Why not just her? A houseful of people I don't know when I'm meeting my daughter for the first time might be too much. I mean—"

Wait. *I* was Divinity? Was that what they'd planned to name me?

A lump formed in my throat, so large I couldn't swallow, and I wished Raffe was awake so we could experience this together. My eyes burned.

"Honey, they're all in danger, not just her. She won't come without them."

"Then bring them all." His voice filled with emotion. "I don't give a damn as long as she comes here. Fane will feel the same."

"Can you run into town and get some blood? They have a vampire with them ... and he's hungry." She swallowed audibly. "And a wolf shifter is severely injured and might need you to stitch him up."

"Jesus, Vi." He huffed. "We went from staying away from all supernaturals to having almost every species under our roof."

"I know. I'm sorry, but—"

"It's fine. Just come home. I love you."

"Love you," she replied. "We'll be there in fourteen hours." She hung up.

I rolled my shoulders and tried to wipe a tear from my eye discreetly. If it weren't for Raffe needing help, I would've changed my mind. Instead, I drove as fast as I dared, hoping like hell we got there in time.

THIRTEEN HOURS LATER, we drove through Salt Lake City, Utah, and headed into the mountains. Raffe had been in and out of consciousness, and I was trying to get him to the doctor.

My only solace was that his breathing and heart rate remained steady. My back was stiff from leaning slightly over the center console so I could touch his arm. I needed the constant buzz of our connection for reassurance.

Between his condition and the fact that I was about to meet my biological father and brother, my emotions were all over the place. I both wanted to get there and dreaded it, but my fated mate's health would always trump my personal needs.

"Turn here." Octavia leaned forward, directing me to turn left onto a gravel road. Under different circumstances, I'd have found this area beautiful. Many leaves were yellow with hints of gold and orange, and the spruce and fir trees retained their evergreen canvas like the dark silhouettes of a painting.

Up ahead, the trees thinned, and a sizable brick house appeared. The buzz of coven magic washed over me.

Heart dropping, I stomped on the brakes. The bitch had set a trap.

CHAPTER FOURTEEN

The tires skidded on the gravel, sending a dust cloud swirling around us. The haze thickened, and I couldn't see through it.

Raffe lurched, and I reached over to keep him in place. His groan sounded so raspy, and the pain that shot through our bond had my breath catching. He wasn't doing well, but I didn't know what the fuck to do about it.

What the hell is going on? I almost rear-ended you, Keith linked. *Did you see Bambi or something?*

I would've found his sarcasm humorous, but between the threat, Raffe's agony, and his current state, my patience snapped. *I just drove through coven magic.*

There was silence as the air cleared around us. Then tires squealed behind us as Adam slung his car into reverse.

Let's get out of here, Adam linked. *Before they attack us.*

We needed to go, but I didn't know what that meant for Raffe. Our bond had cooled ever so slightly. If we left, I wasn't sure where we could take him—an emergency room wasn't an option with his shifter blood and healing.

Worse, we couldn't afford to stay anywhere, let alone

buy food and medical supplies. I wanted to scream and flip off the world, but that wouldn't accomplish anything.

If we left, I couldn't bring Octavia with us. Part of me wanted to keep her as a bargaining chip, but I doubted she meant much to the coven, so there was no true benefit in keeping her with us. That alone made the decision for me. She'd told me I could trust her, and before even reaching the door, I'd felt coven magic swirling throughout the area.

"Get out," I commanded as more tires squealed and Keith backed out. Now I had room to back up too, but I had to get Octavia out of the damn vehicle.

"What?" Octavia rasped, leaning forward so that her head appeared between my headrest and Raffe's. "Why?"

Oh, so she was playing innocent. That was *fine*. Slade had given me plenty of experience in dealing with that. "Coven magic. You told us you weren't part of the Veiled Circle or working with witches, yet coven magic is everywhere here. Get your ass out of the car, or I'll make you."

Raffe's connection faded a little more, and I grew lightheaded.

The front door of the house opened.

Shit, they were making a move.

"*What*? I'm not working with Supreme Priestess Olwyn or her coven." Octavia bit her lip and hung her head. "It must be because I vanished. The witches who live around here probably spelled the area so no other witches can enter, I'd guess."

I climbed out of the car, ready to drag her ass out. My blood went straight to a fizz as I yanked open the back driver's side door. "Well, I don't trust you, seeing as my skin is crawling from the amount of magic out here. This is your last chance. Get out, or I'll make you."

Keith's car stopped ten feet away, and I could feel his

and Lucy's gazes on me. The driver's side door opened, and Keith climbed out as he came to join me.

Two sets of footsteps came from the house, and I turned to find two men rushing out the front door, carrying some sort of bed. My head spun as I took them in. I didn't feel any magic coming off them, and this could very well be my biological father and brother.

What's going on? Keith linked to all of us, heading over to me. *Why are you out of the car? That defeats the point of leaving. Lucy, get in the driver's seat in case we need to escape.*

Lucy didn't hesitate, climbing over the center console to get into the seat.

We can't bring Octavia with us. My stomach hardened. Her presence had impacted me more than I wanted to admit. *We can't afford to take care of another person, let alone ourselves, and Raffe isn't doing well. Where the hell do we go to get him help?*

If the coven is here, we need to leave and quickly. We'll figure out someplace to take Raffe. He's a fighter, so he won't just give up, Adam interjected.

"Is that the injured man?" the older man, who was close to six feet tall, asked. His olive-green eyes glanced at the front passenger seat of my car. Even though they weren't the same shade, the brown in his was close to the brown hint in my cognac eyes. "I've set up the garage to treat him and put a cooler in there with ten blood bags for the vampire."

I hesitated. It genuinely sounded like he would help Raffe and Dave. I homed in on Raffe, noting his clammy and sweaty complexion. Though he'd groaned in pain, he hadn't woken up, and he looked more pasty, challenging Dave for the fairest of them all.

He needed help.

I feared if we left, he might not make it.

And that caused my heart to break and not give a damn about my safety.

"Skylar, I *promise* it's not what you think," Octavia said, getting out of the car and placing a hand on my shoulder.

"Don't fucking touch her," Keith growled, sounding an awful lot like Raffe. He stalked up next to me. "If she thinks we can't trust you and wants you gone, go. Or *I'll* make you."

My heart squeezed, knowing Keith was protecting me because Raffe couldn't. Despite everything, I was beginning to see more and more why the others kept Keith around. Once he accepted you, he was loyal and protective. He'd be a good mate to someone someday.

She exhaled and dropped her hands, but her focus remained on me.

"Why should I trust you?" I asked, torn about what to do. She didn't smell of a lie, and no coven magic surrounded her. Most importantly, Raffe needed help. If that meant I got held hostage, it'd be worth it so long as he didn't die.

Both men came to a stop not far away. The rise and fall of Raffe's chest slowed even more.

I could feel my father's and brother's gazes on me. A shiver ran down my spine.

I'm heading back to you, Adam linked, and the sound of his vehicle grew louder. *If something happens, I need to be there to help fight.*

"Remember how I told you I was aware of all the supernatural goings-on?" Octavia licked her bottom lip. "That's because a huge coven lives down the road. They've helped our family stay hidden for years and have been doing research to help us." She pointed at the gravel road that led past their house and deeper into the woods.

I laughed. "You expect me to believe that with how little you trust covens?" Okay, clearly, people thought I was dumber than dirt. Granted, I deserved that for falling for Slade and Supreme Priestess Olwyn's bullshit.

"That's why I don't trust Olwyn's coven." Octavia lifted her hands. "The coven here is descended from the original ruling coven that took in Foster. His loss changed them fundamentally. They gave me his journal and tried to help him control his magic. For instance, I know that your power ... it's all vibrations. That's why you can shatter glass and cause the ground to shake."

I sucked in a breath, unsure of what to do. What she said made sense. Earthquakes, shaky limbs, causing furniture to break, and even knocking over trees. Hell, even the jolt, fizz, and hum were vibrations. And my connection to animals ... they were attuned to the earth's shifts in patterns and vibrations, which was how they sensed natural disasters before they happened. That one revelation helped me understand so damn much that it wasn't even funny.

Still, that didn't mean it was safe for us to stay here.

Raffe's heartbeat weakened.

"If you want me to help him, you need to decide now," the older man, Dru, said gently. "He's not looking well and likely needs blood."

My heart ached, and that alone made my decision. If Raffe needed blood, he was too close to dying for my comfort. I stared into the man's eyes. They were warm and kind, but I didn't trust my gut anymore, not after being wrong about so many people.

"If you let me help him, I believe he'll be fine." The man appeared to be in his late forties, younger than my adoptive parents. "But I need to know you're okay with me helping him."

"Listen—" Keith started.

"Do you swear you won't hurt him or use him to get even with me?"

Dru's forehead lined with worry, and his Adam's apple bobbed. "I swear I'll do everything I can to help him. He obviously means a lot to you, and the last thing I'd ever want to do is hurt my daughter more." He adjusted the handles he was holding and ran a hand through his warm-brown hair.

With my blood at a fizz, I could read his emotions clearly. He was being honest with me. "Okay," I muttered. *Keith and Adam, do you mind helping them get Raffe into the garage? He's fading fast.*

Sky, are you sure? Keith linked, his body tense.

I snapped my head toward him and bared my teeth. *Would you rather he die?*

Adam's vehicle appeared behind Keith's as Dru, Keith, and my brother jumped into action. The three men hurried to the passenger side and opened the car door. But when the two of them tried to lift Raffe out of the seat, their faces turned red, and Raffe didn't budge.

"Move, please," Keith said curtly. "If you can't lift him, get out of the way so I can."

I climbed back in and tried to help Raffe from the driver's seat. When I touched his hand, the buzz of our connection barely sprang to life.

My mouth dried just as Adam reached the door behind Keith.

"Here, give me his feet, and you take his torso. We can carry him in that way," Adam instructed and glanced at Dru and my brother. "Why doesn't the one who's not a doctor take the bed down to the car at the end?"

My brother swallowed. "The vampire? Won't he try to ... you know."

"He's unconscious, and Josie and Lucy can carry him," Adam replied, taking Raffe's feet and slowly moving backward as Keith slipped his hands under Raffe's armpits.

I wished I could help Dave, but with my blood at fizz level, the worst thing I could do was get close to him.

"Come on." Octavia hurried around the car and took one edge of the bed. "I'll go with you."

My brother nodded, and the two of them took off toward Adam's car as Dru led Adam and Keith to the largest garage door, removing a fob from his pocket. Soon, the door was opening, revealing two beds inside. One had plastic around it and an IV hanging from the pole.

That had to be for Raffe.

Discomfort and stinging pain radiated from my mate, but instead of hating it like I had before, I clung to it, knowing that meant he was still with me. Still, it wasn't intense.

Josie, they're coming for Dave, and they have a setup for him and Raffe in their garage. I wasn't sure why the garage, but I wouldn't complain. *They have blood for Dave there.*

Thank gods, Josie replied. *Dave has begun bleeding from his chest again, and every time I place my wrist to his mouth, he turns his head and refuses to drink my blood.*

Neither of our fated mates was doing well, so at least we understood each other.

"Try not to jostle him." Dru winced, watching the two wolf shifters carry Raffe. "The more he moves, the more he'll bleed, which will exacerbate the problem."

Keith growled, sounding more animal than man. "You try carrying three hundred pounds of solid muscle. Then you can tell us we aren't being as careful as fucking possible."

Dru nodded. "Point taken, but that doesn't make the situation any less dire."

The closer we got to the garage, the more blood seeped from Raffe's bandage. The little bit of healing Raffe's body had done was already reversed. I had to believe my power wasn't lying to me and that Dru was being honest.

Raffe *had* to be all right.

There was no way I could do any of this without him.

My limbs grew heavy, and after what felt like hours, Keith and Adam got Raffe on the bed while Dru put on blue gloves and a face mask. There was an AC unit at his feet, keeping the area cool.

With steady hands, he bent down and grabbed some blood.

"Whoa. No." Adam shook his head. "What the hell do you think you're doing?"

"He needs blood." Dru pointed at the spot on his chest. "He's lost too much."

"Do you know anything about wolf shifters?" Adam crossed his arms, his lips pressed into a line. "We can't take regular human blood. It has to be from another shifter with his same blood type."

Unfortunately, that made sense. Shifters were part human, part animal. I'd bet animal blood wouldn't work for him either.

My heart shattered. After all of this, we wouldn't be able to save him. Eyes burning, I rasped, "Do any of you have his blood type?"

Keith shook his head. "We don't. The royal line has its own kind. His dad or mom are the best people to give him blood."

Vision blurring, I took a ragged breath. "We know that won't happen." I exhaled noisily. "Are there any options left? Can you get him to stop bleeding long enough to let his body remake the blood?"

He gritted his teeth. "I can try."

My world tilted, but I hung on to the bed, refusing to leave Raffe's side.

Dave, Josie, Lucy, my brother, and Octavia joined us. They moved Dave from the transportation bed to the more stable one, and within seconds, they had him drinking blood.

I watched Dru like a hawk as he removed the bandages and dug inside Raffe's wound. Sweat beaded on his forehead, and he breathed heavily through his mouth. He held the edge of a knife to the injury, and blood squirted out. Raffe's heartbeat quickened, and his breathing turned labored.

Something was wrong. "Why is he bleeding like that?"

"I ... I don't know." Dru leaned over, squinting as if it might help him see better. "I see nothing that should be causing this. He should be healing. Something must be causing this bleeding. It's like his blood won't clot, but he's a shifter, so that's not possible."

"Wait." Lucy hurried over to us, her eyes wide. "A coven member stabbed him."

"Yeah. We were all there, Lucy. Damn." Keith shook his head, pacing at the foot of the bed.

What I saw on her face wasn't confusion but fear. My pulse stopped. "What do you mean?" Once again, there was something I didn't know. Add it to the fucking list.

"Don't coven members have a poison that causes bleeding like that?" Lucy rocked on her feet. "I swear King Jovian told us about a poison like that in a *Book of Twilight*?

That's one reason the wolf shifters made the covens destroy the books—so powerful spells like that can't be used against us."

I swallowed.

"And they have access to those books in the secret fucking library." Adam's voice dripped with a malice I'd never heard from him before.

My blood turned cold, and my power wanted to hum, but I couldn't lose control. Not when my fated mate needed me.

"You said a coven lives nearby, right?" I asked, turning to Octavia. "Can they help us?"

She licked her lips. "I ... I don't know, but we can ask them."

That was all I needed to hear. "Then call them, *please*."

"He won't last much longer." Dru swallowed. "If you're going to do something, I suggest you get on it." He began packing the wound again to slow the bleeding.

"Yeah, I can—" Octavia started, but magic filled the air around us.

We didn't have to call the coven.

They were already here, and judging by the amount of magic they radiated, they were here to fight.

CHAPTER FIFTEEN

My power hummed, and I had to get away from Raffe before I lost control. If I hurt him, I wouldn't survive or ever be able to forgive myself.

Protect him, I linked to the others as I darted to the door.

"Wait!" Octavia shouted, but I blew past her. If they kept pushing their magic inside, they could hurt my mate worse.

Dammit, Sky, Keith snarled, sounding so damn much like Raffe that my heart fractured more. *Raffe is out, and if something happens to you, all our asses will be dead when he wakes up.*

I didn't slow as I ran out of the garage door and came face to face with twenty-one coven members.

An older lady stood in the center, her face lined with thick wrinkles and her long gray hair blowing behind her. Despite her age, her eyes were the shade of evergreen needles. Four women of varying ages flanked her with tall men on either edge. Behind them stood another nine women with a man in the center.

They all had their hands lifted. Lightning crashed in the distance, and rain suddenly poured over us.

"Leave now, or you'll force us to attack," the older woman's voice boomed around me, the magic chafing my skin. "Your kind isn't welcome here."

Keith's scent became stronger, and I sensed him behind me just as my power thrummed harder and pulsed outward. In moments, havoc would begin, but I wasn't sure I could take on twenty-one witches by myself.

"My kind? Aren't we all supernaturals?" I asked bitterly. What was up with all these people thinking that because we had different abilities, we didn't have anything in common? That attitude in humans had always perturbed me as a child.

"Yes, we are, but wolf shifters like you think they deserve to make the rules for everyone, and that doesn't work for me." She lifted her chin. "Nor does attacking an innocent family that wants to be left alone, the same as my coven here." She lifted a hand.

My power pulsed out, shaking the ground underneath them.

The older woman tilted her head back when Octavia came racing out.

"Priestess Caroline, stop." Octavia huffed and clenched her hands at her sides. "This is Divinity. She brought me back, and this boy came with her ... pack."

Who the fuck is Divinity? Keith linked.

I think that's ... the name they gave me. Even saying the words via the pack link knotted my stomach. I didn't like the idea of them giving me a name. It made it harder to distance myself from them ... like they might not have wanted to give me up.

"Wait." Priestess Caroline lowered her hands. "How is

that possible? You and Dru are human. She has power, and I can feel a strong wolf presence within her. I thought I was mistaken that she was the arcane-born until the ground shook underneath us."

The other coven members lowered their arms, and the middle-aged woman to the priestess's right tilted her head. She had the same eye color and sharp cheekbones, making me wonder if she was the priestess's sister or daughter.

With the coven's magic easing around me, my power calmed to a high fizz, and my anger flamed without risking the ground imploding. "She can speak for herself, and I was a human with power until Raffe and I completed our fated-mate bond. Then I somehow became a shifter too." I shrugged, not understanding it myself, let alone how to explain it to anyone else.

"The rumors are true." The younger girl beside Priestess Caroline clasped her hands over her chest. She had to be a teenager, but those eyes were the same color as the priestess's.

I scanned the others, wondering if they all had the same eye color. Thankfully, they didn't, or this would've been a lot creepier.

The girl giggled. "The arcane-born is the wolf shifter prince's fated mate. And he chose her! How romantic."

Unfortunately, I didn't have time to be giddy with her. I stepped forward, and the two men on either end stepped forward too.

Keith growled in warning.

I lifted my head. "A coven member stabbed my mate, and he can't stop bleeding despite his shifter healing. We thought maybe you could help."

Priestess Caroline's face turned to stone. Any sense of alarm was replaced with more wrinkles as her expression twisted with worry. "They attacked you." Her jaw clenched. "Of course. Olwyn won't allow you to live if you don't side with them."

"You're not telling us anything we don't know," Keith snapped.

I wanted to smack him. Now wasn't the time to give them attitude. I needed them to help Raffe if they could.

The two warlocks at the end scowled at Keith.

Great, I couldn't get away from the constant pissing matches between all these alpha men.

Pushing away my annoyance, I clasped my hands together, trying like hell not to come off as threatening or demanding. "Can you help him?" I bit my bottom lip, about to drop to my knees and beg them to do something.

"I'll need to confirm if it's what I think it is." Priestess Caroline walked to me, her long, earthy-brown gown skimming the gravel. "If it is, we don't have time to waste. Avalon and Faith, go back to the house and bring me the blood fern concoction immediately."

"But Mother," the woman on the right gasped. "He's the wolf prince, and that's the last bit we have of the—"

Priestess Caroline glared. "Avalon, if the prince dies, Divinity will likely die too. You know what happened in the past. Is that what you want?"

My lungs stopped working. I hadn't been getting as exhausted and struggling like before Raffe and I connected. Even before turning into a wolf, once I'd been with him, physical things had been easier, and his touch always calmed me. "Please help … me." My voice cracked. I hoped that asking for myself would mean more than asking for Raffe.

"Fine." Avalon huffed and gestured toward the gravel path. "Faith, let's go."

"Yes, Mother." Faith glanced at me one last time before following.

"Everyone else, secure the perimeter since they broke through it." Priestess Caroline hurried to the garage and looked inside.

For someone so old, she moved agilely ... more so than I ever had as a human.

She made a beeline for my mate. Lucy and Adam tensed but didn't say anything, likely because they couldn't hear everything outside.

I could see him struggling for breath. The walls closed in on me as I realized how close to losing him I was. The metallic stench of his blood hung in the air, overtaking his normal scent that I loved.

"I need to keep pressure on the wound. He's losing too much blood." Dru shook his head.

"If we want him to have a chance to live, then move. *Now*. This may be magic at work, which means your human doctoring skills could kill him."

Dru stepped back. "Fine, but if it's not magic, I need to stop the bleeding. I've never seen anything like this. Let me get you some glo—"

Before he could finish, the priestess had removed the gauze with her bare hands, and the fated-mate connection cooled.

"Can anyone here give him blood?" I couldn't stand here and watch him die. I had to do something. "Lucy, you're family."

"But on his mother's side." Lucy bit her lip. "It would need to be ..." Her eyes widened. "Sky, *you* could do it. You're a wolf shifter and his fated mate. Normally, fated mates are forged of the same soul and thus have the same blood. It's part of the mate bond."

My heart galloped, and my chest warmed. "Then there's no reason to wait."

Dru's lips mashed together as he came to me with a needle and tubes. I pulled up my sleeve, extending my arm so he could prick me, but he hesitated.

"Dad, what are you doing?" My brother joined us, standing next to Lucy. He glanced at me then at Dru again. "She wants to save him."

"But I can't monitor the amount of blood she's giving." Dru rubbed his hands together.

He didn't get to act like a concerned father. "Do it now, or I'll do it myself. I know enough from my pre-vet studies to get the job done." Though I'd probably wind up stabbing myself several times. I'd never done an IV on a human, but it couldn't be that hard. Surely.

"Do it." Octavia sighed from behind me. "She's an adult and loves him."

"Fine." He prepped a needle. "But I don't know if you can give him all he needs. Got it?"

"As long as he survives." I planned on giving Raffe as much of my blood as I could before they forced me to stop, but no one needed to know that.

Priestess Caroline dug her fingers into his wound. She lifted a bloody hand to her nose. "A spell is keeping the blood from clotting, but the magical properties of the blood fern Faith and Avalon are getting will counter it, so there's no cause for alarm as long as he stays alive until they get here."

"Hook me up." My vision blurred as tears of relief filled them. There was hope, and I wouldn't let my mate die, not like this.

Dru hooked up Raffe to the other end of the tubing and came to me. He pricked my arm, and when my blood trickled down the line, I had to believe everything would be okay.

"Here, sit down," Dru said, bringing over a chair next to Raffe.

I shook my head. Instead, I leaned on the uninjured side of Raffe's chest, needing to feel his skin. Even though the buzz was faint, it was there, which meant he wasn't gone.

"I'm surprised they used magic that would be so easy to counter." Adam's voice sounded rough even for him.

"Oh, Supreme Priestess Olwyn doesn't realize there's an antidote. She believes she has all the existing *Books of Twilight*, but my coven hid the one with the remedy—along with other things." Priestess Caroline laughed. "She doesn't even know it exists since this book was written before her family took over the supreme role."

I turned my head so I could see everyone, but I kept an ear on Raffe's chest, listening to his steady heartbeat. It might have been wishful thinking, but I swore it was already steadier.

"Her family has always been at the head of all the covens," Dave said as he and Josie joined us at Raffe's bedside.

"Here I believed I'd seen it all with Divinity and the prince completing their bond despite the odds, and now there's a vampire in the prince's midst as well." Priestess Caroline smirked. "Maybe the cycle has been broken." She snatched up fresh gauze and packed Raffe's wound again. Before anyone could ask her what she meant by that, she continued, "Olwyn wants everyone to believe that her family has always been in power, but that isn't the case. In fact, she took power after the supreme priestess who was in charge of training Foster, whose family had always reigned. The position changed to Olwyn's coven shortly after the witches fell from power and the wolf shifters took their place."

My brows lifted, but I couldn't concentrate on more than that. I had more important things at hand. "I don't care what happened as long as your coven members get back with the concoction in time." I focused on the rise and fall of Raffe's chest.

When I cracked my eyes open, I noticed Lucy's and my brother's gazes lingering on each other. She wrapped her arms around her waist, and he tugged at his ears, causing his hair, which was a shade lighter than mine, to fall into his face. He was perhaps a year or two older than me, and his complexion was a shade darker than mine. We had similar cheekbones, and he had several inches on me, coming in at around six feet.

Josie rocked on her feet. "How much longer until the witches come back?" Her worried gaze landed on Raffe.

My breathing turned rapid, but I forced myself to take the deep, calming breaths that all my years of therapy had forever lodged into my mind. Just like all the other times, it didn't do a damn thing. The worry and hysteria still dug their sharp claws into my chest.

"They'll be here soon." Priestess Caroline exhaled. "We don't live far."

Hurried footsteps sounded from outside, and I lifted my head.

We'll go check it out, Adam linked, and he and Keith headed back outside.

"Be strong." Priestess Caroline lifted a gray brow. "He needs you to, for him. As long as you are, he'll remain the same."

Some of the weight on my shoulders eased. Not much, but enough not to feel crushed underneath the pressure like before. If my strength helped Raffe, then I'd be strong for him. Even if it was silly, having a task made me feel better, as if I had some control over the situation.

It's the witches, Keith linked. *Nothing to be worried about.*

Words I never thought I'd hear Raffe or one of his friends say. Whether they liked it or not, we were at this coven's mercy. We couldn't get Raffe to stop bleeding without them.

"How do we do this?" I needed to know what to expect.

"We pour the liquid into his wound so it can hit the magic stored there." Priestess Caroline wiped her bloody hands on her gown, leaving her handprints on it.

"Are we sure this is safe? This will definitely work on him?" Lucy wrung her hands. "Like, nothing bad will happen to him?"

Priestess Caroline lifted her hands. "I can't make any promises. I only remember the description of a spell like that being used on us once when Olwyn's ancestors tried to kill our coven. My coven worked together to find a solution, and as we were close to death, they found these rare petals that, when mixed with herbs, eliminated the effects. Based on everything I know, this is the only antidote. But Olwyn could have modified the poison in some way. We have no way of knowing until we use the antidote on him."

All my relief faded away, and the world spun slightly around me. This might not save him after all.

Faith ran into the garage with Keith and Adam on her heels. She held a clear bottle with a putrid smell and black sludge inside.

Sludge that looked gross and like something I wouldn't want to touch me.

Ever.

"Uh … is that still good?" Keith's nose wrinkled. "Because I'm not so sure."

"I'm with him." Dave gagged. "And this is a problem, seeing as I just got full."

"Here, let's unpack him. We need to get the IV out of Skylar. She's probably given him enough of her blood." Dru moved to take the IV out.

I dodged him and shook my head, gritting my teeth. "Not until he's fixed and the bleeding has stopped."

Priestess Caroline unpacked the gauze, and this time, he was bleeding worse than before … probably because they kept messing with it. She held out her hand. "Here."

Faith handed the bottle to her and took several steps back, blinking as Avalon hurried in. Avalon huffed out a breath but didn't say a word as Priestess Caroline tipped the bottle over Raffe's wound.

With bated breath, I watched as the sludge inched out of the bottle. The smell became worse the closer to the opening it came. Then, the material gathered at the tip, thickening until it fell into the wound.

Then something exploded.

CHAPTER SIXTEEN

Black smoke poured from Raffe's wound, his blood boiling as the magic seared through it. A shock shot through my fated-mate connection to Raffe, knocking me back. I almost toppled over until strong arms wrapped around me, keeping me upright ... mostly.

The smell of laundry detergent and the lack of musk informed me who it was.

Dru.

I tried to get my feet underneath me, but my legs felt like jelly. I couldn't take my eyes off my fated mate.

"It's fine, child." Priestess Caroline waved a hand, and the black smoke bent around it as if it had a mind of its own. "It's working. A spell like that is vile magic, so cleansing it is like cutting through soot."

My ears rang, but his blood calming once more kept me somewhat sane. At this point, I couldn't do much more than trust the coven members.

My legs gave out even more.

"I told you that you gave him too much blood. Fane, help me get her into the chair." Dru's arms tightened as he tried to drag me to the chair next to Raffe. He grunted and muttered, "And she's harder to move than I expected."

Out of the corner of my eye, I watched my brother race toward me, shaking his head. "She's a wolf shifter, Dad. What did you expect?"

I needed to be touching Raffe. That was when we were the strongest, but dammit, I couldn't even stand.

Fane came up beside me, and the two of them hoisted me into the chair. The world spun harder, but now that I was back at Raffe's side, I leaned toward him—and began slipping out of the chair.

Placing his hands on my shoulders, Fane held me upright and said, "Get the IV out of her arm."

I moved my arm to touch Raffe and also made sure they didn't take the IV out. If giving him more blood prevented him from dying, then I was on board. Even though I could survive without him, I didn't want to.

"I'm trying." Dru moved to my side, holding my arm.

I shook my head. "He needs—"

Lucy cut me off. "Sky, look."

My brows furrowed, and I turned my head to look at Raffe. His wound had stopped bleeding, and as the last bit of nasty mist came out, the skin closed all around it. He was almost healed. "How?"

"His wolf shifter magic was healing him, but the coven magic prevented the wound from closing. When it left, he healed as intended." Priestess Caroline lowered her hand. "However, he has lost a lot of blood. He'll need rest, but the antidote worked, and he should make a full recovery."

My entire body lightened, and oxygen filled my lungs once more. He was going to be okay.

"Which means he doesn't need your blood anymore, or

you'll wind up in far worse shape than him." Dru *tsk*ed, removing the needle from my arm while I was distracted.

"Hey." I slurred slightly, and my body wobbled.

"Come on, Sleeping Beauty." Keith strolled over and lifted me into his arms. "Let's go find you somewhere to slumber. Your true love is asleep and can't kiss you awake just yet."

Here he went, making another damn princess joke. *You're not funny,* I linked, but my words sounded slurred even inside my head. *And I don't want to leave him.*

We'll take him wherever we put you. Don't worry. Keith moved forward. *But he's lying still and not trying to be a damsel in distress.*

Fuck you. I tried to snarl, but it sounded more like a wheeze. *And stop running.* He was moving so fast that everything blurred around us.

"Here, I'll go with you," Octavia said, sounding way closer than should have been possible with how fast we were moving.

She was human, after all.

A bright light blinded me. *Where are we?*

Outside. What are you talking about?

I exhaled, just giving up. I hadn't realized I'd given that much blood, but I was getting tunnel vision, which wasn't a good sign. The edges of my vision turned black, and before I could link with the others, the darkness took me whole.

"I'm telling you—kiss her," Keith said and chuckled, tugging at my consciousness. "That's how all the fairy-tale princes wake up the princesses at the end."

He was still going on about that? Surely I'd just blacked out for a minute, then.

A very familiar and comforting buzz wrapped around me. My cheek tingled against something hard that smelled of Raffe. I cracked my eyes open to find myself cuddled in his arms and lap. He was shirtless, which had the hairs on the nape of my neck standing on end. Who else was in here?

"Shut up," Raffe muttered. "She's sleeping. You're going to wake her."

"She needs to eat something soon, though the IV fluids I gave her should help tremendously," Dru said from somewhere above my head. "I'm surprised you're already up. You lost a ton of blood, and you'd be dead if it weren't for Divin—er, Skylar."

"And look how that left her," Raffe growled. "You shouldn't have let her do that."

Lucy snorted from somewhere near my feet. "Like anyone could stop Sky from doing something she was bound and determined to do, especially when it comes to *you*."

"In fairness, seeing you like that and watching that gooey shit work isn't anything I want to see again." Adam sighed. "It was pretty awful."

"And speaking from experience," Josie added, "when your fated mate needs something, the other half will give it to you, no matter the consequences. Put yourself in her shoes, Raffe."

"I'm with him on this one." Dave scoffed. "The number one priority is keeping you safe. We'd rather die than have something happen to you."

Part of me didn't want them to know I'd woken up. From the sounds of it, for once, we were all sitting around and talking. We weren't running away or looking for resources. We were discussing risking our lives for each other, but there wasn't an imminent threat.

How much longer are you going to pretend to be asleep? Raffe's voice popped into my head, and his arms tightened around me. *Not that I'm complaining. Octavia, Dru, and Fane have been hovering around you, so I suspect they'll try to steal you away from us once you're moving again.*

Busted. *I guess I can't pretend anymore since you foiled my plans,* I teased. *I'm just glad you're awake and sitting up.* A wave of emotions slammed into me, and a sob built in my chest.

Great, I'd gone from being somewhat content to trying like hell to swallow a sob. The pressure built, making it hard to breathe.

Hey. He leaned down, kissing my forehead. *I'm right here. I'm not going anywhere.*

I opened my eyes and took in his strong jawline, full lips, and caring eyes.

"What did I tell you?" Keith whooped. "All he had to do was kiss her, and boom, her eyes are fucking open."

"He kissed her *forehead*." Fane chuckled. "I don't think that counts."

"True love's kiss knows no bounds," he countered.

I turned my head begrudgingly and saw Keith sitting on the raised tile edge of a fireplace across from me. I lifted a brow. "Someone is obsessed with fairy tales and Disney movies. Bambi is one of the first references you ever made to me. There's a theme, and you always bring it up first. I believe you're a closet fairy-tale lover."

He tilted his head back and puffed out his chest. "*Please.*"

"She's right, man." Adam shrugged from his spot beside

Keith, leaning against a gray-green wall, staring out a window. "You do bring it up often."

"What do you expect when animals come to her like that?" Keith raised both hands. "Not that I'm complaining. It's quite badass. She saved our asses through *that* connection, or whatever the hell it is, but still, that's straight out of the storybooks."

I blinked and took in the living room. Josie was sitting next to Keith on the tile with Dave beside her. Lucy sat next to me and Raffe in the middle of a gray leather couch with Cat-Keith in her lap and Fane on her other side. Octavia was perched on a single seat in one corner, and the TV above the fireplace was on, but the volume was muted.

The screen showed the house we'd been staying at the night before, with firemen and police surrounding it.

My semi-peaceful moment was over. I tried to sit up and wobbled a little. Raffe pulled me to his chest, steadying me.

"Be careful. You have an IV, and you gave me too much blood." He arched a brow, daring me to say something.

I kept my mouth shut ... for once. Anything I said would either annoy him or make the air smell like sulfur. It was best if I took my constitutional right and pleaded the fifth. I glanced down and noted the IV in my arm full of clear liquid. Dru was hydrating me and giving me sugar to give my blood a boost. I probably wouldn't have been awake if he hadn't done that.

I nodded to the television. "What are they saying?"

"They're mainly confused about how no one heard or smelled the fire until the house had nearly burned down." Octavia rubbed her mouth. "And, of course, the medical professionals came on record, claiming that the neighbor the reporters interviewed on-site must have been suffering from carbon monoxide poisoning."

Out of every plausible situation, that was the best one. The older man hadn't been hurt or in danger, and they didn't think he was crazy. I only hoped nothing changed those assumptions even if they aren't able to determine how the fire started.

I suspected they'd never figure it out, but the supernatural world could still be at risk.

Dru came up beside me, and I propped my head on Raffe's chest as he removed the needle and tubing. The sound of Raffe's steady heartbeat and strong breathing made everything worth it, including the stress, fear, and uncertainty. If we hadn't come here, he wouldn't have made it.

"I'll get you some food." Octavia stood and headed out of the room. "You and Raffe should both eat something."

"Remember, nothing too heavy," Dru called. "It could make her nauseous. And bring some orange juice for her to drink."

My chest tightened. Having my biological parents doting on me was very unsettling.

Shit. Parents.

I searched my pockets, but I didn't have my phone. It had probably gotten lost in the fire. Mom and Dad must be worried sick.

What's wrong? Raffe tensed, scanning the area as if a threat had materialized from thin air.

"Mom and Dad. They've got to be worried about me."

Raffe pursed his lips. "The coven could be monitoring them."

That didn't make me feel better. In fact, that made it worse. "I need to call them."

"Okay." He leaned to the side, removed his cell from his pocket, then handed it to me. "Use my phone."

I glanced over to find Dru's lips pressed into a firm line. He moved toward the back of the room to get rid of the tubing.

Unsure if I could stand on my own to get some privacy with everyone around, I decided to text. When I opened the phone, there were ten missed calls from King Jovian and Queen Tashya. I glanced at Raffe and linked, *Are you going to call them back?*

No, I have nothing to say to either of them. If Dad had made it clear that we were welcome at home, Aldric wouldn't have made the mistake of turning us away. Aldric does whatever he believes my dad wants, and Mom will stand up for us but won't go against my dad.

I wanted to push him to reconsider, but we'd gone through enough for one day. On top of that, he seemed resolved, which meant I'd have to handle that conversation more delicately.

I opened a new message and put both my parents' numbers in a text.

Hey, it's Skylar. My phone got fried. Little did they know I meant that literally. **This is Raffe's phone, but I wanted to check in.**

Octavia entered with two packs of Ritz peanut butter crackers and two orange juices. She handed the items to Raffe and me just as the phone dinged.

Mom: Where are you? EEU called and told us you ran off with him.

Dad: Come back home now. This has gone too far.

My back stiffened, and my stomach churned uncomfortably. I didn't like their tone, but I had to remember they didn't understand my world or what Raffe meant to me. They thought I was throwing my future away and didn't know that I'd found my path with Raffe.

Me: There are things going on that I can't explain. Just know I'm fine, and I love you. Talk soon.

Since he wasn't taking his parents' calls, I turned the phone on silent and handed it back to him. I hated the way my eyes burned because I never wanted to upset or disappoint my parents, but they were determined to take me away from the one man I never wanted to be without. There was no question who I'd choose if I had to, but I hoped it never got to that point.

"Hey, you did the right thing," Lucy assured me and bumped my arm.

Unfortunately, I would have toppled over if not for Raffe. Resettling in his lap, I took a pack of crackers and nibbled.

"You all must be hungry too." I lowered the cracker, not wanting to eat in front of them if they were also hungry.

"We ate while you two were passed out." Keith patted his stomach. "Venison, and let me tell you, it was delicious."

I almost wanted to ask if he'd eaten Bambi but swallowed another bite of cracker instead, although meat sounded way more appetizing. "What time is it?" I hadn't checked on Raffe's phone.

"Almost eleven." Fane yawned. "Which means time for bed."

"We only have four bedrooms, so someone will need to sleep on the couch." Octavia frowned. "I'm sorry."

"I'll take the couch." Adam gestured to the front door

about fifteen steps from here and to the stairs where one set led down and the other up. "I can watch all the exits and entrances."

Dru nodded. "Josie and Lucy can stay in one room, and Fane will stay downstairs with Dave and Keith."

"What?" Fane crossed his arms. "What about Skylar and Raffe?"

"They've completed their mate bond, been injured, and won't agree to be separated." Lucy snorted. "Ask me how I know."

Fane rolled his eyes. "Fine. Come on. I'm ready for bed. I can show the girls to their room, too, since I take it you want Sky and Raffe in my room."

Keith stood, happily following Fane with Josie, Lucy, and Dave trailing behind. The five of them headed up the stairs, leaving Adam, Raffe, Octavia, Dru, and me here. Octavia left to grab some bedding for Adam while Raffe and I ate our food. My eyes drooped with every bite, exhaustion kicking in.

Soon, we were done, and Adam made up his bed as Octavia and Dru led us past the kitchen and down a hall. They stopped at the first door on the left.

Octavia motioned. "This is you. The sheets are clean, and we left some clothes that should work until we can buy you some of your own."

I tucked a piece of hair behind my ear. "Thank you."

"Get some rest." Dru patted my shoulder, causing my breath to catch.

It was easier when I hadn't known or liked them. Dru had been concerned since we arrived, and Octavia had come through like she'd promised. Still, I'd thought Slade had my best intentions at heart too, and I needed to remember that.

"Yes, sleep well. Priestess Caroline has asked for you to meet her after breakfast." Octavia gave me a sad smile. "She wants to see what you can do and if she can help you."

My heart raced unsteadily, but getting control over my power would be nice.

"I'll make sure she rests." Raffe opened the door and stepped inside. "I promise."

The two of them nodded and continued down the hall, and I followed Raffe inside. I scanned the hallway for the cat. When I didn't see her, I wasn't surprised. She was as much Lucy's as mine now.

Minutes later, we had taken a shower and crawled into bed. Raffe pulled me into his arms, and I stared at the cream walls and out the window where the moon rose between hazy clouds.

Warmth shot throughout my system as Raffe's body pressed into my back. My ache for him sat heavy inside me, and I turned to him. I needed him so badly after nearly losing him.

I kissed him, but he hesitated.

My chest squeezed as I pulled back. "What's wrong?"

"You're still not well." He traced a finger along my chin and smiled tenderly. "Holding you is all I need for tonight."

I pouted, and he laughed.

Tomorrow night, I'll ravish your body, love. He winked. *Tonight, I'm going to take care of it. Your health is the most important thing to me.*

"Fine," I growled and kissed him once more. Then I plopped onto my side, and his body molded to mine.

Within seconds, I fell peacefully asleep.

The next morning, we all sat in the kitchen. Octavia had cooked pancakes, eggs, bacon, and toast.

Raffe, Josie, Dave, and I sat at the bar across from the square table that sat six. Somehow, the seating here fit our group perfectly.

We were all chattering as if we'd known each other for longer than we had. It helped that I'd woken up feeling normal.

I reached over and swiped an extra piece of bacon from Raffe's plate.

He grabbed my wrist before I could reach my mouth, his blue eyes twinkling with mirth. *What do you think you're doing?*

Eating bacon.

He pointed at the granite counter on the other side of the island, where a plate held several pieces of bacon. "There's plenty over there."

I leaned forward like I was going to kiss him, and his hand relaxed. Then I popped the entire piece of bacon into my mouth. *But it's not as good as the pieces I steal from your plate.*

You pretended you were going to kiss me then stole my last piece of bacon. I require payment of some sort.

I grinned, ready to quip back at him, when something agonizing sliced through me like someone was trying to rip off my skin.

CHAPTER SEVENTEEN

I groaned, hunching over. The once amazing flavor of bacon turned overwhelmingly salty from the pain and nausea that had hit. I gasped for air, but the pain intensified, and I whimpered.

Raffe stood, knocking his barstool into the back of Keith's chair.

"What the *hell*, man?" Keith said loudly as Raffe touched my shoulder, keeping me in my chair.

His fear and concern swarmed my chest, adding to the uncomfortable sensations that made me feel as if my skin was being separated from bone.

"What's wrong, Sky?" Josie asked, turning to me.

I ... I don't know. I couldn't speak out loud. Forming words through the pack link was a struggle through the intense pain. *It feels like coven magic but stronger.* All the other times, coven magic had felt like sandpaper, not sharp like a knife. *I don't know what it is.*

My power jolted, responding to whatever was charging through me, and my wolf edged forward in my chest.

"Can you carry her into the living room?" Dru asked, and I heard chairs scraping the wooden floor. "I'll get my supplies and see if we can determine what's wrong." The concern in his voice was deep and troubled.

I shook my head slightly. *It's nothing he can treat.* My power edged to a hum, and I tried to focus on my connection with Raffe to lessen its strength. I didn't want to rip the house apart.

What do you mean? Raffe bent down so we were at eye level.

Eyes burning, I blinked fast to hold back tears. The more I fell apart, the more worried he'd be, and there wasn't anything he could do about this. *It's magic, but it's superstrong and nothing I've ever felt before.* I breathed through clenched teeth, every breath adding to the agony. I wanted to curl into the fetal position, hoping if I got small enough, it wouldn't hurt all over.

"Get the coven." Raffe's head snapped toward the others. "*Now!*" Alpha will laced his voice, though close to half of the people he was commanding weren't wolves.

"It might be faster if someone calls them," Lucy offered. "I can drive there to get them fast."

Sweat dripped between my breasts, and I realized my heart was racing. I'd take being dizzy from blood loss over *this* any day. I just wanted the agony to end. Even Raffe's touch wasn't making a significant difference. My entire focus hinged on trying not to get skinned, or whatever the magical equivalent was to that.

"I'll go with you," Fane offered as more chairs scuffed the floor.

Each noise pierced my brain like a bomb going off. All my senses were on overload, fighting whatever this was. My control was slipping.

"Hurry," Octavia said, and I heard buttons being pressed on a phone.

She was calling somebody.

I locked my eyes on my empty white plate, my gaze tracing the streaks of grease left by my bacon.

Babe, what can I do? Raffe linked, pressing his forehead against mine.

My chest tightened, adding to my extreme discomfort. I felt like I had yesterday when I couldn't help him or stop him from bleeding.

Helpless.

I focused on the one truth that might comfort him. *You being here helps.* I sure as hell was stronger with him beside me.

A door opened and closed, informing me that Lucy and Fane had left. I hoped Priestess Caroline could help. We'd gotten lucky with Raffe yesterday.

The phone line rang twice before someone answered. The voice was young and sounded like Faith. "Hello?"

"I need you to get your grandmother and come here. Something's wrong with Divinity." Octavia's voice rose. "She's in intense pain, and it came on suddenly."

"Nana left a minute ago, heading that way," Faith answered. "We feel something here as well, but nothing like what Divinity must be feeling."

They needed to stop calling me that. I'd hoped it was temporary, but now the coven was using it. However, I wasn't in any state to address it now.

"What's hurting her?" Raffe's head jerked toward the table.

Thankfully, he'd asked the question. I wanted to but couldn't gather my wits to speak. The onslaught came harder, and I sagged against Raffe.

He wrapped his arms around me, anchoring me to him, but it only added to the discomfort. Still, I'd never complain about being in his arms. They were my safe haven during a storm.

Unable to hold it back any longer, I sensed my power humming inside me. The intense pressure focusing near the top of my skin collided with the magical presence attacking me. I didn't know what sort of hell Supreme Priestess Olwyn was inflicting upon me, but I had no doubt she or Slade was the source of this pain.

Slade.

In all the chaos, I hadn't been able to grieve the loss of someone I'd considered my first real friend. Nonetheless, the lesson he'd taught me would last a lifetime, however long or short that was.

"You should take her somewhere else. Her blood—" Dave gritted out, and Raffe snarled.

"If you don't control yourself, I'll kill you," Raffe rasped and tightened his arms. "I don't fucking care if you're mated to Josie."

"I can't help what her blood does to me." Dave cleared his throat. "Believe me, I'd rather not react to it."

"Josie, get him out of here." Keith spoke low and threatening. "She's in pain and can't control herself. If he's struggling, he needs to remove his own ass while we deal with her."

Deal with her.

Those words added to my agony. That was what so many adults had said whenever my classmates had come to them, scared about me.

"Come on," Josie said urgently. "Let's *go*."

They shuffled off, and I tried to regain my composure.

Still, Keith's words repeated in my mind, crushing me,

and my power increased. *I ... I need to go outside. My power... it's unstable.*

Raffe lifted me like a princess and ran to the door. The room spun, adding to my upset stomach, but I placed my arms around Raffe's neck and held on.

Where are you taking her? Adam linked, footsteps pounding behind us.

Everyone was following us outside, and I wished they'd all stay behind. I didn't want to hurt anyone. I trusted my power wouldn't attack Raffe, but the rest I couldn't count on.

He adjusted me in his arms, and soon, we were out the door and into the cold drizzle of the foggy morning. Raffe ran down the stairs as my power bubbled to the surface. The sharpness of the magic collided with my power, the two strong sensations fighting.

If this didn't stop, I'd be ripped wide open. *Put me down.* I didn't want him caught in the cross fire.

I wasn't surprised when he shook his head. *I'm not going anywhere. We figure this out together or go down together fighting. I'll always be by your side. I can feel your power through our bond, and if being near you helps, I'll never let you go.*

My heart skipped a beat. Even in a moment like this, he made me feel damn special.

Despite wanting to argue with him, my power rose even more. Sparks flickered off my skin, although when I raised my head and looked at my arm, I didn't see any. Each pop and sizzle singed like I'd been burned.

Lucy, where the hell are you? Raffe linked.

We're on our way back, she replied. *She was in a car and heading here before we reached her.*

An engine grew louder, confirming her words.

They wouldn't get here in time.

Not given how the heat was rising.

I felt as if I were being burned alive.

A scream echoed through the air and into my ears. Whoever it was had to be in the same hell I was in. Was it a member of Priestess Caroline's coven?

Raffe whimpered, and my power flashed. Then, as quickly as the pain had come, it vanished.

The scream ended, and I swallowed. My saliva felt like razor blades, and realization chilled me to the bone. I'd been the one screaming.

Raffe loosened his hold, leaning back to stare into my face. A tear trailed down his cheek and into his scruff. "Are you still in pain?"

That one tear ripped my heart bare for him. I shook my head, needing to comfort him. "I ... I don't know why, but the pain went away." I sagged and laid my head against his chest, my magical exertion taking its toll.

Two cars rounded the curve on the gravel road to the house, tires crunching. Raffe's BMW SUV shot toward us in front, followed by an old Chevy.

"Divinity!" Octavia exclaimed, and she hurried to us, followed by Dru, Adam, and Keith. "Where are you hurting?"

She and Dru examined me, and my annoyance flared, taking control. "My name is *Skylar,*" I snapped. "Stop calling me *Divinity.*"

Dru's head snapped back, and Octavia winced.

My stomach soured in an entirely different way than it had moments ago. I hadn't meant to hurt them—they were helping us—but them not using my adoptive name bothered me.

I couldn't bring myself to say sorry.

The doors to both cars opened, and Priestess Caroline, Avalon, Fane, and Lucy rushed toward us.

Even though the last thing I wanted to do was leave Raffe's arms, I placed a hand on his chest and linked, *Can you put me down? I don't want to worry people more than I already have.*

He stiffened, and I felt him struggle with my request.

Don't push yourself. His eyes softened. *I felt some of what you did through our connection, and it was horrible. I can't imagine fully experiencing it. You're not weak—you're strong as hell. Not many could've survived that.*

The corners of my mouth tipped upward in a smile. *I'll be okay, and I need Priestess Caroline to want to train me. I must stand on my own two feet. But don't worry, I plan on leaning on you.*

He relaxed and quirked a brow. *You know exactly what to say to bend me to your will.* He placed me back on the ground.

I winked, trying like hell to come off like my normal self. *That's part of being a fated mate, right?*

That doesn't work for me, though.

Priestess Caroline pushed between Dru and Octavia and stopped in front of me. Her face was strained, showing more lines than yesterday, and she exhaled. "Thank the goddess, you're okay."

"Do you know what happened to her?" Octavia took a step backward like she was giving me space.

"Unfortunately, I do." Priestess Caroline scowled. "That was courtesy of *Supreme Priestess* Olwyn."

"Ha." Keith snorted. "She sounds like one of us talking about the coven."

When Priestess Caroline cut her eyes to him, Keith's face fell into a mask of indifference.

Laughter bubbled in my chest, but I forced it to remain there. Now wasn't the time for jokes, but learning that Keith might be afraid of Priestess Caroline made this entire situation funny.

"It's fitting in this instance." She pursed her lips and regarded him.

Raffe huffed, clearly not finding the situation as humorous. "What did Olwyn do to her? The last time they tried using their magic on her, it didn't work. What made this different?"

"I'm assuming they used a ritual with an item she left behind at the university in an attempt to locate her." Priestess Caroline paced in front of us, allowing Avalon, Lucy, and Fane to come closer. Adam came to my side, and we all watched her like a riveted audience.

"Why?" Lucy stepped closer to Fane, though she didn't seem to realize she had.

"Locator spell." Avalon looked up into the drizzle. "They aren't going to sit idly by knowing she's mated with Raffe and not on their side."

I laid my head on Raffe's arm, feeling sluggish, and my wolf calmed, settling inside my chest like she was as tired as my human part. "But like Raffe said, I've been immune to their magic since we completed the bond."

"They were probably working with several high-ranking priests and priestesses, based on the strength of that spell. There had to be at least five covens backing her magic to make sure their collective magic was stronger than your power." Priestess Caroline smirked. "And they failed. That's why their magic doesn't work on you—yours is that much stronger, and it's arcane-born. You embody the original power ours was derived from. Yours work similarly, but not even a coven member can truly understand the strength of what surges through you."

I hadn't thought of it that way. "But they fought me hard."

"Yes, but I could feel your power fighting back, and it was miraculous." She rubbed her hands together. "They won't try that again. For as much pain as you were in, their pain was tenfold. That's why their magic disappeared the way it did—you pushed them out of here."

Fane rocked back on his heels. "Does that mean they located her?"

"No, they couldn't. Her magic repelled them." Priestess Caroline stood taller. "Normally, when a location spell is performed, the other person isn't aware that it's happening. This had some gusto, which meant they probably tried and failed before."

Even though we were still safe, that didn't make me feel better. "If they have that many covens behind them, what does that say about the Veiled Circle? Could it be growing or already huge and we didn't know?"

"She could've gotten their aid by telling them you're under threat from Raffe or a danger to yourself." Priestess Caroline stopped in her tracks. "Or they could be part of that society. We can't really know."

Once again, we had no definitive answers.

"With Olwyn, always assume the worst." Avalon wrinkled her nose. "Her family has been a menace since the beginning. They're the reason we hid from other covens."

I yawned, unable to hide it.

"She needs a nap." Raffe sighed. "Especially if they try something like that again."

"I don't think they will, but I can't be certain." Priestess

Caroline scowled. "One thing is sure, after *that*—they'll be more desperate to find her. The threat isn't gone—if anything, it's increased, which means we need to prepare." Her gaze landed on me. "We need to train you to get you into the best shape possible." She pointed to the house. "Go, take a nap, and after lunch, head down the road to the next house. Come ready to work."

"We should wait until tomorrow." Raffe lifted his chin. "She'll be exhausted."

"Exhausted is good. That means her power won't be as volatile and will be easier to learn to control. In a way, Olwyn helped us."

Raffe's blood warmed. "I won't risk her life. She won't become another Foster."

"She won't. You completed the fated-mate bond. If she struggles, we won't push her past a healthy level."

The two of them glared at each other, determined to have their way.

"Raffe, you can come with me, and we can try. You'll know if I'm tired, and if I get to the dangerous point, we'll go." I needed to find a compromise so both felt like they were in control.

"Fine." Raffe glanced at me, his face softening. "As long as you promise to stop if it becomes too much."

I nodded. "Promise."

"Let's get some rest." Raffe took my hand and led me back to the house.

We went to our bedroom, and Raffe shut the door behind us. I ran a hand along the dark wooden dresser across from the bed. The wood felt cool under my fingertips.

I lay on the hunter-green comforter, and as soon as

Raffe wrapped his arms around me, I felt safe and drifted off to sleep.

I wasn't sure how long I'd slept, but I woke to the sound of Raffe snoring in my ear. I smiled and turned to face him, his face so serene. Most of the time, when we were awake, we were dealing with threats, and it was rare to see him completely unguarded.

"Take a picture. It'll last longer," he murmured, his eyes opening to slits.

"If I'm taking a picture, I'll need you to remove some clothes." I winked, heat spreading through my body.

My tiredness melted away at the thought of Raffe naked in front of me.

He smirked. "You're supposed to be resting, not trying to seduce me."

I shrugged, trailing a finger along his cheek. The buzz grew stronger, and after this morning and yesterday, I had to connect with him. *I need you,* I linked, still expecting him to say no.

Instead, his eyes darkened with desire. *You had a hell of a morning, but I need you too.*

Then his mouth was on mine, his tongue demanding entrance.

I opened my mouth, and when our tongues met, I moaned. I needed him so much, and our connection demanded that we unite.

His fingers dug into my sides in that way that drove me wild. My heart pounded as I responded to each stroke. He pulled me against him, and I felt him harden underneath me. The world spun, and need knotted within me, driving me to near madness.

His taste and smell enveloped me, and I badly wanted

him inside me. We'd been through so much trauma, and we couldn't fight this any longer.

I yanked his shirt up, and he moved so I could remove it from his body. As I tossed it to the floor, he pulled mine off as well. One hand went around my back and unfastened my bra. His eyes darkened as he ogled my breasts.

His head lowered, and he suckled one nipple, his tongue flicking against the sensitive skin, causing my back to arch. He chuckled.

I gasped as his fingers rolled over the other peak, the buzz shooting between us. He unfastened my jeans then pulled them and my panties off. I yanked on his sweatpants and almost whined over how long it was taking him to toss them and his boxer briefs aside.

He placed his fingers between my legs, but I smacked them away to straddle him.

"But I need to get you ready—"

"Believe me, I *am*." I leaned back, taking in his curves and six-pack.

He smirked as I lowered myself on him, slipping him inside me. Then he moaned, his body shuddering and thrusting inside, filling me.

I rode him, spreading my legs farther apart so he could hit deeper. At first, we moved slowly, but after a few thrusts, we quickened the pace, both hungry for the release and our souls to combine.

He caressed my breasts as I lifted and fell, helping him slide in and out of me. Friction heightened into exquisite pressure, and before I realized it, ecstasy slammed through me.

All through my pleasure, we kept a steady rhythm, and he watched as I succumbed to the sensations.

Damn, babe. He groaned, pumping faster. *You're so*

fucking hot. He flipped me over then stood at the side of the bed and towered over me. He scooted me to the edge and slipped back inside me then settled a hand between my legs, circling as he filled me.

I wasn't sure how it was possible, but my body was already tensing again. The wild need for another release pulsed through my core.

His fingers pressed a little harder, and tingles exploded around them.

Are you close again? His jaw clenched.

I nodded, at a loss for words.

"Thank gods." He grunted, and his body jerked as he orgasmed. *I fucking love you.*

Our bond opened, his pleasure flooding into me, and a second release crashed through me.

I love you too, I replied and moaned even louder as we rode the sensations out together, our bodies completely in sync and our souls merged. We could feel each other, including our pleasures combining, making everything more explosive and amazing.

We and our wolves were all satiated.

When we'd calmed, he slid out of me and climbed into bed beside me, pulling me into his arms. He kissed my forehead as I turned and nestled into his chest. It didn't take long for him to drift back to sleep, but my peace changed to guilt as the memory of how I'd snapped at Octavia and Dru haunted me.

It wouldn't get better until I addressed it with them. I slowly crawled from Raffe's arms. He was still tired from the blood loss of yesterday, and I managed not to wake him as I quietly dressed and covered him with a blanket.

Then I snuck out of the room, ready to search for the two people I'd hurt.

A television was playing in their bedroom, so I knocked on the door.

"Who is it?" Octavia called.

"It's me." I grimaced, knowing the next words would make the entire situation worse, but I had no choice but to say them.

CHAPTER EIGHTEEN

I feared saying the next words, unsure if I could handle actual rejection. "Can we talk?" I wanted to say more and be direct, but nothing could get past my suddenly parched throat. I tried to swallow and nearly choked.

Silence hung in the air, and I tugged at my wolf magic inside my chest to tap into my wolf hearing more.

Then, feet hit the floor and shuffled toward the door.

My lungs moved more freely. They hadn't kept me shut out. They were going to open the door.

As if they'd heard my chants, the door to their bedroom opened, and the first thing I noticed across from the door and above their headboard was a picture of them, much younger, with a little boy and an infant in Octavia's arms.

The walls closed in on me.

Could that be me in the picture? But no. They'd given me up; they wouldn't have a picture of me above their bed. It had to be someone near my age or something.

"Is everything okay?" Dru sat upright in bed, his face creased with worry. "Is someone else hurt?" He swung his feet off the sky-blue comforter and stood. "I should've brought a hell of a lot more supplies. I had no idea how fast we'd go through them all."

My heart dropped. We were causing them problems, and I'd snapped at them earlier. For most of my life, I'd been able to keep my mouth shut, but it was like meeting Raffe had changed me fundamentally. Mostly in good ways, but I needed to remember not to speak in anger, especially to people who were helping us. We'd be a lot worse off if it wasn't for them. "Yeah, everything is ..." I trailed off. I didn't want to say good because that would be a lie. "Well, no one is in imminent danger or bleeding to death." That counted for a lot lately.

Octavia snorted. "I could get used to this change of pace."

"Me too." I smiled, but then it died. I had so much to say, and I wasn't sure where to start. I wrapped my arms around my waist, not liking the uneasy chill that racked me.

"Are you sure you're okay?" Dru asked, tilting his head and heading toward me. "Are you coming down with a cold or something? You did lose a lot of blood, and the thing earlier—it could wear your immune system down and make you more susceptible to illnesses."

I smiled, enjoying having someone with a medical and science degree around who shared my interest. Granted, my limited expertise was on animals and not humans. "Do you mind if I come in, or can we go somewhere to talk?"

"Yeah, of course." Octavia stepped back from the door, gesturing for me to enter. "You're always welcome here. You never even have to ask."

They were being too nice and making this harder for me. I nodded, entering the room, and Octavia shut the door behind me.

Pictures of the mountains hung in another corner of the

room, making me feel slightly more comfortable. The colors reminded me of standing in the woods, surrounded by nature.

I walked toward the dark wooden chest of drawers in the corner of the room to gain some distance.

"Is something wrong?" Octavia asked, now standing next to Dru. They stared at me, waiting for whatever I had to say.

Silence weighed on me, and I straightened, knowing the longer it took for me to speak, the harder it would be. "I'm sorry about earlier." I wanted to avert my eyes, but that would be taking the coward's way out. They deserved better. "When I snapped at you."

Octavia sighed and placed a hand over her heart. "Oh, honey. You don't have anything to apologize for. We've been kicking ourselves for calling you Divinity. It's very selfish of us."

"We didn't consider how that would make you feel, and we were debating apologizing to you or just dropping it," Dru added, placing an arm around Octavia's shoulders.

"You two have been kind to us, opening up your home and giving us medical attention." I extended my arms out from my sides. "You didn't deserve that, and—"

"But we did." Octavia clasped her hands in front of her chest. "We gave you up and allowed other people to name and raise you. The name on your birth certificate is Skylar, and that is what we should call you."

I inhaled shakily, realizing *this* was the conversation I'd always wanted to have. I'd thought I'd be able to speak eloquently and tell them all the ways they'd done me wrong, but things weren't so cut and dried, and definitely not easy. All the things I'd wanted to say seemed harsh. "All my life, I knew why you gave me up. I wasn't normal, and no one understood me. I understand how vicious supernaturals are now and why you wouldn't want that target on your and Fane's backs. But yeah, hearing you call me that name reminds me of everything you chose when giving me up. I do get it, though. I wouldn't want Olwyn and some secret society hunting me down. And you're helping me now, and I do appreciate it."

"Oh, baby girl." Octavia's face twisted in agony. "Is that why you think we gave you up? Because that's not even close to the truth."

"We almost didn't give you up, but we thought the best way to protect you was to let you go." Dru tugged Octavia to his side. "The moment we knew your powers were activated, we knew that supernaturals would want to use you or harm you. There's no in-between, judging by what's been passed down over generations in the arcane-born bloodline."

She nodded. "We believed that if we didn't want you on the run for your entire life, it was best if you weren't around supernaturals. The safest way of doing that was to have a human family raise you. I'd hoped that, by not being around magic, your power wouldn't form and your life wouldn't be at stake. Had we known that giving you up wouldn't work, we would have never let you go."

I tugged at the hem of my white, long-sleeve shirt. "To be fair, I love my parents. Though they don't understand me, they do love me. But growing up, everyone made fun of me, and the more they hurt me, the more out of control my powers became. I ... I didn't feel like I fit in anywhere until I came to EEU and immersed myself in the supernatural." I made the journey sound easy. It hadn't been *at all*, but I'd found a man I was crazy about, friends, and some sort of self-acceptance.

They both hung their heads.

"I'm not trying to make you feel bad." I huffed and fisted my hands. I kept doing this wrong. I wanted to make them see that my life hadn't been horrible, yet I'd done the opposite. "I'm just saying you found good parents for me, but being here at this moment is my destiny. However, I do thank you for trying to protect me." Meeting Raffe had been worth all the pain and confusion because, for the first time in my life, I had someone who truly accepted me, and I wouldn't give that up for the world. "Maybe we can come up with a nickname until we figure out what sort of relationship we're going to have." They couldn't be my parents, but they could be something else.

"Yeah?" Octavia smiled. "You think we can have a permanent relationship?"

"Honey, she didn't say permanent." Dru winced and closed his eyes.

The fact that they wanted me in their lives caused some of the baggage I'd carried my entire life to slip from me. "I meant that if you both want it."

"Of course we do." Dru's eyes popped open. "We've missed you and wanted to know about you every day of your life." He gestured at the picture over the bed. "You've been part of this family in any way we could incorporate you. We loved you before you were even born, and to have you here in the house, not hating us, means more than you'll ever know."

"We just wish we'd met under better circumstances." Octavia nibbled on her lip.

I understood that, but the three of us had to face facts. "If it weren't for these circumstances, I doubt we would've ever met."

Dru rubbed the back of his neck. "That's a fair point. We didn't want this life for you."

"If it makes you feel better, I wouldn't trade it for anything. I have Raffe and a pack, I can handle my power better, and now I've met you two and Fane. The good outweighs the bad."

Both of them smiled genuinely.

Babe? Raffe linked, our connection warming. Then panic filtered in. *Where are you?*

I'd meant to sneak back into the room before he woke. *I couldn't sleep and came to talk to Octavia and Dru about earlier.*

Oh, thank gods. The heaviness of our bond lightened as his relief pushed through. *I thought something had happened again.*

I winced. I did have a habit of disappearing on him and getting into trouble. *I'll be there shortly.*

It's almost noon, so we need to get moving to meet Priestess Caroline. I'll find us some lunch.

Right. I'd almost forgotten about practicing with her. My power was still pretty much extinguished inside, and it probably didn't help that I hadn't gotten much rest. But between needing to reconnect with him and having this conversation with Octavia and Dru, I'd been restless.

I tucked a piece of hair behind my ear. "Well, I hate to do this, but Raffe wants to grab lunch before we meet Priestess Caroline. I just wanted to make sure that the three of us are okay."

"Okay?" Dru chuckled. "We're more than okay. I get that we don't have the right to be your parents, but we're ecstatic to be part of your life in any way you'll have us."

One question did haunt me. "If that's true, why did you want to leave right after we met when Dave was injured?

You said there'd been a mistake." I stared at Octavia, needing answers.

"That wasn't my finest moment, but it was because the royal shifters have never liked our kind, and I feared I would put a target on Fane as well as you." She leaned her head back. "I'm sorry I said it, but the moment I realized Raffe was willing to sacrifice everything for you, I knew that Fate had gotten it right. I wish I could lie, but I don't want to. You deserve better."

That burned, but I had to appreciate her honesty. I did feel as if we'd forged a bond between now and then, and I hoped like hell I wasn't wrong. I wasn't sure I could take another betrayal, especially from my birth parents. "Okay." I couldn't say that was fine, but I could accept it and try not to hang on to the baggage I'd lugged around my entire life. "I'm going to eat with Raffe."

Dru nodded. "Do you want us to come with you?"

"To eat?" I lifted my brows and felt the corners of my mouth tip upward. "I think I can handle that."

"Fair, but I actually meant when you go see Priestess Caroline." He beamed.

His offer warmed my heart. "Nah, I'd like to limit the number of people watching since I'm not sure what could happen. My power has a mind of its own, so I'm hoping she can teach me how to harness it. It'll be safer if no one comes."

"You should've seen her control those animals." Octavia blinked. "There were over fifty raccoons, coyotes, bobcats, and owls that came to our aid before."

My smile vanished. "I didn't control them. Animals aren't meant to be slaves. I merely asked for their help, and they answered." My tone was a little sharp, but I hated when people thought of animals as less than them. "Animals are some of the most authentic creatures on earth, and that's why I want to become a vet—to help protect them."

"I ... I didn't mean it like that. The way they moved around you ..." She trailed off.

And here I was, overreacting again. "You didn't know. It's just ...when I struggled, the only time I felt at peace was immersed in nature. I've always had a connection with animals. It's one reason I plan to apply to vet school." However, considering how much school we were missing, that dream was probably shot. I had no doubt Olwyn would make sure nothing like that happened for me.

"You're going to school to be a vet?" Dru's eyes widened. "That means you're a science nerd like me."

"That I am, but I doubt I'll graduate now." It was silly because it had taken me until this moment to realize that. We'd been going nonstop, and I'd been so focused on the present and our safety that I'd lost sight of the future, the one thing that used to ground me.

What's wrong? Raffe linked, feeling the change within me.

Though I loved our connection, sometimes I needed time to process things on my own. *I'll tell you later. Right now, we need to focus on training.* Wanting to end the conversation before dwelling on it further, I rubbed my hands together. "If you don't mind excusing me, food is calling my name." My stomach gurgled, confirming my statement.

"Okay." Octavia moved, and I headed to the door. When I opened it and stepped out, she called out, "And Sky."

I paused with my hand on the doorknob. "Yeah?"

"Thanks for coming to talk," she said softly.

I glanced over my shoulder. "Anytime. I'll see you later for dinner."

In the kitchen, Raffe had already made us some turkey-and-ham sandwiches, and I slid into the spot at the bar beside him. It was weird that the place was quiet.

Where is everyone? I took a bite of food and almost moaned over how good it tasted. I'd been starving.

Fane is taking Lucy, Dave, Keith, and Josie to the store, and Adam is sleeping. He snagged a bottle of water, chugging half of it. *Why?*

It's just oddly quiet. And is going to the store safe? Normally, when things seemed peaceful, something horrible wasn't far behind.

Octavia assured them that they'd go to a store that most supernaturals stay away from because it's in the center of town. Besides, we need to learn about the area in case something does happen. No one should be out here searching for us yet. It's also quiet because Keith isn't here running his damn mouth. Raffe rolled his eyes. *I swear, he yammers more than a wo—*

I arched a brow at him.

A woefully annoying human. He smiled way too brightly.

That better be what you were going to say. I poked him in the side, causing him to jump. I swallowed, and my mouth dropped. *Wait. Are you ticklish there?* How had I not known this? We'd been together for only a few weeks, but damn, it felt like a lifetime. Moments like this reminded me that we didn't know so many odd little things about one another.

Don't you think about it. I'd hate to be forced to hold out on you.

I snorted. Had he threatened to not have sex with me if

I tickled him? No way. Two could play this game. I shrugged. *That's fine. I can do it better anyway.*

He pursed his lips. *Now that I'd really like to see.*

My face heated. He'd called my bluff. I stuck my tongue out and took another bite as he chuckled and followed my lead.

Unfortunately, we couldn't just spend time like this together. We had somewhere to be.

All too soon, we finished eating and headed out the front door. The drizzle had stopped, though gray clouds covered the sky.

"Wanna take the car?" Raffe nodded to his SUV.

"Let's walk." I'd been cooped up inside and wanted to be out in nature. My wolf nudged forward, needing to be in nature too.

"More than all right with me." He winked.

Interlacing our fingers, we headed toward the woods, stepping into the tree line to walk on mulchy ground instead of gravel.

A few birds made noises throughout, chirping as if they didn't have a care in the world. We followed along, walking at a good pace while enjoying our time away from the house together.

Soon, the road turned, and the first house came into view, the very one Priestess Caroline had told us to go to.

It was a quaint cottage, slightly larger than the seven or so more I could see from here. The gravel road split into a circle where their neighborhood continued. When we had time to explore, I'd be curious to see how large this coven was.

The yards were lush, and each house had a stone pathway to the front door. What I assumed was Priestess

Caroline's house was painted a light green with a matching front door.

Priestess Caroline herself opened the door and stepped out. She shot fire at my feet, startling me back. She then raised a hand, and an apple sat on her palm.

"What the fuck do you think you're doing?" Raffe snarled.

Priestess Caroline didn't even look at him. Instead, she said, "Make the apple explode, or you'll have to fight us."

I laughed. Was this how she expected to train me? "Uh ... shouldn't we do something more conventional and less extreme?" I moved away from Raffe, not wanting him to get stuck in the cross fire of whatever Priestess Caroline had in store for me.

"Then you'll never learn because your power has become too strong for you to control, even in small doses." Priestess Caroline shot flames at me again, but this time, I didn't move, letting the flames engulf me. Just like at the house, they didn't bother me at all.

If she was trying to get a rise out of me, she'd be disappointed. Instead, I found her tactic funny.

Faith and Avalon materialized beside Raffe. Faith had a dagger in one hand, and she lifted her other hand, causing the ground to shake hard underneath him.

He crashed to the ground, and I'd moved to help him when Avalon forced Raffe onto his back and Faith jumped on him, placing a dagger to his neck.

My power went from dormant to a hum. No one threatened my mate like that.

CHAPTER NINETEEN

Power hummed throughout my body, in tune with the heated blood pounding through my veins. My attention turned to the two women on top of Raffe, ready to eliminate them in the most efficient way possible.

"If you want him safe, make the apple explode." Priestess Caroline stepped from the house. "Otherwise, you can't help him."

Fuck all that.

When I realized the real dilemma, I froze. They were on top of Raffe, so if I didn't control my power, he could be injured. A lump formed in my throat as my power pulsed outward.

My wolf surged forward, wanting to join the battle to protect our mate, but I didn't have time to shift.

Raffe tried to fight, fur sprouting on his arms, but Avalon stood over him and lifted her hands. The wind she created was holding him in place. This was a group attack.

These weren't our friends. They had to be secretly working with the Veiled Circle.

The ground shook all over, my power funneling out

Something needed to happen, but we weren't sure what. My focus turned to Priestess Caroline. If I killed her, the others might listen.

"If you make this apple explode, we'll release Raffe. We don't want to hurt him." Priestess Caroline lowered the hand that had shot flames to her side while placing the apple in front of her face. "Just blow it up, and we'll release him."

Raffe's panic flowed into me, constricting my chest painfully and increasing the strength of my power.

I ... I can't shift. The wind is preventing me from doing anything, he linked. *Sky, go back to the house. Get away from here.*

There's no way in hell I'm leaving you. If he thought I would, he didn't know me at all. I took a step toward Avalon and Faith, but Faith dug the blade into Raffe's neck a little more.

"The closer you come, the harder I'll press the edge into his neck," Faith said in a strangled voice. "Don't make me do it. We're just trying to help you."

Blood trickled down Raffe's neck, the copper scent carrying on the breeze. My blood sang, and the ground quaked harder until the trees along the property swayed.

"*Help* me?" If they believed this was help, I'd hate to see what being malicious was like. "That's my fated mate, the other half of my soul you're threatening." Branches fell from the trees, and my power felt like a riptide within me—all-consuming and with nowhere to go because everywhere it wanted to go would only harm my mate more.

Adam, get your ass down here and protect Skylar, Raffe commanded into the pack link. *The coven has betrayed us. Keith, Josie, and Lucy, how far away are you? We need you here now.*

"Listen, just concentrate on the apple before you kill us all." Priestess Caroline lifted the apple higher like she thought it hadn't been visible before. "Blow it up, and your mate is safe. That's all you have to do."

My power became unstable. A crack shot up through the siding of the priestess's house, the foundation no longer able to absorb the shock.

It reminded me of when Slade and I had escaped from the underground bunker and I'd made the rock crumble down almost on top of us. My power hadn't been as strong then as it was now. For some reason, I believed her. I just needed to blow up that damn apple. If that's what it took to save my mate, I'd fucking do it.

Pushing away my frustration, I locked my gaze on the apple, refusing to even blink. I needed that apple to explode —now.

We're leaving the store, about twenty minutes away, dammit, Keith replied, his frustration strong. *I'll run there if that's what it takes.*

A howl sounded from the woods, but it was far away. If something went wrong, they could slit Raffe's throat in a second.

"If anyone interferes, he dies." Priestess Caroline lifted a brow. "Which means you'd better hurry since they've already been summoned."

My stomach gurgled, and the food I'd eaten inched its way up my throat. This was worse than I'd ever imagined, and I wished I'd never asked these coven members for help. When Raffe was free, I would make each of them pay, and if he died, I'd make sure their deaths were slow and painful. *Don't come after all. She's threatening to kill him if you do.*

What? Lucy asked, her surprise filtering through despite the lack of mate connection. *This doesn't make any sense.*

Don't listen to her, Raffe interjected. *Come here and save her. I don't care what happens to me as long as Sky is safe.*

Shit. Out of the two of us, they'd listen to him as the alpha, which meant I had minutes to figure out how to control my power when I hadn't been able to in the past twenty-two years of my life. *Easy-peasy,* I mocked myself internally.

No matter how hard I focused on the apple, nothing happened except for my power fritzing even more. Well, that and seeing *two* apples. My eyes burned, my jaw ached, and I could hear Adam panting as he raced toward us and the sound of a tree crashing not too far away.

He linked, *I'm almost there. Sky, be ready to leave.*

"Listen, you're overthinking it." Priestess Caroline took a step closer. "Picture in your mind what you want to happen. Don't just lock on the object and visualize the end result in your mind. You don't need to tap or pull or anything, not with the amount of power you yield. Your power always protects the ones you want it to because it feels your intention. You need to learn how to streamline it."

The last thing I wanted to do was follow her advice, but my own efforts weren't amounting to anything, and the wolves were nearly upon us. They'd be here in seconds, and I could still feel the turmoil raging through Raffe.

"You can end it." Priestess Caroline nodded at the apple. "Just make it explode." Her voice shook as our bodies lurched, the ground shaking and groaning from my wrath.

I blew out a breath and rubbed my sweaty palms on my jeans. This was the most important test of my life, and I refused to fail.

I stared at the apple again, and against every instinct, I closed my eyes. I needed to block out the noise and chaos the best I could, which meant holding the image in my mind. I focused on the red color of the apple and the small green stem at the top. I imagined something barreling toward it and into the stem, settling right inside the core.

My power stopped swirling within me like normal and merged. I pictured the core exploding and the apple hitting Priestess Caroline in the face.

The collected energy shot out of my body like it had snapped and surged forward. Every ounce of my power left with it, and I heard the sound of something bursting.

My eyes flew open, and I froze. I blinked, making sure it wasn't an illusion.

Holy shit. I'd done it.

"Let her mate go." Priestess Caroline's voice rang with authority despite the bits of apple falling from her hair.

Adam ran from the woods, and I spun toward Raffe and saw them let him go.

The edges of my vision darkened. My legs gave out as the fatigue that struck me whenever I exerted too much power slammed into me. I crumpled to the ground and heard Raffe growl, "What did you do to her?"

I wanted to tell him I was okay. That everything would be all right. But I couldn't find the energy to link with him.

That was fine. Let him kill them all. They deserved it after what they'd done to us.

Sleep enveloped me.

"You KNEW that was going to happen?" Lucy said from somewhere close by. "And you didn't think to tell any of us?" Venom laced each word, making her tone lower than normal.

"Hey, I didn't come up with the plan," Fane replied frantically. "And I didn't know you'd be this upset."

I turned my head, my face pressed against a muscular chest that smelled of sandalwood and amber. Arms tightened around me, and my eyes cracked open to see Raffe's face looking down into mine. The buzz of our bond eased me back toward calm.

Thank gods you're okay, he linked and kissed my forehead. *I was so worried that I couldn't see straight and knew we needed to get you back here.*

I moved my hand to touch his face, but I felt a slight tug. I glanced down to find another IV in my arm, and I followed the tubing to a bag of fluids. My chest warmed at both of their concern.

I don't know how, but blowing up that apple zapped me like my power did before we completed our bond. It was like I'd used too much of my power and drained my entire being.

Lucy's voice edged louder as she said, "Knowing that my cousin was going to be threatened and not informing us is participating in the act too."

Wow. I'd heard her talk like this only once before, when Raffe had been hurt that I'd questioned him about pictures the Veiled Circle had shown me—pictures of him—right after I'd escaped. She'd put him in his place, telling him to think about it from my perspective and pointing out what a jerk he'd been when we'd met. That I hadn't been in the wrong for my questions.

"This was *my* decision. No one else's," Priestess Caroline stated.

My body tensed as understanding sank in. *She* was *here*, and my *brother* had known what would happen and hadn't warned anyone. I pulled out of Raffe's embrace. We were back in the bedroom we'd slept in at my biological parents' house. "That bitch needs to pay." But as I put my feet on the floor to stand, I still felt tired. Dammit, I thought I'd gotten over this, but clearly, that had been wishful thinking.

"Easy." Raffe moved to the edge of the bed next to me and placed an arm around my shoulders. He linked, *I'm all for killing her and hurting him, but my biggest concern is you and your safety. When the rest of our pack got there, twenty coven members we hadn't noticed because of their insane shenanigans stepped out and held them off. Between that and me trying to get you away from them, we all came back here. She showed up a few minutes ago, but I didn't want you to wake up alone. When you passed out like that, it scared me.*

The last time I'd gotten to that point was when the two of us had broken up, and I'd almost imploded at the tree line outside my campus apartment.

I shook my head, the room spinning ever so slightly. "It was the same thing. After I made the apple explode and saw them release you, I collapsed." Even though it hadn't been long since last time, with all the shit that had happened in such a short amount of time, it felt like months. The worst part was being unable to stay alert during a horrible situation.

"You threatened our alpha and alpha's mate," Keith snarled. "And you expect us to sit here and not punish you for what you did?"

Now that I had my bearings, I could tell they were in the living room, so not that far away. I untaped the needle in my arm and pulled it out, wanting to get in there and have my own say to the witch.

"Don't you think, if there had been a better way, I would've done it?" Priestess Caroline bit back. "I do believe in the mantra 'do no harm,' unlike most of today's coven members, so it sickened me to do what we did."

I had a hard time believing that. She hadn't flinched or appeared remorseful.

My power jolted, but that was the extent of it. I was still drained, which made my wolf inch forward in my chest. She wanted to be unleashed and get retribution.

Standing, I waited a moment, making sure I got my balance. Raffe mirrored my movements, hovering close. I could feel his worry and noticed the way his hand kept reaching for mine, but he finally relaxed it at his side.

My heart warmed, and I pushed my love and affection toward him. He understood that I needed to go in there looking as strong as possible, and that reconfirmed he was the man I'd always sensed inside of him. He just hadn't figured out who he was going to become, and I loved watching us grow as a couple.

"That wasn't your call to make," Octavia's voice rang out as I opened the door.

The pain etched in her words caused my stomach to sour. The only thing keeping me together was Raffe standing close behind me so I could feel his warmth on my back. The two of us walked down the hallway, and I lifted my head high as we entered the living room. I might have appeared tired, but I wanted to give the illusion of strength.

"Your actions threatened the very delicate relationship we have with our daughter." Octavia stood in the middle of the room, right in front of Priestess Caroline, pointing a finger at the priestess's face.

Priestess Caroline stood ramrod straight with an indifferent expression.

I wished I could get a read on others' emotions when my

power wasn't at a high level. I'd love to sense exactly how the priestess was feeling.

Dru stepped behind his wife, placing his hands on her shoulders, and rasped, "We *trusted* you, and we told them they could too. Now we look like liars."

Adam and Keith stood near the windows. Adam was looking out, likely searching for signs of threats, while Keith homed in on the threat inside.

Dave, still not back to full health, was sitting on the couch, and Josie towered in front of him, blocking him from the priestess's view.

I brushed past Lucy, who stood a few feet behind my biological parents. She tore her gaze from Fane, who stood next to her and looked at me. Her face softened as she scanned me and linked, *I'm glad you're awake. We were worried.*

"And she completed the task and is standing here." Priestess Caroline gestured at me. "None of which would've happened if we hadn't done what we did."

I growled but held back my wolf. If I shifted, I wouldn't be able to speak to her, and I needed her to hear every damn word. "If you're expecting me to say thank you, then you'll be waiting a long damn while. I won't repeat why since everyone here already has pretty damn effectively. But let me be clear—if you so much as point *anything* at my mate again, I will fucking end you. The only reason I'm not is because you let him go like you promised, but this is where my kindness ends. It's taking everything inside me not to kill you."

Why? Let's kill her sorry ass. Keith pouted. *She's old. This might be her way of asking us to kill her.*

Raffe stepped to my side, his alpha magic pulsing off him. "She might have decided to grant you leniency, but I'm not sure myself." His jaw twitched from how tightly he clenched his teeth. He then linked, *As much as I want to kill her, she has a sizable coven, and they'll retaliate if we do something to her.*

"I didn't do anything to her." Priestess Caroline lifted her hands, palms facing her. "She got tired from having to control the power that was ravaging her and the earth. She was feral and had to use control. That's what exhausted her. Not me."

Unfortunately, that was exactly how I felt. Tired. "But why? I didn't feel anything until I blew up the apple. My power didn't change."

"It didn't, but you had to focus and rein it in. Your power is unruly—that's what you're used to. Now that you're a supernatural and bound to a strong alpha, you can handle its strength. But making it obey and do your bidding takes a whole different skill set you haven't mastered, which is why we had to do what we did. To get your power to ignite, we had to put something dear to you at risk and force you to accomplish the task. The stakes had to be the highest we could get. Otherwise, our help would have been on par with Supreme Priestess Olwyn and her minions. Worthless and futile."

Her words were like a punch to the gut, but my anger from what they'd done to my mate still held on tightly. Unfortunately, I understood her point, but that didn't mean I liked it. "My mate, family, and friends are off-limits. Even one threatening glance, and I don't care how many coven members you have, I will fucking end you even if it takes me out with you."

Raffe shook his head. "There is an easy way to solve this problem. You go back to your homes and don't come near us. If you get too close, she won't have to kill you. *I will.*"

His eyes glowed, his wolf emerging and emphasizing his words. "You're blessed that I'm not ending your life right now, but that's only because I'm sure we'd be attacked if I did."

"Whether you two like it or not, you need me." She patted her chest, fire lighting her eyes, making them greener. "Because of my tactics, an arcane-born managed to control her power for the first time in history. She will need my help to streamline it and see what she's capable of. Do you want to risk her life and Olwyn and the others finding you because you didn't like my tactics? I thought wolf shifters prided themselves on their strength and resilience. Times must have changed since I've been around any."

Raffe snarled, but I placed a hand on his arm. Not to control him but because he needed my comfort to remain calm. He and I were strongest when working together.

At my touch, his anger ebbed, and he breathed through gritted teeth.

Lucy, Keith, and Josie inched forward, circling the priestess, ready to attack.

"You may have a coven, but don't underestimate us," Lucy said and edged beside me. "Even if Fane was okay with your awful plan to hurt my cousin, the rest of us weren't, and we'll make sure nothing like that ever happens again."

From the corner of my eye, I saw Fane flinch.

Good. He deserved to feel shame. In fact, when this conversation was over, I'd have some choice words for him myself.

But right now, we needed to focus on the priestess. I linked with the rest of the pack, *I hate to say this, but she's right. She did get me under control, and I could use her help.* Though it was less than ideal and I didn't trust her, she'd kept her word and released him. Raffe wouldn't be going with me the next time I trained with her.

You can't be serious? Raffe's head jerked in my direction. *You want to train with her again?*

Olwyn won't stop hunting us, and what sort of life can we have together if we're hiding all the time?

A long one, which is exactly what I want with you, he linked, allowing his frustration and anger to course into me.

Between the intensity of his anger and my own, I felt like I might implode but in a different way than before.

She has a point. If she keeps causing earthquakes, they will find us. Josie frowned. *And if they do, it would be helpful if Skylar knew how to use her power effectively.*

Raffe's attention snapped to her.

We don't have to decide now. Adam glanced at us. *We can talk about it when Sky has rested and we've all calmed down.* Then he spoke out loud. "If you aren't threatening us, then why is your coven heading this way?"

"They're making sure I'm okay. I took a risk by coming here, but I needed you all to see that I was sincere." Priestess Caroline huffed.

"You need to leave." Octavia pointed at the door. "We need time to calm down, and Skylar needs rest after this afternoon. If and when we're ready to talk, I know how to get hold of you."

The priestess's pale eyes focused on me once more, and her mouth pressed into a firm line. "My coven has spent centuries studying ways to control arcane magic and learning why each arcane-born has a connection with a wolf shifter. We understand that your power is tied to the earth and its vibrations. The only thing missing is why you're fated to a supernatural.

"Now it's clear—it's the only way you can survive. Your

connection is the bridge between human and supernatural. We believe that, after the original arcane-born passed and created the supernatural, one of her descendants gets their power activated when the balance of the supernatural world is under threat—which means you still need us and our guidance. I vow to you that we will never harm someone you love again."

Some of my hesitation vanished because I didn't smell a lie, but even more, her promise felt magical … more than just words someone said to another.

Still, I wouldn't agree without talking to Raffe, even if we had opposing views. He'd been the one with a dagger to his neck.

"You heard my wife," Dru rasped. "Now get out, or a wolf shifter and arcane-born won't be your biggest problem."

Priestess Caroline kept her gaze on me until she nodded, finding whatever she had been searching for within me. She then walked confidently out the front door, leaving us in silence.

Now that the threat was gone, there was one person who needed to understand how things worked around here. He might be my blood, but that didn't make him my family.

I pivoted, glaring at my brother, and snarled, *"You."*

CHAPTER TWENTY

As he took a step back against the wall, Fane's eyes bulged.

I noticed, once more, how similar our eyes were, reminding me that my own blood had kept the priestess's plan for me and my mate secret. My breath caught when cold realization settled deep within my chest. "That's why you took Josie, Keith, and Lucy to the store, isn't it?" The place had seemed so quiet, but I'd been enjoying my alone time with Raffe.

Fane averted his gaze to the floor, confirming everything I needed to know.

Guilty.

"What?" Lucy asked breathlessly as she turned to him as well. "I mean, you wanted to leave later for the store, but we needed supplies, and nothing was going on, so I didn't think—"

"Faith asked me to occupy you all, so Skylar wouldn't get distracted during her training." He ran his fingers through his hair. "They didn't give me specifics but mentioned that their tactics would be alarming. However that was the only way to get Skylar to learn control, and I needed to get as many of you to leave with me as I could. I didn't know they would threaten Raffe."

"They're *coven*. Of course they're going to use a person's vulnerabilities against them." Raffe stood as still as a statue next to me. "What did you expect from the word *alarming*?"

"I ... I don't know." Fane huffed and jutted out his chin. "And I didn't ask. You all came here, putting my family in danger, so I'll do whatever is needed to protect us."

Octavia gasped. "Fane, you can't mean that. Skylar is—"

"Just stop." Fane slashed out his hand. "I know what you're going to say, but is she really? I don't even know her, nor did I have the choice whether I wanted to or not."

My lungs stopped working. I selfishly hadn't put myself in his shoes. We'd arrived here with Raffe on the brink of death and Dave not doing well, and I hadn't considered how my presence would affect him.

Grabbing Fane by the arm, Dru seethed, "What do you mean you don't know her? We talk about her often."

"Yeah, you two talk about a baby you gave up and how you wish things could be different. She's the child you long for and want to know." Fane's nose wrinkled. "I never said I didn't know about her, but her presence had always hovered over our family, stealing the happiness from the holidays, and even in my own moments of happiness, her absence affects us. It's like you gave up the wrong child."

Lucy gasped, and a hand went to her chest. Guilt weighed on me.

I'd always wanted to know why my parents didn't want me. I'd assumed it was because of my power, and Octavia had confirmed my worst fear. Learning I had a brother had caught me off guard. But maybe he and I had similar issues stemming from opposite sides of that situation. I feared I was the child they'd never wanted, and he'd grown up wondering if they would've preferred to keep me instead.

"Spare me the dramatics. Your choice not to tell us had nothing to do with them giving her up and everything to do with your character as a person," Raffe snarled.

We were ganging up on Fane, and it didn't feel right, not after what he'd said. I stepped closer to Raffe, allowing our arms to brush, and linked with everyone. *I understand you're all upset. I am, too, but maybe give him a break. We've all made mistakes, and no one asked him if he was okay with us coming here.*

She's right. Lucy lowered her head. *I can't imagine how I'd feel if my mom disappeared and came back with a bunch of supernaturals. He even mentioned in the car ride that he'd never been around our kind.*

"Look, I see now that I made a mistake." Fane bumped his head against the wall. "And it won't happen again."

"You're damn right it won't happen again." Keith stepped closer to us. "If any of my pack members get hurt, it won't just be the coven members who'll feel my wrath."

"If you can forgive me for what I did, then surely you can get past what Fane did." Dave cleared his throat and rubbed the back of his neck.

Josie cut her eyes to him and shook her head. "Ignore him."

She wasn't thrilled with Dave's interjection, and if he were my mate, I wouldn't be either.

The only person who wasn't losing their mind was Adam, who kept watch by the window. He was the most rational one of us, which we desperately needed right now.

Raffe's anger spiked again. "Oh, I want him dead. He's the reason Skylar got kidnapped by those crazies.

The only reason I'm leaving him alone is because he means something to Josie, but one more step out of line—especially if it involves Skylar—and I won't hesitate again."

All of this fighting among ourselves was getting us nowhere, and there was only one way to handle it. "Everyone makes mistakes, and Fane is right. We should have made sure that Dru and Fane were okay with us coming here and especially staying. We are putting them at risk because we all know Olwyn won't give up searching for us."

I turned to Fane and noticed he and Lucy were staring at one another again. Something was going on between them.

Wanting to make things as right as possible, I inhaled. "Fane, would you like us to leave?"

"Skylar, no." Octavia clasped her hands. "You're our daughter, and you need protection. We won't make the same mistake again."

I couldn't believe how quickly my heart had thawed toward my biological parents. When I'd first met Octavia and learned who she was, I couldn't have imagined being okay with her presence, yet within days, I'd come to care for Dru, Octavia, and even Fane. "I appreciate the offer." I smiled sadly, hoping they understood I wasn't trying to snub them, but rather, I wanted a relationship with my brother, one that incorporated respect. "But this is Fane's home too, and he needs to be comfortable with us."

Dru sighed and nodded. "I get that and respect it."

"But do I have a choice?" Fane arched a brow, staring Raffe down.

Fair. This was the safest place for us. We didn't have to worry about our limited funds, and the area had been private property for years. Raffe wouldn't want us to leave even though the coven members nearby had soured it all.

Curling one side of his lip over his teeth, Raffe opened his mouth to answer, but I linked only to him, *Please don't push him. If he doesn't want us here, I want to respect his wishes. Think about it from his perspective. If someone showed up at our place wanting protection from powerful people, would you want them to stay?*

I considered myself a kind and compassionate person, but when it came to putting Raffe in danger, I wasn't sure what my decision would be. He was the most important person in my life, and I would never want to take unnecessary risks with his safety.

He must have felt the same way because his anger thawed, though his unhappiness remained stifling. *Fine, but only because this is important to you. But dammit, Sky. I don't know where to take you to keep you safe. This coven has me questioning this place too.*

I believed Priestess Caroline when she promised she wouldn't hurt us again. I didn't know how to explain it to him other than it was as if magic had laced her words, binding her to them and me ... as if I could sense them in my soul.

"See, he won't even answer my question." Fane snorted.

"Don't press me," Raffe gritted. "You're right. I want to tell you that I don't give a fuck. As long as Octavia and Dru don't mind having my mate here, we aren't leaving. But because of Sky, I'm willing to agree. If you want us to leave, we will. No questions asked."

Lucy gasped and bit her bottom lip as Keith linked, *Man, where are we going to go? We have no fucking money. We might as well pony up and go back to your dad's pack with our tails between our legs.*

Shut up. Adam shut the blinds. *That's not an option, and you know it.*

Then what is? Josie asked. *We need a way for Dave to get blood without drawing the attention of other supernaturals.*

Why did everything keep stacking against us? I must have pissed off someone good to be dealt a hand like this.

"Son, it's in your hands," Dru said and rubbed Octavia's shoulders.

Fane leaned forward, catching Lucy's attention, and said, "Of course all of you can stay." His body relaxed. "I don't want anything bad to happen to any of you, but I also want to make sure my parents are safe. I also never imagined the coven would do something like that to you. I've never seen Priestess Caroline harm a fly, let alone another person."

The tension in the room eased, and my lungs filled a little easier. I hadn't been sure what Fane's answer would be, and I was so damn thankful he'd said yes. My body sagged against Raffe, and he wrapped an arm around my waist, anchoring me to him.

Now that this was over, I wanted to rest. I had no idea when the coven would summon me for the next test. Knowing them, it wouldn't be long. With how strongly my magic had fritzed, if any one of the Veiled Circle's disciples had felt it, they'd find us. I could only hope there was a reason the coven members and Octavia had chosen to settle in this spot. It was a ways from the city, and they avoided other supernaturals like the plague.

"Okay, good." Octavia's smile seemed forced, but she patted Fane's arm. "That's settled. I'm going to get dinner cooking. After what Sky and Raffe went through, they should eat and rest more."

Fane winced, but his expression smoothed within a second.

I wasn't sure if his reaction was from guilt or because she was taking care of me again. Either way, I wasn't trying to make his life hell.

"Dave and I can help you cook," Josie offered, taking Dave's hand.

"You don't have to."

"I love cooking." Dave shrugged. "I know it sounds weird, with me being a vampire and all, but food and the way the rest of you enjoy it has always intrigued me. I took some cooking classes in Portland."

"Really?" Josie tilted her head back. "You're full of surprises, aren't you?"

"Good ones, I hope." He shuffled his feet.

Octavia gestured to the kitchen. "How can I say no to that? More hands will make it go quicker."

Josie and Dave followed her while Adam and Keith headed to the door.

Adam linked, *We're going outside to keep an eye out. I understand that the coven promised not to pull a stunt like that again, but I want to make sure they don't do anything else today while Skylar's exhausted. I already fucked up by sleeping through the first attack, and I won't make that mistake again.*

My heart ached. I hated that he felt that way. We could've woken him. None of us had expected them to pull something like that, so if anything, we were all to blame.

As I readied to speak, Raffe linked, *Sounds good. Let me know if you need me out there too.*

With those coven members, it's best if you stay close to Sky. Their sorry asses could cloak themselves and stab her in the back. Keith opened the door and glanced over his shoulder to examine the room again like he expected to find Caroline behind us.

A chill ran down my spine. I truly didn't understand the scope of what the covens were capable of. Slade and Olwyn clearly kept things from me, focusing on trying to get me on their side without revealing too much. They hadn't needed to be vicious ... until now.

Raffe led me back to our room, leaving Lucy and the others in the living room. When we entered the room, he sighed. "That damn cat is taking over our bed. The more time I spend with her, the more I agree with naming her Keith. She's a pain in the ass like him." He held the door open wider and stared at the cat curled in the center of our bed. "Out!"

Cat-Keith hissed but obeyed, giving him the side-eye as she stalked out.

I mashed my lips together, trying not to laugh as Raffe shut the door, climbed onto the bed, and opened his arms.

My attention landed on his neck, where they'd held the dagger against him earlier. Though it was scabbed over, the memory caused cold tendrils of fear to constrict my chest. Once again, I'd come so close to losing him. I didn't understand why; every time we turned around, our bond was threatened.

His face softened, and he patted the spot next to him. *If you don't get your sexy ass over here now, I will make you.*

I laughed, surprising myself. *I might want you to force me.*

He licked his full bottom lip, and warmth spread between my thighs. My mate was the most caring and sexiest man alive, and he was all *mine*.

Everyone is awake in this house, and you're exhausted. His irises warmed to cobalt, my new favorite color, replacing lilac, which had been my favorite color forever. *If you make me, I'll be eager to take you, and then I'd be ashamed of myself. I need you rested because danger has a knack for finding you.*

He knew my weakness and fought dirty, but I found myself crawling onto the bed next to him.

Pulling my back to his chest, he nuzzled his face into my neck, and the buzz of our connection sprang to life and took my breath away. I couldn't imagine a world without him by my side anymore, and the thought of losing him petrified me more than anything.

I don't want you training with those coven members again, Raffe linked, running his fingertips over my arm.

My body shuddered, already melting at his touch. *I don't have a choice. I despised their plan, but it worked. For the first time, I was able to control my power. I've never done that before.*

Next time, they could hurt you and not me. Raffe huffed. *I refuse to let that happen.*

They won't. I don't know how to explain it, but I know she won't. I turned and faced him.

His irises had returned to an icy light blue, revealing his intense struggle with this decision. *Babe, I can't risk losing you.*

I feel the same way about you, but she's right. My power ... it's growing. I refused to consider that Priestess Caroline had been right to use Raffe against me. What they'd done had been too cruel for me to ever approve of it. I'd never wish anyone to watch their fated mate in a situation like that, but it had been effective. *If I thought they'd chance doing something like that to us again, I wouldn't consider risking it. But I believe they won't, and I need all the help I can get. We can't hide forever. Whether it's Olwyn finding us, or the Veiled Circle taking over like they plan, we'll eventually have to come out of hiding. We both know we can't sit back and let innocent people get killed or mistreated. And we can't continue to allow supernaturals to deny their heritage.*

He blinked slowly, and the edges of his mouth tipped downward. *I hate that you're right. All I want to do is hide you away and keep you safe. And maybe if the wolf shifters hadn't been so hard on vampires and coven members, the Veiled Circle wouldn't have gotten off the ground. The coven is the only way you found answers, and my species could have ruined that for you.*

I cupped his face with my free hand and kissed him. I leaned back, needing him to see the expression on my face as I said, "You aren't to blame for any of this. We had a rocky start, but we figured it out, and you've been nothing but supportive of me and our relationship. Hell, you left your pack and future to stand beside me. I don't want you to feel any guilt because our relationship has only made me stronger. But I need to train with the coven, and if they do anything that makes either of us uncomfortable, I won't train with them again."

"I'd do everything all over again as long as I wound up with you." Raffe's hands tightened on my waist. "You're my everything, and my entire goal is to protect you. If training them will make you feel safer, we'll try it one more time, which means that getting rest is most important." He pulled me close to him again, and I nestled my head on his chest.

"Now sleep. I'll wake you up when it's time for dinner." He kissed the top of my head.

Nestled in his arms, safe and secure, I listened to his heartbeat and drifted off to sleep.

The next day, I trained with Priestess Caroline outside

my biological parents' house. Adam, Keith, and Raffe stayed out front with me, keeping an eye out for anything that seemed off. I suspected that Caroline had come here to prove she wasn't up to anything.

Lucy stayed in the house with Fane, Octavia, and Dru while Josie and Dave staked out the back to watch for any coven members trying to sneak in that way.

Luckily, nothing was amiss, but I understood why Raffe wanted to be cautious.

I'd hoped that, after my breakthrough yesterday, I could master my power again. Today, I could actually feel the vibrations merge into one distinct collection, and I managed to blow up two apples and a rock no larger than a golf ball, though it had taken nearly eight hours and a ton of concentration. I'd had to force myself to remember the ways I'd been tormented to get my power to spark. Between the bad memories and the exertion, I could barely stand on my feet.

By that point, the sun had set, which meant I'd trained the entire day and accomplished only three lousy things. How the hell was I supposed to fight in a potential war when manipulating such small things strained me?

"You did well." Priestess Caroline bowed her head. "We'll train more tomorrow. Make sure you get lots of rest."

"We're already done?" Luckily, I was too tired to throw a temper tantrum, so I didn't stomp my feet, but giving up didn't feel right.

Skylar ... Raffe warned, stepping next to me, sensing how exhausted I was.

Damn fated-mate bond. Not really, but this was one of the times the benefits were less than ideal. If I didn't push myself, who knew how long this would take to master?

Keith stood behind Priestess Caroline across the driveway near the tree line. He'd insisted on staying directly behind the priestess in case her "coven-ass tried something sneaky again."

"Uh ... Sky, look at the sky." Keith pointed upward like I didn't know which direction to look in.

From our left, Adam groaned and rubbed his temples. "How long have you been waiting to say that?"

"Don't get upset because I said it first." Keith stuck out his tongue, proving he'd lost his mind to boredom.

"What I think the young shifter is trying to say is ... it's late. You need rest, or you won't be able to train tomorrow." The priestess smirked, seeming more human than supernatural again.

There was no winning against the four of them. "Fine, but I need to do better tomorrow."

"Don't be so hard on yourself." The older lady patted my shoulder. "You've only been able to harness it for a day."

Maybe, but we had too much at stake for my progress to be this slow.

Dinner's ready, Lucy linked to us, and my stomach grumbled.

Priestess Caroline headed toward the woods and her home while Raffe, Adam, Keith, and I went back inside. Raffe stayed close by, no doubt feeling my exhaustion through our bond, but I didn't want the others to worry about me. I needed them to know I could be strong.

Each step was harder than the last, but I managed to make it up the stairs and sit down at the table without collapsing.

You're pushing yourself too hard, Raffe linked, kissing my cheek as he sat beside me. He placed his large hand on top of my thigh, the buzz springing to life even through my jeans.

Octavia, Lucy, Dru, and Fane had lasagna, salad, and

chicken laid out on the counters, and Raffe jumped up and made us each a plate.

Fane slid into the seat beside me, glancing around. He swallowed loudly. "Sky, I'm sorry about yesterday. I know it sounded like I resent you, and that's not fair."

"Hey." I reached over and placed my hand on his arm.

Is everything okay over there? Raffe linked, concern brewing between us.

Yes, you can listen in if you want. I wouldn't ever hide anything from Raffe, but I focused on my brother. "I get it. I had a hard time growing up, wondering why they didn't want me. I can't imagine feeling like you were sharing them with someone you didn't even know. I'm sorry too."

Fane hung his head. "Lucy told me you'd understand. I hoped she'd be wrong. It would be easier if you were upset with me because I was acting like a child."

"Childhood is where we get most of our baggage." I bumped my shoulder into his and smiled. "But I'm willing to help you with yours if you're willing to help me with mine. I know we won't ever have the relationship we'd have if we'd grown up together, but I'd like to have one now if you're open to that."

"Even after how I acted?" He pursed his lips.

"Only if you want. No pressure." Maybe my biological family and I wouldn't have a traditional family relationship, but I'd like to have something with each one of them.

"No, I'd like that." He nodded. "I don't hate you even though it sort of sounded like it. I hated not having a say in them giving you up or in you coming back. But I always wondered about you and what you were like. Growing up here was lonely. Mom and Dad didn't want to risk me going to school or venturing too far in case a supernatural figured out what our family was."

I forced my hands to stay in my lap, but I wanted to hug him. He'd had a lonely childhood too, similar to mine but for different reasons. We had so much in common but under very different circumstances. "Well, you have me now." I wanted to mention Lucy, too, since they were spending a lot of time together, but I kept that off-limits. I needed to take our relationship one day at a time and not push him. I wanted him to set the pace.

"I like the sound of that." He smiled and stood awkwardly. "Uh ... I'll be right back. I'm going to get some food."

As he hurried off, my cheeks ached, and I realized how big I was smiling. Maybe coming here was the best decision I'd ever made.

Unlike the night before, dinner tonight was filled with lively conversation. I was too tired to really contribute, but I smiled and watched as my pack, biological family, and Dave discussed shows, movies, and politics.

The night was fun and flew by.

I'd gotten clean and was crawling into Raffe's arms in bed when exhaustion set in.

When it felt like I'd just fallen asleep, Lucy pack-linked, *The priestess called.*

The door to our bedroom slammed open, and Raffe and I sat upright to find Fane rushing inside, pale.

The perimeter has been breached, Lucy finished as Fane rasped, "Someone is coming."

CHAPTER TWENTY-ONE

Despite the threat, I noticed how swollen Fane's lips were and that his hair was tousled. He and Lucy must have been together when the call came for her to know this information before the rest of us.

Maybe there was more to why he'd agreed to let us stay than just me being his sister. I'd realized there was an odd tension between him and Lucy, but I hadn't expected *that*. And there was no way I wanted them to go through what Raffe and I had—not that they were fated.

Raffe jumped out of bed, bringing me back to the present.

"Did they specify where the perimeter was breached?" Raffe slipped on his sneakers at the bottom of the bed.

I shook my head, trying to wake up and clear my mind. If I didn't get my act together, I wouldn't be helpful to anyone here, especially if Olwyn—she wasn't worthy of me including her title anymore—had found us.

Olwyn.

Had my power fritzing the other day allowed the Veiled

Circle to find us? And if so, what sort of numbers were they bringing this time?

"Uh ... I ... I don't know." Fane blinked, his brows pulling together. "I mean ... they didn't specify. They said to come down there."

"Can you ask them?" Raffe snapped and hurried past him and down the hallway.

When I got out of bed to follow, Lucy appeared at the bedroom door behind Fane.

"Yeah, I'll call them." Fane removed his phone from his pocket, his hands shaking. "We need to get down to the coven houses. That's where they want us."

He should've learned by now that Raffe wouldn't do something because a coven member wanted him to.

Stay here with him and get answers from him and Caroline, I linked as I slid past Lucy, heading to the front door. *He doesn't understand our world enough to know what to ask.*

Where do you want Dave and me? Josie asked as I reached the stairs.

The door shut behind Raffe as I took the stairs two at a time.

Meet me out front, Raffe replied. *We'll go from there.*

When I opened the front door, Adam and Keith were coming up the stairs from inside.

I almost stopped in my tracks as cold, wet air assaulted me, catching me off guard. Luckily, it helped wake me, and I hurried to the spot where Raffe stood in the center of the gravel driveway.

Darkness from thick rain clouds enveloped us. No light from the stars and moon filtered through, which made Raffe's glowing blue eyes like a beacon to me.

He'd tapped into his wolf to listen for the people who I

hoped had accidentally broken through the perimeter. His eyes snapped to me as I rushed toward him, and he frowned.

You're exhausted. You need to stay inside in case we have trouble. Raffe tensed, ready for battle. *I know the witches want us down there, but for all we know, they could be behind this.*

Unfortunately, he wanted to wage war for me and keep me safe in the house.

I shook my head. *If we're under attack, I need to be part of the fight, especially since my little show yesterday could be how they found us.*

That wasn't your fault. Raffe's nostrils flared. *That's on the coven since they decided to upset you like that. None of this is you.*

I reached his side and looped my arm with his to calm him. Though I wouldn't hide, that didn't mean I wanted to put myself in any danger. *Let's figure out if we're actually in danger and go from there.*

Raffe closed his eyes for a second but nodded.

The front door opened, and Josie and Dave joined us. The wind picked up, the rain hitting my face and forcing my dark hair to cling to me. I took a deep breath, ignoring the way my shirt and pajama bottoms molded to my body.

He got hold of the coven, Lucy linked. *The breach is from the main road, coming this way. There's a big problem, and it's why they want us to come down there. They felt coven magic when the perimeter broke.*

Dammit. This confirmed everything. Olwyn had sent people after us. If I'd gotten control of my power before yesterday, none of this would be happening. Our safe haven wasn't safe anymore, and it was all my fault. I'd gotten the people I cared for the most back into trouble.

Wake Dru and Octavia, and get them and Fane down to the coven. I needed to make sure none of them got hurt, especially since they hadn't been at risk until Octavia had decided to show up on EEU's campus.

And you should help her, Raffe added, placing a hand on the center of my back and pushing me toward the front door. *You need to go down there with them.*

And what are the rest of you planning to do? I arched a brow, refusing to be bossed around.

The rest of us will sneak ahead and let you and Lucy know what we see. Raffe turned toward the threat that would be here soon. *That way, we can get an idea of numbers. If there aren't many, we can take them out before they get close to the house.*

Then I'm going to help. Dave should help Lucy since he can't link with the pack like I can. Raffe clenched his jaw, so I added, *I swear I'll stay next to you the entire time. And I can sense their magic if they use it nearby.*

I could see his resolve bending.

Not to state the obvious, but they could be here anytime. We need to shift and scout before it's too late. Adam removed his shirt and tossed it to the ground. *So, make up your mind and stop arguing, or we'll have a fight on our hands before we even get to the coven.*

You stay right *next to me.* His blue eyes glowed again.

I nodded, removing my shirt, readying to shift.

He moved, blocking me the best he could from Adam's, Keith's, and Dave's view as I stripped down and let my wolf free.

She sprang forward, not waiting for an invitation. She and I had gotten to know each other better, and she'd been eager to be released.

My skin tingled as fur sprouted, and Raffe linked as he

called his own wolf forward, *Josie, tell Dave to head down to the coven since he can't link with us.*

Uh ... he can link with me now, Josie replied over the sounds of bones cracking. *We completed the mate bond and ...*

If my bones hadn't been breaking to adjust to my animal body, I might have gasped. No wonder it had taken them a little longer to get out here with the rest of us.

Raffe's shock filtered into me, but after a second, he replied, *Fine. Keep us updated on anything he sees.*

Once we were all in our animal forms, we took off toward the line of thick firs.

Everyone, stay in groups of two, Raffe linked, leading me to the right, away from the road.

Dave and I will stay together, Josie replied, not shocking anyone.

I heard them all split off, with Adam and Keith opting to cover the middle.

A quarter of a mile in, we heard the doors to the house open and close, informing us that Lucy was getting the others down to the coven house.

Good. They would be safest there.

Raffe and I kept pace with each other, and after another quarter mile, the sounds of other animals reached my ears. The smaller animals were scampering off, sensing the threat of an incoming predator.

We were getting close.

The wind rustled branches, and the rain pelted the ground, so I had to strain harder than normal to hear the sounds.

When they came, my heart galloped, and I stopped in my tracks.

I didn't sense magic, but I sure as hell heard at least fifty sets of paw prints just from our angle. Mixed in were the sounds of about five sets of footsteps, which could be coven, vampires, shifters in human form, or a combination of all three.

The fur on Raffe's nape rose, and he spun around, nodding for us to head back in the direction we'd come from. *We need to get to the coven.*

Not wasting time arguing, we took off running as quickly as we dared while trying to remain silent. Adrenaline pumped through my body, burning off whatever fatigue was left.

We found a group on our side—at least fifty supernaturals are heading our way, Raffe linked with everyone.

With the ground muddy from the rain, I had to focus more on my steps to make sure I didn't fall or make a noise. I didn't want to send our location out like a damn beacon; they'd stumble upon our scents soon enough.

Well, that fucking blows because we found a group of thirty, half in wolf form and the other half gods know what sort of supernatural. Keith's voice popped into our heads, giving us further bad news.

We were dealing with over seventy-five attackers that we're aware of.

There are forty this way. Dave and I are heading to the coven, Josie linked.

That makes it over a hundred, and there could be more behind them. My heart sank. The situation was far worse than I'd thought possible. But they wanted me dead, so the numbers didn't surprise me.

My power jolted, the severity of the situation waking it from its slumber. I needed the very essence I once feared to become stronger if we were going to make it out of here alive.

More of the perimeter has been breached. Lucy's voice popped into our heads. *The area about half a mile from the back of the house.*

The house was now in view, so we pivoted and ran close to the edge of the woods, not wanting to risk coming head to head with the enemy. Raffe and I panted softly, and even then, we could hear at least twenty more people coming toward us from the left. They were closing in.

A wolf howled loudly less than half a mile away.

They must have heard us. We shouldn't have run out here, but I'd never imagined we'd be up against these numbers. For all Olwyn knew, there were only seven of us, but she'd brought a literal army.

They've picked up our scent, Raffe linked, his panic slamming into me. *Avoid the house and move your asses,* he informed the other three running in the same direction.

With each step closer to the coven, it felt like the distance somehow grew farther away. The wolves were closing in on us, the wolves behind us speeding up, desperate to catch us.

We ran down the slight hill toward the coven.

The houses came into view with Priestess Caroline, Faith, and Avalon standing at the edge of Caroline's property. They stood ten feet apart from one another, and more coven members continued along the side for as far as I could see, forming a circle around the neighborhood.

They waved us in just as two wolves appeared on our left. A large brown one charged toward Raffe as the smaller white one leaped at me. I dug my paws into the ground, stopping short, allowing the wolf to land right in front of me. I lowered my head and steamrolled it in the side, shoving it into a tree trunk with as much force as possible.

The wolf whimpered just as a dark wolf ran past my right side.

My breath caught as the black fur flashed past me. The wolf's jaws opened and ripped out the white wolf's throat.

Keith.

He'd saved me.

He darted past me, racing toward Raffe as the white wolf's body fell limp, and the sound of more wolves rushing toward us filtered in.

Adam reached my side just as Priestess Caroline called out, "Get behind us. We need you in the perimeter so we can keep them out."

We couldn't do that until everyone was here.

As if there was a higher being that didn't completely hate me, Josie and Dave came into view. Then, four more wolf shifters ran between two trees. Okay, I took that back. Clearly, I'd pissed someone off, and this was their retribution.

We needed to eliminate them while we waited for Josie and Dave to catch up.

All four wolves locked their eyes on me and snarled.

Dammit, Sky. Get behind the coven, Raffe linked as he ripped out the throat of his first attacker.

Adam pawed at the ground. *You heard him. Go!*

I hunkered, readying to fight. *I'm not leaving you to fight four wolves on your own.*

Get in front so we can protect her, Raffe commanded as he moved in front of me, blocking the four wolf shifters' view of me. Adam and Keith flanked him with their fur raised on their backs.

The sable wolf lunged for Adam while the largest gray wolf ran straight at Raffe. The wolf on the far end attacked Keith, leaving the blond-furred wolf to push through the fight to get to me. The blond wolf stood on its hind legs, extending his claws. I rolled onto my side, landing in prickly brush as the wolf crashed onto its feet.

My flesh tore, stinging, but I jumped up as more wolves ran into the clearing. Holy shit, we had to get behind the coven line, or we were going to die out here.

Fire streaked the sky as Priestess Caroline used her magic on the enemy.

The blond wolf snarled and opened its mouth wide, lunging at me. I swiped my claws at it, hitting its snout. The enemy wolf stumbled back a step, whimpering and wiping its nose off.

We're here, Josie linked as she and Dave joined the fight.

Huffing, the blond wolf rushed forward and bit into my left leg. Hot, stinging pain flooded me, but I lowered my mouth and sank my teeth into the side of its neck. My stomach churned as I again hurt an animal. All my life, I'd wanted to be a vet to help animals, and now I'd become part of nature, killing to protect myself and my pack mates.

The wolf whimpered, his jaws slackening, and he stumbled back. The gushing blood told me I'd hit the artery. He'd be dead in seconds.

"Get back here *now*," Priestess Caroline yelled, "before we can't hold them off!"

Raffe sank his teeth into his opponent's side, bringing the enemy wolf to the ground. Adam and Keith fought together, defending against the sable wolf while more wolves raced inward.

Come on, Raffe linked, his gaze landing on me.

I didn't want to leave our pack out here without us. *But everyone—*

Once you start running, we'll all be behind you, Keith

shot back. *Get your ass to safety so we can too.*

I took off. Each time my left paw hit the ground, that leg wanted to crumple. I pushed through the pain and ran like hell.

Priestess Caroline, Avalon, and Faith were using their powers to keep the wolf shifters back. It was the only reason we hadn't been taken over completely.

Raffe and I ran past Caroline, and I spun around. I almost cried with relief as Adam, Keith, Josie, and Dave followed us.

More wolves poured into the clearing where we'd been seconds ago. Wolf after wolf lunged, trying to reach us, and the coven members closed the gap between them, filling in and using their magic to hold them off.

"Priestess, how are we supposed to perform the spell when we can't stop using our magic to keep them at bay?" the white-haired man I'd seen on the first day asked through gritted teeth as wind blew from his palm, throwing a wolf shifter into the top of a tree.

"We can't," Priestess Caroline groaned. "We can only do our best since we can't put up a barrier between us and them."

My stomach sank. Their magic would drain eventually. I understood that all too well because of how my own power worked. I needed to help them.

I closed my eyes, searching for the power inside me. It jolted, but I needed it to be a damn strong hum to get these wolves back so the coven could perform whatever spell they planned to.

Raffe, what do you want us to do? The coven can't handle this much longer, Adam linked.

Get ready to fight when the wolves break the circle, Raffe linked. *Lucy, where are you?*

Heading your way, she replied, *I got Sky's family into the priestess's house.*

If my magic was vibrations, I could cause chaos and make trees fall on them and the earth push them back. According to Priestess Caroline, since that was a wide scope, it wouldn't be nearly as hard as targeting a small object.

I just needed to ignore the chaos and focus.

I'd never been able to purposely make my power stronger but now seemed like a good fucking time to try. I imagined what it might feel like if I lost Raffe and remembered the day the coven held a dagger to his neck, forcing me to believe they'd kill them.

My power sang inside me, the agony of the threat causing the power to flare. I kept envisioning exactly what I wanted to happen. Instead of merging together, the power spread out within me, but it didn't have a chaotic feel as it had before.

Power pulsed from my paws into the ground, and the earth began to quake. Branches swayed.

It was working.

"What's going on?" a woman asked from my left. "Is that the arcane-born?"

A tree crashed to the ground, and a wolf yelped.

"It's working, Sky!" Priestess Caroline yelled. "Keep it going."

Then the ground under my own feet began to shake, and a magic I'd never felt before surged with it.

My eyes opened, and I looked to the right, where I felt the magic coming from. A woman who had to be close to my age stared back at me with her palm raised.

Then, a hole opened underneath me, and I dropped as my power stopped.

CHAPTER TWENTY-TWO

My stomach lunged into my throat, and my paws hit muddy ground. I'd dropped eight feet deep. When I looked up, earth crumbled on top of me, hitting my face.

More and more crashed down on me, my eyes burning from the grit.

Holy shit, I was getting buried alive.

Skylar, Raffe linked, his terror slicing through our fated-mate bond. He appeared at the top, his light-blue eyes glowing. Then more earth fell over me, and I couldn't see a damn thing.

My power roared to life as bigger chunks fell on top of me and the sides crashed in on me, filling the air pockets all around me.

I pawed at the dirt, trying to break through as I gasped a breath of mostly dirt. I hacked, making it hard to continue to attempt to get out from the dirt.

Head spinning, I couldn't decipher which way was up or down as the weight pressed against me from all directions.

My power radiated from me, wild and feral, but I

couldn't let it loose with the people I loved standing above me. I had to be careful, so I didn't harm any of them.

I'm digging you out. Hold on, Raffe linked, but then a sudden, intense pain filtered through our bond.

My world tilted. Raffe was hurt, and I'd come too damn close to losing him once already. I couldn't go through that again.

Lungs screaming, earth filling in the holes around me, I fought against pressure so intense that I couldn't move an inch. The little bit of oxygen I'd taken escaped me, and my head felt as if it might implode at any second.

If I didn't get out of here in the next few seconds, I'd die. Hysteria gripped me, and my head grew fuzzy.

Skylar, stay with me, Raffe linked, and though he was in my mind, it sounded as if he were miles away. *You can fight this. I'm coming.*

Raffe, I tried to reply, but it felt empty even in my own head.

Another shock of pain crashed through our bond, stirring me a little, but I wanted to go back to where the pain hadn't been so intense moments before.

Move, Raffe, Keith linked. *Or you're going to die.*

I'm not moving from this spot until I reach her, Raffe replied as more agony surged through our fated-mate bond, and it felt like he was being burned.

No. He was going to die because he was determined to save me. That wasn't something I could accept.

Raffe, run, I replied, trying to break through the dirt again, but I couldn't move a claw, the crushing weight debilitating.

His determination flared. *Not without you.*

Every inch of me hurt, and I couldn't take in a breath with the surrounding weight. My power sang and pulsed near the top of my skin, waiting to be released, but I kept holding it back to protect everyone above me.

Then, realization slammed into me.

Who said I had to escape directly upward? I was letting panic dictate my thoughts.

My consciousness ebbed, and in a last-ditch effort, I imagined the earth breaking apart and bursting out around the wolves and the witch in the small clearing in front of the coven neighborhood where we'd fought the first few wolves. Then I imagined the earth underneath me pushing me out, so I landed on all four paws, ready to fight the coven members attacking my mate.

My power pulsed from me. The intensity grew, and just when I thought I couldn't survive this any longer, my body moved.

At first, it was mere inches, but I edged upward, the dirt filtering away from my body. I sucked in a shaky breath. Dirt particles still lodged in my throat, making me hack again.

But I'd take it. At least I'd gotten a little air.

The pressure receded, and then I moved so fast that dirt bustled against my fur. I shook my head to get the dirt out of my eyes as the earth shook hard around me.

As my head cleared, I could feel Raffe's agony and pure terror.

I'm coming up, I linked, needing him to back away. He had to save himself, or I'd wind up killing him myself. *Get to safety.*

Holy shit, is that you? Adam asked, sounding more like Keith than himself.

I didn't know what he meant until my body broke through the ground and I soared several feet high, the earth rising underneath me.

Shaking my head, I ignored my aching eyes and took in the scene below me.

At least a hundred wolf shifters were scattered around the neighborhood, fighting Priestess Caroline's coven. About forty wolves already lay dead at their feet, with twenty turning to run toward the house. To the left, ten enemy coven members were gathered, using the firs for protection. They were all women, except for a man whose fire magic poured from his palms toward my mate.

An older witch from Caroline's coven stood next to my mate, water flowing from her hands, protecting Raffe as he frantically dug where I'd been. I could see blisters on his side where the warlock had burned away his fur.

White-hot rage soared into me as I leaped from the elevated earth and dropped ten feet to the ground. My paws stung on impact, with my injured one giving out slightly, but I pushed away the discomfort to focus on one goal.

Killing the bastard who'd hurt my mate.

Babe, I'm out. I'm fine, I linked to Raffe, needing to give him some peace as my power sang from me into the ground. I focused the vibrations into the hand of the warlock who was causing my fated mate such agony. A section of my power circled inside me and peeled off from the rest, which still funneled into the ground.

Then the power left me in a surge, and the warlock's hands exploded, skin, bones, and blood hitting him and the two witches beside him.

His magic cut off, and his piercing scream filled the air.

"My hands!" he shouted. "My hands. They're gone."

Blood poured from his nubs, and he stumbled back, his face ashen.

The witches beside him paused their fight, and when

Raffe spun to look at me, the young witch who'd buried me followed his gaze.

Thank gods. I thought I'd lost you, he replied, our connection lightening from his panic and worry.

The young witch's eyes widened. "It's her."

The older silver-haired witch covered in the warlock's blood gasped. "How is that possible? Neither Aldric nor Supreme Priestess Olwyn told us she could control an element."

My stomach soured. The way she'd put the two names together made it clear they were working together.

Bile burned my throat as everything clicked into place. Aldric was part of the Veiled Circle. No wonder they were gaining strength and weren't worried about overtaking the king.

The man kept screaming. He turned around and ran back to wherever he'd come from. I doubted he'd get far with the amount of blood he was losing, but that was what he got for attacking us unprovoked.

A familiar vibration tugged on my power, pulling me back to the moment just as a dark-gray wolf lunged at me.

I stumbled back, my body weak from the pressure I'd endured underground. I was weak physically, which meant I had to use my power. It was the only way I'd survive.

Skylar, watch out! Raffe linked, his fear once again tangible. *Everyone, Sky is weak. Get to her and protect her.*

They couldn't do much for me now, but I wouldn't dissuade them.

The wolf swiped my uninjured front paw out from under me and I tumbled over. My chest hit the ground just as the wolf lunged overhead. I visualized the vibration hitting the wolf in the chest as it went over me, and my body tensed for impact.

A yelp had me lifting my head. The wolf flew into a tree trunk eight feet away. His head hit the trunk with a sickening *crack* and he crumpled lifelessly to the ground.

My throat tightened. I hadn't meant to do that.

The witch closest to me screamed and raised her hands. Water surged toward me, wetting my face and fur, but the pressure didn't affect me. The water washed the grit from my face and eyes, making me more comfortable.

"Dear goddess," the woman muttered, lowering her hands. "How is that possible?"

Great question, and one I'd like to understand myself, but it seemed no one understood what I was capable of since apparently, no other arcane-born had completed their bond with their fated mate.

"Then we'll do the next best thing." The other woman, with blood splattered on her face, lifted her hands.

A tornado appeared among Raffe, Lucy, and Keith, lifting them several feet off the ground.

I had to end her before they got too high.

"Maggy, have you lost your damn mind?" the middle-aged witch next to her gasped. "Did you see what she did to Tucker?"

"We attacked them—they won't let us walk away," the older woman rasped, her brown eyes turning as black as the sky.

I focused on her hands, but my power sputtered, hitting a high fizz at most. I'd drained myself at this unideal time.

Gritting my teeth, I forced myself back onto my feet as growls, cries, and snarls rang in my ears and the stench of copper damn near made me gag. This was worse than any fight I'd ever been part of, and I suspected if we survived, a worse one would come next.

As I took a step, all four of my legs gave out, and I landed heavily on my stomach.

No. I had to fight her and save Raffe and the others.

Then I heard the sounds of animals, our saviors, rushing toward us. I had to do something to get Raffe and the others down.

I leaned my head back and howled, allowing my agony, fear, and anger to echo in my cry. I wanted the animals to know where to come. Then I snarled as I forced myself back onto my feet.

Refusing to fall, I charged forward, each step sending pain slicing through my entire body. With no time to waste, I hurried toward her.

The witch with water magic sprayed me, but I pushed through it.

"Maggy," the older woman croaked, but it was too late.

My teeth sank into Maggy's throat, and I jerked my head, ripping it out. I crashed onto the ground, my strength giving out.

When I heard Raffe, Lucy, and Keith hit the ground behind me, I linked, *I need help*.

I hated to pull them in my direction, but I couldn't stand anymore.

On our way, Raffe replied, and I heard paws padding toward me.

The older witch removed a dagger from underneath her dress and stood over me, her eyes wild.

Raffe couldn't get here in time. This had to be it. My luck had run out.

She swung her dagger downward.

No! Raffe yelled.

Something streaked across my vision and knocked into the woman's hand.

"Argh," she groaned as the dagger dropped to the ground.

Then, the same fluffy gray blob swooped down beside me, grabbed the dagger in its talons, flapped its wings, and darted into the sky.

An owl.

My chest heaved with relief as animals flooded the area. Bobcats, deer, raccoons, coyotes, and others that I could hear but couldn't see.

"Priestess Diana, look," the younger witch gasped. "Animals."

More owls swooped down, attacking the witches.

"Get out of here while we can!" Priestess Diana shouted. "Only harm the animals to get free."

"What about the girl and the prince?" a dark-haired witch rasped just as a bobcat came at her from one side and a coyote from the other. "Never mind. Let's leave."

The eight remaining witches spun and ran, the bobcat and the coyote racing after them. More animals headed their way as yelps and whimpers filled the air behind us where the wolves had been.

I gritted my teeth. I needed to get back to Priestess Caroline's coven to ensure the animals didn't attack them. As I stood, Raffe, Lucy, and Keith reached me.

Raffe limped from his burns, but he seemed unfazed as he nuzzled my neck. He linked, *You weren't supposed to leave my side.*

Despite the chaos and agony, I laughed, sounding like I was choking. *I didn't mean to. You can't get mad at me for that. The ground disappeared from underneath me.*

I'll be back, Keith linked, rushing after the witches.

Wait, I replied, but he vanished deeper into the woods. I turned to Raffe. *He's going to get hurt.*

He must want to make sure they don't loop around. He'll let us know if he needs help. Raffe nodded toward the neighborhood. *Let's get you somewhere safe.*

My power still fizzed from me, filtering into the ground. I wasn't sure if I could still communicate with the animals, but I needed to make sure the ones I cared about were protected. *The dark wolf that's chasing after the witches, don't hurt him, please. And don't hurt the witches who live in this neighborhood. They've been protecting my pack and me.*

The wolves that smell of you won't be harmed, a weird voice responded, and I couldn't quite put a face to it. *And we know which witches protected you.*

That would work.

Girl, you had us all freaked. Lucy's eyes shone as the three of us headed back toward the neighborhood.

Raffe huffed. *We aren't out of danger yet.*

He and Lucy flanked me as we moved back toward the neighborhood. The coven members were spread out again, and the wolves that had attacked us were either dead or running back the way they'd come from.

I sighed. It seemed inevitable that we would continue to be attacked until I was dead. Olwyn and Aldric were determined, and I wasn't sure how we could defend ourselves with King Jovian's right-hand man involved.

As we moved, I noted all the dead bodies on the ground. A few were from Priestess Caroline's coven, making my body somehow feel heavier. All these deaths were because we'd hidden here.

My chest ached.

Each of them was dead because of me.

I hadn't expected to be found, but I wouldn't make that mistake again.

Everywhere I went, people would die. I had to figure out how to survive without risking more people. Raffe, Keith, Adam, Lucy, Josie, and Dave would remain by my side, and I doubted that Octavia and Dru would want me to go, but they were human and had no powers, so putting them at risk was unacceptable.

As we walked to the coven, I expected to find scornful looks or something close to that, but each coven member stared toward the woods in awe.

I didn't need to turn around to understand why. Wild animals protecting us was something I still struggled to understand myself.

Sky, Keith's voice popped into my head. *I need you. Fast.*

My heart dropped. Had the animals mistaken Keith for the enemy?

Without hesitation, I turned and pushed myself in the direction he'd run.

Raffe stayed next to me and asked, *What's going on?*

A bobcat won't let me pass, Keith replied. *I need Sky here and quickly.*

Adrenaline pumped through my veins, taking the edge off my pain.

I'm coming with you two, Adam linked and caught up to us on my other side.

The three of us pushed through the woods, Raffe taking the lead and using his alpha connection to lead us to Keith.

Then I heard the bobcat hiss just as I passed a thick tree.

The bobcat was crouched, ready to pounce, and Keith stood in front of it.

He's with me, I connected with the light fizz of my power. I wasn't sure how long I could hold on to the connection with the animals now that it was fading. I could only pray it wasn't too late.

I'm not trying to hurt him, the bobcat replied. *It's what he's protecting, but I will attack if he doesn't get out of the way.*

What? I stopped in my tracks ... and then noticed what the bobcat meant.

CHAPTER TWENTY-THREE

I blinked, struggling to understand what I was seeing, but each time my eyes opened, the scene didn't change.

Keith stood in front of the younger witch who had almost killed me. She had a large bite mark on her forearm. Blood poured down her light-brown skin, a crimson stain soaking through her black dress, where she held the arm against her stomach. Her hair, darkened from the rain, looked like strands of blood as well.

What the fuck do you think you're doing? Raffe linked, his anger mixing with mine, putting both of us more on edge. *That bitch tried to kill Skylar.*

Head lowering, Keith moaned. *I ... know, but I can't make myself move from this spot. I have to protect her. I don't even understand it myself.*

I swallowed hard, processing his words. I wanted to run across the clearing and rip out her throat. Of all the coven members I'd come up against, she'd come closest to killing me.

Then I'll take care of her for you. Raffe charged through

the clearing, heading straight for the witch, who bowed over in agony.

A low growl came from Keith as he braced himself for Raffe's attack. When Raffe got within striking distance, Keith slammed into Raffe's burned side and knocked him into a tree. My mate yelped, and my stomach churned. Everything inside me wanted to hurt Keith, but the longer the woman stayed here, the longer this fight would carry on. She must have spelled Keith in some way.

Kill her, I pushed toward the bobcat, hoping he could still understand me since my power had dulled to a high jolt.

The bobcat didn't hesitate and growled, following my command now that Keith and Raffe were out of the way.

"No!" the witch screamed, throwing her uninjured hand high. "Please, don't. I respect the animals of the forest. I don't want to harm you."

Keith backed away from Raffe, spun around, and leaped onto the bobcat's back.

He linked, *Sky, please. Spare her. I think she's my fated mate.*

Even though I couldn't feel his emotions like I could Raffe's, I sensed the fear and heartbreak in his words.

Fated mate.

If that was true and we killed her, Keith would never be the same. The idea of him experiencing a loss like that caused all the anger to leave me. *Raffe, if that's his fated mate—*

I don't give a damn. Raffe pivoted, readying to attack her once more.

"Don't hurt him," the witch gritted, lifting her uninjured hand.

I had to stall them.

Give me a second before you hurt her, I pleaded, pulling on my connection with the bobcat and Raffe.

To my shock, they paused. I pulled my wolf inward, needing to be human again.

Then get your wolf off my back, the bobcat responded. *Or I will kill him.*

Keith, get off the bobcat. He's giving me a minute. My body was already shifting back into human form.

The bobcat plopped over onto his back, putting all his weight on Keith. Keith's breath whooshed from him, but at least they'd stopped fighting.

The witch removed a dagger from her thigh and barreled toward the bobcat.

My heart clenched, and as my spine straightened, I bellowed somewhere between wolf and woman, "Everyone, stop!" My body radiated pain, likely not recovered enough for me to shift comfortably, but I needed to talk to the witch to stop this. Pain sliced through me, but my skin tingled as the fur retreated.

The witch glanced at me, her feet slowing as her eyes bulged. Clearly, she hadn't expected me to shift back into human form.

You shouldn't be shifting yet. Raffe whimpered, stepping in front of me, ready to protect me if the witch threatened me again. His worry tightened my chest, making it hard to breathe again. *What the hell are you doing?*

"Getting answers." I stood tall, the cold rain hitting my body. Even though I was a wolf shifter, I still wasn't the most comfortable with nudity. *If Keith doesn't want us to hurt her, then I need to talk to her and see if we can find a way to trust her.*

The witch lifted her dagger, her gaze flicking between

the bobcat and me. "What are you doing? I can hurt you all. You saw what I can do."

A faint wisp of magic came from her, something I couldn't usually feel until magic was used on me. Now, I could feel it seeping from her soul, telling me everything I needed to know. "You can't hurt us. Your magic is depleted. That's why you're not using it and how you got bitten. And you're injured and weak enough that, even if you attacked us, we could eliminate you easily. Besides, you're outnumbered."

She took in a shaky breath. "You can sense my magic?" Her face lined with concern. "They said you were untrained and would be easy to kill. I don't understand what's going on and why the animals aren't attacking you too." Her face was pale, likely from the blood loss and pain.

"The animals came to protect me, my pack, and my friends." That much Supreme Priestess Olwyn should have known by now, or at least suspected. I wasn't telling her anything that would be shocking. "And who are they?"

The bobcat *hmph*ed as it rolled onto its stomach, freeing Keith. Keith slowly climbed to his feet and moved next to the witch.

"Wait." The witch stepped back, her bottom lip trembling. "The animals are protecting Prince Raffe? That must be why you don't have more shifters with you for protection. We wondered why there were only six wolf shifters, knowing how important you are. We thought it was strange that your dad would allow that."

"You're talking about King Jovian placing more shifters here with us to aid us?" My brows rose.

She nodded. "Who else would I mean?"

Dad wouldn't have notified everyone that I left the pack yet, Raffe linked. *His one and only heir leaving his pack would make him appear weak, and Aldric wouldn't risk it because that sort of information would get back to Dad quickly.*

That made sense, but what the hell was going on? "No, the king isn't concerned about having his people protect us." I wanted to tell her we'd broken away, but that was a decision more for Raffe to make than me.

Her brows furrowed, and she took a hesitant step back.

Adam tensed to my left, preparing to give chase if she took off, while Keith stood in front of her, the fur on the nape of his neck rising.

"Are you going to kill me?" Her bottom lip quivered. "'Cause if you are, I'd rather you get it over with."

Keith growled, his eyes locking with mine as if he were trying to read them.

"For some reason, someone important to me doesn't want me to, so that depends on what you say." By some miracle, we'd gotten the leverage. "Why did you attack us?"

She swallowed audibly, and Keith stepped back, his tail brushing her ankles above her black shoes. "To kill you and capture the prince."

My hands clenched, but I had to admire her bluntness. Granted, lying would be futile around us wolf shifters, and her power was too weak for her to mask a lie from us. "Why? Don't you think the king will be upset if you kill his son?"

"That's sort of the point." She flinched. "Eliminating you and kidnapping his heir will force King Jovian to listen to the East. We want to separate, and we will prove to him that we're strong enough to do it. Between that and the alliance this attack should create among nonshifter supernaturals in the West, King Jovian won't be strong enough to fight us. He'll have enough problems within his own territory to spare us any time."

My breath quickened. "I take it you're referring to the Veiled Circle?"

Her jaw dropped. "How do you know about them?"

Raffe tensed. *Holy shit. How many people does Supreme Priestess Olwyn have working for her? How did she get her hands on the Eastern wolf shifters?*

I suspected I already knew the answer, but I didn't want to throw Aldric's name out until I knew for sure. What I'd overheard could have been pure coincidence, though that was unlikely.

"They tried to recruit me, and I fled." None of this added up. The Veiled Circle wanted to make all wolf shifters pay, so why in the world would the Eastern wolves and covens team up with them? Clearly, they didn't know Olwyn's whole plan, which proved what I'd suspected all along and tried to look past—Supreme Priestess Olwyn was a manipulative bitch.

Or maybe the Eastern supernaturals didn't care, making them worse than the priestess since they were turning on their own kind. "I'm surprised that the Eastern wolves hate the Western wolves so much that they would be okay with their plan." I shrugged, my body aching even from the slight movement.

"We don't hate King Jovian. He's just out of touch with the needs of the Eastern supernaturals." The witch's expression twisted. "Even the supreme priestess doesn't hate the wolves, just that they stripped our rights from us. But honestly, from the stories I've heard, I don't blame the wolf shifters for everything. The covens were awful to them when they needed our aid, and the Eastern wolf shifters have been nothing but supportive of us since then."

Her blood continued to drip all over the ground, but until I understood her plans, we were staying here.

I laughed, causing the back of my dry throat to ache, and I swore a chunk of dirt blew out. Gross. "Trying to kill me and kidnap King Jovian's son says otherwise."

"It wasn't personal." She flinched and tilted her head. "The supreme priestess claimed that you're a threat to everyone because your power is so unstable."

"Killing someone for personal gain isn't a gray area." I shook my head. Even if killing Slade would destroy Supreme Priestess Olwyn, doing so would never cross my mind. There were other ways to hurt someone, like taking their power, imprisoning them, or killing them. There was no need to hurt someone they loved to get to them. To me, that action was villainous. "Raffe and I weren't doing a damn thing to you when you attacked us. We were in bed, resting. We weren't a danger to you. There was no reason for you to want me dead or to take him hostage."

"Look, it might appear that way to you, but if you couldn't celebrate holidays because the people in charge didn't approve of them, or if you couldn't create a council so that all supernaturals had an equal say in things that pertain to them, you'd feel oppressed, too, and desperate to break free." She swayed on her feet, her words slurring together. "But when we saw that coven members were helping you, we realized we would have to fight. We'd hoped to sneak up on you unaware, but seeing these animals protect you ... the goddess showed us we were wrong in our decision, and I'm sorry."

I knew better than anyone that Supreme Priestess Olwyn was a great manipulator, and this girl was losing too much blood. I blew out a breath and walked toward her.

Raffe edged between Keith and me, his gaze meeting mine. He linked, *What the hell do you think you're doing?*

She's losing too much blood. I need to wrap her wound and get her back to Dru so he can tend to it. Even though she'd messed up, every single one of us had done something horrible. If she was Keith's fated mate, I couldn't let her die.

Are you serious? Raffe's wolf head tilted back. *She tried to kill you, or did you already forget?*

I bit the inside of my cheek, trying hard not to say something I'd regret. *She said she was sorry, and I believe she meant it.*

You and your second chances. Raffe shook his head. *One day, it'll get you hurt.*

I think that ship has already sailed. I reached out and rubbed his head to calm him. *And you'll be right beside me, prepared for anything she might try. Do you remember when Keith treated me like a threat and it upset you?*

His eyes narrowed, but I could feel his outrage easing. *She tried to kill you.*

And I bet she won't make that mistake again. If she does, we'll end her without a moment's hesitation. He had to know that, even though I might seem softhearted, I wasn't. After being bullied my whole life, I tried to believe that people did things because they didn't fully understand. With everything Raffe and I had been through together, he should know this as well as I did. *I might want to give second chances, but I don't do it stupidly.*

Fine, but one wrong move and I rip her throat out. Keith can hate me for the rest of his life as long as you're safe.

The way my chest expanded and warmed reminded me how much I'd changed in such a short time. Who would've thought promises of death and hatred would have butterflies fluttering in my stomach? *You do know how to sweet-talk me.*

Yeah, well, let's get this over with so we can continue this conversation with either clothes or fur all over your body. I'm not picky as long as you're covered.

I didn't like standing here naked either, but I had to talk with the witch.

The bobcat hissed as I stepped closer, and my power barely jolted within me. I needed to communicate with him while I could. *I'm going to help her. Raffe will attack her if she does something. You're free to go. My power is almost gone, so I'm not sure how much longer I can communicate with you.*

He bowed his head. *I'll let your mate take the lead, but we won't leave until you're safe. We'll keep watch over you tonight.*

My heart grew heavy. *Thank you.* Before I could tell them they didn't need to do that, my power was extinguished, leaving me cold.

My limbs felt weighed down as fatigue settled back into me. I needed to hurry before I couldn't move.

Avert your eyes, or the witch won't be the only person at risk of dying, Raffe linked and bared his teeth.

Keith lowered his head until it nearly touched the ground. Any other time, I would've laughed, but not right now.

What are you doing? Keith whimpered. *She's been talking to you.*

When I stepped toward her, the witch stumbled back.

"Here, let me help you." I lifted both hands, and they might as well have weighed fifty pounds each. "You're bleeding too much. We need to slow that down, or you'll pass out."

She tilted her head but nodded.

When I moved past Keith, I made sure that my leg didn't touch his fur. The last thing I needed was Raffe getting into a jealous fit, and I could only imagine what he was feeling right now. If he was naked in front of a bunch of women, I'd be losing my damn mind.

I pointed to the bottom of her dress and said, "I'm going to rip off a section and tie it around your bite mark. I won't harm you, though it might not feel great. We need to get you back to ..." I trailed off, unsure what to call Dru. *Doctor* didn't feel right, but *Father* didn't fit the bill either. "My close friend who can help disinfect the wound and stitch you up."

"You're really going to help me?" She dropped the dagger and pressed her hand to her chest. "After I tried to—"

Raffe snarled, and his anger came flooding back.

I tried to push calm toward him, but I was struggling to stay calm myself. "Let's not talk about that right now, or I could change my mind."

She nodded. "Right. That's fair."

Doing as I said, I ripped off the cleanest section of her dress I could find, making sure the strip of fabric was long enough to wrap around twice and tie into a knot. As I worked on her arm, I couldn't help but be a little rougher than necessary, which made me feel better.

To her credit, she didn't complain. She merely watched me with her large emerald eyes. When the makeshift bandage was all set, I dropped my hands.

She whimpered, "Thank you. But I should go—"

I shook my head. "Not happening. We may not kill you, but you're definitely not leaving. We still have tons of questions we need answered. In the meantime, do you mind sharing your name? I don't like calling you *Witch* in my mind."

"Sedona." She bit her lip. "And you're Skylar, right?"

A chill ran down my back. How many people knew my name now and feared my power? Olwyn had to be spreading that information far and wide. "That's right. Now let's get back."

I turned, and Raffe pressed against my side, using his tail to cover my backside. The buzz of our connection sprang to life, calming me more but also making the fatigue set in faster. My body ached, but luckily, during the shift, the injuries on my arm had scabbed instead of ripping more. That had to count for something.

Adam, follow the witch and make sure she doesn't try anything, Raffe commanded as the two of us led the way. Then he linked to Lucy and Josie, *Can the two of you find a dress or something? Sky needs something to wear. She shifted back into human form.*

On it, Lucy replied. *I'll meet you at the tree line.*

We kept a slow but steady pace, but we'd run farther than I'd realized while in animal form.

Footsteps followed us, and I glanced back to see the bobcat several feet behind us, a coyote and a raccoon at its side. Seeing the animals walking like this still blew my mind. For some reason, they all worked together when it came to protecting me.

Right when I thought I couldn't move farther, the trees thinned, indicating we were nearing the coven houses. Lucy's scent filled my nose.

I'm going behind the bush over here. Can you bring the clothes over? I moved toward some thick brush beside a large fir, my feet making a ton of noise from shuffling since I was too tired to lift them.

You all keep going. I'll be with my mate, Raffe commanded.

By the time I reached the brush, Lucy was there, still in wolf form.

She placed a green dress on the ground then trotted back toward the coven.

With shaky hands, I slid the dress over my body. Thankfully, it wasn't white, or there wouldn't have been much point in wearing it with the drizzle coming down. Putting on the dress had me gasping for breath, and I struggled to keep my eyes open. I needed to rest, but I wasn't sure I could with all the dead bodies that needed to be cleaned up.

Hey, lean on me, Raffe linked, pressing against my side.

But he was injured too, though he was trying like hell not to remind me.

I'm fine. Just tired. I sighed.

"What is *she* doing here?" someone shouted.

Shit, I needed to reach the coven. In my weariness, I'd forgotten we hadn't warned them about Sedona.

"Skylar said someone could help me," Sedona said, her voice rising in fear.

I hurried toward them, hearing the animals come out of the woods close behind me. They were keeping watch as promised. The bobcat hissed, and the coyote snarled, sensing the tension. I couldn't communicate with them since my power was gone.

I had to fix this before another fight started. I ran out of the trees with Raffe at my side. Then I lifted both arms. "She's hurt and needs help."

"Skylar!" Octavia exclaimed, her mouth dropping open. "Watch out!"

CHAPTER TWENTY-FOUR

I spun around more slowly than I'd have liked, but my wolf inched forward, listening. I couldn't shift again; I was too tired. Hell, I probably couldn't even fight. When I focused on the perceived threat, my tension vanished.

The bobcat and coyote were snarling from the tension they felt from Sedona and the others. Animals could sense emotions and when something was off, they didn't understand that this wasn't a threat to me.

I attempted to lift both hands, but they were like lead. I raised them an inch, but hopefully, between that and having my back to the coven, the animals would realize I didn't view the people as a threat.

"Everybody needs to calm down," I said over my shoulder, hoping that, with the coven's slightly elevated supernatural hearing, I'd spoken loud enough.

When Priestess Caroline nodded, my eyes burned with tears of relief. Raffe moved closer to me, his tension tightening my chest again. All I wanted to do was take a quick shower and crawl into bed before someone had to carry me because I wasn't sure how much longer I could stand on my own two feet.

Babe, what's going on? Raffe linked.

If everyone calms down, it will be okay. I hated that I couldn't communicate with the animals, especially with tensions so high, and there were bodies we needed to bury.

More animals came forward, their bodies tense as they spread out from one another, forming a circle around us.

Linking with our entire pack, Raffe said, *Josie, tell the witches what happened with Sedona and take her somewhere she won't cause more tension. I suggest the most uncomfortable room for her—maybe a wet, moldy basement?*

Man, her wound will get infected, Keith replied.

And that would bother me why? Raffe snapped. *She tried to kill my mate, or did your dick make you forget that? Because that's the only thing that can explain your sudden aversion to protecting your alpha's mate.*

I flinched, not needing more hostility brewing than we already had. *Babe, we don't need these animals to mistake some of the people on our side as aggressors and attack.* That was the thing with anger and fear—it turned people against one another. Look at what the East was doing to the West. It was a civil war within the supernatural community.

Listen, I can't help it, Keith retorted. *You should understand that better than anyone.*

You two, shut up, Lucy connected. *We have enough enemies without turning on ourselves.*

Focusing on the bobcat that had been trying to attack Sedona again, I spoke low and calmly, wanting him to hear I wasn't worried. "Everything is okay. The coven didn't know we were bringing someone from that side back with us." Even though I doubted he understood my exact words, he should be able to pick up on my cadence and that I wasn't upset.

Just damn tired.

I heard Dave mumbling to the coven, informing them of everything. The bobcat lifted his head, edging back into a neutral pose. I'd count on him to inform the other animals since I couldn't connect with them with my essentially nonexistent power.

Between the animals relaxing and Dave explaining what was going on, I hoped we could get a plan together before I couldn't keep my eyes open. The pain from being buried alive, shifting before I should've, and my now drained power settled exhaustion back into my bones.

Let's get you somewhere covered, Raffe nudged against my side. The comforting buzz of our connection made my eyelids heavy. Sleep was too damn close.

I headed back to the coven. Sedona stood at the edge of the circle with Keith at her side. Keith scanned the group repeatedly, his breathing ragged. He was waiting for someone to make a move against Sedona.

I couldn't blame him. Her group had killed twenty coven members, and I still wasn't sure how I'd survived. The pain had been so horrible that, for a moment, I'd wanted to end my suffering.

I noticed Octavia, Dru, and Fane as they walked toward us from Priestess Caroline's house. Fane's forehead showed deep lines of worry as he scanned the group, searching for Lucy.

Lucy must have felt his gaze like I could Raffe's because her head turned his way and she trotted toward him. When he noticed her, his shoulders sagged with relief.

I made my way to Sedona, wanting to stand next to her like Keith was. I wasn't sure how the coven would react to our decision to bring her here, especially since I'd made it without consulting them. I hadn't considered that, but we couldn't let her go or kill her. We couldn't do anything rash.

"Oh my god." Octavia raised a hand to her mouth, covering it. "Sky, what happened to you?"

Unlike her, Dru raced toward me, hurrying so fast that he stumbled over a rock.

Despite my fatigue, I smiled. In this moment, I saw how much they cared about me. All my life, I'd thought they hadn't wanted me, and being here with them and seeing this proved that hadn't been the truth, though I hated that Fane had sometimes felt second best.

Dru ran to me and touched my shoulder, and I flinched. Octavia, Fane, and Lucy followed and stopped behind him.

My body hurt worse than I'd realized.

"What happened to you? You need to lie down. You're all bruised, and your wrists have thick scabs." His concern grew the more he examined me.

I must look bad. I'd hoped the dirt would come off when I shifted. "I'm fine. We just need to settle things down, and we all need to rest. Sedona is suffering from a deep bite and losing blood." I pointed to the witch, and Raffe growled faintly.

You are the one who should be tended to first, not that bitch, Raffe linked, thankfully only to me.

Babe, I'm fine. I just need to handle this so we can curl up together and rest. That sounded like heaven.

He shook his head, his fur swaying despite the drizzle.

Dru glanced at Priestess Caroline and said, "I don't think I've met this witch before."

The priestess raised a brow. "She's not one of us, and she's the one who tried to kill your daughter."

Sedona's mouth dropped open. "The healer's your dad?

I thought you said *friend*. I knew better than to trust you." She glared at Keith accusingly.

It wasn't me she'd trusted. Fair enough. "He's my biological father, and we just met a few days ago, so calling him *dad* doesn't sound right."

Her head jerked back toward me, and she winced. "Oh. Right."

"Dru, can you please help her? She's given us some very interesting information and hasn't tried to kill me again." I couldn't think of a better way to address that particular instance.

He frowned. "I don't know how I feel about helping someone who tried to hurt my daughter."

I exhaled. I should appreciate his hesitation. "I thought doctors weren't supposed to discriminate."

"Thankfully for me, I'm not in the hospital." He arched a brow. "I'm surrounded by witches, wolves, and various other wild animals, so I'm thinking human rules don't apply."

I know the other one raised you, but I think I like this father better, Raffe linked.

Oh, I'm sure you do, Keith added. *This one doesn't hate you.*

Raffe's anger flared.

"Look, I'm sorry that we brought Sedona here without discussing it, but Keith had run off and sounded like he needed help." I blew out my breath, not up to playing games. All I had left was the brutal truth. "Keith asked us to help her because he thinks she's his fated mate."

"What?" Sedona spun toward Keith, staring into his dark eyes. "You feel it too? I thought I'd gone crazy. I didn't want to leave, which is how the bobcat got me."

"*Fated mate*? Impossible." Priestess Caroline marched

up to stand in front of Sedona. "A coven member has never had a fated mate, and fated mates are always tied to their own species."

Dave laughed from his spot beside Priestess Caroline with Josie on his other side. "Yes, that's the most common thought, but Skylar wasn't a wolf, and she's fated to Raffe, and Josie and I just completed our bond. Things are moving outside the norm fast."

And I think Fane and I are mates too, Lucy added into the link.

That didn't surprise me, and when I looked at them, I noticed Fane's fingers in her fur.

"Grandma, you said our ancestors believed that an arcane-born arrived whenever the balance of the supernatural world was threatened." Faith cleared her throat and rubbed her hands together. "Supreme Priestess Olwyn is creating an army to take down the wolf shifters, flipping the balance once more. But this time, the royal shifter and the arcane-born accepted their bond, so maybe that, along with these cross-species mates, proves the supernatural world could be in true balance once more, like in the time of the ever-powerful first arcane-born."

My heart soared, loving the sound of that, but Supreme Priestess Olwyn had control of the Eastern supernaturals, potentially Aldric, and no telling how many others, like the vampire in the underground bunker who'd hated me, Warin.

We had very limited allies. Every single one of us could be mated with someone from a different species, and it wouldn't mean shit if we couldn't beat Olwyn and her massive army.

The stress was catching up to me. I almost wanted to lie down and give up. Almost. I'd never turned away from a fight before, and I damn sure wouldn't now. Not when I had more to lose than ever.

As if reading my mind, Priestess Caroline sighed and hung her head. "Faith, that sounds wonderful, but look at the loss we took." She waved a hand at the dead coven members and wolf shifters. "We were attacked for no good reason. The prince left his father's pack, the arcane-born is gaining control but doesn't have the stamina, and we lost a sixth of our coven tonight, making us weaker. There's no way we can influence anyone."

"Wait." Sedona held her injured arm closer to her. "Is that why there weren't more wolf shifters here? Did every single one of you leave King Jovian's pack?"

My stomach lurched. Sedona now knew we were isolated from receiving any extra help. If she'd been a wolf shifter and could pack-link with her people, it would've been worse. At least, as long as we watched her, she couldn't inform the others.

"But why?" She turned to me for answers since the rest of them were in wolf form. Sweat had broken out on her upper lip—a sign that her blood loss was getting worse despite the pressure I'd put on the wound.

There was no reason to lie to her now. She knew the truth. "King Jovian doesn't approve of Raffe and me being together. He wanted Raffe to marry the Atlanta pack's alpha's daughter to prevent the East from splitting."

She held my gaze. "Keagan is a great man. He understood as soon as the words *fated mate* were muttered." Sedona swayed on her feet. "Keagan was fortunate enough to find his fated, and he'd hoped his daughter would have the same blessing. The talk of marriage between her and Raffe was a last-ditch effort to make a peace that neither side truly wanted. Then King Jovian came down hard, informing the East that if we tried to break away, he would force Keagan's businesses and some of the other high-profile, successful companies out of their factories and buildings because Jovian's company owns all the property. It made us desperate. That was when Supreme Priestess Olwyn reached out again because Aldric was busy."

I swallowed hard. I'd forgotten about the huge real estate company that Raffe's father owned. All the chaos had made it seem like the king just ruled the wolves, but he owned the largest commercial real estate company in the United States. My dad had been starstruck when they'd met at the football game, and he'd mentioned that he was a ruthless businessman. This was proof of that; he was holding these peoples' livelihoods over them.

Maybe I could understand why they'd teamed up with Olwyn after all.

I still didn't approve of killing anyone, but if Olwyn had made it sound like I could destroy the world, it would be my life for billions.

Some of my anger toward them melted.

My dad is a fucking bastard. Raffe pawed at the ground. *He came down hard on them to get them in line and, instead, pushed them toward action. He should've known better than that. Aldric should've informed him.*

I winced, knowing the question I had to ask next. "What was Aldric busy doing?"

"He was with the king, so he couldn't contact us." Sedona licked her lips, her words slurring more. "Supreme Priestess Olwyn had to make the call and tell us where you were since they placed tra—" She stumbled, and I caught her, but then we both tumbled over.

I turned, allowing my body to take the brunt of the

impact, protecting her from getting hurt. Pain shot through me, and my vision blurred.

Raffe whimpered, feeling helpless as he used his snout to push Sedona off me. Keith snarled and rushed over to us. Her body went slack as she flopped to the side. She'd passed out.

"Fine." Dru glanced around. "I'll help her. We need to get her back to the house."

"No. You'll all be safer here." Priestess Caroline gestured to their houses. "We have some houses available."

My breath caught as I understood why.

"Take two of our vehicles, grab what you need, and come back." Priestess Caroline bit her bottom lip. "Faith and Avalon will go with you to help."

I'm going to run through the woods and check for danger. Keith edged to the outskirts of the clearing. *But if something happens to her—*

My heart ached. *We'll let you know.*

Dave, Josie, and I should go with him. Adam followed after him. *We're the least injured here, and he shouldn't be alone.*

"Okay, then I need someone to go back to the house and get some of the O blood and suturing supplies." Dru grunted as he lifted Sedona into his arms. "I need to find a better way to slow the bleeding."

"The arcane-born family and her fated mate can stay with me." Priestess Caroline pointed at her house. "Take the prisoner there so we can watch her."

"I'll go with Avalon and Faith since I know where everything is." Fane shoved his hands into his pockets.

"You're not going without me." Octavia marched over to him. "No child of mine will go off like that into danger. I went to find your sister, and I'm going with you now."

His brows rose, and a little bit of a smile broke through. If I hadn't been so miserable, I'd have been happy that he saw he meant just as much to them as I did.

I'm shifting forms and going with them. Lucy darted off toward where her clothes must be.

Everyone split off, and I groaned as I climbed to my feet. Pain raged through me.

Priestess Caroline pointed at Raffe then me. "You two, go to the house. You both need rest. In the morning, we'll need to make a plan." She frowned and looked at all the death that surrounded us. "Tonight, we pay our respects to the dead, but Supreme Priestess Olwyn won't stop at this."

"The animals told me they would watch over us tonight." I tried to stand straight, but my body was too weak. Just being upright made me dizzy.

She raised her brows. "You talk to them?"

"It's the vibrations of my power. They understand me. But my power is drained, and I can't talk to them."

"You're more surprising every day." She pointed at her house. "Go. The first room to the left is a spare bedroom the two of you can rest in. Get sleep. We need you and your mate in good form tomorrow."

"But the dead—"

"Are ours to take care of." Her face softened as if she could see me for the first time. "If we need to, we'll get your friends involved, but we like to send our coven members off personally and pray to the goddess for our enemies."

Maybe we were both seeing a side of each other that we needed to tonight because everything she'd said proved she was the complete opposite of Olwyn.

I nodded and headed toward her house, far too tired to argue. Raffe limped beside me, his pain shining through.

I can't shift back to human form tonight, he linked.

That's more than all right with me. As long as he was beside me, I'd take him in any form. *You're a lot softer with fur.*

His body shook with silent laughter.

As we walked to the priestess's house, I noticed the sizable cracks in her yard and that her house had stress fractures in the wood from the day she'd attacked my mate. She must have protected her house with magic but hadn't been able to fix her yard.

Dru had left the door to the house open, and when we walked in, he had Sedona on the blue couch and was tending to her wounds.

"Do you need—" I started.

"Get some rest." He didn't stop removing the bandage I'd put on her. "I suspect you're the one who put this bandage on her, which prevented her from being worse off. You've done enough."

The scent of rosemary eased the heavy copper scent of blood as we walked through the living room to the first door on the left.

As soon as we entered the room, I slid to the floor. Raffe cuddled up beside me, and I moved so that I lay on his uninjured side, our fated-mate bond thrumming. Within seconds, we were out.

A PHONE RANG, startling me awake. I sat up, my body sore like I'd lifted heavy weights. I jumped to my feet as Raffe ran out the bedroom door.

The sound came again, and we rushed into the living room. Sedona was passed out on the couch with Keith hovering over her in human form. He linked, *It's Sedona's phone.*

I don't have time to shift back and answer, Raffe replied. *Sky, I need you to see who's calling her and why.*

A lump formed in my throat, but I ignored it. I reached into the pocket of her dress and removed the cell.

Mom rolled across the screen.

My stomach dropped, but not wanting it to go to voice mail, I answered it. "Hello?"

The phone line went silent. Then the older woman asked, "Who is this?"

I sucked in a breath, but my voice remained calm. "Skylar Greene."

A sob broke through the phone. "You may have the animals on your side, but I won't bow to someone who killed my daughter."

"She's not dead," I bit out, hoping to catch her before she did something rash like hang up.

"Oh, really?" She laughed bitterly. "Then let me talk to her."

Shit. Of course she'd be passed out. I nudged her arm. "She can't talk right now." I winced, knowing how that must sound from her side.

"That's what I suspected." Her voice hardened. I heard her put down the phone.

I didn't want them to hate us more, so I had to do something. "We want to help you break away from King Jovian."

Raffe's shock soared as Keith turned to me and rasped, "What?"

CHAPTER TWENTY-FIVE

I inhaled harshly. I should've discussed this with Raffe first, but if this person hung up, I doubted she would answer her phone if we tried calling her back once Sedona was up. She'd think we were trying to manipulate her since we couldn't get Sedona on the phone now.

Keith, please wake her up while I delay this woman for as long as possible. I rubbed my temple, trying to hold off a cough. Dirt still clung to the back of my throat, courtesy of Sedona. I hadn't known her for twelve hours, and she was already the biggest pain in my ass. That sure seemed fitting, with her being Keith's fated mate.

"You expect me to believe that the abomination fated to the king's son would help the East?" Her voice was laced with suspicion. "You weren't offering to help last night when you blew up one of my coven member's hands."

"Did you really expect us to help you when you attacked us unprovoked after your daughter buried me *alive* and one of your coven members tried to set my mate on fire?" I hoped this was a test because, if it wasn't, this pri ess felt entitled to a level I would never understand

"Let's make sure last night's incidents remain clear. We were sleeping, bothering no one, when you tried to sneak up on us and attack."

Babe, I'm not sure that helping them get their freedom is the right move. Raffe nudged my leg. *I mean, Dad—*

Won't be happy with us? I arched a brow. *We started a new pack because he didn't want us to be together. This would at least get the East to stop attacking us and prevent them from aligning with the Veiled Circle. I get that you don't want to hurt your dad, but we are in an awful situation, and the Eastern supernaturals, or even Olwyn, could attack us again soon. I'm not sure we'd survive another battle with our small numbers despite Priestess Caroline's coven aligning with us.*

He huffed. *You're right. I hadn't thought of it like that.*

Keith sat on the edge of the couch, and his hand shook as he slowly reached for Sedona and cupped her cheek. His brown irises glowed as soon as their skin touched, his wolf surging forward, likely because of the bond that wanted to be forged between them.

"We were told you were volatile and untrained," the priestess replied, parroting the same thing Sedona had said the night before.

Some of the tension in my body released, allowing me to trust Sedona a smidgen more.

At Keith's touch, Sedona's eyes fluttered, and she moaned. It had to be from the buzz of their connection speaking to her soul.

"Supreme Priestess Olwyn has a way of twisting facts in her favor. The coven here helped me understand my power and how it works." I didn't want to tell her that my fated-mate bond with Raffe helped me handle my power better or that I hadn't been a shifter until the past couple of weeks.

She didn't get to know everything, just the bare minimum. "I understand she's your leader, but she hasn't done my fated mate or my pack any favors."

"She may be my leader, but I feel the same about her as the wolf shifters do about King Jovian. Supreme Priestess Olwyn gave us her word that if we help defeat King Jovian, we will all be free. Besides, do you think I'm foolish enough to believe that the prince hasn't informed his father of what happened? Prince Raffe would have informed him about what was going on as soon as you all figured it out. I'm insulted that you think I would be stupid enough to fall for any of this."

Then why is she staying on the line? Not that I was complaining. I needed Keith to get Sedona up so she could speak to her mom and vouch for how we'd helped her.

She's doing exactly what you are—trying to get information that can help them against us. Raffe hung his head and went to the bedroom where we'd slept, shutting the door behind him. *I may be healed enough to shift back into human form, and that way, if she wants to speak to me, I can talk to her.*

My gut screamed that if Raffe got on the line, this conversation would be over. Her staying on the phone with me surprised me, but he'd grown up preparing to be the next king and expected to handle situations like these.

But sometimes, women didn't want to deal with men in power, and King Jovian had proven he wasn't willing to listen to them, especially not to a woman.

"Keith?" Sedona's eyes cracked open, and a faint smile tugged at the corner of her mouth.

"Yeah, hey." He took her uninjured hand and smiled sweetly, no traces of the sarcastic, mouthy man to be found.

"I've been worried about you all night. You were passed out when we got back here."

"Your silence speaks volumes, my dear," the older woman continued, and I realized I hadn't responded. "That's all I have to say—"

"Sedona is waking, and it distracted me." I rushed the words, making sure she heard them.

She swallowed audibly. "If you're messing with me—"

"I'm not." I cleared my throat to get Sedona's and Keith's attention, barging into their conversation and ruining their moment. "She's waking up. She lost a lot of blood last night from her injury."

Sedona turned her head toward me and lifted her brows when she noted I was on her phone. She tried to sit up but moved only an inch before she groaned and lay flat.

Keith leaned over her. "Don't get up. You need to rest."

"Who is it?" Sedona nodded at him before glancing back at me.

"Your mother." I bit my bottom lip, unsure of what to do. I wanted to hand her the phone, but if she wasn't fully awake, the results could be disastrous, like her mom thinking we were tormenting her. "She called you, and I answered."

The older woman gasped. "If she's awake, give her the phone."

"Do you feel like talking to her?" I lowered the phone a little from my ear and covered the mic. "It'd be great if you could."

She nodded and released Keith so she could take the phone with her uninjured hand.

I handed it to her, unsure if this was the right decision, but not giving her the phone would only anger the East further and make them think we'd done something horrible to her. I had to trust that she and Keith were fated mates and the tug of their bond would compel her to protect him.

Keith's foot bounced against the floor, hinting at his worry.

Raffe strutted from the bedroom door, rejoining us as Sedona placed the phone to her ear and said, "Mom?"

I couldn't help but take in the jeans that were one size too small, clinging to every curve of his muscles and his tight ass, and the shirt was even tighter. The area between my thighs heated, and I shook my head to focus back on the threat instead of how badly I wanted to jump my mate. Now that we were in the same form, the tug to reconnect with him had my head all over the place.

His eyes glowed and met mine, and I felt his need for me mix with mine through our bond.

"Is it really you?" Sedona's mom asked with a sob. "Please let it be. We can still feel your magic as part of us, but that doesn't mean you're safe. Why the hell did you turn back around last night?"

Raffe walked over to me and embraced me from behind, wrapping his arms around my waist gently. I felt a twinge of discomfort, but nothing like when people had touched me last night. Add in the buzz of our connection, and I didn't want out of his arms for a while.

I laid my head on Raffe's chest, and he tucked me under his chin, allowing me to sag against him more.

"Uh, well." Sedona's cheeks reddened, and she averted her attention from Keith's face to the ceiling. "I couldn't leave. Something kept tugging me back, and then a bobcat attacked me."

She told the rest of the story about how we'd found her and helped her. The other end of the line grew quiet. When

Sedona finished, silence hung heavy over the line and in the house.

Why isn't she saying anything? I linked with Raffe. I'd hoped that her mom would be relieved and not want to risk making us mad and taking it out on her daughter.

Most likely because it honestly doesn't make sense. Raffe kissed the top of my head. *They attacked us, so the last thing they expected us to do was heal her and let her sleep on a couch.*

Well, when I was taken, they fed me and kept me in a clean room. That was the only comparison I could make.

"Mom?" Sedona adjusted the phone against her head. "Are you still there?"

"Yeah, I'm here." She sighed. "Just processing it all. That's a story I didn't expect to hear."

You can't compare your kidnapping with what we did for her. That damn society wanted you to join their side and turn you against me. Raffe growled faintly, his chest rumbling against my back. *They were isolating you and spending time trying to make you trust them ... as if they were saving you from me.*

I hung my head, remembering the pictures Glinda and Warin had shown me of Raffe leading the slaughter of vampires. They'd told me that the vampires hadn't done anything wrong, and they'd seeded enough doubt for me to question Raffe after Slade had made me think we'd escaped my captors.

Hey, I'm not upset with you. I'm pissed that they did all that shit to you, and worse, I wasn't understanding about your experience. He kissed the top of my head. *Now I just have to figure out how to keep you out of harm's way because I'm so damn tired of you coming close to dying.*

Finally, Sedona's mother blew out a breath. "Why

should I believe a word you said? What have they been feeding you?"

My heart stopped. That was something my own mother had asked me from time to time when I was out and she thought something was wrong.

What's wrong? Raffe's arm tightened.

It's a test to see if she needs immediate help. Mom knew I got bullied, and if I needed her help, I would tell her I'd either eaten or wanted to eat a baloney sandwich. Because, ew, who would ever want to eat that? I shivered at the thought.

"They haven't fed me anything." Sedona closed her eyes and winced. "I passed out from blood loss and just woke up. There hasn't been an opportunity to eat."

Are you sure? Raffe held his breath.

Yes. I had no clue what their code was, but this would pretty much confirm whether her mom gathered more people to attack or didn't feel pressured.

"You should eat peanut butter," her mom said seriously. "It has healthy fats, and they should have plenty."

"Mom, I'm serious. They helped me. You know I'm allergic to peanut butter."

Well, damn. Raffe shook his head. *You were right.*

"Sedona." Her mom's voice became louder. "You're acting like you aren't in the least bit of danger. You almost killed Prince Raffe's mate. He won't let you go unpunished. You saw what the arcane-born did to Jeff."

"One of the wolf shifters is my fated mate." Sedona closed her eyes like she was bracing for a storm. "And you know that's something I wouldn't lie about. He's the reason they didn't hurt me, and everything Supreme Priestess Olwyn told us isn't true."

"What are you saying?" the older woman asked with much more hesitation.

Sedona told her everything she'd learned last night about how we weren't part of King Jovian's pack anymore and how the animals obeyed my commands. As she neared the end of the story, her voice began to slur again.

She needs to eat something before she passes out. I moved to get out of Raffe's arms, but Keith leaped up and ran past the half wall that separated the kitchen from us. Cabinets opened and closed as he searched for something for her to eat.

A minute later, he rushed back with crackers, cheese, and lemonade. As he sat down, Sedona slurred, "Mom, Keith brought me something to eat. I need to go."

"Let me talk to Raffe, then, and yes, eat."

My chest tightened from Raffe's surprise and determination to do what needed to be done.

Keith took the phone from Sedona and handed it to Raffe, then sat back down and held the lemonade to her mouth. He whispered, "The sugar should help you."

She didn't even hesitate, trusting him, and took a huge gulp.

Raffe settled back into place behind me and said, "This is Raffe, and who is this?"

"I'm Ednah, the priestess over the Atlanta area coven. Is it true you left King Jovian's pack? Because I feel like that's something Aldric would have told Keagan."

"Because Aldric is so trustworthy, betraying his alpha and king the way he is." Raffe's hot anger swirled through our bond. "Yes, I left King Jovian's pack. He didn't support me being with my fated mate, and I'll do whatever it takes to protect her."

"Neither Aldric nor Olwyn told us that the arcane-born

had become a shifter, and I do believe King Jovian would have a hard time accepting that. Dear goddess, I'm struggling to accept what my own daughter just told me. A witch and a wolf shifter? That's unheard of."

"We have a lot of strange pairings happening all around us, so we all understand."

"I will give Sedona credit—she learned a lot during her time with you." Ednah clicked her tongue. "Is what your mate offered true? Can you help us split from King Jovian?"

I regretted offering that now because I hadn't considered the odd spot it would put Raffe in. I turned around, placing my hands on his chest.

"Yes, we will, as long as you and Keagan agree not to attack us. Olwyn is a threat to my mate, and believe me when I say she has no plans for any of you to be truly free." Raffe glanced at me, arching a brow, and gave me a tight smile. *You're right. It's better to make an alliance with them instead of having a whole other group wanting us dead.* His warmth floated into me, easing my worry about him being mad at me.

"Are you proposing the Eastern supernaturals submit to you in order to free us from the current king?"

The walls closed in on me. I hadn't considered how we'd free them, and I hadn't considered the Eastern wolves submitting to Raffe as a valid option.

Jaw set, Raffe straightened. "No. I'd help Keagan get things settled, and the Eastern supernaturals could form whatever leadership they want as long as they promise to let my small pack live among you all unharmed."

"How is that going to work with your father owning the real estate properties he's holding over us?" She arched a brow.

"Dad owns forty-nine percent of the company

shares. My grandfather left me a trust, and when I turn twenty-three—in a month—I will receive forty-nine percent of the company as well, with the remaining one percent being owned by newer startups that will want to align with me, the future of the company. So we'll have equal stakes, with Aldric having one percent ownership on the Veiled Circle side. We can make it a stalemate, and I can offer to give Aldric control if he agrees to sell the properties in the East to Keagan. But only if you promise that my pack and my fated mate will be safe."

My head spun. *Wait. You can't do that.*

If it means you're safe and we end the Veiled Circle and can decide our own lives, I'm all fucking for it. Raffe's eyes glowed.

But you'll be poor, and—

Babe, we'll both have amazing degrees. I'm not worried about money. As long as we're together and free, it'll all be damn worth it. You can be a vet, and I can ... well, I can do any damn thing I want, like build motorcycles and own a garage. Yeah, maybe it won't be the future I expected, but it'll be better because you'll be by my side.

"I can't make the decision on my own." Ednah swallowed. "I need to make some phone calls. I'll get in touch when I have something to tell you."

"Sounds good." Raffe nodded.

"But Raffe," Ednah spoke loudly. "If any harm comes to my daughter, everything is off the table."

Raffe smirked. "And if anything happens to us, the same thing goes for you and your daughter's health. She may be fated to one of my shifters, but if you threaten us again, it won't go unpunished. Talk soon." He then hung up the phone.

"What the *hell*?" Keith stood, holding a half-empty glass and cheese. "You can't—"

"I don't plan on it, but man, they can't know they have us by the balls." Raffe pointed at Sedona and growled, "But if you try hurting my mate again, I don't—"

She lifted her uninjured hand. "I won't. I swear. I didn't know all of this. None of us did. We aren't bad people. We just want our freedom, and they didn't paint you in the best light." She glanced at me. "I'm sorry for almost killing you." She winced.

Raffe's ire increased, and my mouth went dry, making the dirt crustier to deal with. I coughed. "I'm not sure how to respond to that."

I do, he replied to me, his arms shaking.

"Where is everyone?" In all the commotion, I realized no one had come out to join us. I sniffed the air, noticing that the only strong smells belonged to the four of us.

Keith sat back on the couch, giving the cup and cheese back to Sedona, and answered, "Caroline never came here, and Dru left a couple hours ago to find Octavia and Fane once he knew Sedona wasn't in danger anymore. Octavia, Fane, and Lucy stayed in the house next door so they wouldn't disturb those here who were worse off."

My body sagged harder. I never realized that Caroline had never come home. That was how out of it I'd been.

I needed a shower and to get out of these clothes before I did anything else. "I'm going to clean up and see if there's anything I can do to help them."

"There's a bathroom attached to the room we're in. I'll go with you to make sure you don't fall." Raffe took my hand and led me to the bedroom.

"Yeah, that's what you're going to do." Keith snorted. "We'll just be right here."

"I'm okay with that," Sedona sighed.

Raffe and I hurried to the bedroom before we all got uncomfortable.

He was right, though—Raffe and I couldn't keep our hands off each other.

I breezed through the bedroom, noting that someone had put a pair of jeans and a lilac shirt on the bed's light-green comforter, along with my underwear. Octavia must have grabbed some of our things while getting supplies. I arched a brow. "How did you get clothes that were too small? Not that I'm complaining."

"She grabbed some of Fane's by accident." Raffe frowned and shut the door.

Some of the heat I felt for him ebbed and I froze. "You're wearing my brother's underwear?"

"Fuck no." He shook his head and unfastened the jeans, dropping them down. He sprang free and hard with no barrier in between.

My breath caught, and I wanted to go to him, to kiss every inch of him and touch him all over, but I felt gross. "I need to get clean."

He nodded. "I can take care of that."

We entered the bathroom, where I almost cried tears of relief when I noticed a shower. I didn't know what I'd expected. Maybe a tub? And I didn't want to soak in my own filth. I turned on the water, and Raffe dug around in the closet to the right and removed two large towels.

I stripped off the dress and hurried into the shower, not bothering to wait for it to get warm. I allowed the cold water to drip all over me and opened my lips, taking big mouthfuls and spitting it out into the porcelain tub.

Slowly, the water warmed, and soon, I was taking gulps of water. My throat had been parched.

The pale-yellow shower curtain shifted as Raffe climbed in behind me. His eyes scanned me, and my breath caught.

Need bloomed within me as I ogled him from head to toe, every inch of him chiseled and huge—pure perfection.

He was sexy, kind, and all mine.

He murmured, "I thought I lost you last night."

Turning toward him, I let the water run through my hair and down my body. "You didn't, so let's not dwell on that." I noted some tea tree oil shampoo and reached for it when he gently grabbed my arm.

He shook his head. "Let me do it. I need to take care of you." He paused. "Please. Sometimes, I need you to need me."

My stomach fluttered. "Of course I need you." I turned around, making it clear that I wanted him to clean me.

His strong fingers tangled in my hair, caressing my scalp and giving me a massage. I moaned, the sensation feeling so good and more sensual than I'd ever known. When I turned to rinse the shampoo from my head, he squirted the conditioner in one hand and took a bar of soap in the other. Turning around, he worked the conditioner into the ends of my hair while his other hand rubbed the bar of soap over my body.

After a minute, he used both hands to clean my body and placed the soap back on its shelf. I turned to rinse off, but he shook his head and connected, *I'm not done yet.*

His left hand cupped my breast, rubbing soap along my nipples, while the other one slipped between my legs. A knot of desperate need clenched inside me, and I leaned against the back wall of the shower, allowing the water to wash over my body. He locked eyes with mine as his thumb caressed my nipples and his fingers slid within my folds.

Friction built deep within me, and I gasped as ecstasy slammed through me.

You are so fucking sexy, he linked, watching every expression on my face as he destroyed me.

After my body stopped quivering, I smiled wickedly and grabbed his dick. "My turn."

He grinned. "Not complaining."

I moved him around, switched spots, let him go, and grabbed the bottle of shampoo.

"Hey!" He reached to grab my wrist. "That's not what you hinted at."

I smacked his hand away. "I'm clean, so now you gotta be too."

He pretended to pout but squatted so that I could reach the top of his head. Just like he'd taken care of me, I washed his hair.

When he spun around to rinse the shampoo, he linked, *No conditioner. I just need my body washed.* He winked, making me laugh.

I didn't complain since this was the part I'd been looking forward to most—cleaning his body. I followed every curve of muscle and slid my hand downward to find him hard.

He shuddered as I stroked him, trying to make him feel like he'd made me feel. His hips swiveled, increasing the rhythm, and he leaned toward me, kissing me.

These were the moments that made me feel sane. With us together like this, the rest of the world melted away. Our connection needed this.

He kissed down my neck, and I moaned, wanting to keep going, but he lifted me, placing my back against the wall as he slid inside me. We were already panting, our souls reaching for each other.

I wanted to tease you longer, I linked, my body tensing, needing that release.

He nipped at my throat and quickened the tempo. *I need to be deep inside you.*

His words had my wolf howling, and I dug my fingers into his back, needing to mark him the way he was marking me. He groaned as his fingers dug deeper into my skin.

Our bond opened and reached out to connect our souls, and he released his hold, taking my hands and pinning them against the wall as he kissed me again.

We orgasmed at the same time, our pleasure blending. Our tongues worked in sync as the strongest euphoria we'd ever experienced exploded between us. I wasn't sure how long the high lasted, but when we came down, the water was lukewarm.

Guiding me back under the stream, he rinsed us off.

We'd climbed out of the shower and were getting dressed when Keith linked, *We need you out here and fast. Keagan's on the line.*

CHAPTER TWENTY SIX

The little bit of peace that Raffe and I had shared floated away, though my limbs were still weak from the amazing exertion.

Raffe groaned, pulling the tight jeans over his legs and carefully zipping up so his dick didn't get caught since he still was going commando. *I'll need to go back to the house and get the right fucking size. I can't handle this any longer.*

Not going to lie; I enjoy seeing you like this, but I won't feel that way when other women get the same courtesy. It wasn't nearly as good as seeing him naked, but I did enjoy seeing all the curves of his muscles in the tight clothing.

Babe, you get to see what's underneath my clothes anytime you want to. He winked. *You don't need me to wear clothes like this. You have special privileges.* He opened the door and marched through the bedroom.

I ran the brush through my hair and glanced in the mirror. My cognac eyes were bright again, likely from Raffe and I reconnecting, but there were dark circles under my eyes from the hell we'd been through the night before.

With our lives hanging in the balance, I didn't have time

to worry about appearances. I put down the brush and hurried after Raffe. I didn't want to miss a moment of the conversation. *I didn't expect a decision so soon.* I wasn't sure if a quick call was a good sign or bad.

Me neither. The muscles in Raffe's back tensed, causing them to bulge through his shirt.

As soon as we stepped back into the living room, I was surprised to see Sedona sitting up on the couch with Dru next to her, replacing her bandages. Octavia sat beside Dru, her face strained, with Adam, Lucy, and Fane standing behind the couch. My nose picked up a heavier rosemary scent, so I glanced into the kitchen to find Priestess Caroline holding a steaming mug while leaning against the doorframe. Her face was pale and wrinkled more than normal from exhaustion.

Octavia homed in on me, and her shoulders sagged with relief. She murmured, "Thank gods, you both look almost normal."

Yeah, it was probably a good thing that I hadn't looked at myself before the shower. I'd have been a lot more self-conscious now if Raffe hadn't made me feel truly loved and cherished. But no wonder he'd wanted to take care of me.

Josie and Dave were missing. That was strange, but they had just cemented their bond and might have needed to reconnect like Raffe and me.

Keith stepped away from the side of the couch where he'd been standing next to Sedona and held out the phone. "Keagan is refusing to talk to anyone but you."

"I sure hope you know what you're doing." Priestess Caroline arched a brow. "Making a deal with someone who attacked you is foolish, almost worse than bringing home the woman who almost killed Skylar."

Raffe's hands fisted at his sides, and his neck corded.

"I'm doing this to *protect* Skylar. There is nothing more important to me than that, so I don't appreciate your accusations."

I hurried to his side, slid my hand into his, making his hand unclench, and pushed calm toward him through our bond. I felt his anger ease slightly as our connection sprang to life.

Priestess Caroline pointed a finger at me and rasped, "The only people protecting your mate effectively are herself and *us*, so why do you get to decide whether we work with the enemy who killed twenty of my coven members last night when you didn't lose anyone?"

"Uh …" Keith cleared his throat. "I don't know how long Keagan is willing to wait, but should I—"

There was no way I would let him finish that sentence with the tension between Caroline and us right now. I stepped forward and lifted a hand. "Priestess Caroline, you're right. You lost people, people you care about, and somehow, we didn't. But Raffe didn't start the conversation; I did. He wasn't happy about it at first, but believe me, it's better to make an alliance—and Raffe is the only one who can make this one because of his position in his family company—so we have somewhere safe to go and none of us have to lose anyone else. This is about protecting all of us and preventing the entirety of the Eastern people from threatening to attack us again and again."

"We didn't want to attack you." Sedona glanced over her shoulder at the priestess. "You've got to believe me. If Keagan and my mother can find another way to break from King Jovian, they'll take it in a heartbeat. Raffe has a way."

"You know I respect you more than anything." Octavia stood and turned so she could see everyone in the room, but she addressed the priestess. "But Skylar's right. If we don't try something, they'll attack again. It's not a matter of *if*. Next time, they'll bring more people."

Priestess Caroline waved a hand. "Fine. Proceed. Though don't be surprised when you get betrayed."

A deep growl emanated from Raffe, and I squeezed his hand. I linked, *Take the call. We both think this is what's best. She's tired and not thinking clearly after losing so many of her people. Imagine how she must feel.*

He exhaled and rolled his shoulders. *You're right. It's just—*

I know. I understood that he didn't like her insinuation. *Just take the call, and let's see what they have to say. We could be arguing over nothing.*

You're doing the right thing, Lucy connected with everyone in the room, giving Raffe a reassuring smile. *I'd tell you if I disagreed.*

This is the safest bet for all of us. Adam nodded, giving his consent.

Raffe took the phone from Keith, unpressed mute, and placed it to his ear. "Hello."

A smooth, older, masculine voice came across the line. "Is this Prince Raffe?"

"Nope." Raffe smirked. "Just Raffe. I'm not a prince anymore."

"So Priestess Ednah informed me, but I find that hard to believe. Why would someone walk away from power like that? Especially a strong wolf like yourself."

My stomach churned, and the weight of the world settled on my shoulders. This conversation already wasn't going well, and all the hope I had about finding somewhere safe for us felt like it was slipping between my fingers.

Hey, it's going to be okay. Raffe's warm eyes focused on me. *He has to ask these questions and hear this for himself.*

He's testing me. If he didn't, I'd be more worried. He then said out loud, "Nothing is more important to me than my fated mate's safety and having a long life together. You should know that since I refused your and my father's plan to bridge the gap between us. You don't want to kill my fated mate—or that's what your coven told us—but you attacked us to find a way to get your freedom. I have a solution that will gain you that without getting more blood on your hands, and I hope that counts for something."

"Yes, I've heard. I find it interesting. But why should I trust you to follow through on your word?"

"There's nothing I can do to make that guarantee. You aren't here, so you can't smell if I'm lying or not, just the same as I can't pick up on whether I can trust you in return." Raffe paused and sighed. "Still, you have more assurances than we do. One of your own that you trust has vouched for our story and how we've treated her."

Keagan laughed darkly. "I'd say you have the upper hand because you have someone you're already aware is very important to us, and of course she'll vouch for you. You're standing around her as she talks to us. Unlike you and the other Western supernaturals, vampires, witches, and shifters get along here. We care for each other like families, and that's something that bothers your father and, from what I've heard, you as well."

"Yeah, well." Raffe closed his eyes. "When you're fated to an arcane-born, the people you love have their own strange fated-mate connections, and your strongest ally is a coven, it puts a lot of shit into perspective."

"Which may include one of our own," Keagan growled in frustration. "May I talk with Sedona?"

Raffe glanced at the witch and scowled. "Why? She's already talked to her mother."

"Because I have a few questions to ask her myself. Or is there a reason you don't want to put her on the line?"

"Fine, but you only have a few minutes." Raffe held the phone out to Sedona.

She leaned forward and took it while the rest of us glanced at each other.

What was your read on the call so far? Raffe linked to everyone here.

I think he's considering it. Adam placed his hands behind his back. *He's nervous, which makes me believe he's more genuine, but I don't know if it's going to work.*

"Alpha Keagan?" Sedona cleared her throat. "How's Mom?"

"She's beside herself." Keagan's tone warmed. "As we all are. Do you trust them? Because his actions sure remind me of King Jovian, despite his words."

His question was so blunt that it took me by surprise. He should know that every wolf near them could hear their conversation.

"They seem sincere, and they did help me last night and have fed me and changed my bandages this morning." Sedona glanced down.

"If they are sincere, they would let you go and not hold you hostage." Keagan's voice hardened. "Keeping you doesn't help them at all."

Unfortunately, he was right. Yes, we might have helped the priestess's daughter, but that didn't mean we wouldn't eventually harm her. They could attack us even if we kept her with us. *We should let her go.*

Keith's head jerked toward me, his jaw dropping. *What? No way. We should keep her here for security.*

That wasn't the real reason he didn't want us to let her loose, and I doubted any of us here believed him.

We're in negotiations because of Sedona. Raffe gestured to the witch as if I hadn't remembered.

Because her mom called her. Otherwise, we'd still be screwed. We can use her mom's relationship with her to get Keagan to listen, but he's still hesitant. I didn't need to be trained to pick up on that, and if I were him, after experiencing all we had with Olwyn and Aldric, I'd feel the same way. *They have no reason to trust anything she says, so we need to give them a reason.*

What? No! Keith shook his head, forgetting all about the conversation Sedona was having. *She needs to stay with us.*

Adam rubbed his hands together. *Unfortunately, I think Sky's right. Just because we have her doesn't mean they won't attack again.*

And hand her back to the enemy so she can attack us again? Lucy's brows furrowed.

You're right. Raffe hung his head. The hope he'd had moments ago vanished. *Keeping her doesn't give us any real advantage. Sending her back might be the only thing that proves we're different from my dad and the others.*

In the end, Priestess Caroline might have been right, but at least we'd tried something. It was better than refusing to speak to the enemy. And though I would never say this out loud, if we were going to be defeated, we'd do it with morals. We wouldn't resort to the same threats and actions as our enemy, and that had to damn well count for something. *We need to show we're different.*

Raffe nodded and held out his hand. "Here, I need to talk to him again."

"Uh, my time's up." Sedona mashed her lips together. "Tell Mom I love her."

I grimaced. Though I knew Sedona realized she wasn't at risk here, those words made it sound as if she was afraid she might not ever get to tell her mom that again. I wanted to smack her, but she had to be scared, and I couldn't blame her.

Muting the phone, Raffe pivoted to Dru and asked, "How long until she's stable enough to move?"

"She's fine now as long as she takes it slow." Dru snorted. "You supernaturals and your healing. She can't walk for miles, but she's fine to move around."

"Good." Raffe unmuted the phone. "Keagan, I'm assuming Priestess Ednah is close by, seeing as we have her daughter. Tell her if she comes to the house that they were going to attack, she will find Sedona there, and she'll be free to take her."

"What?" Sedona gasped, her uninjured hand clutching her chest.

"Is this a joke, or do you plan on attacking my people?"

"Neither." Raffe's hand tightened on mine like he needed to remind himself I was here. "But my mate agrees with you. Keeping Sedona here is pointless despite one of my pack members claiming she's his mate. If they're fated, they'll figure out a way back together, so there's no reason for her not to go home."

"How do I know they won't be attacked? What assurance can you give me?"

Raffe sneered. "None, the same way we have no assurances you won't attack us. If you don't want your priestess pissed at you, I suggest you tell them to be here in thirty minutes. That's all the time we need to get her up to the house, and it will ensure you don't have time to regroup and launch an attack. This is a less-than-ideal situation for both of us."

"What if they don't come?" Keagan challenged.

"Then she's more than welcome to stay with us." Raffe

shrugged. "That'll help me with Keith and his bitching. The decision is up to you. I'm done wasting time and energy talking. You want to see if I'm like my father? Well, here's your chance." He hung up the phone and tossed it back to Sedona.

Keith's face reddened, and his nostrils flared. "What the actual *fuck*? If that was Skylar, you wouldn't be handing her over to them!"

"Wait." Fane rocked back on his heels. "I'm so lost. I get that she and Keith are fated, but aren't we just handing her back to her own people? Why be upset about that unless it's because they attacked us last night?"

"I'm for handing the girl back over." Priestess Caroline walked into the kitchen. "She doesn't need to be here, watching everything we do. Can one of you link with Josie so she can let Faith and Avalon know they'll need to gather some members to go up there with you? Between us and the animals still hanging around the woods, they shouldn't attack right away. Then we need to get some rest."

I hated that they hadn't slept after dealing with the dead, but we needed to try something different. Even if they didn't ally with us, we would need to find another place to hide and hope I could control my power enough so Olwyn couldn't locate us.

"Listen, I can go back to my people and vouch for you." Sedona stood on wobbly feet. "If they see I'm not under duress, it will go better, and any shifter will know I'm not lying."

Keith reached out to steady her, but he scowled. "What if they don't listen and I don't ever see you again?"

Uh … we should give them a minute alone. I caught Octavia's and Dru's gazes and nodded toward the door, wanting them to come with us.

When I went to catch Fane's attention, I noticed that Lucy's and Fane's eyes were faintly glowing at the same time, and they moved toward the door as if they'd spoken without words.

I froze.

What's wrong? Raffe scanned the room for whatever had caught my attention.

Maybe I was seeing things, so I linked with my brother and Lucy and asked, *Did you two complete the bond?*

The corners of Lucy's mouth tipped upward as she made her way to the door. *Yes, we did last night.*

And you can link with him? Is he becoming a shifter? I didn't know how any of this worked anymore since I'd become a wolf myself.

We can link, but I don't know about him turning into a wolf. Lucy held the door open as Octavia and Dru walked out.

Oh, gods. Raffe groaned faintly. *How much more chaotic can all this shit get?*

I smacked him in the chest, but the weight of the world settled. *Stop. I'm glad my brother found her.*

Outside, the sun was out and shining down on us, and realization jolted through me. *Wait. Lucy and I are now sisters!*

She smiled and moved closer to Fane. "We are. I'm so glad you're okay with it. We were worried about how everyone would react, so we told Dru and Octavia this morning. Thankfully, they were fine with it as well."

Adam rolled his eyes. "Unfortunately, I got to be in the bedroom next to them when it happened."

No wonder everyone had been absent this morning, and I couldn't complain; Raffe and I had needed our own time alone. None of us knew how much longer we had left, but I tried to push the worrisome thought away.

"I'm just happy that both my kids found the love of their lives," Octavia sighed while placing a hand on Dru's arm. "Though I never dreamed they would be wolf shifters."

"As much as I hate to ruin this moment, we need to discuss what we're going to do when we get to the house." Adam's jaw clenched. "What if they come here to fight?"

Fair question. I looked around the neighborhood, but I didn't see any of the animals from last night. I closed my eyes for a second and felt a faint hissing inside me from a spot close to my wolf magic.

"The coven members will be with us, and we got some rest," Raffe answered. "You, Lucy, and Josie can be in wolf form, while Keith, Skylar, and I stay in human form to make the swap."

Even as I listened to the conversation, I continued to be puzzled by what I felt inside. I tried pulling on the hiss, and it flared to a faint jolt.

Holy shit. I'd found my power. The jolt had been faint, my power still tired, but it was there, giving me hope I could connect with the animals. I tugged at it a little more and asked, *Are you all okay?*

"Are you sure Keith should be there?" Dru asked. "He might have a hard time letting her go."

Raffe huffed. "He won't be able to stay away. If they are fated mates, I understand damn well how he's feeling. All we'll do is fight if we try to keep him away."

When I was about to give up on receiving a response, the strange, converged answer came through: *Yes, do you need us?*

My heartbeat quickened. I could speak to them again, and for some reason, that made me feel more whole.

We need to meet with people at the house, but we don't want to attack them unless they wish us harm. I swallowed, hating to ask for more from them. *Can you be near us in case they attack?*

Of course. Anything you need, they replied almost together.

"The animals are going to help us again and be there in case Keagan's people try to harm us." I opened my eyes to find all six of them staring at me.

"You just talked to them?" Fane arched a brow.

I bit my bottom lip. "Yeah. Is that not okay? I sorta can feel my power now, even though I'm not upset, and I was able to reach out to them."

Raffe turned to me, cupping my cheek. "You're fucking amazing."

"I'm just glad she won't be breaking our furniture anymore," Lucy teased. "I never replaced the coffee table because she has such a knack for destroying things."

That was the night I'd come home to learn that Raffe was Lucy's cousin, and he'd had his arm around Josie, pretending to be with her. The hurt had taken me by surprise, and I'd lost control. It was so strange that it was not even months ago when everything had gone down.

The door to the house next door opened, and Josie, Dave, Avalon, and Faith stepped outside. Avalon and Faith had dark circles under their eyes, but they headed over.

"We have coven members in the woods heading up to the house, so we should get going." Avalon yawned and rubbed her face. "I just hope we don't have to fight again because we're drained."

"Adam, Lucy, and Josie, shift and join them." Raffe

pointed to a group of women heading into the woods. "We'll get Sedona and head up there."

"I'll stay close to Josie and run ahead to make sure I don't see anything." Dave crossed his arms. "I can let Josie know if something seems odd."

He could run faster than any of us.

"Okay." Raffe gestured to Octavia, Dru, and Fane. "You should remain here."

"What? But Lucy—" Fane started.

Mom cut him off, "If something happens and you get hurt, Lucy will be distracted. She's a supernatural, and you're not, so it'll be safer for her if you stay back. Believe me, I don't like it any more than you do, especially with her and Skylar in danger."

Fane's jaw clenched, but he nodded. He kissed Lucy before he backed away and watched her, Adam, Josie, and Dave hurry away.

Keith, come on. We need to move, Raffe linked and winced, knowing that Keith wouldn't be happy with what was going on.

While we waited for Sedona and Keith, I scanned the neighborhood. If I hadn't been involved in the fight, I never would've known that something had happened. The place looked normal, though something sinister hung in the air that could only be described as death. I hoped that the souls had found peace.

Sedona, Keith, and Priestess Caroline came out, and the five of us followed the gravel road toward the house, leaving Octavia, Dru, and Fane behind.

Our pace was slow since we didn't want to push Sedona. The sun kept the chill at bay, and I tried to enjoy being out in nature.

The animals are arriving, Josie linked. *Dave sees them. That's the only thing as of now.*

Good. We wanted to get there before Priestess Ednah and her group.

Gravel crunched under our feet. Raffe and I held hands, and I noticed that Sedona and Keith kept staring at each other as if this might be the last time they ever saw one another.

My heart ached. I wished I could promise them that everything would be okay.

We reached the spot in front of the house.

Is everyone in place? Raffe linked with our pack.

We are, Adam replied. *There're at least a hundred animals here that we can see, and the coven is circling the backyard.*

The five of us stood and waited, listening to the sound of birds singing from nearby trees.

After what felt like hours, Lucy linked, *I see wolves.*

An engine purred, heading in our direction.

My breath caught. *Why are they coming in a car?*

Sedona's weak. They don't want to make her walk, and they'll want to get her out fast before we change our minds, Raffe answered, brushing his arm against mine.

A black Navigator appeared and came to a slow stop several feet from us.

The wolves stopped moving forward, Adam replied. *They're staying fifty feet back.*

My heart hammered. Maybe they hadn't come in attacking, but I wasn't sure what the future held.

Then, the driver, passenger, and back passenger doors opened.

A tall, burly man with a thick beard stepped from the

driver's side. He was almost the same size as Raffe and alpha power radiated from him. Keagan.

The woman from the front passenger seat stood tall, nearly six feet, with dark-blue eyes that matched Keagan's. She looked close to our age, which made me think she was his daughter.

The one Raffe was supposed to marry.

A deep growl escaped me, my wolf surging forward. My power grew in strength, flaring straight to a high fizz as I studied the woman who could have taken Raffe from me had King Jovian gotten his way. *Is that Keagan's daughter?*

CHAPTER TWENTY-SEVEN

I think so, Raffe linked, and he pushed calm toward me. *Remember, you're the one I chose, and you're my fated mate, the only person who matters to me.*

Some of the anger ebbed, though my wolf remained alert within me. I took a deep breath, remembering what Sedona had said: The girl hadn't wanted to be with Raffe either. That was something King Jovian and Keagan had come up with together.

The older woman in the back stepped forward, her long, silver hair reflecting sunlight. My breath caught as I remembered her from last night. She was the witch who had used water magic on me, and it hadn't worked.

Her eyes homed in on Sedona, and she took a ragged breath. With my power so high, I could sense their fear, hesitation, and wariness. They didn't trust us and were nervous.

"Mom, I'm fine." Sedona gestured to Raffe and me. "What I said on the phone is true. They helped and saved me. They did me no harm."

"Good." Keagan remained at the door and examined Sedona's wrapped forearm. "We've been worried about you. Let's get you back with the others so you can get some rest."

Priestess Caroline cleared her throat from her spot on the opposite side of Keith and almost in front of Ednah. Standing tall, she said, "We may have given her grace this one time, but it's the only time that will happen. Attacking us again will be considered a declaration of war, and no lives will be spared on our front, the same as you didn't spare any of my coven, who'd never done a damn thing to you." Despite her words, I sensed her fury.

"We didn't have a real choice," Ednah rasped.

"No, you made that choice." Priestess Caroline wrinkled her nose. "And broke the sacred oath of doing no harm to others."

"I made that call." Keagan lifted his head high. "If you're angry at anyone, it should be me."

Raffe chuckled darkly. "Oh, believe me, we're furious with all of you equally. The only reason I'm not ripping your throat out is because my mate asked me to be understanding. But I agree with Priestess Caroline. You try harming my mate in any way again, and I won't hesitate to kill you."

Faint paw steps sounded to our right, and I turned my head to see Adam stepping out of the trees in wolf form. The young woman's head snapped in that direction. Her brows furrowed, and she shook her head faintly.

Something akin to interest and confusion swirled from both of them.

"Understood." Keagan waved toward the vehicle. "We should get going."

The young woman frowned and glanced at Keagan as he moved to climb back into the car.

"Come on." Ednah held out her hand to her daughter. Desperation clung to her like a cloak, and her eagerness to leave slammed into me.

I noted Keith's hands clenched at his sides.

My heart ached for him. Even though I could read his emotions, I could only imagine the turmoil he was feeling. Watching Raffe walk away with no certainty of when I'd see him again would be the hardest thing in the world.

"I can't," Sedona whispered and remained still. Resolve sang from her.

"What?" Ednah asked as her brows lifted, her emotions a blend of surprise and terror.

My heart dropped into my stomach, fearing what their reactions might cause them to do.

Alarm rang from Keagan as he tensed and growled to the young woman, "Stephanie, get in the damn car." His eyes glowed, indicating he was linking with his pack. "This is a trap."

Be ready. He's going to attack, Raffe linked and grabbed my wrist, pulling me back.

Out of all the situations, I hadn't expected *this*. Why the hell would she let us set this up only to pretend she couldn't hand herself over? Had she played on Keith and her connection to finish what they'd started?

How had I been so foolish as to give her another chance? My power hummed, and I readied to connect with the animals.

"It's *not* a trap." Sedona took a few hurried steps to stand between the groups. Her determination shot through me like an arrow. She wobbled, proving that her blood loss was still affecting her. "They aren't forcing me to do anything, and they didn't tell me I had to." She turned her back to us, facing the three of them. "I swear to you that everything I've said is true, and I do believe that Raffe can help us break away from the king like he promised."

"We'll take that into consideration once we get you out of here." Keagan's neck corded. His emotions were those of concern and wariness. "We don't have to talk about this *here*."

Sedona huffed, and I watched her hands tremble. "I'm sorry, but I can't leave. I don't want to."

"This isn't a request, Sedona." Ednah rubbed her hands together. "You need to come back with us. We're your family and coven."

If she doesn't leave, we may have to fight them, Raffe linked, his frustration evident. *And this would've been better not to do, but that's where we're at.*

"I know that, but he's my fated mate." She looked at Keith and bit her bottom lip before staring back at them. "And I can't leave him, knowing we might not see each other again because of some misguided quest to break free from King Jovian. They could've let the bobcat kill me, but they didn't." She gestured to me, and her voice rose. "*She* stopped it and convinced the others to help me even after I tried to kill her. If that doesn't show they're different, I don't know what would."

If she wants to stay, I won't force her to leave with them, Keith replied, moving next to Sedona.

"Sedona Butler," Ednah gritted out.

Hand twitching, Raffe leaned forward, readying to grab Keith back.

Instead, I caught his hand in mine. If they wanted to be together, there was no way in hell I would stop them. I squeezed Raffe's hand comfortingly and linked, *Remember what it was like when people tried to keep us apart? We know better than to try to do that, right? They're determined to be together, and who are we to stop them? I can feel their resolve. We don't want to lose Keith.*

Stephanie glanced from Sedona to Adam then back to the young witch. Her emotions flared, and I felt her settle on something.

She shut the passenger side door. "If Sedona trusts them, we should too."

Shock filtered both ways through our bond, and Raffe interlaced his fingers with mine.

That little action told me everything—he agreed. I didn't even need to be around to read or feel his emotions, though I could. We wouldn't prevent her from staying here if that's what they wanted.

"That's not your decision to make." Keagan opened his door wider. Though his face tensed slightly, I could feel panic swirling inside him. "They could attack us at any second. For all we know, Sedona's been coerced to comply."

"Has there been any hint of a lie?" Raffe asked, rocking back on his heels. "Have your priestess come forward to see if any magic has been placed on Sedona to hide her lies or force her to do something she doesn't want to. Also, if we were going to attack, we wouldn't be standing out here, allowing you to doubt us. We would've already taken action. If you don't want to stay here, that's fine. You can leave. But if Sedona wants to remain with us to be with Keith, then we'll accept her."

Keith turned slightly, a huge smile on his face. *Are you serious? I thought you'd alpha-will me to give her up.*

My heart ached, remembering how King Jovian had tried to do that very thing to Raffe and me. The regret that pulsed from Raffe made me confident he was remembering the same thing. Thanks to our fated-mate bond, he'd been able to fight his father's control.

"We both know how well that went when Dad tried that with me," Raffe growled as he tugged me to his side and wrapped his arm around my waist.

Keagan tilted his head back. "King Jovian tried to keep you from your fated mate?"

"In order to marry your daughter." Raffe's hold tightened.

The buzz of our connection eased my wolf, preventing me from getting more upset at the memory.

Stephanie cringed. "I'd never agree to that, especially if you found your fated. I wasn't happy with the arrangement and was relieved when I heard you'd found someone already."

My wolf settled completely, reading that she hadn't been interested in my mate in the least. "Then why agree to the betrothal if you didn't want to?" I asked, needing to understand what had driven her decision.

She bit her lip. "If it was something I had to do in order for the royals to listen to our desires and realize that what we were requesting was actually a need, I would've done it. Begrudgingly."

Adam snarled and shook his fur, forcing us to turn in his direction. Anger radiated from him.

Immediately, Keagan and Ednah tensed.

Stand down. Raffe's eyes glowed, and power laced his command.

Adam's fur remained raised, and he growled deeply.

"But I didn't want to do it in the least. I want to find my fated mate and have what my parents share," Stephanie added softly, focused on him.

His fur lowered on the nape of his neck like those were the words he'd needed to hear.

What in the hell is going on? Lucy connected. *Has everyone lost their damn minds? One minute, the conversation is going well, and the next, it feels like we might attack each other.*

I couldn't argue with her. We did need to get hold of the situation, especially if both Sedona and Stephanie were siding with us. Right now, everyone felt confused. "Look, I get that we don't trust each other, but we have more reason to distrust than you do. You attacked us not even twelve hours ago."

"He's the king's son." Keagan pointed at Raffe like no one knew who he meant and said, "He stands to lose everything by turning his back on his father, so forgive me if I don't trust you all either."

Raffe gritted his teeth. "I told you—"

"Try to link with him," I offered. That was the simplest solution to all of this. We could say words all day, but actions and facts were things we couldn't dispute. "If he's still part of the pack, you'll be able to. When you can't, you'll see that he's left it. Then have your priestess test Sedona to confirm we've done nothing to her." We were wasting time—time everyone needed to rest and recover from a pointless attack.

Stephanie snorted. "That's easy enough to test, especially this close."

I smiled at her, warming to her even more.

"Fine." Keagan shut his door, stepping around the hood of the SUV. His eyes glowed as he stared at Raffe. After a few minutes, his jaw went slack. "I can't feel you." Surprise became his dominant emotion. "You really did leave the pack." He glanced at Ednah. "Check Sedona like they said. They could be telling the truth after all."

Ednah wrung her hands and scanned the area. She seemed hesitant to get closer to us.

"Here," Sedona said and moved toward her. She held out her hands to her mom.

Taking Sedona's hands, Ednah closed her eyes, and her determination was easy to read. It slowly changed to confusion, and her eyes opened. "She doesn't have any magic affecting her."

"I told you." Sedona smiled sadly. "I would never lead you into danger."

Keagan shook his head. "I would've never imagined that any of this was possible. Why did the Veiled Circle send us to you if you aren't with the king? Especially with Aldric knowing his daughter was among you. I thought it was strange when we stumbled upon Josie here."

Raffe flinched, and my chest constricted. This was official confirmation of Aldric's actions, and Josie was nearby to hear it.

"Worse, he put the trackers on your vehicles for the Veiled Circle." Keagan gestured to our three vehicles, which were parked at the edge of the gravel driveway.

"Wait." Keith scratched the back of his neck. "You're saying Aldric is part of the Veiled Circle and helped them track us?"

No, that can't be, Josie linked. *They have to be lying.*

The air remained clear. There was no lie to detect.

Son of a bitch. Adam pawed at the gravel. *That's how they've been finding us.*

I grew light-headed, and I didn't know Aldric the way they did. *Then why did Olwyn try the locator spell? If the cars have trackers on them, they already know where we are,* I linked to our pack.

Probably a distraction, Raffe answered, *so we'd assume they couldn't find us and we'd stay here. She probably knew you'd feel the magic trying to locate you and sense it didn't work. Besides, it's not like any of us expected them to use technology to track us and not magic, so none of us accounted for that.*

"Yes, that's how Supreme Priestess Olwyn got ahold of us." Keagan ran a hand through his hair. "Aldric has been busy with the king, and she called us to offer us this deal. After King Jovian threatened us, it made sense that Aldric would be tied up with him, so we took her word for everything."

I shook my head. "The Veiled Circle tried to recruit me, and when I didn't join, they wanted me dead."

Ednah's brows rose. "Why? They made it sound like you could become unstable and destroy the world, but—"

"The arcane-born influences who will become or remain the leader of the supernatural world." Priestess Caroline clasped her hands together. "That's what my ancestors figured out during the time of the last arcane-born. They tried to manipulate him and his bond to get him to side with the covens, which ultimately led to his demise."

I inhaled sharply. "Foster?"

"Yes." Priestess Caroline closed her eyes. "Him. When he died because of our selfishness, my ancestor repented to the goddess, but another witch stepped forward and took control of the coven and manipulated them. That's when the coven separated, and my ancestor landed here with her smaller coven. They wanted to learn how to right the wrongs when the next arcane-born came along."

"That's not what I was told." Sedona frowned. "I

thought the priestess of that time went mad and couldn't lead anymore, so a new one was appointed." She stared accusingly at Ednah.

Ednah crossed her arms. "Don't use that tone with me. That's what's in the *Book of Twilight*."

"I'm not surprised." Priestess Caroline rolled her eyes. "Supreme Priestess Olwyn comes from a long line of manipulators and users. We wanted to repent, but the wolf shifters took control as punishment from the goddess for us disrespecting the fated-mate bonds and the balance. The other coven members couldn't admit they were wrong and wanted to find a way to keep their power. Clearly, it didn't work, and now we're back to history repeating itself with the arcane-born, but worse, they're actively trying to kill her."

"I'm assuming Olwyn didn't tell you their goal?" I arched a brow.

"Of course she did, to allow us our freedom." Keagan straightened his shoulders. "She doesn't want to dictate what rituals they practice or important things they want us to follow."

I snorted. She did have a way with words. "They, meaning her and maybe the vampires. When they kidnapped me and tried to brainwash me, they made the wolf shifters' future very clear. You are all to be held captive or killed. She wants to punish the wolf shifters for taking power centuries ago, and you're helping her accomplish that by attacking us."

Keagan sucked in a breath. "What about Aldric? Why would he go along with that?"

A deep snarl came from Raffe. "Because he'll be pardoned, or he thinks he will, and they'll need someone to help control the shifters. He has a strong wolf."

No. Dad wouldn't do that. But Josie's conviction felt weak.

Silence descended.

"How do we know that for certain?" Ednah laughed roughly.

"You already tried to kill my mate." Raffe narrowed his eyes. "On campus, with three of your men. I'm assuming Aldric gave the order."

My mouth dried as I remembered that night and the first time I'd ever shifted into a wolf. I'd been cut off from the others with no help.

"Aldric took me and my beta straight to King Jovian to tell us that the agreement was off. He wouldn't let me join the other three wolf shifters and ordered us to make sure my three men watched Josie. While they were there, Olwyn made first contact and told us to kill an unstable witch. They were shocked when she turned into a wolf. We had no clue she was your fated mate until King Jovian showed up in Atlanta, upset and threatening us with the real estate cancelations."

Raffe sniffed, smelling for signs of a lie.

Some of the resentment that had built around my heart toward King Jovian eased. Olwyn had ordered them to kill me, not King Jovian.

"The only way we come out of this strong is to go up against the Veiled Circle together and not fight one another." Now that everything was out in the open, we couldn't put off them deciding if they would ally with us any longer. "Raffe has made an offer so we can both win. It's up to you to accept it."

"I need time to talk with pack members, our coven, and the vampires. Our goal, once we split off, is to form a council to rule and not have one monarch." A muscle in

Keagan's jaw twitched. "A decision like this is too large to make on my own."

"Vampires?" Priestess Caroline lifted a brow. "I don't see any here."

"They remained back in the city because of the food supply. Traveling is harder for them because their food source is limited to blood banks, and we don't have the connections out here for them to eat as they should without risking them needing to feed from humans." Keagan opened the car door. "But they will be part of the decision."

A council where all species had a say. I liked the sound of that. My chest expanded with hope.

"Dad, I'm staying here." Stephanie straightened her shoulders. "While you call and make a decision, I want to get to know them." Her gaze darted to Adam.

We should let her stay if she wants to, I linked. *I think she and Adam have a connection.*

Raffe sighed. *Of course they do. I'm not even surprised.* He then said out loud, "If she stays, I promise she'll be safe."

Keagan winced but nodded. "Fine. Is there someplace I can go to make a call? I'm not leaving my daughter here alone."

"You can use the house." I didn't want them to get closer to the coven and where everyone else was. "There's no one inside."

Pulling on the sleeve of her dress, Ednah rolled her shoulders. "That's fine with me. That way, I'm close to Sedona."

My heart hammered. I wasn't sure what she meant. "The doors are unlocked."

Ednah and Keagan faced one another, and then they walked together toward the front door.

Before the two entered the house, Priestess Caroline

called out, "Priestess Ednah, you know Olwyn. Do you think she would really let the Eastern covens go? It would reduce her power."

The truth of the words knocked the breath out of me, and the two women locked eyes. Then Ednah and Keagan went inside.

Silence filled the area as our nerves teetered on edge. Each moment dragged on like hours, though none of us dared to talk as we waited to find out our future. Unfortunately, the Eastern supernaturals were in control of that.

Several minutes later, the front doors opened, and Ednah and Keagan came out.

They strolled over to us, Keagan's face set like stone. My power fizzed, but all I could read from him was resolve.

When he reached us, he held out his hand to Raffe and said, "We're willing to be allies, but we want a magical contract drafted up."

My heart leaped into my throat. This was everything we'd hoped for.

"That's fine with me," Raffe replied, shaking his hand. "Let's go back in the house and get this done."

"Sounds good to me." Keagan nodded.

FOR THE NEXT SEVERAL HOURS, Raffe, Ednah, Caroline, Keagan, Adam, Keith, Stephanie, and I talked strategy. We decided we would live in Atlanta with Keagan and the others until Raffe could finalize the property sale to them. Once that was settled, we would be given money to help get us established wherever in the East we chose and would be able to form our own pack and be protected.

Though I hated that this would cause a further divide

between Raffe and his parents, it was for the best because the Veiled Circle wouldn't be able to take control.

Overall, it was best for everyone, including King Jovian.

Stephanie and Sedona decided to stay with us in one of the coven houses while Keagan, Ednah, and the other wolf shifters went back to the houses they'd rented here. We would settle everything in the morning so that Octavia, Dru, Fane, and all of Caroline's coven could relocate with us now that we knew Olwyn knew where we were.

When everyone finally left and Raffe and I were in the house alone, some of that relief vanished. Part of me knew not to hope too much because the thought of having a life where I, Raffe, and our pack weren't constantly on the run sounded way too good to be true. No. Perfect.

There was one thing that hovered over us.

When we reached the bedroom we'd been staying in, Raffe changed into his clothes while the information we'd learned about Aldric weighed down on us.

"Should we talk to Josie?" My mouth went dry.

He shook his head. "She's with Dave. I checked on her. She needs time to think before we're all crammed into cars to Atlanta."

Fair. I'd be the same way.

But there was more to it than just how Josie felt. Raffe had a stake in this. His dad's most trusted confidant was working against him. "You should call your dad. You two may not be pack anymore, but the Veiled Circle taking control would be bad. If Olwyn ordered those three wolf shifters to attack me, then your dad wasn't on board with it. She would never do anything to help him."

His shoulders sagged, and I could feel his relief. "You're right, but I don't want to talk to him. He tried to keep us apart and alpha-will me to be with someone else."

I placed my hands on his shoulders. "Then call your mom."

"You're right." He lifted his phone from the nightstand where our phones had been charging. He dialed his mom's number, and I heard it ring two times.

"Hello?" King Jovian answered. "Son? Is that really you?"

Raffe winced. Of course, his father, the person he wanted to avoid, would answer.

"Yeah, it's me." Raffe's jaw clenched.

"Son, I never—" King Jovian started, but Raffe cut him off.

"I don't have much time, but I wanted to let you know that Aldric is working with Supreme Priestess Olwyn."

I swallowed my snort of surprise. Raffe wasn't wasting time on pleasantries.

"Now, son, if this is a joke to get back at me, you're going too far."

Raffe's hurt swirled through me, and I hurried to him and touched his arm, wanting him to know I was there for him.

"It's not a joke. He's been betraying you the whole time." Raffe's face hardened, reminding me of the distant, cold man I'd met at EEU. He got that way whenever he dealt with his father, and I hated it for him, but he leaned against me, using me as support. "Aldric put trackers on our cars, and he and Olwyn keep attacking us. I'm sure you saw the one attack on the news with the house that burned down. We barely escaped. The coven attacked within an hour of when Aldric left. They've formed a secret society and were trying to use Skylar to take you out of power, but she refused. That's why they kidnapped her."

I snagged my own phone, checking it to see if my parents had texted me.

When I opened the phone, I saw a text message from Mom, dated two hours ago.

Shit. I didn't want her to worry.

I clicked on the message, but when it popped up, my heart stopped.

No.

CHAPTER TWENTY-EIGHT

My world stopped.

I blinked, hoping like hell that, when I opened my eyes, the image that was there would be gone, but each time, the stark truth stared back at me.

Mom and Dad were gagged and bound to wooden chairs, their backs to one another.

Raffe moved to my side and stared at the photo.

"Dad, I don't have time to talk." His concern swirled with mine, adding to my panic.

"Dammit, Raffe," his father growled. "This is beyond stupid. You need to stop all this and come back home where you belong. I need your help. I'm tired of you giving me the cold shoulder, and stop trying to cause more trouble—"

Hot anger crackled through Raffe. "I'm not giving you the cold shoulder. Sky's parents are being held captive, and we need to figure out where they've been taken."

"They're at my childhood home." I'd recognized the lilac cushions and those chairs anywhere. When I was younger, I'd complained about the chairs being uncomfortable, so Mom had taken me to Walmart to pick out cushions.

I hadn't noticed I was rubbing my chest until Raffe placed his hands over mine and linked, *We're going to save them. I promise.*

Tears burned my eyes. *You can't promise that.*

"What do you mean her parents have been taken?" King Jovian's voice boomed. "They're *human*."

"Like that matters to Olwyn, Aldric, and the other members of the Veiled Circle," Raffe spat. "I called you and warned you about your beta. The rest is up to you." He hung up the phone and pulled me into his arms.

The buzz of our connection sparked between us, comforting me and also making me feel damn guilty. My chest constricted, and I shook my head. "This is because of *me*. I did this to them." My entire life, they'd loved me and sheltered me when they didn't have to. How did I repay them? The cold claws of panic pierced my chest. "This was two hours ago." Oh god. What could've happened to them since then?

Raffe snagged the phone from my hand and tossed it onto the bed. He placed his hands on my shoulders and lowered his forehead to mine. *Olwyn wanted you to see this picture. She knows the best way to control you is to hold them captive and keep them alive. We will save them.*

I shook my head and took a step back. Breathing rapidly, I lifted both hands. "Not we. *I*. They're in this situation because of me, and Olwyn wants to hurt *me*. No one else needs to be part of this. There's already too much at stake."

Raffe clenched his jaw, his expression turning stony, completely at odds with the way he usually looked at me now that we had completed our bond. An emotion I couldn't read seared between us. He snarled, "*We*. Remember, we're stronger together. Those are the damn words you've said to me ever since you were kidnapped."

Damn him. He wasn't supposed to toss my words back at *me*. It shouldn't work both ways. "I don't want you to get hurt, and Olwyn would be more than happy to use you against me too. I need you to stay here and protect everyone else."

Raffe's face turned red, and he snarled. *Babe, I fucking love you. Try to leave me behind and see what fucking happens. Wherever you go, I'll find you.*

My heart skipped a beat, though part of me wanted him to agree and stay behind. Not only did our pack need him, but so did the Eastern supernaturals. "I don't want to lose you."

"And you think I don't feel the same way about you?" He arched a brow and tilted his head. "What would you say if I tried something like this with *you*?"

I grimaced, giving him the answer he was seeking.

"See?" He booped me on the nose. "And I think others will feel the same way."

Before I could ask him what he meant, he linked with our pack, *The Veiled Circle has taken Sky's parents hostage. We're going to get things together so we can leave and go help them.*

Shit, Keith linked. *I'll let the others know. What do you need us to grab and where do you want to meet?*

Raffe smirked, and I tensed with understanding. He'd known others would join us, and he knew there was no way in hell I was going there alone.

Damn arrogant prick.

I don't know what we'll need. Raffe rubbed a hand

down his face. *They're going to use magic and could have vampires and shifters there.*

That's likely a human neighborhood, Lucy added. *So we'll need to hide the use of magic.*

Of course, Lucy would decide to go too, and now I worried Fane would try as well. But Raffe had a point. It wasn't like I could make sure no one followed me. I didn't have time to waste, and each second my parents were with Olwyn, there was no telling what sort of hell they were enduring. *We live on several acres, and the houses have privacy trees that divide the property. You can't see other houses due to the way they're all positioned.* I'd found solace by slipping away and feeling like I was part of nature when I was younger.

Now, my affinity for the woods and animals made complete sense. The things that had made me feel like I was an outcast now made me feel at peace in this world.

Do we know who took her parents? Josie linked.

Raffe flinched, and a heavy knot formed in my stomach. We both knew what she was asking.

Was it her father?

No, I should call them. I could ask to hear their voices. I reached for the phone.

Raffe snagged my wrist gently. He lifted the back of my hand to his lips and kissed it. "Babe, I *know* you want to call them, but that's the worst thing you could do. We know Olwyn is behind this, along with the society. As soon as they know you've seen the picture, they'll speed up their plan. The best thing to do is not react. It'll keep your parents safer longer."

His words were like a swift kick to the gut, bringing me back to reality.

Since you stopped talking, I'm assuming Raffe is

telling you that calling's not smart, Adam connected. *But if he isn't, don't make the call. Stephanie is talking to her dad and other wolf shifters. What city do you live in so they can book a flight to get more people here to help us fight?*

My chest expanded with so much hope it hurt. *They're going to help us?*

That was the agreement, wasn't it? Keith linked. *Help keep us safe? Ednah and Sedona are making calls too. They're getting a little bit of everyone to come here.*

If the Eastern supernaturals helped, maybe we'd have a chance. Olwyn wouldn't be expecting that. *Dalles, Oregon, so the closest airport is Portland.*

Shit. Dalles. We were over ten hours away since we were close to Salt Lake City. My head spun as I realized my parents wouldn't be saved for at least twelve hours. Olwyn wasn't patient, and I feared what that meant for them. We had to get moving.

Everyone who's going needs to get their shit together and get to the vehicles. We need to move and quickly because we have a long-ass drive ahead of us, Raffe commanded, rubbing his hands on my arms.

The buzzing sprang between us, but my teeth chattered as if I was cold. The only thing that would fix the problem was saving my parents.

We're on it, Josie linked.

Raffe bent down, grabbed a duffel bag, and zipped it open. "Let's pack some clothes. We may not even come back here and head straight to Atlanta instead."

I shook my head to clear it. I should've already thought of that and started packing. If I kept letting fear take control, Olwyn would get what she wanted.

Me, unfocused and easy to kill. And that couldn't

happen. The bitch and Slade needed to die, and if I could help it, they'd go together.

I rushed to the closet and began yanking clothes from the hangers and tossing them into the bag. Doing something other than panicking eased some of the tension in my chest. I needed to focus on tasks that would get me to Dalles faster. That was the only way I wouldn't lose my damn mind before then.

Do you have this? If so, I'll head out to the vehicles to find those damn trackers. Raffe paused at the door. *I don't want them to know we're heading that way.*

I've got this. I dropped a shirt into the bag then rushed to him and kissed him on the cheek. *Thank you for getting me through this.* Not only was my mate sexy and smart, but he also understood what I needed at that moment.

You never need to thank me for that, he replied, kissing my lips quickly. *Now, make sure you don't accidentally pack your brother's clothes for me. I don't want to worry about my pants ripping during the rescue.*

I chuckled, the image not all that disturbing in my mind. I still didn't understand how Octavia could've mixed up his and Fane's clothes. Raffe wore several sizes larger. I then linked with the others, *Don't worry about coming to get things. I'm getting enough for all of us.*

After grabbing what I needed for the others, I headed outside to find ten more vehicles pulled up alongside the three we'd brought and Keagan's SUV.

Priestess Caroline, Avalon, Faith, and thirty-five other coven members stood around their vehicles. Raffe, Adam, Keagan, Dave, and Keith were spread out among the other three, examining their undercarriages, while Lucy, Josie, Stephanie, Sedona, Octavia, Dru, and Fane stood around, watching them.

I'd wound up with three bags full of items to pack in the back of Raffe's black BMW SUV. I tossed the bags into the trunk, trying to keep busy and not stand around.

"How are you, child?" Priestess Caroline frowned.

Good question. I shrugged. "Just eager to save my parents. Who's coming?" There were so many people here.

"Everyone." Lucy strolled over, bumping her shoulder into mine. "Why else would we be here?"

I swallowed and took in a quick inhale. I hadn't expected this many people to be willing to go up against Olwyn for my parents, especially Caroline and her coven. "For humans?"

"Well, we're doing it for you." Josie smiled tenderly. "If Dad had a hand in this, I should—"

"No." I lifted a finger and pointed at her. "Don't you dare finish that. You aren't your father, and you don't have to pay for any of his bad decisions. Do you understand?"

Dave crawled out from under one of the vehicles and saluted me. "That's what I told her, but she worried you wouldn't think that way. I mean, I helped kidnap you, and you still forgave me. She hasn't done a damn thing."

"And you helped me when you should've killed me." Sedona bit her bottom lip and frowned. "The least we can do is to help you save your parents."

"Besides, Priestess Caroline had a good point." Ednah steepled her hands. "Olwyn won't want to give up her power, and the East doesn't want the secret society to get stronger and take over our cities either. We need to take a stand, and what better way than to help the arcane-born, who can connect with animals? That's near goddess-level power."

"I'm nothing like a goddess, so let's never use that

comparison ever again." I laughed nervously, but now that I was standing around, I became anxious.

"Found the last one." Raffe scooted out from under the vehicle, dirt smudged on his face.

I loved it when he got all dirty and manly.

"We're ready to roll?" Keith climbed out from under the white SUV and dusted off his jeans.

"The rest of our group makes ninety-five people and sixteen rental vehicles. They're waiting for us at the Walmart at the bottom of the mountain. We'll follow Raffe and Skylar to the house, where four vampires should be waiting for us nearby to help fight."

Raffe used his shirt to wipe off his face but only made the smudge worse. "So we'll have over a hundred and fifty people. Okay." His concern floated into me.

We could hope that was enough, but Olwyn would want to make sure she left a mark. No matter what, we couldn't just let my parents die.

"Okay, let's move." Raffe headed over to my door and opened it. "Everyone, switch out drivers and try to rest. We need to be as prepared as we can once we arrive."

"Savannah from the coven is staying here to keep watch and said she'll watch your cat. Do you mind if we ride with you?" Octavia asked as she and Dru headed to our back seat. "Or we can take our car."

I breathed a sigh of relief that they'd thought about Cat-Keith. I really was frazzled.

Raffe shook his head. "We have enough vehicles—riding with us works." I could feel his relief. Having them with us, we could keep an eye on them easier.

Everyone climbed into the vehicles, and soon Raffe pulled ahead in the lead.

He leaned over and squeezed my hand. *Get some sleep. You didn't get much last night.*

He hadn't either, but the best way to get him to rest eventually was if I didn't fight him. I leaned the seat back and closed my eyes, Raffe's hand on my thigh.

Still, the image of my parents kept popping into my mind. My chest tightened, and a sob built in the back of my throat.

Octavia leaned forward from her spot behind me and ran her fingers through my hair. She whispered, "Baby girl, you aren't alone. We're all right here."

Between Raffe's hand, the buzz of our connection, and Octavia petting my hair, darkness took me unexpectedly.

Twelve hours later, I was driving the car, my hands tight on the wheel to the point that my knuckles blanched. I'd slept for five hours, and then Dru had forced Raffe to switch spots with him. Thirty minutes outside of Dalles, we'd picked up three of the vampires who had been waiting for us. Apparently, one of the other vampires had taken an earlier flight and texted us instructions on where to meet him. I took the driver's spot since I knew my way around. The rest of the vehicles drove behind me, and I had to force myself not to stomp on the gas.

With each mile we drove out of the city and closer to the house, my stomach became tighter. Raffe seemed to feel the same way but for different reasons.

You're going to stay next to me the entire time? he asked for the tenth time in the last ten minutes.

I'll try my best. I couldn't promise because we weren't sure what would happen, which was why he kept asking.

We were in a cycle I wasn't sure we could break at this point.

I pulled into a section near the lake where people went fishing during the summer that had enough spots for all of us to park. It was about two in the morning, and no one else was out here. Plus, it was a mile from the back of my parents' property.

Everyone climbed out, listening for any sounds of the enemy.

"There's a back way into the yard." This was one of the places where I used to hang out because animals came here to drink. "We need to go on foot from here." I glanced at the three humans in our midst. "Maybe you three—"

"No, we're going." Dru reached into the back and pulled out a bag I hadn't noticed him carrying. He removed three guns and handed two of them to Octavia and Fane. "We can use these since we don't have magic."

I exhaled. I'd been nervous about them coming.

My phone dinged, startling me. I removed it and saw another message.

I swallowed and opened it.

There was a dagger pressed against Mom's neck and a text underneath. **You better get here. Our patience has run out. Tell Keagan he'll regret this.**

"Son of a bitch," Raffe snarled, and his gaze landed on Keagan. "Someone told her you're with us."

Keagan shook his head. "Impossible. I told only the people I trust. Everyone here, Chuck, Earl, and Samuel, who we picked up." He gestured at the three vampires. "And Warin, who should be nearby."

Bile inched up my throat, and I rasped, "Warin?"

CHAPTER TWENTY-NINE

Every ounce of hope I'd had vanished, leaving me cold and hollow. Memories surged from the days I'd spent trapped inside the bunker, being threatened and drunk from by that very vampire.

"Yes. Warin." Keagan lifted a brow. "He's one of the oldest vampires in existence. I just don't know where the hell he is. He said he knew the spot and would meet us here."

My blood turned to ice, his response confirming everything I already knew.

Raffe froze, feeling my emotions.

I hung my head, and my knees weakened. No wonder Olwyn had texted me. She'd probably known the moment we left Salt Lake City. "They know we're here." I scanned the trees for the enemy, but if coven members were there, they could be cloaked. "They've had ten hours to prepare."

"There's no way they could know. The priestess probably texted because it's been so long since you saw the text." Stephanie laughed quietly. "Maybe she couldn't sleep and wanted to nudge you again."

I inhaled deeply and put the phone into my back pocket. They weren't mind readers. I needed to tell them, but foolishly, it felt like if I didn't speak the words, maybe what I knew wouldn't be real. I murmured, "Warin works with them. He's part of the Veiled Circle."

"What?" Ednah pursed her lips. "No. You must have him mistaken—"

The memories of his fangs biting into my neck made me shudder. "No, I'm not. He was one of my captors in the underground bunker. He and a witch named Glinda were my handlers."

"*Glinda.*" Sedona blinked. "No. That can't be right. She's one of the coven members in Missouri who's been working on a solution to help us separate—"

"Holy shit." Keith grimaced. "They've been around longer than any of us have ever known."

We should've known not to underestimate the Veiled Circle, especially with how they'd taken me from campus, but it had made sense once I'd learned about Slade and Olwyn's involvement.

Keagan looked back at his people standing behind him. His eyes faintly glowed, and his group dispersed, heading toward the water and near the tree line. They sniffed, searching for any sign of Warin.

I suspected they wouldn't come up with anything. I'd bet Warin and Olwyn had determined exactly where they wanted us to arrive, and he'd never set foot here.

Bastards.

Worse, they now had a dagger to Mom's neck. My lungs stopped functioning as the entire situation hit me. We had no element of surprise, and Olwyn had my parents. The panic I'd felt back in Salt Lake City came crashing over me. Being busy and believing we might be able to save them had gotten me through, but now the future looked damn bleak again. "It doesn't matter whether you all smell Warin or not. They know we're here."

Raffe nodded. "The only thing we might still have on our side is if Warin thinks there's a chance we haven't put everything together."

I bit my bottom lip. "No. They want us to piece it together." My heart dropped into my stomach like a bomb. "That's why they sent me the text now—to trigger this conversation." Once again, we'd played right into their hands because we hadn't seen the full picture.

"Maybe we should go," a taller man who stood behind Keagan said.

I gritted my teeth to keep my frustration at bay. Losing the numbers we had was the worst thing that could happen to us since Olwyn and the others would have prepared to face this many, but this wasn't their fight. Olwyn had brought it to me and targeted my family. Yes, the rest of the supernatural world would have to deal with the fallout, but that didn't mean they had to face the firing squad right now. "If that's what you all need to do, so be it. I can't leave my parents. Not like this. Not after everything they've done for me."

Raffe stood firmly next to me, though I could feel his dread and worry.

"Well, I, for damn sure, am not going anywhere." Keith stepped forward. "I will fight alongside my alpha and alpha's mate."

My heart doubled in size. And to think, just over a month ago, he would've been the very one to suggest they leave me here alone. How far our relationship had come astonished me.

"I'm staying as well." Sedona lifted her chin and moved next to him. "If it weren't for Skylar, I'd be dead."

The rest of Raffe's and my pack, including Dave, joined Sedona and Keith, which didn't surprise me. We were all pack and family, and when Sedona completed her fated-mate bond with Keith, she'd joined us.

Priestess Caroline and her coven had stayed several feet away, but she chose this moment to clear her throat and add, "My coven will always stand with the arcane-born and right our past mistakes." Her eyes cut to Ednah in daring.

"None of this is needed." Keagan raised a hand. "We promised to protect you, and that's what we'll do. The supreme priestess knowing that we're coming doesn't change a damn thing. If anything, it makes this fight more important." He pivoted to face his men. "We've allowed these people to manipulate us into attacking innocents. Are we going to walk away and let innocent humans die? A species that isn't even supposed to know we exist? Obviously, this organization doesn't care about keeping our secrets."

The tall man who'd made the original suggestion averted his gaze to the gravel road and nodded.

Eyes glowing, Keagan huffed. "As you suspected, Warin's scent isn't anywhere near here. They can't pick up the trail."

"I don't feel any coven magic around here." Priestess Caroline closed her eyes. "We aren't in immediate danger, but that could change at any time."

The longer we stood here, the more antsy I became. There was no telling what they were doing to my parents. "We need to go before she ..." I trailed off, the sound dying in my throat. I couldn't say the word on the tip of my tongue; it was way too permanent. I inhaled, hoping my voice remained steady, and tried again. "Before she hurts them."

"We should split up." Adam turned in the direction we'd be moving. "Groups of around twenty-five each since there are a little over a hundred and fifty of us. People from each pack group should mix together so we can communicate between groups via pack-link bonds."

Stephanie rubbed her hands together. "That would put around nine witches in each group, though two groups won't have vampires."

"Does that matter?" From beside Lucy, Fane furrowed his brows.

"Vampires move quicker than the other species, so having them is an advantage, especially since we'll be fighting vampires here." Josie smiled and glanced at her mate.

I bit the inside of my cheek to keep my smart retorts to myself. Fane didn't understand this world completely, and I didn't want us to take the time to teach him now. Yet, he did need to know more so he'd be prepared to face them.

"We should make sure there's at least one wolf shifter in each group that can cross-communicate, but the six of us should remain together." Raffe tugged me against his side. "If there's an attack, we need to be able to link and strategize with each other. We can't do that if most of the people we're with can't speak to us in animal form or telepathically."

Even though I understood the merits of both ways of splitting up, I agreed with Raffe. "He's right. Last time, things were chaotic, and coordination may be critical." I hadn't been as worried about that when we'd believed we were taking Olwyn by surprise, but everything had changed.

"My pack stays together with Dave," Raffe said and tightened his hand on mine. His nerves churned.

I suspected he feared that Keagan would not want to listen, and he believed this was the best route. He'd never had to worry about that when he was the prince and heir, except with his father. Keagan could go against what he said.

Keagan blew out a breath. "Okay. I'm assuming the seven includes Octavia, Dru, Fane, and Priestess Caroline."

Octavia nodded. "Yes, I want to be with our daughter."

"And I know Stephanie and Sedona will want to be with you as well. So, with Dave, that will make thirteen, and I would like to stay with your group as well, if possible. That way, we can coordinate easily among alphas if needed."

"Then the rest of each group should be made up of my coven," Priestess Caroline added. "We're used to interacting with each other. I understand wanting to pack-link, but if both alphas are together and we split up so that most of us are with the people we're most familiar with, it will be for the best."

"I can see it both ways. We need to get moving so they can't attack us all in one place." Keagan's eyes glowed as he turned to his pack members.

We started splitting up, with eleven of Priestess Caroline's coven members joining the fourteen of us. We had a group of twenty-five.

The rest formed another five groups, and we were ready to go.

"The house is a mile north. Our yard is five acres, so there're tons of room to spread out. We'll come up to the backyard. The back of the house has a sliding glass door on the ground level, and stairs lead to a porch overhead with a door that enters into the kitchen." I rubbed my hands together to get rid of some nervous energy. "They have my parents tied up in the kitchen. That's where we need to go."

Everyone nodded.

"We'll head straight to the house." Raffe glanced at everyone. "The rest of you can fall in where you like."

"At least two wolf shifters stay in human form so we can communicate," Keagan added.

Something meowed at my feet, and I looked down. I sucked in a breath.

Of course, Cat-Keith had snuck her way into coming here with us. Part of me wanted to find a way to keep her safe, but knowing her, she'd locate us again. I didn't have time to worry about that when my parents were in danger. This cat was proving to be smarter than I'd ever have expected and probably wanted to help us. I'd let her.

Now it was time to move, and I was more than ready.

I took the lead, hurrying to the woods. I felt the faint hiss of my power, so I tugged at it to make it stronger. There was no telling when I'd need to use it.

My wolf edged forward, but I held her at bay. I needed to stay in human form so when I reached my parents, they'd know who I was and listen. I could only imagine the sort of hell they'd been through in the twelve hours it had taken us to get here.

I'm going to shift, Josic linked, *since most of our group is human.*

It'd be best if we all do, Raffe answered. *We need to be in our strongest form.*

I looked at him and linked, *I don't want to. My parents ...* I had to believe we were going to reach them and save them.

It's fine. Raffe's expression softened. *With your power, you're just as strong in human form. I didn't expect you to shift, and besides, you're my mate. I expect you not to listen to me. Never have before.*

I chuckled, unable to stop myself. Even in a dire situation, he knew how to make me grin.

The others peeled off, and Keagan watched them run toward the firs.

"We should go shift with them," Stephanie said.

"You go." Keagan nodded. "I'll stay in human form because I need to understand what the hell is going on." He lifted his shirt, revealing a pistol. "That's why I brought this."

I lifted my brows. That was one way to protect himself.

The coven members, Sedona, Dave, Octavia, Dru, Fane, Keagan, and I kept moving forward. The wolves would catch up once they were in animal form.

Our group formed a circle with the coven members in front. After a minute, I heard the sound of paw steps as the wolves hurried to join us. The groups on either side of us were made up of half witches and half wolf shifters, with one vampire. We were close enough to see one another but unable to speak without shouting.

My heart raced faster with each step. I wasn't sure when the enemy would pop out or if one or both of my parents were near death. All the potential situations had my stomach in knots and my power increasing. I swallowed, trying to keep it under control as much as possible. I didn't need to drain myself before we even got there.

We've almost caught up to you, Raffe linked, though he didn't need to. The base of my neck tingled, telling me he was watching me.

Static weaved through the air in front of me, and my wolf howled inside me.

"Coven magic," I whispered, but it was too late.

Priestess Caroline and the other coven members slammed into an invisible barrier. They bounced off the wall, and Priestess Caroline fell hard backward. I rushed forward, catching her, but by righting her, I stumbled forward and I braced to hit the wall.

Static rubbed against me as I went through the barrier and dropped to my knees.

Skylar, Raffe linked, and his panic slammed into me as he tried to race through the perimeter spell they'd cast, but he was flung onto his back, snarling.

The same thing had happened that night at campus when the three Eastern wolves had attacked me and I'd shifted for the first time.

I spun around, searching for my attackers, but all I heard was silence.

No animals were nearby, which meant they felt danger. I noticed that all the groups had stopped and couldn't get through. They'd isolated me.

Dammit, Sky. Raffe jumped back on his feet, baring his teeth. *If they touch you, I'll kill them all.*

"Calm down," Priestess Caroline bit out. "We need to bring down the spell, so stop running into it. It won't vanish on its own." She held out her hands toward the other coven members, who took them.

A shiver ran down my spine just as Dave yelled, "Vampires!"

I spun, searching for the attackers, and saw ten blurs charging toward me through the trees.

I yanked, my power humming as I lifted my hands.

"Focus on big targets, but don't blast your power into the ground!" Priestess Caroline shouted. "If you can hold them off like that, your power will drain less quickly than forcing it into small or massive areas."

I took a deep breath to center myself. The vampires were almost on me. I pushed the power from my palms, aiming for the closest blurs I could see. The coven members behind me chanted, though I couldn't make out the words over the roaring in my ears.

Then, the fastest two blobs were on me, so I funneled the power from my hands. I knocked the first blob down, a hiss resonating, and blasted the second one, causing a sickening *pop*. The smell of copper hit my nose.

But I had no time to see what I'd done because four other blobs were already on me.

A loud wolf howl came from behind me, and Raffe's fear pummeled me, making my power surge to a song. I hated that he was seeing everything that was going on but couldn't reach me. I could feel the edge of hysteria clawing between us.

And that made me miss the third mark.

One vampire wrapped his hands around my neck, choking me, as a second vampire snagged my arms and forced them behind my back. I kicked backward, nailing him in the knee, and heard a crack. Then I grabbed the pale, sinister arms of the one strangling me.

Power soared into his body as I stared into his dark eyes, dug my fingernails into his wrists, then kneed him in the crotch. He grunted and dropped to the ground, so I kicked him in the face. His head jerked to the side before he landed in a heap.

Two other vampires appeared at my sides, their teeth extended. The woman fisted her hands in my hair, dragging my body toward her. The male vampire kicked me in the stomach. Acid burned up my throat.

I had to do something before they killed me or worse.

So I allowed my power to go feral.

The power soared through me into the ground, and the earth quaked underneath me.

The vampire that had my hair hissed, and sharp teeth sank into my neck. Raffe's snarls and whimpers echoed in my ears as the woman gulped and then gagged, the combination of my power making her crazy but my wolf blood poisoning her.

She released her hold and stumbled back as the man backed away, pinching his nose as if trying not to smell me.

I placed my hand against my neck where the vampire had bitten me, and warm liquid slipped between my fingers.

Babe, I'm so sorry, Raffe whimpered, and a dark void of helplessness opened deep within him.

I spun around to see him pawing at the ground like he could go under the barrier, but then I felt a shift in the magic. My attention flicked to Priestess Caroline. Her eyes were glowing. I knew I couldn't move forward without everyone, but I was desperate to reach my parents.

Then I remembered how I'd taken the barrier down before. I could help them, and maybe it'd be quicker.

I released my neck and placed my hand against the barrier. Just like when I'd slipped through, it passed through.

My heart skipped a beat. I could get out there with Raffe and help the coven.

As I stepped forward, something stabbed into my shoulder.

CHAPTER THIRTY

Pain exploded in my upper back and wrapped around the front of my shoulder as I stumbled forward. The static of the magical barrier chafed against my skin.

I got my feet underneath me, but then a gigantic wolfy body crashed into me, forcing me to my back. My body jarred, and vomit surged upward as the pain became worse than anything I'd ever experienced before.

Then I heard gunshots.

Get down and hide behind the trees. The coven members are using weapons, Raffe linked and pressed his entire weight on me. He then connected to only me, *Babe, I'm sorry, but you've been shot.* His body jerked, and sharp agony tore through him.

No. This wasn't how we were going to die, unable to get through a barrier. Chaos rang around me. If I didn't do something, we *were* all going to die.

Every single one of us.

I yanked on my power, no longer worried about moderating it. It was now or never.

My body sang and allowed the power to pulse from me.

I used the trick Priestess Caroline had shown me, closing my eyes and envisioning my power attacking everyone to my north and none of us here. I felt the entanglement of my magic with the barrier, the way my power pressed against the static, swallowing it whole, and how it seeped into the ground.

"The barrier's down!" Priestess Caroline yelled. "Use your magic against them. If they win, nothing will ever be the same, and the arcane-born will die. Pass the message along to all. We need to act now."

I gritted my teeth, shoving Raffe off me. We were in the open. *Get behind a damn fir,* I commanded as I crawled the two feet to the nearest tree. Each time I moved, my shoulder felt like it was ripping in two, but I pushed past the pain. At least I was still breathing, and my power was working. At the bare minimum, I needed to stay alive long enough to save my parents and protect the people who'd decided to stand with me.

The vampires I'd injured yelled, "Let us get out of the way before you continue shooting!"

But the gunfire didn't halt.

The ground quaked, and I propped myself against a trunk and glanced up to see the branches swaying. I groaned, the pain pulsing almost in sync with my power. I kept a strong grasp on my power, making sure it didn't stop.

The gunfire continued.

Two of the vampires that had attacked me lay dead on the ground from gunfire, while the two others had taken shelter like the rest of us.

Raffe limped over to me, blood trickling from his side. Some bastard had shot him. I'd figure out who it was and make them pay.

He lay at my feet, positioning himself so that the sizable

trunk protected him as well. He linked, *Did the bullet come out?* Then he raised his head to sniff my shoulder.

I swallowed my whimper, knowing he could feel my pain. Making noise would only put him more on edge, and he had a wound of his own. "I don't think so." Even speaking made the pain worse, but I didn't have time to dwell on that. "I need to stop them long enough for us to get close and attack them."

Suddenly, something *yank*ed on my power—the animals of the woods answering my call.

I fought against the urge to hunch over from the agony. I hated asking for their help, especially since they were truly innocent in all this.

We're on our way, the merged voice replied in my head just as Priestess Caroline and the other witches began to use their magic as weapons.

Keagan hunkered down and ran to our trunk, and bullets were fired at him. The trees blocked him, and he dropped next to Raffe, a bullet hitting the dirt just a millimeter away from him.

He glanced at the bullet and scoffed. "That was damn close."

"Those who can control the wind help Skylar take the others down!" Priestess Caroline shouted.

Five coven members with us eased around the tree that protected them and made the wind gust against the trees, knocking over a few between the quaking ground and my power. They were able to aim for a specific tree and take it down.

Out of the corner of my eye, I noticed Octavia, Dru, and Fane were five trees over to the right, with Cat-Keith darting through the brush and disappearing again. Dru and Fane ran across, spreading out to hide behind two other trees. Lucy stayed right on Fane's heels, the fur on the nape of her neck rising.

I didn't need a fated-mate connection to know how she felt. I was experiencing the same damn thing.

The three humans got settled and began firing.

"Tree!" a woman shouted, and some of the gunfire stopped as something came crashing down.

"Now that some of the gunfights are stopping, I'm telling my pack members to move," Keagan rasped. "Otherwise, Olwyn will have time to bring reinforcements."

Raffe nodded then linked with the five of us, *We're moving. Be careful and stay close to the trees. If you come across one of the Circle members, kill them. Don't try to take a captive or let them manipulate you into thinking they're innocent. They are our enemy, and they'll kill us if we don't kill them.* His eyes locked with mine, making it clear that those words were mainly meant for me. *Even if we once considered them friends. And make sure Dave doesn't get near Skylar—we don't need him going blood crazy and dying.*

My stomach roiled. I hadn't considered those possibilities, but he was right. My blood could affect even the vampires on our side, and we had no clue who was working against us. For all I knew, Hecate, Zella, and anyone else could be here.

Even *Slade*.

The damn traitor. Still, his betrayal cut deep.

Understood, Adam replied as he and the others in our pack surged forward, leaving Raffe and me behind.

Keagan's group followed their lead. With my good side, I grabbed Keagan's hand, tugging him back into place even though the pain wasn't that much better since the back muscles were connected. Keagan's head jerked back, and his forehead lined with worry.

"The vampires. They shouldn't get near me." I gestured to my neck, where the blood still soaked my shirt. "They won't be able to stop biting me even though it'll kill them."

"That's what Olwyn said and why we didn't bring vampires on the attack. They know to stay clear of you." Keagan's lips pressed together. "But thanks for the warning." He took off.

Skylar, do you understand what I said to the others? We can't let our sympathies get the best of us. They're okay with attacking humans. Raffe edged forward, blocking me from moving around him easily.

Yes. I opened up my connection to him so he could feel my sincerity, including my concern. My body had started to feel heavy, but I wasn't sure if that was from the weight of the decision I'd made or from blood loss.

Good. Now stay with me. He trotted ahead, his discomfort increasing from his injury. *I don't want to lose you in this mess.*

Swallowing hard, I pushed myself off the trunk, and the pain pulsed. Darkness clouded my vision. Most of the secret society coven members had abandoned their guns and were back to using their magic, which somehow comforted me, even though it was just as deadly.

A few gunshots still rang through, indicating not all our attackers had abandoned their weapons.

I focused internally on the sounds of animals coming toward us. I didn't know why they felt the need to protect me, but I wouldn't complain.

My head grew dizzy, and I tripped on a root. I caught myself, and my entire body jerked, causing the vomit to come up. My stomach emptied, and the sound of fast footsteps had my head tilting forward.

The shorter man who'd attacked me earlier raced toward me, fangs extended. I tried to prepare myself to fight, but it was impossible.

I'd have to use my power.

I lifted my good hand, ignoring the way my back felt as if it would separate, and focused on his dead, milky-brown eyes. I needed him to die, and before I understood what happened, my power had shot out, and his head exploded.

Pieces of tissue and blood splattered the nearby trees and the vampire's body as it sank to the ground.

Thank goodness I'd already vomited, or I'd be upchucking right now.

Some of the Circle coven members had seen what I'd done to the vampire.

"Dear goddess." A middle-aged man paled as he froze.

I turned my attention to him and focused on the ground. The earth split open underneath him, and he vanished.

A lump formed in my throat, and the horrible taste in my mouth got worse. I'd killed two people in under a minute. My heart ached, but at least it distracted me from my injuries.

Babe, what's wrong? Raffe linked as he hunkered down, readying to attack a woman shooting flames at Lucy. *It doesn't feel like you got hurt.*

I'll be okay. The last thing I needed him to worry about was the fallout of the fight. He needed to focus on the threat in front of us. *I'm still not used to all the blood and violence.*

Once we've saved your parents, we'll get away from all this shit, he vowed and lunged at the witch just as the flames burned Lucy's paws.

Lucy whimpered. A warlock three feet over spun in her direction and smirked. He raised his hands, and the earth shook harder underneath her.

The prick wanted to use my power to help kill one of my own. Oh, fuck no.

I imagined the earth shooting from the ground and tilting toward him so Lucy could rip out his neck. My power inched stronger, obeying my command. I yanked my power back in, not wanting the earth to shake as hard with us fighting the enemy coven members, and I especially didn't want to allow them to leverage it against my pack.

Just as I wanted, as the man stumbled back, Lucy jumped from the ledge and ripped out his throat.

Something slammed into me.

I spun around to find Gavyn. His hands were raised toward me, and the static of his magic swirled around me, but the wind merely blew my hair. His normally warm forest-green eyes were darker, and his expression hardened so much that he didn't even resemble the man I'd known on campus.

Good. Maybe that would make this easier.

He turned his hand, the tornado following the direction and lifting Raffe off the woman he'd attacked. Gavyn lifted him higher and higher.

My stomach clenched, and my body went numb.

Yet another person who wanted to hurt my mate and had to die.

Screams, cries, and the stench of blood intensified around me, but there was one clear thing I had to do. We hadn't even gotten to the house, and there was already so much death and destruction around us. This had to end *now*.

Lowering my head, I kept my gaze locked on him and

pushed my power straight at him. It hit him in the chest. His eyes widened, and he lowered his hand, reaching for his heart. His ash-blond hair hung in his eyes as he clutched his chest and dropped.

Shit.

Had I imploded his heart?

Cold tendrils of fear clenched my chest as I jerked toward Raffe and saw his body slam down from fifteen feet off the ground.

"No!" I shouted, my emotions and power heightening like never before, and I rushed to him. Everyone who wanted to hurt us needed to die. We hadn't done a damn thing wrong.

Pain sliced through our bond, and I ran to him and dropped beside him. "Raffe," I croaked, and my power gushed from me, blowing up like a bomb. I could hear the vibrations as it hit the ground, trees, and even the air around me, crackling like lightning.

Then there was silence.

What the fuck just happened? Keith linked. *All the people we were fighting just dropped dead.*

I suspected it was because of me, and my heart clenched. What if I'd killed those on our side too? But as I glanced around, it looked like everyone on our side was okay. I touched Raffe's face, hanging on to the warm bond in my chest. That was the only thing keeping me from losing my damn mind.

People gasped, but none of that mattered.

Raffe? I linked, desperate for him to answer me.

His eyes cracked open. *You fucking saved me.*

My body sagged against his. *Dammit, are you okay?*

Yeah. He whimpered, getting his legs underneath him. *I'll be fine.*

Don't— I started.

He stood even though I could feel how much his body ached.

We need to get to your parents. He nodded. *Which we might have a chance to do now that you killed every enemy in the clearing.*

What? I looked around and noticed all the dead bodies. Mostly it was the secret society, but I also noticed several of Keagan's pack, two vampires that had come with us, and a handful of coven members from Caroline's and Ednah's covens. Luckily, both priestesses were still alive, along with their immediate families.

Worse, every one of them was looking at me in a way I didn't understand, with a combination of terror and awe. The same way the kids used to look at me in school. My heart squeezed.

I'd have to tend to it later.

"We need to go," Keagan said, waving his hand. "While we can."

Can you keep going? I linked to Raffe, not wanting the others to hear this question.

He answered, *Let's get this the fuck over with.*

Amen to that.

I stood, my back screaming, and forced myself to put one foot in front of the other. Soon, our entire group was moving.

Dru rushed to me, his face twisted into a frown. "Where are you hurt?"

"It's nothing." The doctor in him was coming out, but we didn't have time to deal with injuries. We needed to keep going. "I'm fine."

"But—" He reached out.

Octavia took his hand and said, "Come on. We need to keep an eye out."

As we moved toward the house, I took stock. Fane and Lucy were side by side. Fane looked fine though Lucy had blood trickling from claw marks. Josie and Dave were in the lead, also seemingly fine. Keith and Adam were with Stephanie and Sedona, and none of them looked too bad off, though blood coated both wolves' fur. It didn't seem to be theirs.

All in all, our pack was okay, except for Raffe and me.

My power fizzed inside me, having taken a huge hit from the large amount of energy I'd expelled, and I could again hear the rustle of animals scampering toward us.

We pushed forward. The animals would know where to find me.

But my power ebbed with every step I took, lessening to a faint buzz. *Shit.*

After what felt like way too long, we reached the edge of the woods by the backyard. Keagan and Ednah stopped in their tracks, rushing to take a few steps back.

Something was wrong.

I darted forward, the adrenaline numbing the pain.

I couldn't believe what I saw.

Fifty people were gathered in the backyard, wearing armor and with guns pointed at us. Olwyn, Slade, Aldric, and Warin stood on the wooden porch above them.

I swallowed. This was bad, and it was just the people outside. *If you can still hear me, only attack the people connected to this house. Read my body for cues. I may not be able to talk.*

"Please tell me you have animals coming," Priestess Ednah rasped. "We're low on our magic from the last fight."

That had been Olwyn's plan—to drain us and, if we

made it through, force us into another battle against fresh fighters.

"I do—" My power vanished, and my body sagged with fatigue. I hadn't heard an answer.

My connection to the animals was gone, and Supreme Priestess Olwyn screamed, "Attack them!"

CHAPTER THIRTY-ONE

My body tensed as I tried to figure out what the hell to do. The coven members were low on magic, and my power was gone. The animals were our last chance to catch them off guard, but even then, that must be why they had weapons—to fight all of us, including the animals.

This could have been a suicide mission.

Josie whimpered as a blur blew past me.

Dave.

With his vampire speed, he raced forward. The coven members couldn't keep up with him, and he descended among them.

My heart ached, knowing the turmoil Josie was going through. And this confirmed what I'd always suspected—Dave was a good guy, just misguided.

The witches tried to fire at Dave as the other two surviving vampires followed his lead, one coming from the left and the other from the right, creating a distraction.

I gritted my teeth. The inevitable had come, so I searched deep within myself, found the faint fizzle of my power, and *yank*ed at it.

"Some of Ednah's coven members are going to attack," Keagan rasped. "But they can't hold everyone off. We need more distractions."

I had no choice. I had to be the one to do it. I yanked at my power again, and it hummed. It'd have to be enough to do ... something.

Warin hissed. "Shoot them. You may not see them, but they aren't invincible to bullets. Just fire. We want to kill them *all* anyway."

A few of the gunmen fired but missed the three vampires, who reached the front line and broke three of their necks.

Panic ensued. Other society members backed up, firing their weapons randomly.

Then coyotes, bobcats, foxes, deer, and raccoons flooded the area, adding to the chaos. They didn't directly attack but rather impeded the battles going on, giving our allies a chance to turn things in their favor.

Dave tried to move away, but with the constant shots, a bullet hit him in the chest. He stumbled back several steps, and Josie yelped and raced forward.

"No!" Aldric shouted. "Hold your fire!"

A few stopped, but the ones closest to the vampires didn't hesitate; they kept shooting. Fortunately, they weren't aiming at Dave but at the other two vampires. One of the vampires dropped dead when a bullet hit the top of his head, and the second stumbled after getting hit in the leg.

I yanked at my power once more, and it reached a high fizz, but it wouldn't stay that way. I was running low, and it might not get that high again.

Imagining what I wanted to happen, I forced the power forward, using every bit I had, and aimed it at the porch.

The power surged, and fatigue hit me, my knees going weak. I'd exerted myself too much.

As my butt hit the ground, the porch shook and shattered, collapsing the entire structure. Between the large pieces of wood, Warin, Olwyn, Slade, Aldric, and a third of the guards were taken out. The others near them spun around, searching for the threat, while the remaining fifteen continued to shoot while dodging animals.

I'd done everything I could.

"Holy shit," Keagan gasped. "Was that you?" His gaze landed on me, his eyes wide.

I nodded. "Now, we need to attack before they recover."

His eyes glowed as his side and the coven members on our side surged forward.

Lucy, I need you, Fane, Octavia, and Dru to stay with Skylar and protect her, Raffe linked as he ran forward.

My heart quickened as I watched my fated run into danger. I should have been there beside him. Still, when I tried to stand, my body sagged even more.

Octavia and Dru flanked me before Lucy had a chance to speak with my brother.

Dru scanned me. "What's wrong?"

"I'm drained and hurting, but there are more important things to focus on. I need you all to fire at the guards so the others have less of a chance of getting shot," I gritted out through clenched teeth, trying not to snap. "Avoid the animals." My physical state could be addressed later ... if we lived.

"But—" Dru started.

Octavia lifted her weapon and interjected, "She's right. Let's clear them out so we can actually save her parents and take care of her."

Lucy hurried over, eyes forward, searching for a threat, with Fane right beside her.

Gunfire continued, and I watched as three wolf shifters from Keagan's pack were taken down. Two raccoons grabbed the hands of one of the wolf shifters in animal form on our side that was injured, half guiding, half dragging him toward the woods to safety.

My stomach roiled. This was a bloodbath.

There was no way in hell I'd stay here and not fight alongside them. I just needed to find a damn way to get enough strength to stand.

The coven attacked. Priestess Ednah and Priestess Caroline stood side by side, taking on the enemy together. Water shot from Ednah's hands while flames expelled from Caroline's.

A few screamed, but the twenty-ish who'd stopped to help the people impacted by the collapsed porch were engaged in battle once more.

Raffe, Adam, and Keith barreled forward, attacking three of the people in front who'd pivoted to fire at our witches. Octavia, Dru, and Fane fired, though they struggled to find clear shots with our witches and wolf shifters fighting.

I took a deep breath to steady myself. I had to find the strength to get up and fight alongside them.

Two bobcats tugged Dave from a spot in the center of the yard, heading toward us. He groaned, his face white, and did his best to push himself along and help them. A warlock yanked on the second vampire to get him out of harm's way as well.

Now that my adrenaline had worn off, the agony from my wound crept back in, making it feel as if my muscles were ripping apart.

Then I watched in horror as a woman turned her gun on my mate.

Fear strangled me, and I jumped to my feet. *Raffe, watch out,* I linked, trying to run toward him, but my feet moved way too slowly.

When the woman pulled the trigger, my world stopped. Raffe's body jerked backward, and he flipped onto his back.

I swallowed past a large lump, yanking like hell against my power. It wasn't even flickering. Still, I had to get to my mate before he got hit again.

My wolf surged toward the location of my power and pulled on the fated mate connection. Something flared inside me, causing my power to hum.

I pushed my power toward the woman with her gun trained on my mate, and her head exploded. Blood and tissue flew out, and her body crashed to the ground.

Knowing that my power wouldn't last long, I pulled as much energy as possible into myself and linked, *Get Raffe out of there.* Acid burned in my throat at the state he was in, and worse, I knew this was a battle we couldn't win, which meant I had to do everything I could ... even if I died in the process. Everyone here had risked their lives for my parents and me, and they deserved me doing my best for them.

Blurry images came from both sides of us as wolves raced behind the vampires, heading toward us, and more animals ran into the clearing, distracting our enemies.

I suspected more Veiled Circle coven members would be coming forth shortly, using their magic against us.

I lifted my arms outward, imagining the twenty vampires knocked back as Olwyn, Aldric, and Warin pushed their way out of the porch disaster.

My power blasted the twenty vampires, tossing them back several feet into the side of the house with sickening splats. I didn't have time to think about what I might have done to them.

I raced toward my mate and funneled my power around me.

Skylar, stay put! Raffe linked, his eyes widening as he twisted around, trying to get back on all four paws. *You're too exhausted. Just wait there, and I'll be back to you soon. I need you safe.*

His pain pulsed through our connection as he stood, confirming what I feared. He was hurt just as bad as I was. For the moment, I rode high on power, not feeling my pain. I linked, *There's no way in hell I'm staying back when you're injured. What would you do if it were me?*

He stumbled, and fear stabbed my chest. I had to reach him. He was one of their main targets.

"This ends now!" Olwyn exclaimed and lifted her hands to unleash her magic. "Caroline, you should have known not to get involved. Slade, take care of Ednah, the fucking traitor. She has water magic like you." Her face twisted into a sneer, and she unleashed her fire power at Caroline.

Priestess Caroline didn't hesitate, their flames colliding. Sparks shimmered from their streams together while Slade focused on the other priestess, wanting to take out the strongest of both covens, which would impact all of them.

Sedona hunkered to one side, causing the ground to quake underneath them as new enemy wolves attacked.

There had to be at least a hundred of them fighting against us. I heard the sound of tires squealing in the distance, indicating reinforcements were arriving.

Warin appeared in front of me, his coal eyes dark as night and wooden splinters sticking out of his dark, wavy hair. Just seeing him with his tan complexion, a sign of his ancient age, still shocked me.

"You *bitch*." He sneered, his teeth elongating. "I told them you would cause problems, but no, they wanted the *arcane-born*." He lunged.

From seemingly nowhere, Cat-Keith jumped into Warin's face, halting his progression as she clawed at his face and bit his nose, yowling and hissing.

As Warin yelled and tried to shove her away, Raffe leaped, sinking his teeth into Warin's neck and jerking his head.

Warin dropped, and Cat-Keith ran off. Raffe leaped toward the next attacker.

Scanning the area, I noted we were more even with so many animals creating distractions and our coven members using their magic effectively, helping us stand our ground. However, several vehicles squealed to a stop in front of the house.

Something weighed on my shoulders. How could we keep going when we were low on magic and half of us were injured?

Octavia, Dru, and Fane ran forward, using their guns now that they weren't risking us all, and Lucy hurried toward the new wolf shifters.

"Do *not* harm my daughter!" Aldric shouted. "That was part of the deal."

"Fuck the deal, Aldric," Olwyn spat. "She's fighting against us on the side of the prince."

Doors slammed shut, and I could hear people running toward us.

Faith stepped up beside her grandmother, adding her magic and creating a water tornado. The two of them pushed their combined magic toward Slade. They were going to win against him.

Skylar, Raffe linked. *To your left.*

I spun just in time and took a step back, causing the wolf to miss my neck and bite into my chest. I yelped, agony taking hold as my back jarred from the impact.

Pain sliced through me, and the connection I'd been pulling from stopped.

Suddenly, Fane appeared at my side, shooting the wolf before it could slash my neck.

Blood coated me. "Thank you," I gasped.

I turned to find Raffe fighting for his own life with two wolves flanking him.

I noticed he was moving slowly, and it wasn't due to his wound. I could feel his fatigue, and realization slammed into me. I'd accessed my power ... by funneling strength from him.

No.

I hadn't even considered that I'd been using him.

More people ran around the corner of the house, and I stumbled toward my mate.

"Move," Fane rasped as he pushed me aside and shot the wolf nearest me before it hurt Raffe. He then shot the wolf in the back of the head, killing it.

A loud, familiar voice commanded, "Stop at once. No more fighting."

My heart skipped a beat as the alpha will, laced into the words, brushed past me, and I blinked, taking in King Jovian and ten other men alongside him, including Valor and Finley.

Raffe's dad was here.

The chaos stopped as his orders swirled through the wolf shifters, forcing them to stand down. Even some of the guards lowered their guns, confirming that not all of them were coven members.

But the coven members on both sides didn't stop their battles, and I glanced over in time to see Slade get pushed over stray pieces of wood from the fallen porch and land on his ass.

Her son's fall didn't affect Olwyn, who continued to fight Caroline, taking a few steps toward the other priestess and pushing her flames closer to the older lady. Ednah turned her water magic on Olwyn, dosing her flames and her entirely.

Priestess Caroline pulled back her magic, not killing Olwyn even though she could have.

My respect for the priestess grew, especially with the number of bodies from both sides littering the backyard. In some cases, because they were in animal form, I couldn't tell which side the wolves were on as I didn't know Keagan's pack well. Still, the numbers didn't lie, and I wanted to vomit. This loss of life was completely pointless.

I couldn't help but feel relieved that the people I cared about were okay, including Sedona, Stephanie, and Keagan —though Keagan had a large gash on his upper arm that was so deep I could see tissue.

King Jovian's steel-blue eyes widened, and his nostrils flared as his normally olive complexion turned red. He marched toward the center of the yard, several feet away from me, taking in the chaos. "What the *hell* is going on here?" Somehow, his hair seemed more salt than pepper this time, and his beard had gray streaks throughout. "And who *shot* my son?" His eyes landed accusingly on Aldric.

"I ... I—" Aldric started.

"Your reign is over, *Jovian*." Olwyn scowled and shook the water from her arms. "It ends here, and everyone will be relieved that we don't have to cower in your presence anymore." She lifted her hands.

Raffe's terror slammed into me, tightening my chest.

I couldn't let Raffe's father die, not like this. He'd never forgive himself.

Though I knew it was futile, I had to try, so I pushed through my agony and raced toward the wolf shifter king.

I waited for the flames to flash across, but instead, I smelled the rancid stench of burning flesh.

A yell of agony echoed, and a wolf whimpered, with Josie linking, *Dad! No!*

CHAPTER THIRTY-TWO

"I'm drained," Priestess Caroline shouted, informing our side that she couldn't use her magic.

It had been dangerously low before that, so it wasn't surprising.

I slammed into King Jovian just as heat warmed my back, adding to the excruciating pain that burned like fire in my chest from the wolf's claws. The only blessing was the fact that I was immune to their magic, so the sensation was merely warming and not charring my skin ... unlike King Jovian if it had hit him.

The king grunted as he landed on his back, and my body covered his, but his grunt was cut off by a cry of pain as my body jarred. Pain pulsed through me, overwhelming me, and fatigue crashed over me.

Raffe's hot anger boiled, and he snarled. *I'm so damn tired of people trying to hurt you. This ends now.*

Panic ripped through me, giving me enough energy to lift my head. Raffe leaped at Olwyn and sank his teeth into her throat. His paws hit her in the chest, causing her to stumble back, her eyes widening. The flames receded from her hands.

Josie hovered over her father, who lay on the ground, rolling to extinguish the flames torching his clothes. The stench of burned flesh and the way his skin had charred told me he had severe burns.

My body cooled, and Slade yelled, "No! Mom." He tripped, trying to get over the fallen wooden pieces from the porch, then fell over a dead body.

Olwyn gurgled, her hands clutching her neck, blood seeping between her fingers. I lowered my head, unable to lift it anymore.

Raffe hadn't been injured again.

Some of my panic receded.

King Jovian huffed and gently rolled me off himself and onto the ground. When my back hit, I whimpered as my pain doubled. My vision darkened. I could no longer ignore the exhaustion and the torture my body had endured.

Sky, Raffe linked, and I heard his unsteady paw steps as he hurried toward me. His concern swirled through our connection, along with his own fatigue and pain.

I cracked my eyes open as he ran past his father and laid his head on my stomach. His pain mixed with mine. We'd both been injured, but the buzz of our connection flared between us, comforting me.

King Jovian cleared his throat and rose to his feet, then turned to the chaos behind him. "This is over *now.*"

Sobs echoed in my ears as Slade mourned his mother. I hated that my heart ached for him and his loss after everything he'd done, not only to me but to all of us. He'd never been a friend, not a real one, and I shouldn't let his sadness affect me. We'd done what we had to because his mother had attacked *us.*

"Does anyone else want to fight against my family or my species?" King Jovian's voice echoed with authority. "If so, let's finish this and kill all the people who want to rise against me."

A lump formed in my throat as I waited for the fight to commence again. I didn't see a way we would get out of here, not like this. Raffe and I were completely drained.

"You son of a bitch!" Slade screamed. "I'll kill you for what you've done to my mother."

My eyes flew open, my power pulsing through me at the mere thought of losing my mate. Raffe flinched, moving so he protected me. I locked gazes with Slade as he lifted his hands, aiming at me and my mate. I pushed my power at him.

"Kill him," King Jovian commanded, and his ten men rushed toward Slade.

Water hit Raffe, the force of it driving his body onto me, making my chest and back throb.

Then Slade's body lurched, and he clutched his chest, cutting off his magic. He dropped to his knees as his body shook then fell.

I had no doubt he was dead, but that last little push had taken me over the edge.

I sank into darkness.

MY HAND BUZZED, and I heard slow, steady breathing to one side of me and purring on the other.

Something tickled my brain, but I couldn't quite access what it was. I opened my eyes to familiar lilac walls and a poster of the woods right above me taped to the white ceiling. The picture I'd used to calm my power when I couldn't get out into the woods.

I turned my head to find Raffe beside me. He sat in my leather office chair, which he'd pulled over from my purple desk on the other side of my childhood room. He was shirtless and holding my hand, and he'd listed sideways in a way that couldn't be comfortable. Faint scabs dotted his side.

Some of my tension eased. His wound had been taken care of.

Parched, I tried to sit up, but pain stung my shoulder, and my chest burned despite my fuzzy head. Cat-Keith jumped from her spot at my feet, glaring at me like my movement had offended her.

Raffe woke and winced. "Hey, careful." He squeezed my hand and leaned so that his shoulder brushed my arm. "Your injuries were awful, so it'll take you time to heal even with your shifter magic running through you." He kissed my shoulder, the warmth of his love and worry flowing into me. "I'm so damn glad to look into your eyes again. It's been fucking awful to see you like this. I thought I was going to lose you."

I'm sorry. I didn't mean to scare you. I tried to swallow, but nothing happened due to how dry my mouth was.

He tensed. *What's wrong?*

Water. Please.

His forehead lined. *I'll tell Lucy. Do you need anything else?* His guilt swirled in my chest, tightening it.

I shook my head.

His eyes glowed quickly before he continued, *Dammit, Sky.* A tear trickled down his cheek, and his eyes glistened. His turmoil swirled between us. *Do you know what that did to me when you blacked out? Your heart was barely beating, and it's a miracle you're alive.*

This time, when I winced, it was from the heaviness in my heart. *I'm sorry. Slade was going to hurt you, and I—*

I was alert enough to know that I'd better not finish that thought. My words would only upset him.

Oh, I know what you thought, and I fucking feel the same way about you. His shoulders slumped. *Luckily, everyone was arrested while Dru performed surgery on you to get the bullet out. With how much blood you lost—* He stopped and took a ragged breath. *At least, it was my turn to return the favor and give you some blood to get you through it.*

I cringed. *I'm sorry. It's just, I love you and—*

He exhaled. "Don't. I'd have done the same thing. I'm just fucking glad this is over." He leaned over and kissed my forehead. "You better never do anything like that ever again. Do you hear me?"

I gritted my teeth, ignoring the discomfort as I reached up and cupped his cheek. *I love you.*

I love you too. He arched a brow. *But when you get better, you're getting a spanking.*

Even feeling off the way that I was, I couldn't help but smile. *Promise?*

He straightened. *Don't keep teasing. There's no telling what I might do since I fucking need to be inside you again after damn near losing you.*

As much as I loved the sound of that, even the thought of doing too much had me damn near in tears. *Let's try tomorrow.*

His face softened. *I doubt you'll be able to even then, but at least you're awake, and we can talk. That's better than the way you've been sleeping the past two days.*

Two *days?*

Mom and Dad. Panic clawed in my chest, forcing me

upright. Agony shot through my body, but I pushed past it, needing to see what had happened to them. *Josie, Dave, and Aldric?* Dave had been shot, and Aldric hadn't appeared well.

My door opened, and two of the very people I was concerned about walked in.

Mom held a glass of water and hurried to me. She'd pulled her short blonde hair into a small bun, and the skin around her russet eyes tightened. She had a scab on her neck where the dagger had been held against it in the picture. "Here, honey. Lucy told us you needed water."

I took the glass from Mom and sipped, then turned my attention to Dad. His forehead was lined all the way up to where his hairline used to be, and his brown eyes darkened. "We're just glad you're all right. You gave all of us a scare."

The water felt like sandpaper going down my throat, but I took another gulp, which went down a little smoother.

Josie went back with Dad to bury her father. Aldric didn't survive the burns. Dave is with her and fine. Mom has been blowing up my phone nonstop, worried sick about us, but Dad needs her there next to him with all the fallout from Aldric's betrayal, Raffe answered during a moment of silence.

My chest ached for Josie's loss. I could only imagine, and I was thankful she had Dave with her through the process.

A knock came at the door, and I turned to find Dru standing there.

"Oh, come on in." Mom took a few steps back, giving him room. "She's finally awake."

"I heard." He smiled. "Go easy on the water. You haven't had anything to drink in a few days, and even though we gave you an IV for pain relief and fluids, you could get nauseous."

Reluctantly, I placed the cup in my lap. "Noted. Where is everyone? Are they all okay?"

"There were about fifty deaths, including the key players in the Veiled Circle—Olwyn and Warin." Raffe took my hand and sat on the edge of the bed next to me. "And that damn cat is finally growing on me. She prevented Warin from reaching you so I could finish him."

I swallowed my groan, not wanting him to move. I laid my head on his shoulder, needing to feel his touch. He rubbed a thumb over my hand. "Keagan and his pack went back to Seattle with Dad to determine their next steps, and both covens went with them, though Stephanie, Sedona, and Faith stayed behind."

Do my parents know? I linked, not wanting to ask that question out loud.

He mashed his lips together. *They do, and they don't want their memories taken from them. They want to know about your world, but ultimately, Dad and I agree that the decision is yours to make. If you want us to get a vampire to alter their memories, we can do that. We already repaired the porch and took care of the dead. So we could do it at any point, you just name it.*

That was a tough question and something I needed to discuss with them first.

"Are you doing that pack-link thing?" Mom asked, her gaze darting from him to me. "Because both of your eyes are glowing."

I snorted, caught off guard that she'd noticed. Pain sliced down my chest, and I glanced down, ignoring the way my back screamed, to see deep scabs on my chest. "I asked if you knew about us."

"Yes, we do, and we don't want to forget it, Skylar Greene—er, Wright." She clenched her fists. "I'm not even sure which name to say when you're in trouble."

Dad scowled, but he let out a breath. "We just wish you hadn't kept anything from us."

"In fairness, you would've thought I was insane. You were already worried about my attachment to Raffe." I could still imagine them dragging me from EEU, thinking I'd lost my mind or joined a cult. "The only reason you don't now is because of what you experienced."

"That was something." Dad shivered. "And you're probably right. Though I'm still not thrilled about this man claiming you as his own without discussing it with us." He glowered at Raffe.

"Dad, it was both of us, and I don't want to talk about how we formed our connection"—I wrinkled my nose—"with my parents. Even if you had told him no, we'd still be with one another. He's the other half of my soul, and I know it's hard to understand, but we *feel* one another, thoughts and all."

"And sir, I'll do anything to protect her." Raffe's shoulders sagged. "I know it doesn't look like it in her current state. She's just so damn stubborn."

Dad raised both hands in surrender. "Now that, son, I can agree with you on. And the animals circling our home made everything sink in. I always knew Sky had an affinity for nature, but I never imagined this. She's the closest thing to a Disney princess that anyone could be."

I snorted, remembering so many of us thinking the same thing.

Octavia stuck her head into the room, Fane and Lucy behind her. Octavia chuckled and said, "I'm not sure if that's a strong enough description when it comes to her." She winked at me.

The three of them joined us, standing in front of the desk.

"You have no idea." Mom rolled her eyes but wore a huge smile. "Let me tell you some stories."

Raffe settled closer into me, and we lay back with his arm anchoring me to him. Mom and Dad launched into stories of my childhood and how I wouldn't take no for an answer when it came to things I wanted.

For the first time in my life, I felt like maybe everything would work out after all.

Two DAYS LATER, the rest of our pack, which now included Sedona, Stephanie, and Fane, arrived back at Evergreen Elite University to meet with King Jovian, Queen Tashya, Keagan, Josie, Dave, Priestess Caroline, and Priestess Ednah.

Being back at the university was strange, but it also felt right.

The school was on fall break, so most people were off campus. The eight of us headed into the brick administration building, passing through the evergreen-painted halls to a back office used for board meetings.

A dark wooden, rectangular table took up the center of the room, with seats for up to twenty. Two things struck me as odd. First—Lafayette was there, and second—there were two open spots in the middle of the table. One on Keagan's right and the other on King Jovian's left. Queen Tashya sat on his other side.

"Please, come sit here, son." King Jovian pulled out the thick wooden seat next to him. "We saved these two for you and Skylar."

Queen Tashya jumped up and ran to Raffe and me, pulling us into a hug. She murmured, "Thank gods, you two are all right. I wished I'd forced my way into coming that night, but your father conveniently left out who he was rushing off to help, wanting to protect me."

Raffe hugged her back tightly. "It's okay. I need to learn his ways of doing that so Skylar won't keep ending up in danger."

Good luck with that. I cut my eyes to him. *Not happening.*

I detangled myself, my body slightly aching from her hug, to give them a moment together and sat down in the open spot beside Raffe.

Soon, Raffe took the seat between the king and me, across from Priestess Caroline and Priestess Ednah.

Raffe intertwined our fingers and rubbed his thumb over my wrist. He linked, *Babe, I swear, I won't let anything bad happen. Dad said he wanted to talk to all of us, including you and me.*

I smiled tensely at him and nodded. I wasn't sure if King Jovian still hated me, so I was a little on edge, but this was something we had to do, at least for Raffe. I didn't want to come between him and his father.

Josie and Dave sat on the opposite side of King Jovian, and the others filled in spots, with Stephanie sitting next to her dad and Sedona taking the spot next to her mom and their mates beside them. Lucy and Fane sat on the end across from Stephanie and Adam.

When we were all settled, Keagan turned on the large

screen on the wall at the end of the table. A female appeared on a live feed.

"Thera, so glad you're here." Keagan smiled and introduced each of us, except for Ednah, Stephanie, and Sedona.

The woman pushed her long black hair over her shoulders and smiled. "I'm honored to be chosen to take over for Warin. Hopefully, I can do a better job than him."

That wouldn't be hard.

"We wanted to have this meeting before Keagan headed back to Atlanta." King Jovian placed a hand on the table. "I don't want to drag this out since my decision is quite simple. My wife and I are stepping down as king and queen and handing the reins over to my son and his mate."

My jaw dropped. Raffe tilted his head back, and his shock mixed with mine, but he smoothed his expression into a mask of indifference, whereas I couldn't.

"Really?" Raffe's hand tightened on mine, and he laughed. "What made you come to that conclusion? Not too long ago, you told me I wasn't fit to lead and my mate was a liability."

"Which is why you two should be the leaders." King Jovian hung his head. "I was stuck in the old ways, and I let fear dictate my decisions. I trusted someone I shouldn't have —though he did try to protect me in the end—and I didn't listen to the one person I should've respected more than anyone. You and Skylar have proved that I was completely in the wrong and that now it's time for new leadership to take over. I mean, Skylar did jump in front of the fire to protect me after I'd been so awful to you both." He turned to Raffe and smiled. "If you and your mate are willing, I'll submit to you, and you can take over officially."

Warm hope spread through Raffe and flowed into me.

This was the future he'd always planned—taking over and leading his people.

What do you think? Raffe linked and turned to me.

Out of all the possible scenarios, I had never imagined this. Not only was his dad accepting me, but he was also okay with me ruling beside his son. However, there was one problem. *I don't want to lead the same way. I don't want to hinder the other species, so—*

Maybe, at one time, I wouldn't have agreed with you, but I do now. He turned his back on his dad and took both my hands, his blue eyes glowing brightly. *We'll make decisions together and figure out how* we *think our reign should be. You and me. Together. Forever. The way it was always meant to be.*

I really like the sound of that. To make a difference, to help the rest of the species, and to allow each person to have a voice sounded better than being a vet. Maybe this was what Fate always had in store for me. *Together. Forever. That's the way I always want it to be.*

Raffe stood, turned to his dad, and whispered, "I accept."

When his dad lowered his eyes, submitting to him, thousands of pack links soared into my chest, and Tashya beamed.

For once, I felt balanced, inside and out.

A year and a half later

I HELD on tightly to Raffe's waist as he took each curve of the road, his bike moving smoothly and the wind blowing in our faces and hair.

We were heading back to campus to check in with Josie and Dave and meet up with my parents later for dinner. We'd wound up not removing their memories, and I was thankful we hadn't. After getting past the nightmares of their capture, they'd acclimated easily to this world.

We'd all graduated from EEU, and I now had my bachelor's degree in science. Raffe had stepped into the family business, working alongside his dad while I worked in a vet's office as a technician, though not as the vet I'd once planned. I was happy with that because I could focus on learning how to use my power and finally controlling it. Between all that and my duties as Raffe's mate, I found a new sort of future that felt even more complete. The best part was shifting into wolf form and running while communicating and connecting with animals and learning more about their species and how Raffe and I could make changes to better help everyone.

We'd set up a council with each supernatural species equally represented. Adam had moved to Atlanta to be with Stephanie, and having one of Raffe's right-hand people there helped to bridge the gap between the East and the West. Problems were addressed and not discounted, and every species was free to honor their heritage in any way they saw fit, including the covens having access to the *Books of Twilight,* which we'd removed from the hidden library and made available to any supernatural, not only coven members.

Caroline took over as the supreme priestess, her family's legacy falling back into the rightful hands, with Sedona joining her coven, though she and Keith stayed with the shifters to help with the West's problems. Lafayette had quickly gotten on board with our plans, though we'd kept a watchful eye on him at first, unsure if he'd ever been part of the Veiled Circle. From what we could tell, he hadn't been, but Dave and Josie joined the college board to make sure it was never used for recruiting again.

Surprisingly, Hecate and Zella were still friends of mine, though they'd graduated and gone back to their hometowns. They'd both acclimated to the way things ran now and seemed to enjoy it.

Overall, things were settled, and most everyone seemed happy with the changes.

Raffe pulled into the spot where he always used to park. Once we'd removed our helmets and stowed them, he took my hand and led me past the women's apartments.

I tugged on him to stop him in his tracks. "I thought we were meeting Josie and Dave."

"We are. I just want to check on something first." He winked and nodded. "Come on. It won't take long. I'll make it worth it."

I snorted. "Fine. But I don't want to be late if they're expecting us."

"They'll be okay." He wrapped an arm around my waist, and we headed toward the woods where so much had happened, both bad and good.

As we stepped through the tree line, a strange emotion wafted from him, something he normally didn't exude. "What's—" I started, but a few feet away lay a lilac blanket on the ground with purple roses all around it. Raffe headed straight to it.

I inhaled sharply. "What's this?"

We stepped onto the blanket, and Raffe rubbed his palms against his jeans. Then he dropped to one knee.

My entire world stopped, and I placed a hand on my chest.

He looked up at me through his thick eyelashes and

cleared his throat. "Skylar, we've gone through a lot of shit in the last year, but ever since the day you ran into my chest here on campus, one thing has never changed. I fucking love you, and I fall more for you each and every day. I not only want you as my fated mate but as my wife and the mother of my children. I want you to be *mine* in every way." He reached into his pocket and removed a jewelry box. "Skylar Greene, will you marry me?"

My vision blurred as tears filled my eyes. My chest wanted to explode from how damn happy I was. I'd never imagined I'd have a friend, let alone a man like him who wanted me by his side forever. Not only was he kind, loyal, and caring, but he was also the sexiest man I'd ever known.

He fidgeted, our bond shrinking. "Uh ... for the record, you saying no would probably kill me."

I snorted and threw my arms around his neck as tears spilled down my cheeks. I kissed him and linked, *Of course I'll marry you. That wasn't even a question with everything we've gone through. There's no one else I'd ever want by my side. You're the perfect other half of me and have always had my back when no one else did. I love you, but let's wait a few years on the children.*

He laughed, kissing me back. *Fine with me.*

Pulling away, he slipped the three-carat oval diamond ring on my finger, and it fit perfectly. My heart couldn't be happier. "We need to call my parents."

"Oh, don't worry." He stood and pulled me to his chest. "Everyone is waiting for us at the student center to celebrate. There was no way I was pissing your dad off again and not asking his permission first. Not when he just started liking me."

"Everyone?" I arched a brow.

"Everyone." He kissed me again, his tongue slipping

into my mouth. *The whole damn crew, including Octavia, Dru, and my parents. Adam, Keith, Stephanie, and Sedona even flew in from Atlanta.*

And that right there made this moment even more perfect.

Best of all, I had the most caring mate in the entire world ... for the rest of my life.

ABOUT THE AUTHOR

Jen L. Grey is a *USA Today* Bestselling Author who writes Paranormal Romance, Urban Fantasy, and Fantasy genres.

Jen lives in Tennessee with her husband, two daughters, and two miniature Australian Shepherds. Before she began writing, she was an avid reader and enjoyed being involved in the indie community. Her love for books eventually led her to writing. For more information, please visit her website and sign up for her newsletter.

Check out her future projects and book signing events at her website.
www.jenlgrey.com

ALSO BY JEN L. GREY

Fated To Darkness

The King of Frost and Shadows

The Court of Thorns and Wings

The Kingdom of Flames and Ash

The Forbidden Mate Trilogy

Wolf Mate

Wolf Bitten

Wolf Touched

Standalone Romantasy

Of Shadows and Fae

Twisted Fate Trilogy

Destined Mate

Eclipsed Heart

Chosen Destiny

The Marked Dragon Prince Trilogy

Ruthless Mate

Marked Dragon

Hidden Fate

Shadow City: Silver Wolf Trilogy

Broken Mate

Rising Darkness

Silver Moon

Shadow City: Royal Vampire Trilogy

Cursed Mate

Shadow Bitten

Demon Blood

Shadow City: Demon Wolf Trilogy

Ruined Mate

Shattered Curse

Fated Souls

Shadow City: Dark Angel Trilogy

Fallen Mate

Demon Marked

Dark Prince

Fatal Secrets

Shadow City: Silver Mate

Shattered Wolf

Fated Hearts

Ruthless Moon

The Wolf Born Trilogy

Hidden Mate

Blood Secrets

Awakened Magic

The Hidden King Trilogy

Dragon Mate

Dragon Heir

Dragon Queen

The Marked Wolf Trilogy

Moon Kissed

Chosen Wolf

Broken Curse

Wolf Moon Academy Trilogy

Shadow Mate

Blood Legacy

Rising Fate

The Royal Heir Trilogy

Wolves' Queen

Wolf Unleashed

Wolf's Claim

Bloodshed Academy Trilogy

Year One

Year Two

Year Three

The Half-Breed Prison Duology (Same World As Bloodshed Academy)

Hunted

Cursed

The Artifact Reaper Series

Reaper: The Beginning

Reaper of Earth

Reaper of Wings

Reaper of Flames

Reaper of Water

Stones of Amaria (Shared World)

Kingdom of Storms

Kingdom of Shadows

Kingdom of Ruins

Kingdom of Fire

The Pearson Prophecy

Dawning Ascent

Enlightened Ascent

Reigning Ascent

Stand Alones

Death's Angel

Rising Alpha